THE CON CODE

SHANA SILVER

Swoon READS

NEW YORK

A Swoon Reads Book
An imprint of Feiwel and Friends and Macmillan Publishing Group, LLC
120 Broadway, New York, NY 10271

Our books may be purchased in bulk for promotional, educational, or business use. Please contact your local bookseller or the Macmillan Corporate and Premium Sales Department at (800) 221-7945 ext. 5442 or by email at MacmillanSpecialMarkets@macmillan.com.

Library of Congress Cataloging-in-Publication Data is available.
ISBN 978-1-250-26681-1 (hardcover) / ISBN 978-1-250-26680-4 (ebook)

Book design by Liz Dresner

First Edition, 2020

10 9 8 7 6 5 4 3 2 1

swoonreads.com

To Mom,

For being my best friend, for instilling in me a love of art
that inspired much of this book, and for not becoming a fugitive.
(That I know of.)

CHAPTER 1

My sneakers squeak like a warning as I breeze through the lobby of the Hotel Galvez and Spa in Galveston, Texas, keeping my eyes focused on the painting at the far end of the long downstairs hallway.

The painting I'm about to steal.

While most parents teach their kids to read and write, mine schooled me in the fine art of forgery and theft. By five, I could pick the most complicated of locks. By seven, I'd perfected my stealth by slipping into forbidden places without notice. For example, the teacher's lounge after hours. By nine, I could re-create every brushstroke of the masters in exact replica. To this day, one of my paintings hangs in place of Chuck Close's at the Schack Art Center in Washington after the lead art expert authenticated the wrong one. Or the *right* one if you're looking at it from my perspective.

By ten, my mom had disappeared, leaving behind only a delicate silver necklace and a vacant hole in the more dangerous cons. The hole I now fill.

Rule #1 of the con code: Look like you belong. My expensive suitcase (fake) and my expensive taste (born with) fit right in with this glitzy hotel. Pearls hang heavy around my neck, settling into the groove of my throat as if they're trying to strangle me. I've traded my school uniform and mom's necklace for . . . a different school uniform and a varsity jacket. Sunglasses conceal my eyes, and my long blond hair is stuffed under a bald cap. Instead, an auburn wig twisted into two fishtail braids helps conceal the earbuds situated in my ears.

The concierge doesn't even glance in my direction. The other guests pass right by me without a second glance.

Beams of sunlight splash in through the large bay windows, drenching the open space with golden light. Posh, white wicker love seats line the hallway leading up to the painting of Bernardo de Galvez. Guests claim it's haunted because his eyes seem to follow you around the room. Most people report feeling queasy after only looking at his face. Weirder still, the painting always appears blurry in photographs. The hotel capitalizes on this phenomenon by pimping it out with full-on ghost tours and elaborate macabre sales pitches.

Too bad the painting currently hanging is a fake.

When my mother disappeared, she left behind a legacy of forgeries strewn across the country before she fled said country (allegedly) with the originals, never to be heard from again. Even though she abandoned me, I can't bring myself to lead the FBI right to her trail by leaving her forgeries out there like arrows pointing directly to her. So my dad and I have spent the last few years tracking down the fakes and replacing them with ones that can't be traced back to her.

"You got this, kiddo," my dad's voice buzzes in my ear, and my steps get a little lighter.

"Mr. Spangler, with all due respect, Fiona doesn't need encouragement," my best friend, Natalie, says in my ear. "She can do this in her sleep." There's a hint of a French accent in her words.

"Sure, but a little accolade never hurts," I whisper back, trying not to move my lips too much, so the security cams don't capture me talking to myself.

The end of the hallway darkens as though the painting itself is clouded in shadow. I've been staring at the image so much for the last few weeks while painstakingly re-creating every brushstroke, every speck of dust, that the creep factor doesn't make me flinch. But even though I plan to steal it today, it's not the first stop on my tour of this hotel. Before I reach the painting, I veer toward the right into a small alcove and jam my finger against the elevator button. A college guy wearing a fraternity sweatshirt steps besides me, and both of us stare forward.

"Oooh, cute guy alert," Dad says in my ear. "Don't get distracted." Whistles and whoops from the rest of the crew follow.

I stifle the scowl demanding to break free on my lips and give the guy my best smile, waving him ahead of me. There's nothing worse than your father and two of his best professional-criminal friends trying to amp up your nonexistent dating life in the middle of a long con. Two thousand miles from home. While *your* best friend bursts into laughter.

"Don't stray from the plan, kiddo," Dad teases.

There's a pang in my gut at the words. They're supposed to mean *goodbye* if we're ever on a heist and one of us becomes compromised. But today he means it for real.

I make sure to look away from the cute guy quickly, but not so quickly that he takes notice. I want my dad to see how I can keep my eye on the ball during the game. Cute Guy presses floor seven, and I let out a breath that he's headed far away from where I need to go: floor three.

On floor three, I stash my (empty) suitcase near the ice machine to keep it away from the security cams and waltz down the carpeted hallway until I find exactly what I'm looking for: the maid's cleaning cart perched outside room 307. Right on time. For a week, I patrolled these hallways in different disguises created by Natalie, automatically memorizing the maids' individual schedules. The swing of the keys on their waistbands like hypnotism devices. Routines. The locations that offer the best chance to be discreet: not the rooms close to the elevators, but the ones toward the back of the hallway, where there's no place to run. Rule #2: A good criminal never rushes.

Some students spend their spring break working extra hours at the mall. I'm spending mine pulling a different kind of job.

I pause in front of the cart and clear my throat until the maid inside the room takes notice of me.

"It's showtime," Dad says, and I swear I hear the crunch of popcorn in my ear as he watches on the hacked security feed.

"Excuse me." I crane my neck toward the maid. My hands vibrate, but I knock some sense into them by slapping them against my varsity jacket.

The maid sets down her rag and bottle of cleaning spray and ambles toward me in her beige top, brown pants, dark hair slicked back in a bun so tight, it tugs on her skin like horse reins.

"I'm so sorry to bother you." I force myself to inject sweetness into my tone instead of my usual default setting of snark. "But we're out of towels in room 323."

Her dark eyes roam over my body as though I might have smuggled contraband in with me. Cash. Diamonds. The crown jewels.

My pasted smile wavers, and my heart starts to beat a little faster. "Please." *Please fall for this.*

"I'll swing by your room in ten minutes. Wait there." She shoos me away with her hand.

My jaw twitches. I bite down on my tongue. "I, um—"

There's silence in my earpiece even though this is the one moment I need advice.

"I really need to shower. Right now." My pulse pounds, sharp and loud. I can't falter. Not with my dad watching. Not with so much riding on this. What would my dad do in this situation? He'd blabber. "You see, my boyfriend. He's about to arrive. And it's going to be a special night." Oh God. I can't believe I'm saying this with my dad listening. "And I really want to shower before he—"

The maid grunts in annoyance and plucks two towels from the storage compartment beneath her cart. The tension drains from my shoulders. When she hands me the towels, I spin fast to accidentally bump her in the shoulder before she has a chance to head back into the room. The towels fly from my hands, and we both bend down to pick them up. I knock into her again accidentally (on purpose). If this were a romantic comedy, we would have just experienced the cutest meet-cute that ever existed.

"Sorry! I'm such a klutz." I let out a self-deprecating laugh. While she helps gather the towels and the movement distracts her, my hand snakes out and lifts her master key card from her waist. I tuck it into my jacket pocket and stand up. "Thank you. Seriously."

Rule #3: Criminals have to get really good at being polite.

"Nice save, but we're going to have a little talk later about boyfriends and hotel rooms," Dad says.

"Don't worry, Dad." I hustle back toward the ice machine. "If I ever manage to snag one of those elusive creatures, I'll be sure to sneak around and hide him from you. Word on the street is I'm really good at that."

Natalie giggles while Dad's comrades cheer at my comeback.

"Dad, you're up. And don't worry, I'll try to find lots of ways to make you uncomfortable, too."

I stuff the towels inside the empty suitcase and leave it by the ice machine. I retrace my steps and breeze right through the lobby once again. As I exit onto a cobblestone driveway, hot sun beating down on my shoulders, a van pulls up, screeching tires. The man in the passenger seat gives me a quick nod, so brief, you'd have to know to look for it to notice. But I know where to look for all of Dad's cryptic signals.

A white hard hat covers Dad's slicked-back black hair. Thanks to prosthetics, his cheekbones sit slightly higher on his face, his stubble a little thicker, nose more bulbous. The driver beside him now boasts a lumberjack beard on what was smooth skin an hour ago. I take one quick second to admire my handiwork on the van. The perfectly replicated logo for the Texas Gas Service with swirling waves surrounding a circle. The hand-lettered contact info stretching across the plain white body. The van looks totally legit, even though a few days ago it sat rusting on the lot of a used-car dealer, plain white and boring.

Dad gets out of the van, while Jorge, our newly bearded getaway driver, crosses his burly arms over the tats that didn't exist yesterday and stays in the car. They wear matching protective jumpsuits and carry official-looking clipboards with official-looking documents. I know because I'm the one who forged said documents. In the back of the van, Johnny, our electronics guru, works diligently to replace the live feed of most of the hallways with still images of empty hallways now that I'm safely captured on camera exiting the building.

While Dad heads inside, I round the perimeter to the back of the hotel, where my best friend and fellow do-no-gooder, Natalie Babineaux, waits. Her parents think my dad is taking her on a lavish vacation to Texas out of the goodness of his heart. And part of that is true. There's some part of his heart that is good.

Two years ago, Natalie was just a girl who liked designing elaborate costumes for the school theater productions, winning cosplay contests at various nerd conventions, and dressing up in disguises daily to fool her teachers. But then I plucked her out of the costume slush and trained her in all methods of subterfuge so she could use her skills for good, like tricking bank clerks. She thrives on the challenge . . . and the profits. I love corrupting someone who seems impossible to corrupt.

Now Natalie wears the same beige top, brown pants, and hair-net as every other maid in this place. I squint, and when I do, I see the edge of a wig and a lump where the putty sculpting her breasts is uneven. I pin the stolen key card onto her uniform.

Rule #4 of the con code: The trick to impersonating staff at a luxury hotel is simply to find out where they purchase their uniforms and then order the same one.

"Next time," I tell her, knowing full well my dad can hear, "let's give Dad defective earbuds."

"Now that's a con I can get behind." Natalie gestures toward the cleaning cart. "Your chariot awaits, my dear."

Towels tower on the top, but behind the curtains that should conceal cleaning products and extra sheets, I squeeze my thin frame into the space carved out for me, careful not to squish the rolled-up replica of the painting of Bernardo de Galvez. On a small shelf above my head, a variety of tools rattle: crowbar, lock-picking set, drill. The usual accoutrements you might bring on vacation with you.

"Thanks, driver. Now step on it! I always wanted to say that." I slide the curtain closed and grip the metal bar above my head for dear life.

She laughs. "You're so dramatic."

The cart bounces, and the wheels spin on gravel, sounding louder than an airport runway so close to my ears. A beep indicates she successfully opened the back door, and she wheels me over a ramp into the basement. I jam my eyes shut and concentrate on the conversation beginning in my earpiece as Dad approaches the front desk.

"Sir," he says in his best Texas accent. It took a week of practicing with YouTube videos to knock the San Francisco out of his voice.

"You sound partially Texan, partially Australian," I whisper, but Dad doesn't falter. He's the smoothest criminal there is. Next to me, of course.

According to the government, my dad's a lawyer who specializes in personal injury cases. According to reality, the black market for art sales funds the upkeep on our historic three-story Victorian house with the manicured yard (paid labor) and the white picket fence (cliché).

"I'm afraid you've got a gas leak."

There's a scrape, and I imagine Dad sliding over the clipboard containing "official" paperwork regarding the gas work his team has been performing for the last few days. Johnny backed this evidence up with a long con involving back-and-forth emails between the gas company and the hotel to warn them of upcoming improvements to the gas lines in the area. "We're going to need you to evacuate." Dad clears his throat. "Immediately."

"Evacuate?" the desk clerk says.

"One of our guys accidentally punctured the line. Smell that?" Dad sniffs loudly, and Johnny makes a disgusted sound. Dad's pockets contain mashed-up rotten eggs as well as a layer of automobile gasoline to fool the people inside the hotel into smelling natural gas. Dad and his crew also strategically placed rotten eggs along the perimeter of the hotel to carry the scent outside. "Natural gas. Highly flammable."

"How long?" The desk clerk sounds nervous.

"We need to get into the basement to access the main line. Should take an hour, tops. Hopefully less. But it's best to take precautions. One wrong move and *boom*!" Dad shouts the word, and even I jump beneath the cart. "Guest soup." He lets out a hearty laugh as if that's the most hilarious joke he's ever told. "I'm going to need you to make sure all staff and guests remain at a safe distance from the hotel. We recommend at least one thousand feet. Better hurry, though. The longer this leak festers, the bigger the explosion." He waits a beat. "Unless we can get in there to prevent it."

"Oh my God. Let me talk to my manager."

"Oh, one more thing!" Dad says as though he forgot this tiny detail. "We're also going to need you to turn off all electricity and gas. Don't want any wires short-circuiting and flattening the entire building. Am I right?" he laughs again, and there's a slight pang of jealousy in my gut. Dad has always been so good at the charm, at bending people to his will with only a few words. I'm only good at re-creating someone else's work and then slinking behind the scenes, unnoticed.

A minute later, the fire alarm wails, followed by an announcement to vacate the premises immediately. The cart stops in a hallway, and I hear the trampling of feet rushing across the carpet. Natalie offers directions to fleeing guests, pointing them toward the nearest exit. She wheels the cart into an empty room identified by Johnny earlier and then flees with the guests. Her job now is lookout. If any of the staff decides to check up on us, she'll be our eyes.

"They're checking rooms to make sure everyone's out," Johnny says. He must be watching the security feed. "Fiona, heads up, coming your way. Sorry, though, it's not a cute guy."

"It's okay, I'm still getting over my breakup with the fake boyfriend who just stood me up on our hotel date," I deadpan into the mic before clamping my lips into silence.

We hear sharp knocking as the manager slams his fist against doors. Beeps and blips indicate he takes the extra precaution to check each room for vacancy himself. The pitter-patter of a few more feet reveals that some patrons didn't get the memo the first time.

The whole process of clearing the hotel takes approximately ten minutes. Being a criminal involves a lot of waiting around.

The lights suddenly switch off, plunging me into darkness.

"Confirming the electricity's been cut," Johnny announces. "You guys are on your own now."

I push myself out of the cart, my knees digging into the rough carpet. I grab one of the flashlights and beam a circle of light onto the dark wall. After I throw all the tools into a tote bag stashed in the cart for this specific purpose, I carefully grab the rolled-up painting and head down the stairs.

At the end of the long hallway, Dad has already managed to liberate mom's painting from the wall. The two of us work as a team to unscrew the gilded frame and pop the stretched canvas free.

"Bad news, guys," Natalie's voice rings in my ears.

Dad and I freeze. I imagine her telling us one of the employees is on his way back right now, giving us less than ten seconds to run for cover. My heart hammers in my chest, and my head whips around, taking in all the exits, all the possible ways out of this.

"Cute Guy's here with the evacuees . . . but he has his arm around another cute guy."

I let out a breath. Tension visibly drains from Dad's shoulders.

"Too bad. I'll just have to find a boyfriend on the next heist, then."

We get back to work, our pace amping up thanks to Natalie's

scare. Dad plucks each staple out of the woven-linen canvas until the entire painting falls away from the wooden slats that gave it shape.

I push him out of the way and desperately shine the flashlight along the back of the painting. My body thrums in anticipation. Familiar scratchy handwriting on the canvas catches my eye. My *mother's* handwriting.

> *Your age when I left, now with the standard term. Paint an inch thick, bugs instead of eyes. You belong on the surface. Or so it seems.*

My heart squeezes, and I hug the painting to my chest. It's so very much my mother's voice. This is more valuable to me than money. Another scavenger hunt clue that I hope leads to her whereabouts. My dad's crew hopes the clue leads to the *real* versions of the stolen paintings so they can exchange those on the black market for cold hard cash.

"Not now, honey." Dad rubs my shoulder. "We'll decipher it later."

I swallow hard, but he's right. I get to work rolling up my mom's forgery while Dad spreads *my* forgery over the wooden slats and secures it in place with a staple gun. Five minutes later, my painting hangs proudly in the hallway, a masterpiece no one will ever attribute to me.

I head back upstairs to stash the painting in my suitcase and then hide inside the cleaning cart. Dad waltzes outside to announce the gas leak has been contained. Once all the guests start streaming back into the hotel, I slip out of my hiding place, grab my suitcase, and mosey outside with the painting, successfully pulling off one of my greatest heists to date.

And all before lunch.

CHAPTER 2

Dad makes me wait until we're back in San Francisco, safely ensconced in our historic house, before he lets me start working on deciphering the clue. I sit at the table in our drafty dining room. We recently had the intricate crown molding polished and refurbished in the places it needed a little twenty-first-century love. Dad brags about the renovation process to all his friends even though he has to stay quiet about how he got the cash to fund the work.

I squint at the clue, trying to make sense. *Your age when I left, now with the standard term. Paint an inch thick, bugs instead of eyes. You belong on the surface. Or so it seems.* My mind circles around all the possibilities, going over every last memory in case any of it contains the key to cracking her cryptic words. Nothing comes to mind, so I try a cipher.

My mom's favorite cipher was Nihilist, which starts with a five-by-five grid that assigns each letter to a two-digit number by cross-checking which row and column the letter falls in. In Nihilist, *I*s and *J*s are treated as the same letter since there are only twenty-five boxes.

	1	2	3	4	5
1	A	B	C	D	E
2	F	G	H	I	K
3	L	M	N	O	P
4	Q	R	S	T	U
5	V	W	X	Y	Z

Nihilist creates an encryption on top of the grid by replacing each letter with a different one using a key. My mom always used the key of *FIONA* when I was a kid, so I use that here as well. With the letters switched based on the key, I try to plug in the clue phrase to figure out the code. But her phrase is far too large, and the first part—*your age when I left*—provides the guide I need to condense the phrase to a more manageable size. The age when my mom left me was ten, so I circle every tenth letter to reduce the clue to *wthdiesooe*.

When I cross-check the shortened phrase against the newly created grid, I get this number sequence: *73 68 57 47 35 36 67 68 67 26*.

"But which number is it?" I growl in frustration at the sheet, my heart beating fast. If I can't solve this, I can't find my mom. I can't be whole again.

Dad leans over my shoulder and points at number 47.

I look down at the sheet and notice 47 is the fourth number in the sequence.

"But how? Why?"

"'Now with the standard term.' Don't you remember government class?" Dad taps his lip. "Well, maybe not. If I recall, you only got a C plus in it last year."

I let out a small gasp. Standard term must refer to the standard *presidential* term, aka four years, aka one of the many lessons my mom sent me via postcards. I rush over to the stack in my room and flip through them until I find the one with random facts about elections. I thought she had just wanted me to know about electoral colleges for my grades, but maybe she was preparing me to decipher this particular clue.

The electoral college wasn't the only homework assignment she doled out to me on a regular schedule long after she disappeared, each arriving in an unconventional way. A yearlong tuition paid in full to gymnastics. Postcards with the periodic table on the back, stamped from a different country and containing a single pop-quiz question about chemistry, as if my mother once held a teaching degree. A book about lasers typed and sent via a dedicated email address, one paragraph at a time.

Even before she disappeared, Mom put more stock in my criminal training than my education. Every day after school I'd forgo homework in favor of art lessons with her, during which she taught me how to replicate the brushstrokes of the masters in intricate detail. Other art students learned the difference between linseed oil and turpentine, but I learned where to find vellum canvas in the same material used in the 1600s. In fifth grade, she pulled me out of school for a weeklong surveillance operation where she tasked me with following an anonymous target of my choosing (a boy from school) and learning everything there was to know about him, from his routines to his breakfast cereal preference. I then used that info to break into his house and leave behind a single rose. It was a practice assignment, after all, not a con. All I had to prove was that I could succeed without being caught.

And after she left, we found cryptic handwritten scraps of paper with her plans strewn around like a grocery list for a witch's brew. It's how we pieced together her trail of forgeries and replaced

75 percent of them so far. Only three left to go and then I hope, hope, hope she's the pot of gold at the end of the rainbow.

With all this info she's been sending me from wherever she is, I've been clinging to a stupid fantasy that maybe she's my own personal guardian angel, guiding me to be the person she always dreamed I'd be. And when I find her again, I need her to know I became that person.

Now, my stomach flips with guilt that I let down my mom somehow, that I'm not good enough to be worthy of this quest because I couldn't crack the code as fast as Dad did. That I couldn't do it without him. *Forty-seven.* It's what my mother wanted me to know. The number should spark a memory. But my mind comes up blank. "Does it ring any bells?"

Dad purses his lips. "But neither do the others." We add forty-seven to our growing roster of clues: *11, D5, Hesiod, 2nd, 92.5.* We know Hesiod is the author of an ancient Greek poem, but what that has to do with the other numbers, who knows? We do have faith it will come together once we track down the remaining clues. After all, the first cryptic message we found in the house said:

Find the clues, then find me.

Dad places his hand on my shoulder. "We'll find her, though. I promise. Just three more heists to go."

Just three. It seems so close, yet so far before I can wrap my arms around her again. They're the three hardest heists. Save the best for last and whatnot.

I've already started molding a replica of a notorious prop from a ride at the world's most famous amusement park, painstakingly re-creating the binding of an ancient book, and distressing a famous and well-loved guitar. Still, there's so much left to do. The Hotel Galvez heist took us months to plan, and there's a pang in my gut that tells me if we take that long for the other three, we're going to run out of time.

I clutch my necklace in my palm, grounding myself by touching the last gift Mom ever gave me. Silver twists into a complicated matrix of swirls, folding over one another to form a circle engulfed in metallic flames. Touching it usually comforts me, but today it transports me back to the moment that punches me in the gut every time it resurfaces, when I learned my mother had disappeared. Ten-year-old me sat by the front door waiting for her to come home. I stayed there off and on for three days before Dad placed a hand on my shoulder and whispered, "Sorry, kid. She's gone."

"I miss her so much," I say now. My voice is small, and I feel like I'm ten years old again, needing my mommy.

"Me too." Dad plants a delicate kiss on my forehead. But then his face grows serious. "But Fiona. I need to tell you something."

The tone of his voice makes my stomach drop. "Oh God. Did something happen to Mom?"

A million terrible thoughts float into my mind, all ending in the same scenario: cold metal handcuffs slapped around her wrists and a life sentence robbing me of her forever.

"It's not about her. Well, I guess it sort of is. Maybe. It's too coincidental not to be." He rakes a hand through his black hair. My dad, who can sweet-talk anyone, who can stand in a courtroom and make every single person inside cower in fear, looks terrified.

I brace myself.

"I didn't want to say anything in Texas because I didn't want you to lose focus, but—" He swallows hard and looks away for a brief second like a coward. "I've heard through the grapevine that Ian O'Keefe moved to town this past week, and his son Colin is scheduled to start at your school tomorrow." He says the words as if they carry the kind of weight that could sink someone to the bottom of the ocean. But the names are meaningless to me.

I blink at him. "Okay. I'm guessing we aren't interested in bringing them home-baked muffins to welcome them to the neighborhood?"

"Mr. O'Keefe recently accepted the job of head of the white-collar branch of the FBI, heading up the Northern California region."

"Oh crap." I sink onto the couch. "You think he's after Mom?"

Dad nods. "Or us."

"Double oh crap." My skin goes cold.

"I don't want you giving Colin any intel he can take back to his dad. So please be careful around him, okay?"

"Okay." But perhaps Colin's the one that needs to be careful around me.

"So." Natalie stops at my locker, and I nearly jump from her abrupt approach. I might be just a little too on edge right now, thanks to the news of Colin's arrival. A deep fake scar that hadn't been there yesterday and won't be there tomorrow covers one side of her cheek. A long wig made up of different pastel-colored strands falls in cascading curls down her shoulders. Every day I come to school and have to pick her new appearance out of the crowd, *Where's Waldo?*–style. Of course, to adhere to school policy, all her disguises have to be easily removable in the form of wigs instead of prosthetics. They don't compare to the ones she uses in private with me and my dad's crew. "Your dad sent me a text to lay low for a bit because of the new guy, but the one thing we're really good at is not following rules." She grins. "So, we're still taking con jobs, right?"

"Shh." I dart my head around, sweeping my eyes past the familiar faces roaming the hallway. "Yes, of course, but we need to be as quiet as possible about it."

Most freelance criminals would kill (not literally—at least not this criminal) to have the freedom of homeschool. But I love the confinement of high school. It's the perfect practice environment for small cons, especially at Amberley Academy, where the students' pockets run deep, and their desire for rebellion runs deeper.

Natalie and I have a good side hustle helping our classmates pull one over on someone of their choosing for a small fee or favor. We have a few regular customers who use us to provide them with foolproof alibis to rebel against their parents. My kind of people. I've also forged front-row concert tickets for a girl in my bio class. We orchestrated fake parent-teacher conferences—with Natalie playing the lead role of teacher—to prevent the parents from meeting with the *real* teachers and learning less-than-ideal information. We've even staged a fire drill to give poor Regina Clemmons time to run home and change after an unfortunate time-of-the-month-meets-white-pants incident.

As if on cue, one of our regulars, Olivia Rossdale, fluffs her sandy-blond hair and beelines toward Natalie and me, clutching her violin case like a shield. She leans against the beige locker beside me and beams a pageant-worthy smile, complete with Vaseline slicked on her teeth for extra shine (I'm guessing). "Hey!" Her voice is full of cheerleader pep. "I need your help."

"Fake hall pass?" I whisper, spinning around to open my locker. She asks for these so often, I have a stack already forged and ready to go tucked beneath a false bottom in my locker. I've mastered the art of passing these to her with a quick sleight of hand.

Olivia shakes her head, curls jangling. She leans in conspiratorially. "This time I need a permission slip from my music teacher."

She does a little tippy-toe ballerina twirl as she looks behind her toward the music room across the way. "For an overnight in two weeks. A concert performance at another school or something. Whatever sounds the most believable."

Natalie's eyes light up. "Where are you really going?"

Olivia's cheeks turn pink. "Ski lodge with friends"—she bites her lip—". . . and my boyfriend."

Natalie raises her brows a few times in succession, and I elbow her in the ribs.

"Do you have an example of a previous permission slip?" I ask Olivia, still trying to keep my voice as low as possible.

"I turned in all the previous ones, but . . ." Olivia scrolls through her glittery phone. "I found a pic online." She holds up the blurriest photo imaginable of a pink permission slip, the lettering completely illegible.

I purse my lips and refrain from groaning. "Give me two days."

A chuckle resonates from behind me. "Two days? That's practically an eternity."

Spinning around, I narrow my eyes at the annoying smirk attached to the even more annoying boy wearing a scarf knitted by blind orphans (I presume). Thanks to my internet stalking last night, I instantly recognize him as Colin O'Keefe, my new mortal enemy. He pushes his long bangs out of his face and wiggles his eyebrows in a way that indicates he knows something I don't. And he's gloating about it.

"Hi, I'd introduce myself, but something tells me you're going to wish you hadn't met me." He pops a wad of gum in his mouth, completely against school rules, but he doesn't seem to give a damn.

Natalie flips him off in lieu of an answer, stealing the move I was about to use. My blood turns to ice. How much did he overhear . . . and is he planning to divulge what he heard to his father? Not even three minutes into the school day and already I've failed my dad's one request to be careful around the new douchenozzle.

Still, I can't let him see me falter. I straighten and do what I do best: recon. "What are you doing here? Besides gloating."

Colin peers over my shoulder at the image on Olivia's phone, and I fumble to hide it behind my back. It's too late—he's seen enough and arches one brow at Olivia. "I'll steal the permission slip for you before the warning bell even rings." He doesn't bother lowering his voice.

My eyes widen. Isn't he supposed to operate on the *other* side of the law? I hastily rush out a *shhh*.

Colin sidles closer to Olivia, and her cheeks turn even brighter. She ducks her head and bats her eyelashes. I consider poking her to remind her about that boyfriend of hers. "Then all you have to do is type what you want and print it out. No forgery required." He grins at us with all his teeth.

Natalie gasps.

I sputter. My eyes dart throughout the hallway, locating each camera with the precision of an expert thief. I tilt my body at the exact angle needed to shield my lips from surveillance view. "Wait, *you're* going to run her con?"

He strokes his chin with his forefinger and thumb. "I guess you know *exactly* who I am." He lifts a brow. "Go ahead, tell my dad. But please note: I know exactly who you are, too." He winks. Then turns to Natalie and winks as well.

I cross my arms. "This is my territory. So—"

"*Was.* I already know your asking price is one hundred," he says, then directs his attention toward Olivia. "I'll do it for fifty."

Olivia straightens, clearly intrigued.

"Will you lower your voice?" I snap, and let out a growl of frustration.

Colin hits me with a megawatt charming smile before spinning back to Olivia and dropping his voice an infinitesimal amount. "Where does she keep the permission slips?"

"In her desk. But it's locked!" Olivia's voice is equal parts nervous and excited. And definitely not quiet.

"Not a problem." He struts toward the music room with the kind of confidence that makes people pay attention. Students part the hallway for him, all of them swiveling their heads at the new guy. Even the overhead lighting appears to be angled just right to shine a spotlight directly over his skin.

In the doorway, Mrs. Caldwell stands with her arms crossed above her ill-fitting skirt, a permanent scowl etched on her face. "Jasmine, tuck in your shirt!" she yells at a girl whose shirt is actually tucked in, but not well enough apparently. Mrs. Caldwell has a way with the students, and that way is yelling.

But Colin disarms her with politician-worthy charisma and some magically charming *hello* that makes her visibly relax. She quickly smooths down her skirt as though she, too, needs to impress the new student. I scuttle closer, only catching snippets of his smooth intro among the din of chatter in the hallway. "New student . . . personally introduce . . . interested in the music program." She leads him inside her classroom, her face beaming, nodding along to his every word.

I wedge myself just outside the door, close enough to hear a little better, but angled so that Mrs. Caldwell doesn't spot me. Across the way, Natalie shakes her head at my petty spying, her pastel wig dancing. I ignore her as Colin casually leads Mrs. Caldwell toward her desk, chatting her ear off about the various types of instruments he wants to pursue. "I've always loved the idea of playing a piccolo. Took piano lessons for years, but the piccolo, man. I love how such a small object can produce such brilliant sound." He lets out a long sigh as though he's imagining wrapping his long fingers around the body and experiencing pure bliss as he presses his lips to the embouchure. Mrs. Caldwell pushes her frizzy bangs out of her eyes as if to see him better.

"We're actually in need of another piccolo player for our band next year. Our last players are graduating in two months."

"How lucky is that?" He forces a chuckle, and I think he somehow already knew this information. Perhaps recon on me isn't the only research he did before day one at Amberley. "Do you think if I practice a bunch this summer, I'd be good enough to make the band in the fall?" He sounds so hopeful, so devoted. She buys every damn word of it.

Mrs. Caldwell nods. "If you start right away, you have a real chance."

His eyes quickly flick to me in the doorway, and I use the opportunity to thrust my middle finger high in the air at him. Anything to try to trip him up.

"Would it be possible to change my schedule to add music class to my electives? I want to start today." He covers his mouth to hide a giddy smile, as though this is a secret, and it's one he can't wait to reveal.

"The office will need to make that change with my approval." Her eyes fly to the clock, checking that she has exactly ten more minutes before the warning bell rings. "If you wait right here, I can talk to them quickly to see if I can get you into my second period."

"Oh my gosh! That's so amazing of you! I really, really appreciate it." He circles around to a desk in the front row, taking a long route, but one that forces her to brush past him on her way out the door. As she does so, he quickly plucks her keys from her belt with a sleight of hand so smooth, Vegas magicians would be envious.

My breath rattles out of my throat. I'd been hoping he was bluffing. That this was all a ruse to get a rise out of me. But he's so damn charming, so good at the kind of cons I've never excelled at: the ones that require you to talk people into doing your bidding rather than doing it yourself behind their backs.

Though judging from the volume of his voice in the hallway and his too-public antics, he may have a thing or two to learn in the stealth department.

Mrs. Caldwell hustles out the door and toward the office, and a few students squint in confusion when she doesn't bother to scold them for minor dress code violations. As soon as she's gone, Colin flies into action, twisting the key into the desk drawer and plucking a yellow permission slip from the top of the pile. He locks the drawer and then slides her keys into her purse. Before he exits the room, he scrawls a quick note on her desk.

He steps outside and presents Olivia the permission slip with a flourish and, damn it, he looks incredibly sexy doing it. She squeals in delight as she hands him the fifty bucks.

"Guess I'll be upgrading to the new iPhone sooner than I thought." He shoots me a wink and starts to brush past me.

"Wait!" I yell, then immediately clamp my mouth shut when several people whip their heads toward us. Damn him for making me forget to be quiet. I lower my voice. "What did your note say?"

He leans toward me. So close I can smell his amazing musky cologne. "I'm not sure I should tell you," he says in a volume so low that I have to drift even closer to hear him better.

"I'll just go into the room and read it myself after you leave."

He purses his lips together as if considering this. "It was an apology." He lets out a heavy sigh. "I've regretfully changed my mind about the piccolo." The expression on his face morphs into one of sadness, as though he truly feels terrible about what just happened.

"Oh." I blink, trying to make sense of this. For a minute there, I thought there was a small chance he actually wanted to play and had just been using the fifty bucks as bonus incentive. But of course, it was all part of the con. Of course.

"Anyway." He backs up a step. "Hope I see you around, though I'm sure you're hoping for the opposite."

He brushes past me, and when I straighten up, I realize I was leaning toward him, falling right into his trap.

I stumble back to my locker and bury my head in my hands. "Crap. This is bad, Nat. He's bad news, but of a totally different kind than we thought."

She aims a death stare down the hallway at his retreating back. "I'll say. I've never seen you so thrown off your game."

I thought I needed to watch out for him catching me stealing . . . not that he'd be stealing clients from me.

CHAPTER 3

A few days later, I race into school just as first period lets out, covering my mouth to catch a yawn. I was up way too late last night working on one of the forgeries and overslept. Thankfully my dad didn't hesitate about calling me in tardy. School always comes second to criminal activities.

I stop short as soon as I round the corner into the wing that contains my locker. The hallways of Amberley Academy are usually kept sleek and pristine, but today posters containing the smiling face of Colin O'Keefe and his stupidly chiseled cheekbones worthy of Renaissance sculpture follow me down the school hallway. He hasn't even been here for a full week, and already it seems like my hold is slipping, my world tumbling. I swear his smoldering brown eyes watch me as I weave through the crowd. Each poster contains a simple phrase written in bold block text: I WILL GO AN EXTRA MILE TO MAKE YOU SMILE. Combined with the cocky smirk, it looks more like a pickup line than a campaign slogan. In smaller letters, so tiny I have to step up close to one of the posters to read, it says VOTE FOR COLIN O'KEEFE FOR STUDENT BODY PRESIDENT.

I can't catch a break.

I hustle my pace to outrun his glorious smile as it follows me to the end of the hallway, but I freeze a few feet away from my locker.

His assigned locker's nowhere near here, and yet he's standing right beside mine, holding court among a crowd of students surrounding him in a semicircle as though he's telling ghost stories at a campfire. Football players, cheerleaders, burnouts, and even middle-of-the-road gals like Jessica Sanchez unite as one to listen to him.

I march up to him and cross my arms. "Move."

He scoots over an infinitesimal amount, and the crowd follows suit to clear the area in front of my locker. Jessica uses the opportunity to take a step closer to him so that she's no longer part of the audience, she's beside him. He turns back to his fans. "This one time, I posed as a valet car parker at a swanky restaurant. Got some idiot to give me the keys to his Ferrari."

I shoot him a death glare and catch him staring at me. Is he seriously bragging about a con in the middle of a hallway with an audience of gossip-happy teens? Someone needs to give him a firm lesson in Criminal 101: You fly under the radar, not show off.

But of course, he's not bragging to Jessica or the crowd of lapdogs.

He's bragging to me.

"Wow." Jessica is breathless. Her red lips part, and she glances up at him like he's a celebrity she follows on Instagram, beside her in the flesh. "Did you drive it?"

"Took it out for a spin and"—Colin whistles through his teeth—"it was sweet. Had it back in the parking lot before the guy even finished his entrée."

"That's so cool," she says, and Vance Whitford nods in awe.

Vance Whitford, resident burnout, owes me twelve different

favors thanks to all the parental signatures I've forged for him, but he doesn't seem to be doing me any favors right now.

I slam my locker so hard, I startle all of them.

Colin swivels his head to grin at me. "It's so exhilarating to get away with something, isn't it?"

His words sing in my heart. He's speaking my language.

I hate him for it. "Fuck you."

"Fiona!" Mrs. Caldwell snaps as she passes by me on her way toward her room. Of course she hears *that* and not his dumb humble brags. "That's two days' detention!"

I resist the urge to scream while Colin and his cronies sing out the requisite "OoooOOOOoooh" song when someone gets in trouble.

I storm into the bathroom, my hands curled in fists, whispers of all the girls wondering if he's single or not echoing in my head. My breaths come fast and hard, whipping through my chest with the force of a tsunami. I haven't been this rattled in a long time. Not since my mom fled.

Hiccups and sniffles resonate from one of the bathroom stalls. There's a quick flush of the toilet, a clear attempt at covering the sound of a sob.

"Hey, you okay in there?" I knock on the stall.

"Yeah," a meek voice sounds back. "No." The door opens, and Amelia Thomas steps out, pushing her glasses up the bridge of her nose. They're foggy from her heavy breathing. She shudders again, and my heart tumbles. Until this morning, she was the front-runner for the student council election, running on a platform of delegating money to arts and sports. It was a platform everyone cared about, but my guess is they'll soon care more about certain perfectly coifed bangs.

"He's not going to win," I assure her. "No one's stupid enough to vote for him."

She hiccups and clutches her books closer to her chest. "Ye-yes. They are. People have been telling me to my face they're no longer voting for me. Even my sister!" She lets out a sob. "I need this on my résumé so badly. It's my only shot at getting into Harv—" Her eyes light up. "Wait." She clamps a hand over her mouth. "Oh my God."

I straighten, my body on high alert. "What?" I half expect her to tell me she's just realized her sister's right, that Amelia herself is going to vote for Colin, too.

She grabs me by the arm, squeezing tight. "You can help! You can rig this!"

I wobble. My first instinct is to say no. I don't accept cons that will hurt another student, either physically or emotionally. But it would be so easy, forging paper ballots for three hundred of my (least) favorite classmates. I've written all their names so many times, I can mimic their handwriting in my sleep. Then it's just a matter of switching them out.

Besides, Colin winning would hurt *everyone*. I don't know how, but I know his motives are the ulterior kind.

"But oh." Amelia bites her lip. "I don't have any money on me. I can bring it tomorrow, I promise."

I grin at her. "Don't worry. This one's on the house."

I intended to go straight home and keep working on the remaining three forgeries for the heists, but instead Natalie and I march into the computer lab as soon as the final bell rings. Well, I march; Natalie flutters while simultaneously attempting to fix her turquoise wig and smooth down her uniform. She pops open the top button on her shirt, revealing just a little bit more cleavage than Mrs. Caldwell would like.

A girl wearing oversize headphones, a fedora, and a fierce glare taps rapidly on the keys at one of the farthest desks. Tig Ramirez.

She's also a junior and sometimes helps us out with any cons at school that require the use of electronics . . . or lack thereof. Such as when we require a convenient blackout to shutter the security cams. I personally don't think we need an electronics whiz to screw over my new best enemy, but Natalie insisted.

"Hey, Tig," I say.

Natalie bats her eyelashes and ducks her head to hide her giggle. The corners of Tig's lips quirk in the hint of a smile, but that's as much of a greeting as we'll get from her. She's the strong-and-silent type.

I wait a second for Natalie to kick off this convo, but she's too busy trying not to make moon eyes at Tig. I clear my throat, and Natalie quickly shoots another smile in Tig's direction before ducking her head again.

I sigh and launch into it myself. "Need your help on a gig."

Tig leans back, studying us with her pursed lips, painted a distracting shade of violet. Another thing Mrs. Caldwell would freak over during school hours.

"During Colin O'Keefe's election speech at Thursday's assembly, it would be awesome if there were a few"—I cough for emphasis—"audio problems."

She holds out her palm, and I place two twenties into it. Money well spent.

Tig turns back to her computer, not giving us another second of her time. Natalie's face deflates. After we exit, I nudge her in the ribs. "Girl, you're really good at disguises, but really bad at flirting. Next time, I suggest actually speaking."

She rolls her fake-green eyes. "Like you're any better. You practically melt whenever you're in Colin's presence."

I scoff. "I don't *melt*! I fume!"

I stomp out the door and to my car.

At home, I set up my printer to spit out three hundred ballots and get back to work on the forgeries while they print. Last week Colin showed me his skills.

Now it's my chance to screw him over with mine.

In the auditorium the day of the student council election speeches, the crowd erupts in applause while Colin struts toward the podium. I snicker at the awkward way he readjusts the mic to his height after the squat girl before him had nearly brought it down to the level it belonged: his crotch. He waits a full ten seconds *after* the crowd's applause dies down before he graces us with his speech (probably plagiarized).

He sets his brown eyes on me, dark hair flopping into his face. Giant posters with his smiling face hang behind him, although these are unfortunately missing the devil horns that adorn the ones in the hallway (thanks to me). I fight back a groan at how effing gorgeous he looks up there onstage.

"Homework," he says. "I hate it. We all hate it. Am I right?"

Teachers shift uncomfortably, but the students erupt in claps.

"New research indicates that homework may be doing more harm than good. Too much of it can result in physical and emotional fatigue. This is a health risk, folks." His words might be dry, but his delivery is infectious. He leans in and enunciates each syllable as if our lives depend on it, punctuating it all with a glorious smile. "And so, I propose we do away with homework entirely and take back our afternoons!" He slams his hand against the podium gavel-style.

Whistles and whoops flood the air. Olivia Rossdale and Vance Whitford are the loudest. Olivia's boyfriend slumps in the chair and looks like he wants to punch Colin.

I notice Colin's "research" doesn't include any sources, just wild claims delivered with gusto. I also notice he doesn't make any actual promises. If he's elected, homework is going nowhere. I wish Natalie were here to witness this absurdity, but she's currently huddled in a bathroom stall, transforming herself into someone else.

"Even more important, the ban on students leaving campus for lunch is restrictive and unfair." He paces the stage like a rock singer riling up an audience. "If I'm elected, I'll try to convince the staff that we should be allowed to jet off to In-N-Out for a Double-Double on our lunch break."

More cheers erupt, and the claps increase. Vance Whitford leaps to his feet in an attempt to start a standing ovation. I aim a phallic gesture at Colin that earns me a sharp glare from Ms. Jensen. Every day for the last three years this lady has doled out my homework with equal parts algebra and disdain, and today's no different.

Right as he's about to blab about more ridiculous school requirements he wants to stop, the audio screeches, a high-pitched wail bleating from the speakers. Everyone rushes to cover their ears at the nails-on-chalkboard sound. Colin stands there, palms flat on the podium, elbows bent, sleeves pushed up, staring me down. He waits patiently as the audio rises to a crescendo of uncomfortable screeches. He remains cool, calm, and collected, and my own screech wells deep in my chest that this didn't manage to faze him. I clutch my necklace in a tight fist.

When the audio problems cease—likely because someone came

to check it out and Tig had to flee—Colin continues blabbing about more issues, all ones that seem to benefit him: new uniforms for the teams, bigger budgets to hire bands instead of DJs at dances, a school-sanctioned mental health day that's just an excuse for students to play hooky. The clapping increases in volume and fervor.

Colin's dimples indent his cheeks from his ginormous smile. "And last but certainly not least . . ." The students quiet down, waiting for what would surely be the most exciting declaration yet. "I also propose Pizza Thursdays." He checks his fancy, expensive smartwatch. "Oh look, it's Thursday."

On cue, the back doors burst open, and several pizza deliverymen march down the aisles, balancing white boxes piled higher than their heads. One by one they deposit a box of pizza at the end of each row. The scents of gooey cheese and spicy tomato sauce drift to my nose, drowning out the overwhelming peony of Jessica Sanchez's signature perfume. My stomach gurgles, and I grit my teeth against my own betrayal. Beside me, Jessica grabs the box from the boy next to her and lifts a steaming slice, hearts in her eyes.

Join the club, girl.

My jaw clenches. Whoever said the way to a man's heart is through his stomach was dead wrong. They should have replaced *man's* with *voting constituent's*.

Jessica sets the warm box on my thighs, and it takes all my willpower not to indulge. Biting my cheek, I pass the box to the kid next to me, who's practically slurping at the sight of it. I focus only on Colin and not the students chomping on garlicky goodness around me.

He marches off the stage, and Amelia Thomas timidly takes her place behind the mic. She looks green, knowing if the voting today were actually counted, she'd lose. And lose big.

After the assembly, everyone drops their ballots into Mrs. Caldwell's wooden box located next to the doors. Sauce and grease drip onto their recently dry-cleaned uniforms. Mrs. Caldwell nods to each student as they drop in their ballots, guarding the box with her life. For an amateur con artist, this would be a deal breaker. But not for me.

Because, thankfully, I have an advantage that Colin doesn't have for his cons: I have Natalie.

I walk right on past Mrs. Caldwell, past the stacks of leftover pizzas, hoping to convey that I don't care. That I won't be jetting straight to the first pizza parlor I can find after school. (Okay, fine. Pizza Thursdays sound amazing.)

Once everyone has voted, and the students scurry off to third period, Mrs. Caldwell takes the box back to her empty classroom to count the ballots. Natalie and I spring into action. I carry a trusty hall pass, this one obtained the legit way: by raising my hand and faking period cramps, much to the embarrassment of my teacher, Mr. Linker. I trudge through the empty hallways and pause at my locker across the way from Mrs. Caldwell's door. That's when the "new" substitute teacher stumbles past, winking at me in the process.

Constellations of age spots connect on her orange-tanned face, her white-blond bangs falling into her eyes. Her overly pushed-up breasts jiggle from her bouncing feet. She looks like a middle-aged woman who just got divorced and now has to work a job for the first time in her entire life. Tears stream down her face, and she lets out a hiccup.

She looks nothing like Natalie . . . but that's entirely the point.

Her fist bangs against Mrs. Caldwell's door. I keep to my locker but watch the exchange through the mirror. Mrs. Caldwell opens the door with a look that could fry ants on contact.

“Hi!” Natalie shrieks, altering her voice by an octave and speaking in a heavy Boston accent. “Oh God, this is so embarrassing. I’m a new substitute that just got called in, filling in for Western Civ?” She hiccups and then sniffles a few times. “And I can’t find the classroom. E602.” Of course not, it’s nowhere near this hallway. In fact, it’s on the clear opposite side of the school. “And I don’t want to look like an idiot to the office by asking them and, oh man, I’m already three minutes late for class!”

Mrs. Caldwell lets out a huge sigh but then steps out of her classroom and locks the door behind her. “Follow me.”

“Oh my gosh! Thank you so much! You saved my life!” Natalie hustles after her, and I roll my eyes at how thick she’s laying it on. She loves the drama.

But so do I.

Too bad when they get to the Western Civ classroom, it’ll be empty, and Natalie will clamp her hand over her mouth and apologize for completely messing up the schedule, because she has a free period now.

But this gives me approximately five minutes to pick the lock on Mrs. Caldwell’s door, slip inside, switch the ballots, and then slink away unscathed.

I unzip my black case until I’m reunited with twenty little silver tools. My best friends. Unlike Natalie, they don’t try to meddle in my love life (or lack thereof). I plunge my tiny tension wrench into the bottom of the keyhole and apply slight pressure until the pins inside the keyhole start to shift. I’ve done this so many times, my pulse doesn’t even dare to race. With my tension wrench in the bottom, I slide a Bogota rake into the top of the keyhole all the way to the back. Still applying pressure to the wrench, I twist the rake back and forth in the keyhole until all the pins set and I hear the magical click.

Too bad no one can see the grin on my face.

Mrs. Caldwell hadn't gotten very far in counting ballots, only about ten so far, so I leave those where they are and simply pluck the remaining pile from the box and shove it into my waistband. I drop the forged ones inside the box and spin on my heels to leave, but before I do, I quickly pick the lock on her desk drawer and swipe a yellow permission slip from the pile. I manage to stash the real ballots in my locker before Mrs. Caldwell even returns to her room.

At lunch, Colin hovers at the entrance to the cafeteria, shaking hands (and probably flirting) with every girl who cast a vote to thank them. He even holds out his hand to me.

"I'd say good luck, but you're going to need more than that to win today," I say in lieu of shaking his hand. And then I drop a permission slip into his palm. It only contains one sentence, written in my best interpretation of *his* handwriting:

Luck is for losers.

Colin's mouth drops open, and I bask in the glory of having him realize I beat him at his own game. But a moment later, his eyes flash and a slow grin spreads over his face. "Wow, okay. How did . . . ? Wow."

I do an internal victory dance. Not only did I surprise him, I knocked the most charming guy around so far off his game that he can't even string together a coherent sentence.

CHAPTER 4

"How are the forgeries coming?" Dad hovers over my shoulder at the dining room table a week later as I slave over a crime worse than theft: algebra. "I hope you're not letting that boy distract you? I can't have him blabbing anything about us to his father."

I pull my math book closer like a shield. "He's not a distraction!"

"You sound mighty defensive right now." Dad slides in across the table from me and lifts his brow.

I let out an aggravated sigh and rush in with details. "The amusement park skull prop is nearly complete." It's a painstaking sculpture modeled out of clay that took me over two months. "And the guitar just needs a little more distressing before it's good to go."

Dad taps his fingers against the wooden table. "And the book?"

I hesitate, twisting partially away from him. "I've run into a bit of an issue, but I'll work it out. It'll be ready in time."

Dad's face suddenly grows concerned. "What kind of issue? Is it too difficult to re-create?"

"No, I can do it." This time I'm not defensive, I'm confident. "But—" I shift in my seat. I was hoping to solve this on my own instead of admitting to him that maybe I don't have this completely under control. But we're a team. Maybe he can help. "I can make it *look* perfect. Except I can't help think about all the stuff Mom taught me. That it's not just about appearances, it's about texture. Feel. Smell. *History.* All the stuff that's impossible to re-create without the right materials."

When I helped her with an Artemisia Gentileschi forgery, she traveled all the way to Italy to steal canvas made in the sixteenth century.

"If anyone ever touches the pages, it'll be obvious that I'm using modern paper instead of paper made in ye olde olden times. It's a risk, because if they ever get suspicious and test the fibers, they'll know. And then they'll link it to us."

Dad massages his jaw. "Then we need to use paper that will pass the test."

I laugh. "Easy peasy. I'll just go to my local art supply store and buy some sheets made in 1492."

Dad chuckles. "Fiona, we're thieves. We're not going to *buy* anything." His fingers fly across his phone, and a few minutes later, he shouts, "Aha!" He slides the phone across to me.

I squint at the website. "A rare-book store?" The one on display on his phone is only an hour away.

"Read the top listing."

Guest Book kept at Tabard Manor, Southwark, the home of Sir Bartholomew Godefryd of Schleswig-Holstein and his wife Lady Elizabeth, from 1498–1501.
Price: $15,000.

"Quite a book title." My eyes bug out at the price. The description indicates there are only four pages of signatures from noble guests, and the rest of the pages are blank. "And quite a book to steal."

He shakes his head at me. "We're not stealing the entire book. There are only two pages on display in the case at the Hesburgh Library because the book's propped open, so that's all we need in order to make a convincing forgery. Two pages plus a few for contingency."

"And a lot of prayers," I mumble.

Excitement rushes through my veins at the start of another con. On Saturday, Dad parks the car in front of a brick bookstore squeezed between two glossy mirrored office buildings in the heart of downtown San Fran. Big window displays showcase rare first editions of books. A little bell jangles when we walk inside, and an old man at the counter perks up. Colorful selections of hardcover spines pack the mahogany shelves that line the walls. The musty smell of literary perfume surrounds us.

An X-Acto knife waits in the pocket of my jeans, my only weapon in this con.

Dad came with his own set of weapons: trustworthy fake blue eyes, expensive tailored clothing that screams wealth, and a firm, politician handshake. Natalie traced my eyes with heavy kohl liner and doused my waist-length blond hair with temporary black hair dye. Goth chic. Dad marches right up to the desk.

"Hi, sir, I called yesterday about—"

I act annoyed and bored, crossing my arms for emphasis and sighing so loudly a lock of hair flies away from my face.

The man nods. "Right this way." He emerges from behind the large checkout counter, where vintage posters of artwork hang behind the wall, each one depicting the original illustrations that became the covers for classic novels. "I've already set it out for you."

"Thank you, thank you," Dad says. "I've spent years collecting incunabula such as the *De pollutione nocturna*." Rule #5: The best way to convince someone you know what the hell you're talking about is to throw around words that a normal person wouldn't know. *Incunabula*: a term coined in the seventeenth century that refers to books printed during the first fifty years of the invention of the printing press. "I'm absolutely thrilled to take a look at it today." Man, he's good. His eyes even light up on the last sentence, like he can't believe his luck—even though we make our own luck by controlling the variables as much as possible.

"This gonna take long?" I poke Dad's arm and jut my head toward the door. "I thought we were going on a tour of Alcatraz. I want to see the prison." His feet won't budge, of course. This is all part of the strategy.

"We will. After we finish here. I'll just be a sec, okay, hon?" He flicks his wrist dismissively at me and turns back to the clerk. "Sorry about that. I promised her a fun family vacation, and here I am, dragging her to a bookstore. That's like a teenager's worst nightmare!" He chuckles and earns a reciprocal smile from the clerk.

The clerk needs to think I'm just an accessory, completely not interested in the rare books. This way he'll focus all his attention on Dad.

And forget all about me.

"So, the *De pollutione nocturna*? When I saw your recent acquisition"—Dad kisses his fingers—"I knew I had to drive up here and buy it." Dad's asking about the *De pollutione nocturna* because he can't be asking about the guest book. We need to lure the clerk's attention *away* from the guest book, and the *De pollutione nocturna*'s rare enough that the clerk won't want to remove his eyeballs from it. It was one of the first books ever printed by printing press, all the way back in 1466. The book's written in Latin and deals with the subject of morals, so maybe not the best choice for an epic con, but beggars can't be choosers.

"Yes, recently acquired at auction in Cologne. I thought I'd be able to hold on to it longer than three weeks, though!" The man laughs, dollar signs popping in his eyes. His knees wobble with every step on the rickety spiral staircase, his elbow rattling as he clutches the wooden bar for support. The steps creak with each footfall.

I follow behind them, striking my combat boots against the wood loud enough so he knows I'm there. So he can keep track of me peripherally.

When we reach the top floor, the owner unearths an old key from his pocket and slides it into an unmarked, locked door. With a push, he shoves the heavy wood open into a room so filled with old leather-bound copies of books, the entire place takes on a sepia tone. Dust swirls in the air, making me cough. Wooden tables hold several rare books, but the rarest, the first editions, the manuscripts so old they can't be exposed to the air without consequences, wait inside glass cases, face out, mocking me.

I spot my target: the guest book filled with glorious pages made from linen rags and animal glue that rests on the middle shelf in one of the big glass cases.

The owner leads Dad to a podium in the back of the room where the *De pollutione nocturna* waits. Dad's fingers reach out for it, slowly, as if he's too afraid to touch the pages. His sharp intake of breath does a great job of showcasing his intense interest.

"This one!" I exclaim. Both heads whip in my direction. "I want to see this one." I jab one hand toward the guest book, my other cocked on my hip. "I need a new notebook for my lyrics." I croon what sounds like a verse of an angry parents-cover-your-ears punk song. Mostly it's just swear words.

"Miss, that guest book is an antique from the fifteenth century. One of the only bound manuscripts with most of the pages left blank." The man turns back to the *De pollutione nocturna* and opens the cover for Dad to see, mumbling something about the author, Jean Gerson.

"Dad." I cross my arms. "Are you just going to let him ignore me?" Some people say you catch more flies with honey, but sometimes you can do it with belligerence.

Dad holds up a finger to the old man, and then crosses the room to where I'm standing. He leans toward me, and we engage in a fierce whisper argument, both of us saying nonsense and trying not to laugh at the other's acting skills. After a moment, he spins back to the clerk. "How much is the guest book exactly?"

The man rattles off the price, but the question isn't about cost anymore. It's about how far this clerk will have to go to keep me happy in order to snag Dad's sale of the bigger-ticket item. After all, the *De pollutione nocturna* costs two hundred thousand dollars. The man's hesitation is written plainly on his face. A choice. A sale or preserving a rare piece of history.

His keys jingle in his palm as he ambles over to us, limping and clutching the tables in the middle for support. Dad stays by my side to prove he's trustworthy by not studying the priceless first edition alone while the clerk's back is turned.

The glass door screeches as the owner slides it open. He lugs the guest book off the shelf, and a cloud of dust puffs into the air. The manuscript sits heavy in his palms, his back bending.

The man's chest bulges in and out as he wheezes. He ambles to another podium and sets down the diary for me. He keeps his hand tight on the book and steps aside to give me only enough space to run my finger over one of the pages.

"The oils from your fingers can ruin the paper." He snaps the book closed, and the wrinkles around his mouth deepen. "I can't allow any more touching without purchase. How would you like to pay for both?" he asks Dad.

"Do you like it?" The smile Dad offers me comes complete with a little twinkle in his eye. It's the kind of smile any whipped parent would make to buy their child's love.

I shrug. Gotta play up the part.

"We'll take this for sure," Dad says. "But I have a few more questions about the *De pollutione nocturna* if you don't mind."

The man beams. "I don't mind at all."

Now that he's got a hefty sale locked, he turns his back on me and leads Dad over to the other book. "I need to make sure this edition is authentic. I came across a seller a few years ago in Mississippi who tried to pass a twentieth-century edition as a first printing."

The man laughs at the absurdity of that idea, and I know Dad has him under his spell.

While they bend over the book, I slip the silver X-Acto knife out of my pocket and hum fake punk lyrics to cover the sound of me flipping through the pages of the diary to the very center of the book. There're no cameras to worry about, not when Johnny already hacked in and disabled them. I slide the knife along the inner seam of the linen pages until the top ten blank pages lift from the book as easy as peeling a sticker. I only need two, but a good criminal steals enough in case of mistakes. Given the total price on the manuscript, each blank page in my palm could pay for a semester of college. Quick as a fox, I shove the pages under my blouse and drop the knife back into my pocket.

"On second thought," I say in my most uninterested voice. "This is rather heavy." I bounce the book up and down until the men turn back to me. "I changed my mind." I pinch the corner between my thumb and index finger as if I'm carrying a smelly diaper to the trash can. I shove the book back into the man's waiting palms.

The man gasps and flips through the book with urgency, clearly checking for damage. But I'm good at what I do. He won't find any evidence of the missing pages unless he deliberately counts them. After his quick comb-through, he gingerly sets the book down on the shelf.

"Are you sure you don't want this anymore?" Dad asks loud enough for the clerk to overhear.

I nod. I'm very sure. And I'm also positive that Dad is about to lose interest in his book as well.

CHAPTER 5

The following Wednesday, I grab a plastic tray and set it on the metal counter in the cafeteria kitchen, dreaming of Double-Doubles from In-N-Out and not the glob of mashed potatoes the lunch aide slops onto my plate. It's been almost two weeks since Amelia Thomas won the election, and people are still griping about the loss of those burgers and Colin's promise to free everyone from cafeteria sloppy joes, none louder than Vance Whitford, who's been mourning like he lost a dear loved one. As the lunch aide drops steaming carrots beside the potatoes, someone shoves their tray above mine and commandeers the last carrot.

"Hey!" I turn to the thief and groan. Colin. "I wasn't actually going to eat something that nutritious, but that carrot belongs to me."

He grins at me. "Mine now. Along with another one of your clients."

My eyes widen, and I stomp on his foot to get him to shut the hell up in front of the lunch aides (who probably don't care) and fellow students ahead of me (who definitely do).

"Any chance my girl Fiona here can have another carrot?" He sets his megawatt smile on the lunch aide and winks. "Please?" I watch in horror as the lunch aide's sourpuss face melts into a smile of her own, and she drops not one but three carrots onto my tray.

"I'm not your girl." I scrape my tray along the metal counter toward the next station while Colin bullshits his way into an extra helping of meatloaf. When I exit the line, I veer left to get as far away from him as I can manage, but he keeps step with me.

"So listen. I had an idea."

"Was it to transfer schools?" I bat my eyelashes in hope.

He rolls his eyes. "Admit it. You'd miss me too much."

My phone vibrates, and when I glance at my smartwatch, a text from Jessica Sanchez appears.

Jessica: Sorry, Fiona, but I need to cancel later.

I stop dead. Jessica Sanchez is one of my best customers, but I can't help but think back to what Colin said a few minutes ago. *It's mine now. Along with another one of your clients.*

That's the third thing this week he beat me at. In debate class, he took me down with an eloquent speech about why the driving age should be raised that even had our licensed classmates cheering. In biology, he finished dissecting his frog 2.7 seconds faster than me. At least in gym he trailed behind me in number of pull-ups and get-out-of-class excuses.

I don't even care about my grades, I only care about getting better grades than *him*. But that's probably impossible, considering the way he has the teachers eating out of his hands. They're already clamoring over him because of his goody-two-shoes bullshit and how he twists his uniform tie into fancy European knots. He even started a trend of looking prim and proper. I prefer to give a big ol' *eff you* to the administration by testing the limits of what they deem appropriate for the dress code. Red lipstick? (Check.) Safety pins added to lining of plaid skirt? (Check.) Ironing a drawing of my teacher's face in effigy on the back of my blazer? (Detention.)

"Oh good," Colin says, reading over my shoulder. "You got Jessica's text. That makes this easier."

Mr. Linker shuffles by us and nods hello.

"We could keep doing this," Colin says without dropping the volume of his voice. "Stealing from each other. Or we could—"

I balance my tray in one hand and clamp my other palm over his mouth. "Shut up. We're in the middle of the cafeteria. Are you trying to get us caught?"

He shrugs and pries my fingers off him. "It's not a big deal. Everyone already knows."

"Our classmates, yes. Our teachers, no." I let out a huff. "If you want to talk to me about this, you have to find a way to be discreet."

I storm off, my knuckles turning white as I carry my tray toward Natalie's table. For someone supposedly acing his classes, he sure sucks at being smart.

"What did Colin want?" Natalie asks when I slide my legs onto the lunch table bench. Today her lips are plumped to Hollywood collagen standards using contouring techniques, not prosthetics, giving her a stung-bee appearance. She's chosen blue contacts and a long blond wig that grazes her waist, making us look like twins. Imitation is the sincerest form of flattery.

"To remind me how much he sucks."

She snickers, and when Colin doesn't try to ambush me in an empty hallway by the end of the day, I consider him defeated. But a few hours later I'm sitting at the dining room table with Dad, going over the plans for the last three heists while I sew the newly acquired book pages into the distressed cover I made out of a mix of clay and fabric, when the doorbell rings.

We bolt upright and look at each other. Dad slides the notes we've made and the book forgery off the table and flies down to the basement to hide them with the rest of Mom's stuff in a locked cabinet. I head to the door.

It's probably just a delivery man, but when I swing open the door, Colin's brilliant smile greets me. "This discreet enough?"

I slam the door in his face.

The doorbell rings again, but I make no move to answer it. When Dad comes up from the basement, he squints at me. "Who is it?"

"The school douchebag," I say, even though Colin can't hear me make fun of him, then add, "Our friendly neighborhood FBI agent's smarmy son."

Dad scratches his chin. "Well then. Let him in. Everything's hidden now, and I'm curious what he wants."

"I'm sure whatever he's here for, it's bad news."

"If Ian O'Keefe sent him over here to snoop, then I want to make sure he leaves without anything to report back."

I groan. "Can't we pretend we're not home? I mean, I realize I just opened the door and he saw me, but we've dealt with worse ruses before."

Dad gives me a look, and I sigh. He shuffles back to the living room.

I crack open the door again, and Colin shakes his head at me while wearing an amused expression.

I cross my arms. "Take off your shirt."

Colin tilts his head at me. "Whoa, okay. I mean, my abs aren't that great, but if you really want to see them . . ." His fingers grip the bottom of his cool anime T-shirt. Gah, why can't he be wearing something awful, like a shirt with a cheesy saying? *FBI: Female Body Inspector.*

I roll my eyes. "Calm down. I'm making sure you're not wearing a wire or anything. And leave your phone out here so you can't record any convos."

He mock scoffs and places a hand over his heart. "Are you saying you don't trust me?"

"That's exactly what I'm saying." I step forward to intimidate him, but he doesn't back down.

He lifts his shirt quickly to give me a brief view of his bare chest, and I have to force myself not to stare. During my momentary distraction, he sets his phone on the porch swing and then brushes right past me into the house. His shirt falls back down, and he breezes right up to Dad with his hand outstretched. "Mr. Spangler, it's so nice to meet you. I've heard a lot about you."

"Really?" Dad looks suspicious. "From Fiona or from your father?"

"Fiona of course. She told me you two have a fantastic relationship and she loves you very much."

Dad beams, but I have to break up the party here. "I never said that."

Colin flicks his wrist dismissively. "She's just embarrassed. She went on and on about how much she adores you today at lunch."

I start to interject again and remind him that the only thing we discussed at lunch was his ineptitude at all things covert, but when I see Dad's smile growing larger, I can't help it—I concede. Damn, Colin's good.

"Anyway, we'll be in Fiona's room." Colin leans toward Dad. "Don't worry—we'll leave the door open, and you can check on us every few minutes if you'd like."

My feet stay planted. "We're not going in my room."

Colin lifts a brow. "Afraid to be alone with me?"

"No—it's—" I open and close my mouth but can't seem to find

the right words, if they even exist. "Let's stay down here. Where there's a chaperone." I gesture my hand toward Dad and try to give him my best *put an end to this right now* glare, but he retaliates with a firm *find out what he wants* nod of the head. I imagine normal parents probably don't encourage their teen daughters to spend time alone in their rooms with rebellious heartbreaker boys, but normal parents also don't prioritize recon over everything else.

I groan. "Give me one second to . . . clean up all the dirty underwear from my floor." Or more accurately, hide any evidence about my mother from that room, too.

I race upstairs and take a quick sweep of my room. The guitar's already hidden in my closet and looks normal enough in the case, but the stack of postcards my mom sent me rests in my drawer. There's also a notebook lying on top of my bed. It's mostly filled with schoolwork, but I did write out my mom's clue answers on one of the pages, because I'm a visual person and I like to stare at them every night to try to decipher them. I shouldn't leave any evidence in this room at all.

Pulse amping, I grab the notebook and postcards and run into the guest room next door. I shove the notebook under the guest bed mattress and the postcards on top of the closet, under a spare pillow. I let out a relieved breath. Coast's clear. He has no reason to go in here.

I smooth down my shirt and, okay, my hair, and then head back downstairs to beckon Colin. He swaggers toward me, shaking his hair out of his eyes in the same move shampoo models use in commercials. I have to force myself to look away from this, too.

We take the stairs side by side, neither of us speaking, and something in my stomach starts twisting. I tentatively point toward my bedroom door, and he stops in the center and pivots on his heels to take in the three-sixty-degree view. Suddenly I wish I'd thought to yank my old childhood porcelain dolls—the ones Mom gave me—off my shelf and hide those, too. Colin nods approvingly at my *Ocean's 8* poster and the floor-to-ceiling mural landscape scene I painted on one wall, but squints questioningly at my frilly purple bedding and sequined throw pillows.

"The pillows were a gift from Natalie," I mumble.

"She has good taste." He plops down on the bed. "So do you." He grabs a Funko figurine of Frida Kahlo from the shelf above my bed and turns it over in his hands. His eyes flick to the mural on my wall. "You're a really amazing artist."

My cheeks ignite. When I hoist myself onto the bed, the mattress wobbles, and Colin shifts closer to me.

"Hey," he whispers in a velvety voice.

I bolt to my feet and wipe my sweaty palms on my skirt. Colin lifts his brow in question. Oh God, I can't do this. I can't act normal around him.

I need help from the one person who would know what to do. Natalie.

"Can you give me a sec? I'll be right back." I swipe my phone from my nightstand and squeeze it tight in my palms.

Colin nods and grabs another figurine from the shelf to study.

I head (more like flee) to the doorway. Because the guest room is right next door and I don't want him to eavesdrop on my conversation, I hole up on the third floor in my dad's room. My throat tightens, and I correct myself in my head. My *parents'* room.

I stab in Natalie's number with shaking fingers.

She picks up on the first ring. "Hey, lady. What's up?"

"Colin's in my room," I whisper. Even just saying his name makes my pulse spike.

"Bow chica wow wow."

"You're lucky you're not next to me, because you deserve a jab in the ribs for that." I let out an exasperated sigh. "Please. I need help here."

"Are you asking me for help because you don't know what he wants and think he's out to get you . . . or are you asking me for boy help?"

My heart beats faster when she says that last part.

"Because if it's the latter, I should remind you I'm way better at girl help than boy help." She tacks on a laugh.

"It's the former!" I say too fast, my voice too high-pitched. "I swear."

Natalie keeps laughing. "Sure it is. But either way, my advice here is the same. Just be yourself."

"So steal from him, then? Because being myself means being a thief."

Natalie clucks her tongue. "Talk to him. Flirt with him. Find out what he wants."

"I prefer to find out that sort of information via surveillance and spying."

"And you wonder why you're single!"

I scoff. "I don't like him like that."

There's a momentary pause before she whispers, "Then why did you call me?"

I slam my finger down on the end call button. It takes me several seconds of deep breathing to calm myself enough to head back, not feeling any better about the situation. But I stop short when I get to my room.

Colin's not there.

In a panic, I fly to the guest room, clutching my mom's necklace for comfort, but he's not in there, either. I fling myself at the mattress and lift it. The notebook remains under it. The postcards are still in the closet. I let out a breath.

There's a flush from the bathroom, and then the sink turns on. I wipe sweat from my forehead and coax myself to get it together.

In my room, I flop onto my bed right before Colin returns. He settles in the spot beside me and shoots me a giant smile.

It makes a smile wobble onto my face, too. Damn it!

Talk to him. But what do I even say? My fingers itch to dial Natalie again and ask, but I know I have to strap on my big-girl panties and have a conversation with the one guy who can sweet-talk anyone.

Flirt with him. I think back to how he waltzed in here and complimented my dad, then did the same thing to me in my room. So I start there. "You're really good at charming people," I say, and I can see the tips of his ears turn pink. "But seriously. Are you *trying* to get caught?" Okay maybe that flirtation attempt took a wrong turn.

He lifts a brow. "What do you mean?"

"Your dad's an FBI agent. You're practically shouting through the hallways that you're a criminal. What if he catches you?" I know I've asked this before, but that was in the cafeteria when he was talking loud enough to show off. Maybe alone, he'll give it to me straight.

Colin swallows hard and scoots away a few inches. "Then maybe he'll finally notice me."

He says it low. So low I'm not sure if he intended me to hear it. But I think it's exactly what I needed to hear. He has a reason to do this, and that reason has nothing to do with me.

Our eyes meet. We stare at each other for a few seconds, and my skin tingles. But then he breaks the moment by stretching his legs and rubbing his palms over his thighs. "But I didn't come here to talk about that."

Whatever emotion he'd let escape in his confession vanishes. His voice comes out cool and calm. Collected.

"Listen, I know we've got a game going here. I stole Olivia. You screwed me over in the election. I stole Jessica . . . which makes the next move yours."

I purse my lips, considering. "Okay, so you came to tell me you know you have to watch your back?" Also, probably not an appropriate flirtation attempt.

"I could keep doing this. Turning every one of your clients over to my side, and then you try to retaliate . . ."

"Please. I'm not *trying* to retaliate. I'm succeeding very well in retaliation. Plus, you only stole two of my clients. That's hardly a majority."

"Fiona." His brief gaze burns right through me. "Let's end this once and for all."

I push a tangled blond strand out of my face, my chest stilling. I'm on edge, not sure where he's going to take this. Not sure where I *want* him to take it. Suggest we ignore each other from now on? Suggest we work together?

"How 'bout a challenge?" He raises his brow. "A competition to prove which one of us is the better con artist and thief. Winner gets all the student clients from now on. The other backs off empty-handed."

I flinch, and something inside me deflates. He's not here to become friends. He's here to become enemies.

I scoot a few inches away from him on the bed. My body becomes all hard angles instead of soft, relaxed limbs. "What are we stealing?" I snap, the bitterness evident in my voice.

"I have some ideas, but—"

No. I'm not letting him control this. If he's suggesting a challenge, then I'll challenge every damn thing he says. "If we're doing this, it has to be difficult. Dangerous even. It's got to be something we can't access easily." Rule #6: A good con artist knows how to get people to do what they want by planting the idea in *their* heads.

Colin snaps his fingers. "The principal's office. He's always in there, and whenever he's not, one of the secretaries sits guard right outside the door. It's on the second floor, so it's impossible to get into from the outside."

Unless you're me, of course.

"His framed PhD diploma?" I wrinkle my nose the minute the suggestion comes out of my mouth. I need something small enough to fit in my pocket if I'm thinking in terms of exit strategies.

Colin must be on the same page as me, because he casually throws out, "A USB drive."

It isn't something I could forge, but it's still small. "A USB drive containing what?"

He doesn't even hesitate. "This semester's grades."

I narrow my eyes. This was the exact con Jessica wanted to hire me for but paid Colin instead. Find out her grades before her report card travels to her house, so she can decide next steps: accept her fate or go for con number two and hire me to create a forgery. Or I guess now con number two might involve Colin talking his way into the school office, stealing a blank report card, and printing out new grades for Jessica. The final grades are due from the teachers today, and mailings won't start until Friday, giving us a two-day deadline to complete the task. And if I'm the one to complete it, I'll make my next con stealing back the pile of cash Jessica already paid Colin.

"Whoever gets them to Jessica first wins," I say.

The two of us agree with nods of our heads and matching glares. And then he stands up and exits my room without another word.

My dad pokes his head into my room a few minutes later. "What did he want?"

"To get his ass whooped."

CHAPTER 6

Part one of my plan to beat Colin involves Natalie disguising herself as a prospective new student coming to tour the school. My dad even agrees to act as a pinch hitter, letting Natalie color his slicked-back black hair into distinguished salt-and-pepper gray and alter his features just slightly—longer nose, plumper cheeks—to disguise him as *her* father. It's nice to have a dad who understands the importance of an education, and he values nothing more than me learning how to orchestrate the perfect crime.

He also understands the importance of screwing over the family who likely moved here to screw over *my* family.

When I first suggested it, Dad cracked his knuckles as a devious smile quirked his thin lips. "I haven't been this excited about a job in weeks. And that includes the nasty workplace-injury case I'm about to win." He suddenly grew serious. "But, Fiona, I need you to promise that once you win this challenge, you'll forget about Colin and focus on finishing the forgeries."

I waved him away dismissively. "That's the plan." The amusement park skull prop and the guitar are ready to go. Now that I have the proper material to work with, I can complete the ancient-book forgery in a week or two. And we have five weeks until we leave. Once school ends, we're hightailing it out of San Francisco (okay, we'll drive the speed limit to the airport so as not to cause suspicion) to take back what's rightfully ours: my mom's last three forgeries and the clues written on them. And then we'll finally have all the tools to find her.

Now, gray clouds lurk behind the pitter-patter of heavy rain colliding with the sidewalk, sending water droplets splashing upward like dribbled basketballs. The crisp scent of moisture lingers in the air. I hunker outside on the ground floor beneath Principal Van Lowe's window, which is located on the side of the school. The window faces the football fields, but the rain ensures they'll be empty today. I lean close to the brick, catching bits and pieces of the persuasive argument Fake Dad makes through the cracked window (thanks to Natalie claiming she's stifling). ". . . sizable donation . . . new school wing . . ."

Thankfully, the dollar signs popping in Principal Van Lowe's eyes help persuade him to ignore any similarities to one of his most detention-happy students. "Registration is usually closed this late in the school year, but I'm sure we could find a spot—"

Just like they "found a spot" for Colin with a little monetary persuasion, I'm sure.

Fake Dad clears his throat. "We're looking at several options. Any chance we could have a campus tour?"

"Of course. Right this way."

Chairs scrape.

Now all I have to do is wait for the signal that the campus tour has taken them far away from the office.

In this case, the signal is a text from Natalie with a ghost cat emoji, which arrives a few minutes later.

I swipe my damp hair out of my eyes and slip on black fabric gloves, the kind used for elegant celebrity awards dinners and preventing fingerprints.

Rain pummels my legs, making them glisten like stolen diamonds. I'm soaked enough to enter (and win) a wet T-shirt contest. My eyes lock on a formidable challenge. Ivy curls around a steel-lattice trellis next to the window. The school feels it gives an air of history, but I view it as an invitation to upstairs. I push away the wet leaves and grip the slippery steel bars underneath, my feet finding purchase easily.

Fat raindrops pound against my face as I heave myself upward, the trellis rattling under my weight. I pause, squeezing my eyes shut until the shaking stops. The smart part of me itches to go slow and steady on the rickety structure, but the smarter part races in case Colin beats me to the punch and steals the grades as soon as the office empties.

A crunch of leaves makes my heart pound. I whip my head around, expecting to see my buzzkill rounding the corner. But only the wind gusts and plasters my drenched hair to my cheeks. Since the window's cracked a tad, I easily slide it open all the way and spread out a towel on the floor. That's the good thing about breaking and entering in the middle of the day: The alarms aren't activated.

The air-conditioning turns my skin to ice as I shimmy inside. I strip off my soaked school uniform and replace it with a fresh one I folded neatly at the bottom of my purse to limit incriminating drips on the gray carpet. Stuffed at the bottom of my bag there's a third set to change into before I rejoin my classmates in fourth period. There's also a wig that's a perfect replica of my blond hair to cover my soaked locks. The same wig Natalie wore a few days ago. Rule #7: Thieves must be good at packing in small bags. After removing my shoes and squeezing out the ends of my waterlogged hair onto the towel, I tie it back into a low ponytail and cross the room to Van Lowe's computer.

I'm not a tech genius, but I know a thing or two about people who use passwords: They tend to forget them. I only need to lift up his keyboard to find the Post-it Note stuck to the bottom that reveals the sequence of gibberish that unlocks his files. My USB purrs when I drag the folder with the grades onto it. With a satisfied smile, I eject the USB, stuff it in my skirt pocket, and reverse my entrance until my feet land with a wet splat onto the grass.

Victory never tasted so sweet.

I spin on my heels to flee but run smack into Colin O'Keefe.

Beads of water stick to his hair and eyelashes, making it seem like he's posing as the romantic lead in the climax of a movie. He blinks at me as though he can't believe what he just saw. "I admit, I'm impressed."

"Good." I turn to leave, but he places one arm against the brick wall, blocking me.

"Tell me how you did it. I clearly could use some tips." He lets out a self-deprecating laugh that sounds almost endearing. Almost.

"I'm a better criminal. That's how." I wheel around to go the other way, but he falls into step beside me.

"Hey, wait. I'm serious. How did you manage to open the window from the outside?"

He actually sounds sincere this time. I think back to when I first found Natalie, a lowly cosplayer capable of so much more. It only took the promise of fun, cold hard cash to fund her cosmetics obsession, plus a little bit of training with the methods my mother used on me to convert her. Maybe Colin could be the same: an ally instead of an enemy. It would be good to know someone with a connection to the FBI. He could spy for us.

I stop short, blinking against the pounding rain. "Tell me what your plan was first."

He leans against the trellis, his white button-up turning see-through from the rain. My mouth goes dry at the way it sculpts against his abs. The same ones he was embarrassed about yesterday. I force myself to look away and cross my arms over my own see-through shirt.

"I was going to do it at night," he whispers. He's speaking so low, I have to inch toward him to hear. And even when I stand a foot away, I still have to come closer. I lean next to him on the trellis, both of our shoulders pressed into the metal lattice, facing each other in spite of the rain. "I already swiped Ms. Jensen's keys and had a few feelers out to some electronics people I've heard about to help with the security alarm. Someone named Tig."

"She wouldn't have helped you," I whisper.

He shrugs, clearly trying to downplay how utterly terrible his plan was. "But seriously. Climbing up the trellis was badass."

My cheeks ignite, wet hair clinging to my torso. For some reason I want to duck my head and giggle—and I banned giggles from my vocabulary years ago. "Thanks," I whisper back, surprised at the sincerity in my voice. Even though the pounding rain demands shouting, I keep my voice to trading-secrets levels.

"I've been thinking." He scoots even closer. Our shoulders brush, sending crackles of electricity through me. "Maybe this challenge was a mistake. Maybe we can work together instead. Be a team. I have a few tricks I can show you, too."

The way he says the last part makes it seem like his tricks have nothing to do with cons but rather his lips. And when he hits me with his spectacular grin, I suddenly understand how he captivated Olivia and Jessica so fast. I'm swooning, too.

I want to nod along to everything he says, but I force myself to respond. "I'm—I'm not sure."

Colin tilts his head at me as if he's just noticed something and purses his lips. "Hey." He reaches out a hand toward me, hovering it in front of my face. "Can I?"

I nod to this, too, even though I have no idea what he's asking until he brushes his fingers softly along my cheek and sweeps a wet lock of hair behind my ear. Tingles follow in the wake of his touch, and my eyelids flutter.

My own fingers instinctively reach up to push his matted-down bangs off his forehead. When his eyes briefly close and he sucks in a shaky breath, my hands keep going, fingers knotting in the hair at the base of his neck.

Following suit, he trails his hands down my neck, along my collarbone, wiping water away even as it sloshes right back. My mouth parts at the amazing feel of his touch. *Friends*, I think, then correct myself. *More* than friends.

He wraps one arm around my waist while his fingers continue their exploration down my sides. My hands interlock behind his neck. Bending down, he brushes his lips along my ear instead of the place I want them to land: my lips. My breath comes out shaky, but his voice sounds confident when he whispers, "When I told you my plan before, I lied. *This* was my plan."

And then he drops his arm from around my waist. My arms fall to my sides in surprise. He backs away from me a few steps and flashes the USB drive at me, because of course Colin won't do anything unless he can brag about it. I reach into my pocket to confirm, but I know the drive's gone, stolen while Colin distracted me with something I didn't know I wanted and definitely don't want anymore.

A grimace tightens my lips. I launch myself at him, trying to grab it. He lifts his arm high in the air and keeps walking backward toward the side entrance while I try to swipe for it.

"By the way, does the number forty-seven mean anything to you? What about *Hesiod*?"

I freeze. The list of my mom's clues: *11, D5, Hesiod, 2nd, 92.5, 47*. We may not be able to discern the connection, but something tells me the expert code crackers at the FBI can.

"Nothing," I snap. My pulse increases, limbs turning to Jell-O.

"Never mind, then." He shrugs and wrenches open the school door during my momentary distraction. He slips inside and leaves me behind with nothing except resentment.

By the time I catch up to him, he's already nudged the drive into the slats of Jessica's locker, effectively stealing her and all my other clients in the process.

"I hate him." I slam a curled fist against my dining room table that evening. Above us, the fluorescent light trapped behind a glass cylinder buzzes like a wasp caught in a spider's web. "Any ideas how to create a forgery of *him* and replace him with a replica? Preferably one that doesn't talk back."

Natalie purses her lips, now sporting a delicate gold lip ring. A few other clip-on hoops line her ear, which has been shaped to pointy elf standards. "At least let me slip him some crushed-up laxatives first. It'll make for a fun debate class!"

Only my best friend would view poisoning someone as a good thing.

"Girls." Dad stops pacing in the dining room and pulls out a wooden chair across from me. "He doesn't know anything. He saw a list of random things in Fiona's notebook—"

"The notebook hidden under the guest room mattress," I remind them. Colin must have clued in that I'd hidden something important when I went upstairs. He's smart enough to know if I left him alone in the room, it wasn't there. With only a bed and a dresser in the guest room, it probably didn't take him long to find the notebook and thumb through it. I don't know how he found *that* particular line of text hidden among a bunch of math problems and history notes. Either Colin knew what he was looking for . . . or he somehow knows me so well already to pick this line out.

Dad whirls on me. "Why would you leave him alone? Even for a second?" He shakes his head in shame at me, but it's something I've been beating myself up about, too.

"The bottom line is he's sniffing after Mom. Maybe blabbing everything he learned to his dad. *And* he's won control of my turf."

"Forget about the school cons for now." Dad pushes the half-completed ancient-book project toward me. "Finish the important stuff so we can find the remaining clues and reunite with your mother. You've already taken things too far, and I don't want anything else drawing the attention of Ian O'Keefe."

His words sink in, and a renewed sense of purpose washes over me. Finding Mom is what's important. Not getting revenge on the douchebag that one-upped me.

But still, it doesn't need to be a choice. If I'm right, and Colin really is onto us, then I need to show him what happens if he messes with my family. He needs to know that if he goes after Mom, I go after him.

"Okay." I paste on the sincerest smile I can muster. Dad can usually smell my bullshit from a mile away, but I take a cue from Colin here. To get someone to believe you, you have to convince yourself you believe it, too. And turn on the charm, of course. "You're right, Dad. You always are." I pluck one of my trusty paintbrushes from my stash and hover it over the book.

Natalie squints at me.

Dad rolls his eyes, seeing right through my bullshit. "We leave three days after school lets out. I need you focused."

"I *am* focused. I want Mom back, too." I nod to reinforce my resolve.

Dad studies me for one long second before letting out a sigh and walking away.

As soon as he's out of earshot, Natalie leans over. "Okay, how are we taking him down?"

"We're not taking him down entirely, we're just going to show him we're capable of doing so."

"A threat." Natalie's mouth practically waters. "I like it. But how?"

"You know all those favors Vance Whitford owes me? I'm about to cash in."

Twenty minutes later, we're at the mall one town away, next in line for Vance Whitford's register at Mama Burrito's fast-food kiosk. Vance may act the part of ritzy prep-school student with his expensive jeans (thrift store) and his bro-y accent (watching too many reruns of "The Californians" sketch on *SNL*), but his ticket to preppiness came complete with a tuition-free scholarship. He prefers not to announce that fact, though, because everyone knows good grades are a one-way path to Loserville.

"Vance! My man." I slap my palm down on the counter. "Word on the street is you owe me a favor or twelve."

His face drops at the sight of me. Wispy red hairs poke out of his blue-and-yellow ball cap. "I'm working," he whispers through gritted teeth, as though I may not have noticed that fact. But what he's really telling me is *Not here*.

"When's your break? I can wait." I gesture toward the empty table right in front of the burrito kiosk.

Natalie taps her lip. "Yeah, it'll probably take me that long to decide what to order anyway." She grins at him. A challenge.

"Um." He tugs at his collar.

The girl at the register next to him eyes me up and down and then flicks her eyes toward Vance, a small smile playing on her lips.

She clearly thinks he's tongue-tied over me and not, you know, terrified about what I'm going to ask him. "You can go now. I'll hold down the fort." She juts her chin toward the last straggler in line.

With a sigh, Vance unties his apron and exits through the side door. He doesn't wait for us as he traipses straight through the food court, out the front exit, and then over to a small alcove guarded by large garbage bins. Even he knows more about stealth than my mortal enemy.

The rain from earlier has subsided, but dark clouds lurk in the sky like eavesdroppers, setting the mood a dreary gray. My long hair whips around my face.

"Whatever it is, just please don't tell anyone I work here, okay?" He shoves his hands in his pockets, biting his lip.

I hold up a palm. "Secret's safe. As always." The only reason I know he works here in the first place is because one time I offered him a deal: He tells me a secret in lieu of payment for a forgery. You never know when blackmail might come in handy later. Like today!

"What do you need?" He ducks his head as though he needs to brace himself.

"This one's just as much for you as it is for me. I know you're still upset about the ban on leaving campus for lunch, so I want you to hire Colin for just that. Ask him to sneak off campus during lunch on Monday and buy you as many burgers from In-N-Out as he can get his slimy little paws on."

Natalie rolls her eyes at my theatrics. I didn't even get to my evil *mwuahaha* laugh yet.

"Just ask him to get you one or two burgers, okay?" she clarifies. "And you can't brag about it. You have to eat them in private."

Vance blinks at me, waiting for the punch line. "I mean, that sounds delicious, but I don't get why you need me to do this. Why can't *you* hire him?"

"If he knows the burgers are for me, he'll never agree. Plus, he already knows you want them."

Vance bites his lip. "I'm not going to get in trouble, am I?"

"You?" I wave my hand dismissively. "Nope. Promise you won't get in trouble at all."

Can't say the same for Colin, though. The standard infraction for breaking a school rule like sneaking off campus is an automatic three-day suspension. Three full days where Colin will stew over how I did this to him . . . and how if he messes with Mom, I can do so much more than just get him suspended.

On Monday, I linger in the hallway, pretending to riffle through my locker, while I watch Colin in my mirror as he talks to the security guard. With lunch starting in less than a minute, the hallway's almost empty. I'm not exactly discreet, but neither is Colin's choice of location. Or the fact that he continually flicks his eyes toward me as though he wants me to overhear how great he is at subterfuge.

"Smokers," Colin says. "Heading toward the woods. I think they're seniors."

Mr. Porter's face blanches. "How many?"

Colin shrugs. "A bunch. Five? Fifteen?"

"Wow." Mr. Porter rakes his hand over his mostly bald head. "Thank you. Really appreciate the tip."

Colin shakes his hand and grins. "Happy to help keep the students safe. My grandma died from lung cancer," he adds unnecessarily, but Mr. Porter's face turns even more grave, as though he totally understands why Colin cares so much.

He waits until Mr. Porter exits through the back door and hustles toward the woods before he twists around and winks at me.

I respond in the only way that seems appropriate. I wink back.

Unfazed, he lopes outside, heads straight past the picnic tables near the parking lot, and proceeds to get into his car and zoom onto the main road without the threat of a security guard to catch him.

I turn on my heels and head in the same direction as Mr. Porter. Thankfully, I'm in shape and he's . . . not. I catch up to him near the entrance to the grand woods that expand behind our school. A year ago, a few students got expelled for being caught in the center of the woods, over a mile from the school, smoking in the middle of the day. I guess that was Colin's entire plan: send Mr. Porter on a wild-goose chase that could last miles and keep him away from the parking lot for the full forty-five-minute lunch period.

"Mr. Porter!" I yell. "Wait!"

He pauses just long enough to swivel his head toward me, wheezing. "Sorry, miss. But I've got—"

"I just saw Colin drive off campus. He mentioned something about burgers?"

Mr. Porter stops in his tracks. He casts one long glance toward the woods and another at me before his face melts into one of anger. He marches back in the direction of the school and does a quick sweep around the tables to confirm Colin's absence. And then he parks himself at one of the tables in the back to keep watch but not be seen when Colin first returns.

I hunker down at a table closest to the school parking lot, far away from my usual table indoors. The freshmen at the table all eye me like I'm crazy when I slide my legs onto the bench and then proceed to ignore them entirely by twisting around and facing the parking lot entrance.

Something in my stomach hollows out, but it can't be nerves. I never get those on any of my con missions.

Still, I squirm in my seat. I half expected all the tension to drain from my shoulders once I ratted Colin out, but I feel even more anxious than before.

My phone vibrates with a text from Natalie.

Natalie: How's it going?

Fiona: Most of it's going according to plan. Except one thing . . .

I bite my lip and nearly type out a joke instead of what I actually want to say. But she's my best friend. I can tell her anything.

Fiona: . . . I might be developing a conscience.

Natalie: Don't feel bad. Just remember why you're doing this. To keep your family safe. And to show him that you can fool him, too.

Natalie: Also, remember there will be juicy delicious burgers at the end of this! Sure, no one's going to get to eat them, but they'll still be juicy!

I swallow hard and hug my phone to my chest. My resolve returns. She always knows the right thing to say. Especially the part about the burgers.

A new text pops up on my phone from Tig, but it's just the emoji of two eyeballs staring intently at something to the left. I groan and bang out a text to Nat.

Fiona: Did you tell Tig about the plan?

Natalie: Um.

A GIF of men with bunny ears pops onto my screen.

Fiona: Nat!!! Men with bunny ears is NOT an answer!

Natalie: I wanted to impress her. Think it worked?

I send an emoji of a head exploding in lieu of an answer.

Each time a car drives toward the lot entrance, I flinch. My leg rattles up and down until Colin's sleek, silver Subaru pulls into the lot, engine revving, and I bolt upright. As Colin parks in his assigned spot, Mr. Porter hustles over to him.

I stalk toward Colin's car, too, careful to stay out of Mr. Porter's line of sight. I duck behind the next car. The body of the car shields me so Mr. Porter can't see me, especially not with his back to me, but I can still view enough of the action by peering through the windows. I want to see Colin's face when he realizes *I'm* the reason he got caught.

Mr. Porter knocks on Colin's driver's window, and Colin rolls it down.

"Colin O'Keefe," Mr. Porter says. "I'm afraid I have no choice but to report this. Violation of rule number seventeen in the school handbook carries a three-day suspension." He tugs at his collar. "You're just lucky pranking staff doesn't carry additional time."

While Colin chews on that news, I shoot off a text.

Fiona: Enjoy your mandatory vacation! It's my gift to you. Or should I say . . . my warning.

His gaze shifts toward his phone on his console, and his eyes narrow.

"I'm going to need you to hand over those bags." Mr. Porter juts his chin toward what I presume are two white paper bags oozing with grease. The scent of meat and cheese drifts toward me, and my stomach growls. Judging by the way Mr. Porter's licking his lips, his stomach's growling, too.

Colin hands over one white paper bag through the window.

Mr. Porter dips his head through the window. "That plastic bag, too. The one you just knocked onto the floor."

"That's not part of the burgers. That's—"

"Don't care." Mr. Porter sets down the bag of burgers and crosses his arms. "Hand over the plastic bag, son," he says as though he's taking his job of security guard as seriously as if this was a cop show on a big-five network.

Colin's fingers tighten on the wheel. "Can I start my suspension immediately? I'll leave right now and—"

"You hiding drugs in there, boy?" Mr. Porter presses his forehead against the top of Colin's window. "Out of the car or I call the cops. Now."

Reluctantly, Colin pushes himself out of the car. He shoves his hands in his pockets and ducks his head. An uneasy feeling washes over me. I've only ever seen him be cool, calm, and collected, but right now he looks as if he's one second away from freaking out.

Mr. Porter crawls into the driver's seat to grab the plastic bag from the floor.

Colin squeezes his eyes shut, bracing for something.

My stomach winds up, coiling tight. What did he do?

"Holy crap." Mr. Porter ducks back out of the car. He holds up handfuls of small plastic rectangles, and the sunlight reflects off them in a prism of colors. One of the rectangles falls out of his hands and skids beneath the car I'm hiding behind, stopping at my feet. My eyes widen. California state IDs, complete with holograms. The only thing missing is the portrait and information, but that's probably the point. Colin just needs to type it in, print it out, and bam! Fake.

"They're not mine." Colin holds up his hands in surrender. "I was just transporting them, I swear."

Vance's gig must not have been the only one he agreed to do at lunch today.

A muscle in Mr. Porter's jaw twitches. "Whose are they, then? I have to report this to the cops. No choice there. Creating and selling fake IDs is a serious offense." He steps into Colin's line of vision, forcing Colin to look at him. "But I'd rather report the person who these really belong to. So tell me a name, and I won't tell them yours."

Colin clamps his mouth shut, and for some reason this makes something painful shoot through me. He's not a rat.

But now I am.

"All right, come with me. We'll call the authorities from inside." Mr. Porter takes a step toward the building.

My heart leaps into my throat, and I feel like I'm going to throw up. I only meant to teach Colin a lesson so he would step back a little. Instead, I ruined his life.

I get out my phone and type words I've never said before: *I'm sorry*. But before I can bring myself to hit send, a text pops up on my phone.

Colin manages to steal the last word without ever opening his mouth:

Colin: I guess this means you won the turf war after all.

CHAPTER 8

I stare into my locker in a daze, barely registering which book I'm taking out. I've been a walking zombie for four days now.

Natalie nudges me with her shoulder and gives me a sad smile. She's wearing her most subdued disguise yet: simple fish-tail braid in a shade of brown that would never stand out from the crowd, cat-eye plastic-rimmed glasses, and nude lipstick. "I thought you'd be doing ballerina twirls in the hallway now that Colin's out for the count, not . . . moping."

I swallow hard, unable to stave off the guilt eating me inside the past few days. "I wish I didn't feel so guilty."

Natalie bites her lip. "This is what you wanted, though, right? To get him out of your hair."

A gaggle of girls congregate at the locker next to me, and when I spot Olivia, I straighten. I don't want to be like her, or Jessica, or all the other girlies swooning over Colin. For the last few days, they've been sniffling into tissues, big fat tears streaming down their cheeks as though they're mourning his death and not his suspension.

"I heard his dad negotiated a reduced sentence," Olivia says to her friend near my locker. "Three months' house arrest. He'll be free by the time school starts next year!"

Olivia's friend's smile increases. "Maybe his dad will do some 'negotiating'"—she even uses air quotes—"with Principal Van Lowe in the form of a hefty donation."

Tension drains from my shoulders at this news. Maybe I didn't ruin his life forever. Only his summer vacation. But then I remind myself that it doesn't matter if he comes back here in three months. By then I will have already found my mother and joined her wherever she's hiding out. In three months, I won't be here, either.

For the next three and a half weeks, I throw myself into finishing up the last forgery and helping Dad finalize plans for the remaining heists. We're going to hit them all up consecutively for a summer of wham-bam-thank-you scams. Everything looks rosy colored for our departure next week . . . until Dad drops a new bomb.

"Funds," he says, drumming his fingers against the desk in my bedroom. "By my calculations, we're at least twenty thousand short."

"But how?" I tilt my computer screen to show him the elaborate Excel spreadsheet that tracks all the costs we've anticipated, all written in code, of course, in case the feds ever snoop around. From apartment rentals to gas mileage to disguise fees, it should all be accounted for.

"Johnny and Jorge. They're demanding a bigger cut. Immediately—or they won't help." Dad lets out a sigh and runs his palm through his dark hair. "We can't do the heists without them, Fiona."

My eyes flutter shut, and I breathe in sharply through my nose. An IOU won't work in this scenario, because that's the currency we've been paying them in, knowing that finding Mom means finding the real versions of her stolen art and the buckets of cash we can get after Dad fences them all on the black market. We don't have time to find anyone else. "Is there anything we can sell to get that kind of cash?" We have a lot of nice things in our house. Maybe we have 20K worth of nice things.

"Well, it's not just a bigger cut. It's another job they want to hit to get that cash. *Tonight*. But it's dangerous."

Apprehension knots in the base of my throat. "What job? How dangerous?"

"Stealing a statue from a wealthy owner before it goes to auction." Dad swallows hard. "The auction is tomorrow."

My stomach lurches. A wealthy owner means a fancy alarm system. Maybe even security guards. And maybe those guards will carry guns. Not to mention no time to fully plan this out so we can come up with an exit strategy for every possible scenario. "I'll come with you." My voice sounds a little less confident than I intended it to.

Dad shakes his head. "We don't need a forgery on this one. Standard smash and grab. Jorge, Johnny, and I got this." He points at my stack of textbooks. "Besides, don't you have finals tomorrow?"

I let out a sigh. "Only in English . . . and AP History." I try to bite my tongue, but it doesn't work. I can lie to strangers just fine, but I can't ever bring myself to do it to the one person I trust with my life. "Okay, fine, and pre-calc."

Dad pats me on the shoulder. "You focus on studying tonight. And then tomorrow, we'll both celebrate a job well done."

I can't help but feel a little jealous at missing out. FOMO and all that. I wear all black to study, in solidarity.

By 11 p.m. when I finish studying, Dad's not home, but that makes sense. The best smash-and-grab heists are performed during the cover of night, where fewer eyeballs might rest on your misdeeds. I attempt to crawl into bed and go to sleep, but my mind has other plans. I lie there, waiting for the telltale sign of a car pulling up, engine switching off, footsteps pounding up the stairs, and the relief that comes from knowing my dad's okay.

But 11:10 p.m. passes in silence. 11:35. 11:50.

By midnight, I propel myself out of bed and start pacing the floor. A quick check-in text to my dad yields no results. Same for Johnny and Jorge.

Dad sometimes doesn't text back during the middle of a heist, but Jorge's the getaway driver. He's just sitting in the van, waiting to put pedal to metal.

12:18.

There's a knot in my chest that won't subside. Overnight jobs usually don't take *this* long.

12:49.

My stomach squeezes in fear that something happened to Dad, something involving a gun.

1:23.

I park myself at the kitchen table, eyes trained on the door, leg rattling under the table. I'm going to fail my finals from exhaustion at this rate, but I can't possibly sleep until I know Dad's okay.

2:01.

My nerves grow even more raw. This is late. Even for a dangerous heist. Even for Dad. But I can't shake the feeling that something bad happened. I'm giving it one more hour before I start calling hospitals to check if Dad's been admitted.

At 2:57 a.m., headlights swing into the driveway and beam spotlights through the window so bright, I have to squint. I bolt to my feet, eyes stinging. My bare soles skid against the cold hardwood floor as I race to the front door and wrench it open so fast, it slams into the wall behind me.

I'm expecting to wrap my arms around Dad in relief, but instead a man in a suit aims his dark soulful eyes at me, eyes I'm probably supposed to trust. He flashes an FBI badge at me, and all the breath leaves my lungs. My gut was right. Dad's not okay.

"Hi, Miss Spangler. I'm Ian O'Keefe."

I freeze; my blood beats in my ears. Ian O'Keefe. The guy who had the gall to spawn my biggest nemesis.

My arms fly to cover my chest like a shield. "Wh-what do you want?"

"I want you to step aside." He shoves a sheet of paper in my face. "Search warrant."

My stomach drops. "But—you need probable cause to get one of those. You need—"

"Miss Spangler, I'm sorry to tell you that we've taken your father into custody along with his accomplices."

I back up a step, shaking my head, as cold hard panic sluices through my blood. Ian goes on to tell me what I already figured out. They've caught them stealing the statue and have reason to believe my dad's hiding other stolen goods inside the house. Goods that might reveal the location of my fugitive mother. Goods that helped expedite the search-warrant approval process.

Hot tears press against my eyes, and a strangled sound I don't recognize breaks from my throat. I've already lost my mother to the lam. I can't lose my father, too.

"How?" My voice comes out all pitched, so I try again. "How did you know my dad was going to hit the statue?"

Ian doesn't even blink. "Because I'm good at what I do, Fiona. I know a lot more than you think."

My skin turns to ice. Does he know where my mom is?

The FBI agents carry evidence out of our house in clear plastic bags, all neatly numbered and labeled. Our laptops. Random notebooks (though thankfully not the one with the clues. But they did take my US history one, which I need to study with, damn it). My mom's forgeries, each one containing the very clues we worked so hard to retrieve. All the postcards. They even take the ancient-book forgery with the two stolen pages as well as the eight other blank ones I didn't need, though they thankfully leave the guitar and amusement park skull prop behind, likely mistaking them for my high school pastimes or fandom collectibles.

And they don't take me. The handcuffs never materialize around my wrists. I'm not the fish they're here to fry.

Instead, I stumble through school the next day, trying to distract myself with my finals and staying awake while Dad's whisked off to his arraignment. I rush over there straight from school and barely make it in time to hear Dad's lawyer's speech about circumstantial evidence, how they only confiscated forgeries and not the real things, and those forgeries were created by my mother, Lianne Spangler, and not my dad.

My heart gives a little tug at all the narrowed eyes in the room. At the way the lawyer sells out Mom to try to save Dad. But it doesn't work.

"How do you plead?" the judge asks, his face void of expression. Every head in the room turns to Dad.

I hold my breath.

He squeezes his eyes shut, swallows hard, and then mutters, "Not guilty."

He sounds so utterly defeated, and he hunches forward like a withering flower. I want to rush over and wrap him in my arms, tell him it'll be okay.

But the judge slaps his gavel with a thwack that makes my teeth snap and announces that bail will be set at one million.

One. Million.

Six big fat zeros following the number one.

Holy shit.

Even if I drained our bank account and sold our belongings. Even if I pooled all the spare cash Natalie and I have raked in. Even if I started an online fund-raiser. We wouldn't come close to a tenth of that.

Dad deflates even more, tilting his back toward me as though he can't bear to face me.

Since Dad doesn't have a way to pay for his freedom, the judge decides to ship him off to the state penitentiary to await his trial. Jorge and Johnny join him in separate vans, their bails set equally high. My throat closes at the sight of the prison van, and I gulp down desperate breaths of free air to savor like souvenirs of this last moment with my dad.

My esophagus stings. My fingers twist my necklace—a good-bye gift from my mom—but I have nothing from Dad except this moment, this memory, and the realization that I'm only seventeen. I'm still a minor. Which means without any proper guardians, they might try to punt me into the foster care system for the next few months.

Just before Dad steps into the idling van, he twists on his heels and glances back at me. His gaze pierces mine. "Don't stray from the plan, kiddo." Dad gives me one last smile before they shove him into the van.

I straighten, my heart beating fast. It's not just a goodbye . . . it's his blessing.

I have to act now. Finish the heists. Find the remaining clues. Save Mom.

Before the FBI finds her instead.

Later that day, I bang on the door to Natalie's house, hopping up and down on her front steps because I can't stay still. After the van drove away, my dad's lawyer managed to convince the judge to let me stay with a friend for a few days until they get something more permanent in place. Something with curfews most likely.

I'll be long gone before that happens.

Natalie wrenches open the door, and her face falls. "God, Fiona. You okay?"

She engulfs me in a hug, and for one brief second, I allow myself to lean into her embrace and breathe in her jasmine perfume before I straighten up again. "I will be."

She pulls me inside, past her younger brothers playing loud video games in the living room. From the kitchen, I can hear her mother bumbling around as pots clang. Natalie starts to head upstairs, but I pull on her elbow to stop her. "Can we go in your backyard?"

She eyes me skeptically but obliges by sliding open the glass doors. Orange koi slither beneath the murky water in the large pond occupying the center of the spacious yard. Bright green grass tickles my feet as I duck underneath the volleyball net. A set of tables and metal chairs with gingham cushions rings the perimeter. Beyond that, dense trees stand guard, a barrier made of nature. Once I'm safely ensconced in the shade of the elm and maple trees, tension starts to drain from my shoulders. This is the safest place to talk freely. I can't be sure the FBI didn't plant bugs in our houses.

Natalie drops into one of the chairs, and I pace in front of her while banging out a text. My eyes continually fly to the gate in the fence and the time on my phone, my body full of jitters.

Natalie's brows knit. "Fiona, you're acting crazy. What's going on?"

"Hold on. We're waiting on one more person." Wind blows my hair into my face, sticking it to my coral lip gloss.

Natalie squints at me. "Should I tell my mom one more for dinner? Besides you, I mean."

I shake my head, and Natalie clamps her mouth shut.

A minute later, Tig Ramirez opens the gate and scurries to the chair farthest from us, closer to the woods. She's wearing men's work pants with suspenders that dangle at the sides and a tight, fitted white T-shirt. She flicks her eyes toward Natalie for only a second before she ducks her head low beneath her fedora and refuses to look at either of us. Natalie's eyes widen, and although she keeps her hands at her sides, they twitch. I know from experience that she's itching to fix her luscious purple waves and make sure she looks as adorable as possible.

"Okay, here's the deal. We don't have our con man or our getaway driver, but between the three of us, we can re-create the team." I point to Nat. "You're the master of disguise, as always." I glide my finger toward Tig. "You can replace Johnny as our electronics guru." I pat my chest. "And I'll be the stealthy one, plus I have to re-create the forgery the FBI stole."

"Whoa, whoa, whoa." Natalie holds up a palm. "You still want to go through with the heists? Without the professionals?"

"*We're* the professionals now. We're just as good as them. We can do this."

We have to.

"But the FBI—"

I shrug. "They know a lot, but not everything. Which gives us a limited window to carry it all out."

The FBI left behind the guitar and amusement park skull prop. Maybe they don't know *where* the last three clues are hidden, or even that there *are* three clues left. They probably just seized anything that resembled a forgery in case it was linked back to my mom, like the ancient book. And who knows? Maybe they think the book was a forgery already retrieved and not a place we still have to hit.

Which means I have a slight advantage over them right now.

Tig dons a scowl, and for her that's as much as shouting her disagreement. Natalie bolts from the chair. "Fiona, this is insane. This is—"

"Please, Nat." My voice cracks on her name. "I need to find my mom. I can't give up. I just can't." My eyes flutter shut. "And I can't do it alone."

Natalie rubs her hands down her face, stretching her Silly Putty skin. She lets out a long sigh. "Okay." She laughs to herself. "I can't believe I'm saying this but okay. I'll help."

We both turn to look at Tig, and she shrugs. I take that as consent.

The first smile I've felt since today's arraignment jumps to my lips. "Here's what I'm thinking. We hit up the amusement park first, using the plan Dad and I concocted." The plan that the FBI shouldn't have found much evidence for, because other than the cost-and-supply sheet, we stored all the important bits in our minds. "Swipe some access cards from staff members. Sneak into the underground employee tunnel system. Steal a few uniforms from the storage room. Then voilà! Wear the disguises and smooth-talk our way—"

"And who's doing the smooth-talking?" Natalie raises a brow. "Because it's not you. I've seen you try to be charming. Let's just say that would be a one-way ticket to getting caught."

Tig holds up her palms as if to say it's not her, either.

"And if you remember correctly," Natalie continues, "I have too many other tasks to perform to make the plan work. You do, too, actually. Tig will be occupied with cutting the ride electricity and hacking the ID system to plant our pictures when the stolen IDs are scanned. We can get away without a driver on the team, but we need a con man. We need a fourth."

I sink into the chair beside Nat, cold metal gripping my thighs. "Okay. We can find another way to—"

"The guitar heist has the same issue. Actually, it's even worse. In that one, the plan involves us convincing them to literally walk out the front door with the real guitar in hand. Tig works behind the scenes to plant backdated emails into their system. I'm the distraction. You're the stealthy one who switches the guitars during the distraction. How is that going to be possible without a con man doing the initial convincing?"

I let out a growl. "We'll rethink that one, too. We'll—"

"And don't even get me started on what it's going to take to replace the book in an alarmed glass case at the Hesburgh Library. Spoiler alert, but we need a con man there, too."

"Well, we don't have one!" My hands curl into fists, and I leap to my feet, stomping hard on the soft grass. "And we don't know anyone else who can pinch-hit here, either."

"Yes we do." She meets my eyes. "Colin."

I start shaking my head frantically. "That's the most ridiculous thing I've ever heard."

Natalie arches a brow. "He's the most charming con man I know. He needs a little training, a little reining in, but he could be even smoother than your dad. With his help, we'd be unstoppable."

I fight to keep my jaw from falling to the floor. Tig nods in agreement, and the two girls share a small smile. A scream claws its way up my throat, but I stifle it. "No. No way." There's a hard set to my chin. "I don't trust him. He doesn't have a stealthy bone in his body. Not to mention his dad works for the FBI!"

"Right. His *dad* works for them, but he doesn't."

Blood whooshes in my ears. This is insane. But none of it matters, because of one vital fact. "Need I remind you that Colin's on house arrest? Because of me?"

She waves her hand dismissively like this is just a minor inconvenience. "So, we break him out. Cut his ankle monitor and go on the run. We'll still have a head start on the FBI, especially if they think those locations have already been hit by your mom. They won't know where to look for us."

I sputter a cough. "Okay, fine. I'll pretend that's not the most absurd thing I've ever heard and humor you for a second. Let's say I agree here. And let's say we manage to get away after we cut that blinking, alarmed anklet that will instantly alert every police station in a fifty-mile radius. He'll never agree to help us. Not in a million years."

Her lips curl into a smile. "I think he will. You got him caught. He's got something to prove now. And I think he wants to prove it to *you,* specifically."

I cross my arms and slump in the nearest seat.

"Fiona." Natalie's voice softens, and she pushes out of her chair to stand beside me, stroking my hemp-blond waves. "If you want to have any shot at finding your mom, we need him."

I bury my face in my hands, my heart thumping so loud in my ears I can barely think straight. If she's right and we need a fourth, and if we need that fourth to be someone who can talk our way into anything, then he's our only option. Which means that even if he refuses to help, I need to find a way to convince him.

I need to talk him into this.

"Okay." Something in my chest loosens. "Colin's officially been promoted from royal douchebag to team member, but . . ." I drum my fingers on the metal armrest. "If we cut his anklet, that severely limits our transportation options. The FBI will be notified instantly. We can't fly down to Anaheim like we planned, not to mention our tickets to LAX have been confiscated. They'll be stopping cars at every major highway entrance, checking pedestrians, Metro riders, train, bus. We won't even make it out of the city, let alone all the way to the land of roller coasters."

Tig's chair rattles as she rises out of it. She thrusts her phone into my face and shows me a website for a teen tour:

Coast-to-Coast Connect Teen Tour:

An educational adventure across the nation!

They seem to have a warped idea of what requires an exclamation point.

"Travel camp?" I cross my arms, resisting the urge to full-on scoff. "In case you forgot, we'll be *on the run.* Which means we should be, you know, running. Not kumbaya-ing."

"It's brilliant." Natalie's eyes light up, and she grins at Tig. "The FBI will be so focused on checking cars on the freeway or bus stations, they might not think to look for us on a legit student expedition." She slides her silver fingernail down the page. "Look, first stop is the same amusement park we need to hit. And they're even going to the Gibson Guitar Factory, and the Hesburgh Library later on the tour!"

Ugh. They're right. It's brilliant. Even if they search the tour roster, any fake names we use will mask our identities, and disguises Natalie whips up will cover the rest. This is the perfect way to flee the city and stay incognito.

I gasp and point my finger toward another sentence. "The tour bus leaves in two days. And we still have one day of school left."

"Then we better get cracking. If we pool the cash we made from the last few cons, we should hopefully have enough to cover the funds." Natalie turns to Tig. "Can you create fake identities and populate internet search histories with some fake backstories for us?"

Tig snaps her fingers. Piece of cake.

"I'll be in charge of supplies, disguises, and registering us for the tour. Fiona, give me a list of art stuff you need to re-create the book, and, Tig, same for you for electronics. I'll make it happen."

Tig starts jotting down items on her phone.

Great, I know what that leaves me. "And I get the joy of breaking Colin out of house arrest."

CHAPTER 9

I reach for the doorbell, but then snap my hand back. Standing on the porch of my mortal enemy is not exactly how I would have chosen to celebrate completing my last day of school. My fingers shake, and I rub them against my jeans. I've never been nervous for a con before, so I'm not sure why my body decides now is the time to go full-on hummingbird wings. But I can't stay on this porch forever. Not when the fancy doorbell contains a small camera right above it and a light that shines directly on me in the darkness. Not when I've just witnessed Ian O'Keefe's car pulling out of the driveway after an hour of stakeout, crouching behind a bush across the way. Not when I have no idea how soon he'll return.

Don't stray from the plan, I coax myself. My throat tightens because the words swim into my mind in Dad's voice. It's this reminder that renews my resolve.

I straighten my shoulders and press the button.

The musical little *ding* seems to hang in the air for an uncomfortable number of seconds. I hear the stomp of footsteps growing closer behind the door, and then the peephole darkens.

I hold my breath.

The door swings open, and Colin shakes his head at me, dark

bangs swaying, before he slams the door in my face . . . just like I did to him when he showed up at my house unannounced.

I jam my finger against the bell again, a little more frantically, but then yank my hand back. I can't seem too desperate.

There's an even longer pause, and my pulse starts to amp. If he doesn't let me in, I can't convince him to upend his entire life to help me. But just as I reach for the doorbell again, he pulls the door open a little.

He crosses his arms. "I guess if we're replaying this, my next line is to ask you to take off your shirt?"

"I will," I say, his voice somehow sparking my latent need to snark over all the nerves swimming in my gut. "But not yet."

His brows shoot way up, but he doesn't get my meaning. Because if I somehow manage to convince him, whatever we're wearing when we run out of here has to go. Which means my shirt's coming off. "If you'll let me inside, I can explain."

He lets out a ginormous sigh and pushes the door open. I step into a rather bare entryway, nothing to greet me except a small wooden end table, polished to a sheen but holding nothing on top. Not even a speck of dust. Colin leads me through a long hallway where a few chaste gray-scale art prints of intertwining cubes hang on the wall but don't breathe much life into the place. Gray-stained hardwood flooring stretches the entire length, only a shade darker than the gray walls. Colin's gray sweatpants (pajamas?) match the monochromatic ambience, but the flash of red light that peeks out from beneath the bottom of his pants provides the only spark of color in the entire room. His steps seem normal, though, not dragged down by the heavy anklet. It must have taken weeks to get used to.

We reach a sleek, minimalistic living room decorated in steel grays and stark whites, as though his dad took decorating tips straight out of a black-and-white film. Even the big bay windows showcasing the dark night sky add to the effect. In the center of the room, the coffee table remains bare except for a single TV remote that blends in to the black surface. The entire place gives off that lemon-fresh tinge of Lysol.

The blaring TV projects subdued colors on the white wall until Colin shuts it off. He plops down onto the plush gray couch and leans forward as though bracing himself for what I might have to say. I set my backpack down at my feet and perch on the other side of the sectional, my back ramrod straight. I open my mouth to speak, but then clamp it shut. Natalie's advice from when he came to my house floats in my mind. *Talk to him. Flirt with him.* And then his own actions at my house: *Shower him in compliments.* But none of that seems like the right way to start. The only way to start this is with the truth. "Look, I'm really sorry you got arrested."

He flinches and then grips the armrest on the sofa with white knuckles. "Would have been nice to hear a month ago."

I wince. My heart beats fast, and I start to look away, avoiding his eyes, but I force myself not to wimp out here. "I'm sorry about that, too."

A muscle in his jaw flutters. "Is that why you came? To tell me you're sorry a month too late?" His voice cracks, and something inside me falls apart at the hurt leaking through his words.

But of course, what I just said isn't the actual truth. I didn't come to apologize. I never would have.

"I need a favor." I deliver the words straight like an arrow, my face void of expression. Just the facts, ma'am.

There's a flash of annoyance in his eyes. "Sorry, I don't do sexual favors."

"Well, darn." I swing my arm in an aw-shucks way. "Guess I'll be going, then." I start to stand up and earn the hint of a smile on the corners of his lips. Progress. "For real, though." I sit back down. "I'm putting together a crew, and I need a con man. You're the best one I know."

He ducks his head, a little less confident than I've ever seen him before. "Am I, though? I mean, you won the territory. And all I got was a spiffy new anklet as a consolation prize."

There it is. The hint of doubt in his voice. The need for validation. Natalie was right: He has something to prove.

"You *are*," I say emphatically. "But I'll be honest. You need a little training, and that's where I can help."

He strokes his chin as though considering this. "What's the job?"

The taste of dust coats my mouth. If I tell him, I'm giving him a weapon to use against me. But how can I convince him to help me without exposing myself at the same time? How can I show him I trust him if I don't trust him enough to tell him the truth? Of course, that's the entire problem. I *don't* trust him.

My hands twist my phone over and over in my palms, jittery. I can't answer his question, not yet, so I ask one of my own. "Did you tell your dad what you found in my notebook?"

"Hesiod and all that crap?"

I nod, my chest stilling.

"No." His voice hardens. "Don't get me wrong—I was going to. Especially after . . ." He waves his hand at his ankle again. When he speaks, his voice is slightly lower. "But he never made time to hear what I had to say."

I squeeze my eyes shut. He was going to sell me out, but he chose spiting his dad over spiting me. I can only hope he continues to make that same choice. "If I tell you the job, I need you to keep it secret. From your dad and the rest of his dirty henchmen."

The corners of his lips stretch into a full grin. "Can I at least tell my dad you called his fellow agents *dirty henchmen*, because that's pretty hilarious?"

"I'm sure he already knows how I feel."

"Okay. Secret's safe." He waves his wrist to coax me to get on with it.

I hesitate, hands trembling in my lap. His voice is so confident, so infectious, but he delivers both his lies and his truths with the same gusto. It's a gamble. Throw down my cards and reveal my hand . . . or walk out of here empty-handed.

I lean forward and ante up. "I need to find my mom. And the only way to do that is to find the rest of the clues she left behind."

His eyes flash. "When you say 'find the rest of the clues,' you actually mean steal them, right?"

I hold his gaze. "I wouldn't be here if I didn't."

"What are we stealing? Where are the rest of the clues? How many are there?"

I hold up a hand. "I'll tell you that information when you need to know it. Right now you only need to know that these heists are not going to be easy. In fact, they're going to be downright dangerous. If you get caught, you'll be trading in your anklet for an orange jumpsuit."

It's only fair to tell him what he's getting into, even if I can't divulge what we're after.

"Why would I possibly help you, then?" He lounges back into the couch cushions, showing off just how good he has it here at home. "I only have to deal with two more months of this thing." He taps the anklet. "I'm not willing to trade that in for years behind bars."

"If we can find the art my mom stole, there's some money at the end of the rainbow, but I don't think you care about that. I think you care about honing your skills as a con man, proving that you can do it without getting caught, and . . ." *Then maybe he'll finally notice me,* he said in my bedroom. *He never made time to hear what I had to say,* he said only a minute ago. My voice rises in volume. "Getting back at your dad."

His mouth drops open just a little, and there's a sparkle in his eye.

"But we need to leave now. What size boxers do you wear?"

He does a spit take even though he isn't drinking. "I'm not sure which part to react to first, because they're both insane. *Now?* Boxers?"

"I need your T-shirt and pant size, too. I just led with boxers for funsies." I'm smiling, but his eyes are wide, staring at me like I'm crazy. "Natalie's heading to the store now for the final supplies. You can't exactly wear any of your real clothes, because they might be traced back to you."

He sputters a cough.

"For future reference, the part about leaving *now* was the one you should have focused on. We have a lot to do before nine a.m. tomorrow when the tour bus leaves, so it has to be now."

He just stares at me, clearly waiting for me to clarify.

"Coast-to-Coast Connect Teen Tour. An educational adventure across the nation." I fist-pump my arm in the air halfheartedly. "Get ready for the best summer of your life! You might even get to make s'mores by a campfire if you're super lucky."

"But—but I can't leave now." He jabs his finger at his anklet.

I reach into my backpack and pull out a giant pair of garden shears. I'm really enjoying dragging this out and watching him freak out the same way I did when Natalie first suggested this. It's kind of fun to be on the other side. "The anklet won't be a problem."

Colin stands up and starts pacing the carpet, treading footprints along his path. "Are you crazy? If . . . if you cut that, it'll alert the authorities. It'll—"

I purse my lips. "Then I hope you're good at running."

"So let me get this straight. You're not just asking me to perform a few heists. You're asking me to become an escaped convict!"

When he says it like that, it sounds pretty bad. "But did you hear the part about s'mores?"

He rakes his hands through his hair and continues pacing.

"Colin," I say, all hints of humor leaving my voice. "I have your back now, okay? We're in this together. You, me, Natalie, Tig. You won't have to be alone anymore. We're a family now, and we're not going to let you get caught."

It's the only thing I can offer him that truly matters. Sure, it's a family by choice rather than by blood, but it's a choice he can make.

My words stop him short. His chest puffs in and out.

"Okay." He laughs to himself. "Holy hell, I hope I don't regret this, but okay. Except . . . can I grab something from my room?"

"You can't take anything from here. It's too dangerous. I'll let you keep the clothes on your back . . . for now."

"It's just a photograph. You're going to find your mom . . . and I want mine with me on this journey." His voice catches on the word *mom*.

My heart tugs and I nod, my fingers twirling on my mom's necklace dangling at my clavicle.

"Okay, but be fast. We've got anklets to cut, hair to dye, and FBI to evade."

Colin's eyes widen on that last part, but he rattles off his sizes and then treks up the stairs. I bang out the information to Natalie with my new burner phone, and by the time I've finished, he's back downstairs clutching a photograph.

"Can I see it?" I'm not sure why I whisper this question, but it feels like something I should tread lightly on.

He holds the photo out to me. It's of a woman with dark brown hair smiling down at a toddler as he sits on top of a green plastic slide.

"She died a week after this was taken." There's such rawness in his voice that a lump instantly lodges in my throat. "Car accident."

"I'm so sorry," I say, and this time I'm glad to be able to say it instead of holding on to it for a month, wielding it like a weapon.

He takes a shuddering breath and then stands tall. "Okay. Let's do this. I need to get the hell out of this house."

My heart pounds, the crime we're about to commit solidifying like a thick ice cube blocking our path. We're in this together. No turning back.

He squeezes his eyes shut, lifts his sweatpants up to his knee, and clenches his teeth. I snap the anklet in two.

CHAPTER 10

Streetlamps illuminate circles on the deserted road, and pinprick stars are scattered across the inky black sky. Giant, colorful houses line the lane in front of us, each sealed away by curtains or fences. A slight wind seizes my long hair, sending it flying, and for once I let the strands stick to my lips and crowd beneath my neck. I'm going to miss my long locks.

Everything looks so peaceful, even though we just spun our world into total chaos. No turning back now. My head pounds as I place one shaky foot in front of the other, my backpack hanging heavy on my shoulders. A sense of camaraderie with my long-lost mother nestles into my chest, burrowing there to keep me strong. She chose a life on the run over one huddled in a six-by-eight rectangular box. Her last words to me blink in my mind like neon lights. *I hope you grow up to be exactly who you want to be.*

Who I always wanted to be was . . . her. The kind of person who wields middle fingers instead of guns, who steals what they want from those who don't need it, who never gives up or gives in.

The kind of person who follows the clues.

A car ambles down the road, swinging headlights that force both Colin and me to squint. "Please tell me that's not your dad's car."

"He doesn't drive an SUV, but just in case . . ." He rushes to duck behind a bush.

I tug on his shirt to lift him upright. "Act cool, dumb-ass. Not incredibly suspicious." Something in my chest swirls at my use of the word *dumb-ass*. I shouldn't have said that. Not after promising him we're family now.

But when the car passes us by, we both let out heavy breaths.

"Sorry I called you a dumb-ass."

"Wow, you don't apologize for a full month, and now they're freely flowing from your lips."

"I meant what I said earlier. We're family now. Come on." I wave him forward. "Let's not chance that happening again."

We run for a single block before we slide into the waiting seats of an idling taxi. The cushion squishes under my weight, and my head hits the back seat with the same relief as a pillow after a long day. I drop the heavy backpack at my feet.

Colin squeezes in beside me. "Our perfect escape . . . involves a taxicab? Can't this be traced back to us somehow?"

"Shh." I lean forward and brace my hands on the plastic window that separates us from the driver. "Sorry about the delay, we're ready now."

The driver guns the engine and swerves toward a preplanned destination Tig helped me pick out. Streetlights sweep over the car, dropping temporary spotlights onto my worn-in knees. What better way to get rid of old pants than to plant them as evidence in the wrong place to throw the FBI off our scent!

Colin's eyes bug at the hefty number displayed on the running meter. "How long was he waiting here?"

I pull a thick wad of bills out of my backpack and fan them. "The meter is nothing compared to the size of the tip I promised my new buddy."

"Cha-ching!" The driver rubs his thumb and index finger together.

"So a payoff," Colin whispers.

The car bumps along the roads, obeying all traffic laws and the exact speed limit. We lurch to a stop at yellow lights as if even crossing through might be taboo. After twenty minutes, the cab pulls to an abrupt stop at a random corner in the Mission. The heavy beat from a nightclub pulses so loud, the sidewalks vibrate. Black lights in the windows cast purple highlights on the lingering crowd, and plumes of cigarette smoke curl into the air.

I pass the driver a stack of folded bills so thick, my fingers extend to their limits. "I trust this covers both our agreement and a little extra for—" I press my index finger to my lips in the universal sign for *shhh*. None of this would be possible without the generous donations of my cheating classmates.

"I picked up a couple of generic-looking kids to go to a nightclub. Nothing more, nothing less."

I pile out of the car and crook my finger toward my chest in a come-hither way to coax Colin to follow me. I'm really enjoying this dose of control and power over him. He hesitates for a moment, but follows. The people standing on the nightclub line swivel their heads in our direction, sizing us up. We keep on strolling right past the line, crossing the next street, where we stand on the corner and I lift my hand. Another yellow cab pulls up, and I throw my backpack onto the seat before shuffling inside.

Colin grunts and plops down next to me. "Where are we going this time?"

"Thirty-Fourth and Moraga Street," I tell the cabbie.

"Why there?" Colin squints at me.

"It's away from here." It's also a street with no cameras. A true blind spot. Just like this one.

Neon signs blur into streaks from the velocity of the car.

We switch cabs two more times before the third drives another forty-five minutes on the straight and narrow to an address that makes Colin's eyebrows shoot way up. All the way in San Mateo. Residential houses line the destination, each one perky with alarm systems that would freak if they knew criminals lurked outside. Once the cab drives away, I fumble in my backpack and yank out two baseball caps. I toss him the 49ers hat, and he pulls it low over his eyes without question.

I twist my long hair into a messy French knot and dump my own Giants cap on top to cover the escaping strands.

"How many more cabs are we going to take?"

"None. Now follow me and stay close. This stretch of sidewalk is blind to cameras."

He lets out a little laugh. "Of course it is."

At the end of the block, an ARCO gas station glowing with bright lights comes into view. Cars swerve in and out of the open gas lanes. To seem like we belong, we amble past the drivers filling their tanks and circle around the station to the single-occupancy bathroom on the side. Colin twists the knob and holds the door out for me, proving the incongruity that sometimes assholes can also be gentlemen.

I stomp past him and wait a beat until he follows. Once he's inside, I flip on the lock and the light in quick succession. Air leaks from my lungs. We're safe. Which means my mom's safe.

"Do you take all your conquests to such romantic places?" He pinches his nose.

It's the equivalent of a cell, complete with a toilet and sink, and lacking any dignity. Dirty gray tiles lead up to the toilet overflowing with mushy white paper. I cough against the overwhelming stench of urine and kick the toilet handle to flush it.

"Only the special ones."

I drop the backpack onto the tile with a loud *thwap*, missing a puddle of yellow liquid by only an inch. I crouch in front of the bag, forcing Colin to hop back a step and slam into the wall from lack of space to maneuver. I unearth an electric barber's razor and stand to face him. "Turn around."

"Thanks, but I think you've already stabbed me in the back enough times for one lifetime." He rakes a hand through his own beautiful hair. I admit, he's been blessed in the follicular department. Ugh, and the face department, too.

I roll my eyes. "You'll get your revenge. Scissors in my bag. You can cut it short."

My hand flies to my precious dirty-blond hair, still tucked beneath the baseball cap. My dad used to urge me to chop my long locks. *It'll be easier to stuff under a wig*, he'd claim. I'd dangle a bald cap in his face in retaliation. My forgeries defined me anonymously, but my waist-length hair helped me stand out in high school, the only place safe enough to indulge in being recognized. Plus, I haven't cut it since my mom left, as if keeping my strands the same length was a gateway drug to putting everything back to normal if—no, *when*—she returned.

Colin reaches into the bag and grabs the scissors. We glare at each other in a dumb staring contest neither of us has the balls to lose.

"Ladies first." He gets up right in my face, so close I can smell his brand-name soap above the lingering stench of urine. His smirk does the talking while his hand flies toward me and knocks against the underside of my cap. It hits the opposite wall before sinking to the floor. When my long hair flops against my shoulders, I feel the urge to fight him off but force myself to surrender. This was my choice, after all. But I can still give him a hard time during it.

He grabs a clump of my hair from my side and yanks it away

from my arms. The sickening metallic scrape of the scissors across my hair also cuts a figurative hole through my gut.

He waves a fistful of at least fifteen inches of my glorious locks. "I won that round."

My chest cinches tight, but I combat the feeling with a fierce glare. "It's not a competition. I literally gave you permission." My shoulders tremble. "You better not make me look ridiculous."

"Hey, don't go blaming your natural appearance on me." He crosses to the garbage, but I shake my head. "Flush it."

A tilt-o-whirl of hair swirls until it disappears down the drain. If we leave the hair behind in the garbage and the cops find it, they'll be able to deduce what I look like now.

I kneel on the floor in front of him, my knees sinking onto a towel he laid out from the bag. Each snip of his scissors tears my heart in two. Long strands flutter to the floor like snowflakes that melt as soon as I scoop them up and destroy the evidence, each one forcing me to stifle a whimper.

"Ta-da! I tried to make you look better, but even *I* can't work miracles."

On shaky legs, I take tentative steps toward the streaky mirror, cringing. Choppy ends crest my chin, and sharp angles frame my face, dancing when I shake my head in a way my heavy locks were always too lazy to do. I allow myself only ten seconds to mourn the loss before I reawaken my stiff fingers by wrapping my hand around my revenge weapon. "My turn to castrate you."

This time he gets to be the submissive one. I force him to kneel in front of me on the towel that will catch his strands. A pang of regret swoops through me, and for a split second, I almost toss the razor out the window instead. I may hate him, but that doesn't mean I hate how stop-traffic good-looking he is with this particular style. The way he's always pushing it out of his eyes, like he's revealing a secret.

"Don't worry," he whispers. "It'll grow back."

That does it. I flick on the razor, and the static buzz grounds me. I run my fingers through his silky hair for the first time, for the last time—and then I exact my revenge by gliding the device over his scalp. Strands fly in all directions, dropping onto the towel in clumps. Each piece that falls gives me a satisfaction I've never felt before. He's my enemy, but he trusts me with what could potentially be a weapon. I brace my hand on his shoulder, gripping tight. "Thank you," I whisper, even though he can't hear it above the buzz of the razor. "For helping me."

I switch off the razor, cringing at the abrupt silence.

He pushes himself up and heads to the dull mirror and purses his lips at his reflection. Damn it, he's still incredibly good-looking with his head completely shaved. Sometimes hotness is wasted on the undeserving.

"So, you mentioned hair dye earlier, but I'm assuming that's only for you. Considering I'm now lacking in the hair department."

"Wow, nothing gets past you."

He riffles through my bag, unearths three boxes of hair dye, and lines them up along the sink. "They say blonds have more fun, so it's a good thing we're about to dye your hair. It sounds like we have a lot of work ahead of us." He nudges the first box, where an orangey-red head beams at me. "What'll it be? Ariel mermaid hair?" He taps the second box. "Rebellious blue. It'll make you stand out, yes, but in that cliché teenage rebellion way that adults will roll their eyes at." He tosses the third box in the air and catches it. "Or maybe you want to go dark, like your personality?"

I snatch the third box out of his hands. Dark brownish black is the most natural. Most realistic. Most likely to be ignored. "The other two are going to be planted evidence."

Rule #8: You can't just plan for your main exit strategy, you have to plan your decoys as well. My plan is to empty the other boxes out in the sink and then abandon the auburn box with my clothing and the blue box with Colin's at two different locations. One in this bathroom and then one at whatever rest stop we pull in to on the teen tour. Hopefully, they'll assume I'm now a redhead and he's now a Smurf.

A rush of water sends his strands down the sink drain while he shakes out the towel into the toilet to destroy the rest. I slide on crinkly plastic gloves and rub the black tar all over my locks. My burner phone ticks off the twenty minutes. Some getaway. Usually people who break out of jail run like their ass is on fire. Not wait around. I kill the time by splashing drops of the auburn dye around the sink and floor in case the FBI link us to this bathroom.

A *thump thump thump* on the door makes my teeth snap together.

We freeze like mannequins, the only sound the tick of my phone timer.

My mind supplies only one scenario: the police, standing right outside with shiny new handcuffs dangling from their fingers.

Colin risks a step toward the door and presses his ear against it just as someone bangs again. He hops back, rubbing his ear.

"Someone's in here," Colin shouts in a deep voice that would probably earn him lead baritone in choir.

"Hey, man, you almost done?" a muffled voice shouts from outside.

I sag in relief. Not the police. Just a guy who has to pee.

"Could be a while," Colin yells back, then groans as if he has stomach cramps. A moment later the patter of footsteps outside retreats.

The timer goes off, and I nearly have another heart attack. I head toward the sink and dip my head under the tiny faucet. Cold porcelain presses against my neck as black swirls of dye mix with the clear water.

Colin braces one hand against my neck while his other runs through my hair, squeezing out the dye under the faucet. His soft hands glide against my skin, and the incorrigible part of me loads a snarky comment on my tongue (*Haven't you done enough already?*), but the criminal part of me allows his aid because it means my disguise kicks in faster. And there's a third part, the girl part, which enjoys every second of his touch, even if I'm still bitter about what happened the last time he ran his hands through my wet hair. After a few minutes, the water runs clear.

I toss him a change of clothes despite not being quite the right size, since we had to guess earlier. I rummage in the bottom of the bag and pull out the only clothes left. A way-too-short skirt and a cleavage-happy V-neck top. Ugh, Natalie. These were *not* the clothes I'd packed!

Colin's eyes bug out. "Whoa. I think you have a warped idea of what being incognito means, because you're going to be showing a lot of skin."

I groan. "Scratch what I said earlier about a crew of four. Natalie's just been demoted."

"Ah." He holds up his new T-shirt to me. It's got Pokémon characters plastered all over it. And his boxers have heart-eyes happy faces. "Guess that explains why you brought me a T-shirt purchased from the kids' section."

"For someone so good at costumes, she has a warped idea of what constitutes a proper disguise."

"But more importantly . . ." His eyes light up with an amused expression. "I haven't forgotten your promise to take off your shirt. Is this the part where you strip?"

I make no move to look away. "No, you do. Go ahead—change." My eyes zoom to his crotch in challenge.

"Count of three we both turn around. No peeking." He holds my gaze. "One."

I sigh.

"Two." The corners of his mouth lift.

I spin around before he gets to three. In a mad dash, I shrug out of my jeans and shirt. The air conditioner hits my bare stomach for one open, exposed moment, but I duck my head into the V-neck shirt. As I'm doing so, I flick my face behind me and sneak a glimpse at Colin.

I catch his eye.

He's peeking, too.

We both whip our heads back around at the same time. My cheeks and neck burn. With trembling fingers, I glide my legs into the way-too-short skirt and clear my throat when I finish.

My skirt grazes just below my no-frills cotton underwear, and the four-inch strappy wedges my (soon to be former) best friend left me are definitely not running-from-the-law appropriate.

I find a note from Natalie pinned to the inside of one shoe. *The wedges are in case you need to kick him in the nuts. I was too afraid to arm you with stilettos, though, because you can't actually stab him. We need him.* I drink in the words three times before I stuff the note in my bra to keep Natalie close, as if she's still beside me. Okay, fine, she's back on the team.

Colin twists around, his gaze lingering on my new outfit for a beat too long. His too-tight jeans sculpt his muscular legs in a way his school dress pants always hid. Biceps bulge beneath his polo. He must have been working out during all that time cooped up in his house.

"I feel like I'm wearing a Halloween costume," I say. "Sexy fugitive."

He laughs. "Does that mean I get to be Sexy Pikachu?"

"Well, you'd have to be sexy for that to be true," I say, and he rolls his eyes at me. "But you can totally be Loser Pikachu without even trying."

"Okay, enough making fun of me." Colin bounces on his toes. "Let's go."

I lean casually against the wall, legs crossed at the ankles. "And where do you think we're going?"

"Wherever the next stop is in your near-perfect getaway plan."

There's no hint of sarcasm in his voice, and my skin prickles with goose bumps at his use of the word *perfect*. That's the highest compliment you can give a criminal. Even if he did downplay it with a *near*.

He juts his arm toward the door. "Besides, we can't stay in here forever. People need to use it."

"As long as those people aren't the police, this is our best bet for the night."

His eyes widen in utter horror. "I'm not sleeping here."

I raise a brow. "You have a better idea?"

"Of course I have a better idea." And then, softer: "Can you please trust me for once?"

His words make something in my chest loosen. He's right. I'm asking him to trust me. *Help* me. The least I can do is return the favor. "Okay, fine, we'll do your idea. But first—" I slide two thin cards out of the front pocket of the backpack and toss one to him. "Memorize it."

On mine, my old school picture scowls back at me from a fake

California ID, photoshopped to transform my blond hair into a shoulder-length black bob.

Colin's eyes land on the birthdate on his ID. "You made me a fake ID but didn't even make it legal for me to drink? What kind of criminal are you?"

I grin. "That the only thing you noticed?"

His vision slides to the lines above. His name. His *new* name.

"Colton Buttz?" He groans. "What are you, five?"

I run my hand through my short locks. "Trust me, it's better than my first choice. You should be thanking me."

"Wait, let me prepare for the bad joke." He sticks his fingers in his ears.

"Colton McLoser."

"Yep. There it is. My ears are now scarred forever." He snatches my new ID out of my hands and barks out a laugh at what I coined myself. "Fiona Queen? At least you've got your ego in check. Wait, why do you get to keep your first name and I don't?"

"Because I wasn't arrested."

With an aggravated sigh, he wrenches the bathroom door open and stomps into the night air. It's the first time all night that I've lost control.

Once we leave the gas station bathroom, cricket melodies cut the silence. My stupid wedges wobble on loose gravel that skids across the parking lot. Colin darts right past the gas station entrance, where bright lights spill from the tiny restaurant that houses several slumped-over truckers. A few large trucks are parked, engines off, their drivers passed out in their seats. He stops behind the largest truck's trailer.

Someone else slinks inside the bathroom. Cars zoom past us,

each one shining a spotlight directly on us. I'm even more open and exposed here, in my skimpy clothing, standing next to the boy I . . . can't hate anymore now that we're on the same side.

"And your plan is . . . stopping in the open parking lot?" I invade his personal space until I win the battle and his heel slides an infinitesimal amount backward. Checkmate. "You're right—this is so much better than a locked bathroom."

He shoots me a dirty look and pulls my backpack toward him. "Tell me you packed lock-picking tools."

I release a sharp, anguished sound into the night. "Yes, but—we can't just hide out in the back of a truck. We're trying to lay low. Not attract attention when we're found trespassing!"

"Calm down. It's only for a few hours, just to get some sleep before the s'mores adventure begins."

I sigh and hastily unzip the front pocket of the backpack to grab my tools.

I kneel on the uneven gravel, the rocks indenting crop circles onto my knees, and slip the rake into the lock, just like the first time my mom taught me to do this. I was five, and we made a 3 a.m. adventure out of picking all the front doors in a neighborhood full of complicated locks. We didn't break into the houses, just cracked their doors to prove we could. "You're a natural," she told me, her voice full of gusto as my small fingers worked. Her words seeped into my psyche, floating me on a puffy cloud. When she let me test my skills in a department store, where I pretended to be lost while she caused a panicked distraction so I could unlock the office and swipe the spare cash, I knew she loved me.

Now I make quick work with what I've got and pop the lock on the back of the trailer in two minutes flat. I spin around in time to catch Colin's impressed blink.

We climb inside the dark trailer. Shelves line the entire cargo space, packed floor to ceiling with boxes, separated by only a thin row of space barely big enough for my shoulders. I squeeze into the recess of the trailer but stick close to the door to prevent the driver from hearing any movements. My back leans against the row behind me while my knees jab the boxes in front of me. Colin twists his body to stretch out his long legs, pressing his back into my shoulders.

I dig my elbow into his spine. "What about me makes you think, *Yes, she looks like she'd be a good snuggler*?"

He shifts until an inch of space separates us, his head leaning on a box in what looks like the world's most uncomfortable position.

After a few moments, his snores fill the truck, echoing off the metal walls.

Darkness surrounds us, concealing us and hiding the most incriminating thing of all: the way the tension flees my shoulders. He was right. This is a way better hiding spot.

CHAPTER 11

I wake to the rumble of an engine purring beneath my thighs. The truck bed swerves, boxes gliding along the tracks. I bolt into a standing position but topple onto Colin, my hands gripping his shoulders like handlebars. His eyes fly open in confusion, then dart in panic. "What—"

"We have to get out of here!"

We scramble to our feet, gripping the metal rim of the shelves to keep from falling again. The truck gains speed, and my feet surfer-balance in the center.

"Hold on tight," he says. "We're gaining speed. If the doors open and you're pressed against them . . ." He bangs one palm against the door for a sound effect. "Splat!"

His words grind deep into my chest like a drill. My hand tightens on the metal bar that hangs above the door, and his trembling fingers cover mine. He braces his other arm against the door and pushes, biceps bulging. Grunts escape from his mouth. On any other guy, this level of exertion would look sexy. But I prefer to attribute anything he does to slimeball.

The door doesn't budge, and panic rockets through me.

"Count of three we kick," I shout. "One. Two."

"Three!" he finishes before I can, snatching the last word.

Our legs swing back in unison like we're performing a choreographed routine with the rest of the Rockettes. Two feet slam into the doors. They pop open, and we lurch forward, our clammy fingers straining against the bar like a current is trying to tow us out to sea. An orange streak of morning light blasts in, making me squint against the butt crack of dawn. The yellow dashed lane lines speed beneath the truck so fast, they blur. We catch a glimpse of perky houses before they whip out of eyesight, replaced by a silver guardrail edging the road. No other cars, thankfully.

Colin gasps. "We're on the freeway ramp!"

If we don't jump now, the truck will reach deadly speeds. Without hesitating, I throw myself out of the truck. My feet hit the pavement with a hard slam that ricochets through my entire body. My torso falls forward from the impact, and I tuck my head into a somersault, rolling several times before I come to a stop. I splay flat on the ground, panting. Scrapes and tender skin throb all over my body, but I manage to push myself upright and hobble off the road.

Most parents send their kids to gymnastics for the fun of it. Mine sent me there to improve my getaway skills.

Colin flies out of the truck bed at a superhero angle, as if he's soaring toward a daring rescue—and not his own. He twists his body too early, aiming for the small patch of grass that lines the freeway ramp. His shoulders crash into the grass, but his legs smash onto the hard pavement. He basically did a belly flop from a speeding truck directly onto a hard surface. His moans announce his failure.

"Colin! Are you okay?" I run to him and rest my hand between his shoulder blades. My palm rides the waves of his shallow breaths as the scent of exhaust dissipates in the open air.

He whimpers. "Okay, fine. You were right. Sleeping in the bathroom would have been a much better idea."

"Oh thank God." The tension in my shoulders eases. Both at the fact that he's okay and that he conceded.

He squints at me. "Wait. You were terrified that I was hurt just now. Do you actually care?"

I flinch. "Of course I care. I need you."

Something in his face deflates. "Ah. You only care because if I got hurt, your whole plan goes to shit."

"No, it's . . ." I wipe sweat from my brow. "You're part of my crew. I *care* about my crew." I jab my hand toward him to help him up, but he grips the silver railing for support instead, just to spite me.

A bloody scrape covers the entire length of his shin. He rests his weight on one leg at first, limping a few steps before walking at an almost normal gait. "Small sprain, I think."

I offer him my elbow for support, but he shakes his head. "I can handle it."

"We'll go back to the bathroom to get you cleaned up," I suggest.

"Your dream come true! I know how much you miss that place."

I roll my eyes. "It's like you can see into my soul." I stop dead. "Wait." A cold, cracking sensation creeps up my spine. I spin around frantically, taking in the uninterrupted panorama of the empty freeway ramp. "Tell me you have the backpack."

He performs the same revolution as me, wincing with each pivot of his heel. "Tell me nothing important was in there."

I rake a hand through my hair, surprised when the strands end so abruptly. "A couple burner phones. Most of the cash for today. Breakfast." I set my eyes on his brown ones. "Oh God. Your ID?"

I pull my own ID from my bra, where I stashed it before I fell asleep last night. Phew, but remind me to tell Natalie that next time she packs a getaway outfit for me, it better have pockets.

Colin pats the pocket on his cargo shorts and pulls out two items. "Still have mine. And my mom's photo." He studies the photo for a moment and lets out a shaky sigh before sliding both back into his pocket.

I sag in relief and clutch my mother's necklace, still tight around my neck. "Good. Everything else is replaceable. Natalie has extra burners." Maybe this will be a good thing. Maybe the cops will find the backpack wherever the truck stops next and think we fled from *there*, not here.

He pulls out two twenties from his shorts pocket. "Glad I grabbed some cash from my room before we left."

I groan. Why does he always have to one-up me? Even if this time it's to my benefit. "Breakfast is on you, then." As soon as I say it, my stomach growls.

We hobble down the freeway ramp, flattening ourselves against the railing when a car speeds by. After several blocks, we come to our good old neighborhood staple: the gas station. A little bell jingles as he leads me inside.

". . . O'Keefe escaped last night . . ."

My eyes fly to the TV, where Colin's smoldering mug shot fills the screen. Because he can't do anything without being aggravating, he looks gorgeous on his official record, too. Blood drains from my face. Every head in the place swivels toward us in the three seconds it takes for Colin to pivot and run right back out the door.

I rush after him. "Hey, you look different now. They won't know."

He lets out a howl of pain from his sprained ankle but charges forward. I surge my pace despite the stupid uncomfortable wedges. My pulse pounds loud in my ears with a thought that plays like a metronome, ticking down the seconds until my demise: *He's a wanted criminal, and I'm the accomplice.* We run for several blocks, cutting through backyards when we can. Each step he takes causes a grunt of pain. I grit my teeth against the ache in my burning lungs. After about five minutes, I clamp a hand on his shoulder.

"No one's—" I pant. "Following us."

I lean against a tree in a gorgeous backyard with a tire swing hanging from a branch. My chest aches at the sight of it, at all my mother missed of me growing up, but it also serves as a reminder of what I'll find at the end of this rainbow: a chance to fill the void she left with new memories.

"What—" He doubles over, bracing his hands against his knees, coming away with a smear of blood. He gulps air. "What do you suggest?"

"Lesson numero uno in being stealthy: Act normal. Don't look guilty. The people in the gas station only noticed you because you ran like you were on fire."

We mingle with large crowds of suited people heading to work on busy streets, the roads the police would assume we'd avoid. A quick stop at a drugstore provides us with a bathroom to clean Colin's leg and some sunglasses to conceal our eyes. We split a few pastries from Starbucks, and each down an iced coffee as we walk. Our first date, how ridiculously quaint. We kill time by not staying in one place, always moving.

My police-radar eyes scrutinize every person we pass and evaluate them on a scale from one to undercover cop. I guide him several miles to a Safeway parking lot, where a large charter bus idles at the curb. Puffs of exhaust fumes curl up into the sunny air, rendering everything in my view blurry. Faces peer out the darkened windows as if we're approaching a museum attraction filled with caged animals. I stop in front and rap my knuckles on the glass door.

"Listen, if the head counselor gives us a hard time about any of this, like the fact that we're late—"

His eyes widen. We would have been on time if we hadn't had to stop for first aid. Or breakfast.

"I need you to sweet-talk her into letting us on, okay?"

"Wait, but—"

The accordion door opens with a sticky *squish*, the entire vehicle sighing. An Asian woman trudges down the stairs, her dark hair twisted into a low pony. The clipboard pressed against her chest sums up everything: She's someone to avoid. Her lips set in a thin line as she drags her gaze down to my extremely inappropriate skirt.

"Hi." I try to sound bubbly, but it comes out as flustered. "We're—"

"IDs?"

We hand them over, and my pulse increases, a steady *tick tick tick* that she must be able to hear. For years I've been using fake identities for both crimes and good times at bars, but when I breeze up to those, I'm usually cool, calm, and collected. Here I shift my weight from foot to foot and try not to collapse. If this doesn't work, we're screwed. No other options. No other way to get my mom's remaining clues.

"Colton and Fiona," she says and shoves the IDs back toward us. "You're thirty minutes late."

"Yeah, sorry about that." He gives her a sheepish chuckle. A line of concealer does a poor job of covering his new wound. "This one over here took forever getting ready." He nudges me with his elbow, and then leans in toward the brunette. "Tell her she looks pretty—she's always fishing for a compliment."

My enemy cheeks betray me by blushing, even though he's just doing what I told him to do.

Her stare hardens. "Consider this your warning. Next time, we won't wait."

Colin ducks his head and nods, as if he's just been reprimanded by the principal for acting out in class. "No problem. We'll be good. I promise."

"I'm Abby Ito, head counselor." She swings her arms toward the door. "Come on."

The dark bus swallows us whole, a sharp contrast from the bright sun baking our skin. Loud jabbers of conversation cease as eager faces spin forward, each one boasting some kind of trademark cliché: nose piercing, Mohawk, salon blowout, Burberry headband, natural makeup, glittery glam makeup, varsity jacket, and pentagram necklace. I'm pretty sure every teenage clique is represented here from stoners to rich bitches, goths to preppies. Each camper sizes us up, too, all their eyes roaming from Colin's pretty face to his slight limp.

Velvet seat backs promise more comfort than the squished interior of a commandeered truck. I march down the aisle, my eyes searching for Natalie and Tig, and though I spot Tig right away, Natalie's nowhere to be seen. Panic shoots through my gut. Maybe she hasn't arrived yet, either. The two planned to arrive separately just in case. Which means . . . there's a chance the FBI got to her first.

There are only two unoccupied seats on the whole bus, across the aisle from each other. Colin plops down next to Tig before I have a chance to. She's wearing a purple fedora, large mirrored sunglasses, and oversize headphones. The fact that Natalie isn't sitting next to her makes my stomach queasy.

"Tig?" I whisper-shout, but the girl doesn't budge.

Abby clears her throat, instructing me to sit down. I have no choice but to plop next to a girl with a frizzy mop of dark curls that covers half my seat. Her giant nose attempts the same. She sets her big, unnaturally violet eyes on me and watches my every move with great interest. I turn away.

"Tig?" I whisper over Colin again, but the girl still ignores me. Colin taps on her elbow, and she glances at us, but then turns back to the window, not humoring us further.

The bus jerks into motion, and I leap to my feet. "Wait! We can't leave."

"Fiona!" Abby snaps. "Sit down this instant or I'm going to have to—"

I plop down faster than she can finish her sentence. Colin's eyes close as though he no longer has a care in the world now that he's safely ensconced in the bus.

My spare burner phone is in the backpack in the back of the truck. I have no way to contact Natalie and see if she's okay. Tig ignores me entirely for no real reason. And my new seatmate's intensely staring at me, her face hovering only an inch away from my cheek. Her surplus of hair brushes against my cheek, forcing me to swat it away. "Can you give me some space?" I turn back to the aisle. "Tig!" I hiss.

My seatmate continues to study me as she pushes sheets of curls away from her face, securing them behind her ear for a futile three seconds before the hair pops back into place. Silver rings glint in the dim light, pierced through her lips and eyebrow.

She gives herself a satisfied nod. "Success."

Her voice is a little too high-pitched, as if she's speaking entirely in falsetto, but there's a hint of something familiar encased in her voice. Too fast, too clipped. I squint at her, this time the one doing the staring.

"Say that again."

"Success." Her high-pitched voice notches down a few octaves to sound exactly like a voice I've listened to in my earpiece for years.

I grip the girl's arm, pulling her upright. She rolls her ethereal eyes at me. "Finally."

Up close, caked-on makeup conceals putty-sculpted cheeks and a prosthetic nose. The faint gray ring around her irises gives away the telltale colored contacts. An ornate swirling tattoo stems from the giveaway heart-shaped birthmark on her inside wrist. My protégé. My partner in con. "Natalie! I thought you missed the bus."

She poofs her wig with her palm and bats her false eyelashes. I tackle-hug my best friend so hard, we both tumble into the window. "I was wondering how long it would take for you to figure it out. I'll consider this my best disguise yet."

"Why is Tig ignoring me?"

She lowers her voice. "After you changed Colin's name, we started to worry her name was just too unique, so we lengthened it. She'll only respond to Teagan now." Natalie purses her lips. "Well, maybe not *respond* with actual words, but, you know, with a glance or two."

I clamp a hand over my mouth to stifle my laughter. "Teagan? There's nothing about her that screams Teagan."

"I've been calling her T in public, and she does this cute little smile when I say it." Natalie lets out a swoony sigh. "Except of course she didn't want to sit with me, so maybe I'm reading her signals way wrong."

"Maybe she just wanted to save the seat for Col . . . um . . . Colton?" I say in a hopeful way. That maybe Tig's rebuff wasn't a sign of disinterest but all part of the job she agreed to.

"Maybe." Natalie bites her lip.

I rush to change the subject. "What did you end up telling your parents, anyway?"

When I left her to get Colin, we'd told her parents that my aunt (who doesn't actually exist) had arrived at my house to become my guardian. (Hallmark, here's your next movie plot). Natalie was still trying to figure out how to disappear for a month without her parents suspecting mischief.

Natalie jerks her thumb toward her oversize backpack stuffed into the overhead compartment. "Backpacking through the motherland." For Natalie, the *motherland* is actually Canada. French Canada. Montreal, specifically. "They were really happy I was taking an interest in my heritage, and since I'm already eighteen, they couldn't exactly stop me. Tig helped photoshop one hundred pictures and schedule them to post on Instagram throughout the summer." She scrolls through a burner phone and shows me photo after photo of her having the time of her life in poutine country and kissing a girl with supermodel bone structure.

"I see you found yourself a stock-photo girlfriend on this fake trip."

Natalie beams down at the picture. "Well, the whole trip *is* a fantasy after all."

Abby stands up and claps her hands. "Listen up, people!" She introduces the other counselors, two males both named Dave, one who is cute, with muscles for brains, and the other who seems to have taken a firm stance against anything related to cuteness or muscles.

After the pleasantries, she gives an over-rehearsed speech about all the fun we'll have this summer on C2C tours, although all the rules she follows that with say otherwise. "No leaving your room past curfew. On location you must check in every two hours with a counselor. No drugs, alcohol, or other illegal substances."

I guess it's a good thing she said only *substances* are illegal and made no mention about crimes.

CHAPTER 12

The bus speeds down the freeway for several long hours. Each time we pass through a toll, Colin and I duck low in our seats, expecting the FBI to swoop out of the booth and wrench our hands behind our backs. A quick glance at Natalie's burner phone reveals the trucker found the discarded backpack at a rest stop in Reno, Nevada, but police are combing both Nevada and Northern California in search of us. *Both* of us.

> Colin O'Keefe is expected to be traveling with Fiona Spangler after she was caught on home security footage leaving the scene of house arrest with the suspect.

I stroke my necklace and shut my eyes to try to calm down. The image of my mother's face forms against my lids, her dark blond hair spilling over her thin shoulders, her wild eyes searching mine as she presses the same necklace into my palm. *I made it especially for you.*

The whole memory overtakes me. I'm ten years old again, hugging the necklace to my chest, mouth parted in awe. "But it's not my birthday for another four months and twenty-three days." *She loves me,* I think.

"It's not a birthday present." She stands up, her face dissolving into stoicism, all traces of emotion sucked back into her stare. "Remember that," she says, turning the gift into a warning.

A few days later I discovered what the warning was about: her departure. It wasn't a birthday present. It was a farewell gift.

The cacophony on the bus draws me out of the memory. The other campers spend the ride jabbering in a desperate attempt to one-up each other. Tidbits and brags are traded like hot commodities: a pre-college class taken at MIT over winter break, a coveted scholarship, a horseback-riding prize, Miss California, and one whose claim to fame seems to involve tying a cherry stem with only her tongue.

"Hey!" A perky girl with long dark hair expertly curled into luscious waves hovers over us, her voice so peppy I can practically see the extra exclamation points tacked onto her words. "I'm Lakshmi Kumar, and I've taken it upon myself to be a welcoming committee around here." She giggles, but when Natalie and I don't react, her pink-lipped smile wavers. "Anyway, I thought it might be fun to do a little get-to-know-each-other icebreaker. Two truths and a lie. Ready?" She sucks in a big breath, and I brace myself as her words come out in a rush. "One: I'm on track to become valedictorian. Two: I turned down an internship at the White House to go on this trip. Three: I can speak five languages."

I yawn. "All true. Although computer languages don't count, so you can really only speak four."

Her smile flatlines on her face. "How did you—?"

I shrug. "I'm good at reading people." And eavesdropping on her earlier conversations.

Her pep returns in full force. "Okay, then. Your turn!"

I supply a one-sentence entry into her makeshift contest: "High school dropout."

It's not true yet, but it will be as soon as I don't return to Amberley in the fall. When I say nothing more, and Natalie makes a grand show of pretending to sleep, Lakshmi shuffles along to her next victim: Tig. When Tig refuses to even look at her, and Colin is legit snoring, she sighs and moves to the row ahead of us.

The bus finally arrives in Anaheim, where palm trees sway in the distance, the sky bans all clouds, and people in powerful business suits and bulging arm muscles march down the street. We stop in front of a conference hotel a few miles away from the land of thrills and stomach drops. Natalie hands Colin and me new burner phones, his number already saved into mine in case I'm hankering to hear his snark at 3 a.m.

The other campers stroll out of the bus, stretching and yawning, but my legs zing with adrenaline, amped and ready, like they should still be on the run. I scan the crowd, searching for anyone staying in one spot, pretending to be blending in when they're really undercover. As my feet land on the pavement, Abby hands me a scowl and a key card folded in a little white packet with a room number on it—354. "We're all meeting in the mall food court next to the hotel for mandatory dinner at six. There are meal vouchers waiting for you in your room."

I clutch the key card in a tight, overprotective fist. It's a key to my room, but it offers me so much more than that. An alibi. Sanctuary. A place to finally breathe. Natalie, Tig, and I are all assigned to the same room, which will give us a safe place to plan our next steps. There was no way to get Colin into our room, too, without a full-on makeover of the drag-queen variety, so he's unfortunately (or fortunately, depending if you're me) stuck with random roomies.

Abby hands a key card to the girl behind me, then taps my shoulder again like an afterthought. "Lights out at nine tonight," she tells me. "Understand?"

Translation: The other counselors will be checking to make sure you're in your room promptly at nine. And probably several times throughout the night as well.

Translation: You're probably going to be up to no good.

Translation: Watch out.

Snarky comebacks bubble to my lips, but Colin subtly shakes his head at me before I get a chance to engage in a verbal battle with my new second worst enemy. How does he know me so well?

"I know we've got shiny hotel rooms for tonight." Colin flashes his key card. "But we *could* find another truck to sleep in if you want. For old times' sake." He raises his brow a few times.

"It's no gas station bathroom, so hard pass."

Nearby, the bus driver heaves colored luggage onto the sidewalk, and campers grab the retractable handles, eliminating my options one by one. Natalie loops her arm through mine and leads me toward a pair of suitcases, side by side, as if even our bags are in this together. Her foot nudges me toward the one covered in multicolored glitter, so stuffed it leans onto Natalie's chic gray one for support.

I raise my brow. "Glitter? Really?"

"It matches your disguise." She plucks the strap of my too-revealing tank top. "Sorry, lady, but your old style of ripped jeans and clever T-shirts didn't work for me."

"Hey, my style was actually deconstructed school uniforms as an *eff you* to the faculty."

She shrugs. "Now you have some girly flair to work with."

I groan. She's always trying to get me to dress to impress . . .

boys, that is. In my case, anyway. "I hope your intent is for me to be mistaken for an underage prostitute." I smooth the skirt over my butt, trying to cover as much ground as possible.

"Hey, the way I figure it, might as well put the *ho* in *last hoorah*." She pats me on the back. "Besides, it could be worse. That gaudy leopard-print bag over there belongs to your bathroom buddy."

An oversize pink leopard-print suitcase complete with Hearts for Vandals stickers covering the front leans against my black guitar case. I chuckle, because Hearts for Vandals is the biggest boy band on the planet right now, with a screaming fan base of eight gazillion twelve-year-old girls and a music video so saturated with neon colors that it makes my eyes bleed. One of the girls shrieks with delight when she spies the sticker on Colin's bag and starts prattling on about how swoony the lead singer, Jackson, is. Colin gives us a death glare.

In our room, Natalie slides open the curtains as if she's parting the Red Sea. Sunshine floods the room, dust particles dancing in the beams. I catch a glimpse of myself in the mirror. The short black bob with sharp angles at the front makes me gasp. The style Colin coiffed for me actually looks pretty good, not that I'd ever tell him.

Tig hustles to the far bed and starts unpacking various pieces of electronics equipment. I heave my suitcase onto the closest crisp white bed, the entire mattress sinking under the weight. "What did you put in here, a dead body?"

Natalie bites her lip, her gaze shifting between my bed and Tig's. I nudge her toward Tig's bed with a quick jut of my chin. After all, we both win in that scenario, since this way I can sprawl out diagonally across the queen-size bed. Natalie hesitates for one more second before setting her stuff on the other side of

Tig's bed. They share a quick glance and then focus back on their own suitcases. I can't tell for sure, but I swear I can see the corners of Tig's lips quirking upward.

The lid on my suitcase flops open to reveal more uncomfortable and inappropriate clothes, all made of lace or sparkles. "I hate you. I hope you die in polyester pants and cotton underwear."

"Don't hate me too much. You haven't seen everything I packed for you!" Natalie tosses the top layer of clothing aside to reveal my skull-prop forgery carefully wrapped in gauze and Bubble Wrap.

I start to peel off the layers of gauze to check for damage. We've got eight hours at the amusement park tomorrow to make the swap, and if anything's amiss with the skull, I won't have much time to fix it.

"There's a false bottom beneath your clothes." Natalie juts her chin. "All the art supplies you asked for and then some!"

"The 'then some' comment scares me a little, considering your penchant for glitter."

Natalie goes back to pretending not to look at Tig, while Tig pretends not to look at her. Damn it. I didn't account for extreme hormones when I put together this crew.

Natalie starts cataloging all the wigs and disguises she brought, including the maid's uniform from the Hotel Galvez con in case it might come in handy later. Just as I remove the layers of gauze from my skull-prop forgery, an electric blip signals the door opening. I dump the skull into the suitcase, heart hammering, and throw a bunch of clothes on top. Tig freezes in place, but Natalie quickly yanks the bedspread off the bed and tosses it over the array of electronics Tig has been setting up on the desk. It looks like a giant pile of up-to-no-good.

The perky girl who can speak four languages (five if you count HTML) skips toward us. My stomach drops like an anvil to the floor. Not her. Anyone but her. She rushes over to us with two hands extended, clearly attempting to multitask a handshake. "Hi, roomies! I'm Lakshmi Kumar," she says, even though she introduced herself earlier. "And you're Fiona." Her dark eyes sweep over me from top to bottom. I never told her *my* name. "The high school dropout who made us all late."

I snub her handshake. "My dad always told me to make a grand entrance."

Well, technically he said *exit*. And not *grand* so much as *inconspicuous*.

Lakshmi purses her lips. "Hmm, I think I got the short end of the stick. My parents always told me promptness equals politeness." Her smile somehow widens even more in an attempt to break her cheekbones at her veiled barb. "And that I should always be prepared."

Mine said that, too. Of course, they meant *be prepared to flee at a moment's notice*. I cross my arms. "Then I hope you're prepared to stay out of my way."

Natalie gives me a dirty look and deflects with a sweet, innocent tone. "I'm sorry, but I'm a bit confused. It's supposed to just be the three of us in here. I called yesterday and confirmed." She points her hand between herself, me, and Tig.

Lakshmi shrugs. "Everyone else has four to a room. They must have realized they had an odd number, so they put me in here!" She practically bounces on her toes in excitement at this. "I can't wait to get to know you guys!" Her eyes land on the giant, conspicuous pile of blanket on the desk.

Tig twists her back to Lakshmi in an *I can't see you, so you can't see me* defense. Natalie's face turns red. "Oh," she says. "Hotel bedcovers gross me out."

Lakshmi nods. "Agree completely. Shall we remove this one,

too?" She starts to tug at the bedspread on top of my bed. The bed that I'm going to be sharing with her. Ugh. My suitcase wobbles, and the clothes inside jostle, revealing part of the skull.

"No!" I shout a little too aggressively. I place my hands on the suitcase to steady it. "Please leave the bedspread. I, uh, I love it." Oh God. This is why I can't be trusted at the con part of cons. I'm the worst liar.

Lakshmi squints at me like I'm insane, and the shaky laugh I let out doesn't exactly prove my sanity. "Sure, that's fine. I'll just push it toward your side tonight." She claps her hands and squeals. "Seriously, I'm easygoing. Promise. I've had some horrible roomies on other teen tours, and I won't do any of that." As she says this, she pulls out a giant CPAP contraption that looks straight out of medieval times and sets it next to the bed. It comes complete with headgear and a face mask. I'm positive it's loud as hell at night. "Sleep apnea," she explains.

Natalie and I exchange a concerned glance. If she's in this room, how the hell are we going to plan tonight?

Lakshmi spins, and her eyes land on the guitar. "Oh my gosh! You play?" She claps her hands as though I've already performed an entire concert. "I can't wait to hear!"

"I, uh . . ."

"She hurt her hand!" Natalie says. "Real tragedy."

I don a frown. "Maybe later in the tour." Like, when I'm no longer on it.

Lakshmi lifts her side of the bedspread and gingerly pushes it toward mine, then lounges on the bed with her hands clasped behind her head. "So, which stops are you most excited to go to?"

"None of them," I say. Rule #9 is never giving away vital information about your targets if you don't have to.

Lakshmi's eyes go wide. "Really? Not even the roller coasters?"

I shrug. Noncommittal. Behind Lakshmi's back, Natalie juts her chin toward the electronics, and I get the message.

"Hey!" I say way too excitedly. So much so that Lakshmi flinches on the bed. "I just realized we haven't gotten ice yet." I grab the ice bucket off the counter. "Lakshmi, want to go with me?"

She squints at me. "I don't think that's a two-person job."

"Sure it is." Natalie tugs her arm, forcing her to slide off the bed. "Didn't you just say you want to get to know us? Now's your perfect chance!"

I hold open the door for Lakshmi, and she reluctantly steps outside. I follow into the hall. The door shuts behind us, and I hear the click of the double lock setting into place.

Now that she can't get back inside, I head toward the ice machine, not even bothering to wait for her.

She hustles to catch up. "So, what do you think of the other campers?" she says. "Teagan—or is it T?—seems cool but antisocial. And Colton? My God is that boy swoon worthy. You know him, right?"

"Yes, but I'm trying to forget him," I mumble.

Lakshmi hops up and down, clapping. "*Squee!* Can you put in a good word for me?"

"I'm not sure I have any good words to say about you. Or him, for that matter." I set the bucket under the ice machine and hit the button.

Her lip quivers, and her eyes well up.

I scramble for a way to save this. She seems like the kind of person that gets right up in your business and then tattles said business to the counselors. "I, um." Crap. "I have a crush on him," I blurt for lack of a better lie. "Sorry, I was putting up my defenses a second ago," I say dryly. "I'll fight you for him." I cringe inwardly.

Lakshmi blinks at me, then cups her hand over her mouth, her eyes widening in horror. “Oh my gosh. I’m so sorry. I didn’t realize.” She holds up her hands in surrender. “I’ll back off, I promise.”

“I’m going to take that promise literally,” I say, and then grit my teeth. “I mean, thank you.”

“Do you want me to help you write a love note?” Lakshmi hops up and down, clapping her hands. “Oh, this is so romantic!”

“Um, no, that won’t be necessary. He already knows how I feel about him.” And that feeling is toleration.

Her eyes light up, glinting beneath the overhead light. “He does? Does he like you back?”

Damn it. This rabbit hole is going way too deep. If I say no, she’s going to try to convince him. If I say yes, she’s going to demand details. So I do the only thing I can do. I deflect. “I—I’m not sure. I mean, he’s not sure.”

“Got it. Well, I’m making it my mission to make him fall in love with you this summer.” She winks.

I try not to vomit.

As the ice clinks into the bucket, Lakshmi goes on and on, listing every single camper on the bus as though she bonded with all of them in only a few hours, including ones she never even spoke to. One thing becomes very clear to me. Lakshmi is nosy, which means I need to be careful around her. We all do.

When we get back into the room, my suitcase is neatly organized, no skull prop in sight. The electronics on the table are gone, and the bedspread is folded on the desk. So much for using this afternoon to prepare for the heist tomorrow.

How can we possibly pull off a complicated heist if we can’t even discuss it?

CHAPTER 13

Tig continually flicks her eyes toward her suitcase and then at Lakshmi, who has not stopped blabbering since she first got in the room. I can now list the exact ranking order of every TV show she's ever watched in her life, recap the entire history chronicling the rise and then fall of her friendship with her former BFF Kylie, and name every single member of her extended family, down to her second cousin twice removed's hamster.

I've tried everything to coax Lakshmi out the door for longer than a few seconds, but she's not budging, and Tig has had no time to hack into the park's electronic systems and set everything up for tomorrow. In related news, I'm now sporting a beautiful chevron-pattern friendship bracelet thanks to Lakshmi's insistence that this isn't just a teen tour, it's *camp*, and so we must indulge in all the usual camp pastimes. I'm sure she's got ghost stories on the tip of her tongue for tonight.

At ten minutes to six, Lakshmi swipes the food vouchers off the desk and doles them out to each of us. "Should we head down to dinner?"

Natalie glances at Tig. "You go ahead, Tig and I are going to skip it. We're not that hungry."

"Same," I add, even though my stomach's growling. Vending machine Snickers bar, here I come.

Lakshmi bites her lip. "But Abby said dinner is mandatory."

I wave my hand dismissively. "I'm sure it's fine."

Lakshmi shifts her weight from foot to foot. "I don't want to get in trouble for disobeying the rules. Not on day one!" She taps her lip. "Actually, not ever." She starts scrolling on her phone. "Let me just clear it with Abby."

Great, we don't just have a roommate. We have a narc.

Natalie, Tig, and I all look at one another and sigh. We can't risk getting in trouble, too. Reluctantly, Tig pushes herself out of bed and gives Lakshmi her greatest death stare to date.

The din of chatter and the zesty aromas of pizza and tacos welcome me. Tig beelines onto one of the concession lines. She loads up her tray with several slices of delicious-looking pepperoni pizza, baked ziti, a few tacos, a salad, a slice of cake, and three different sodas. Natalie takes Tig's cue and copies her dinner choices.

Lakshmi widens her eyes at their trays. "Whoa, I thought you weren't hungry. Can you eat all that?"

"We'll find out, I guess!" Natalie says.

I squint at her in question, but she just shrugs, clearly going with whatever game Tig is playing here.

I hesitate between the baked ziti and tacos, debating if I should add both for whatever ruse is about to go down or stay here. Keep an eye on Lakshmi. And Colin.

Ugh, I need to be the lookout, don't I?

I reluctantly only grab the baked ziti and then push my tray behind the girls as they wait at the register.

"That'll be forty-seven dollars and thirty-five cents," the cashier tells Tig.

She hands the cashier the ten-dollar voucher, then checks her wallet but only pulls out a five. She frowns at her tray.

Natalie catches on quick. "Let me see how much I have." She searches as well and pulls out a single dollar, hiding the rest of her cash with her palm. "Oh crap," she says sheepishly. "We don't have enough. Not even if we pooled our vouchers."

"I've only got a five," I add unnecessarily.

"We'll run back to the room and get more cash. Can you guys snag us a table?"

Before we can respond, Natalie and Tig shuffle out of the cafeteria, not running, because that would draw attention, but moving fast enough to ensure Lakshmi will choose not to follow.

I pay for my pasta, and Lakshmi pays for her pizza. Ten bucks says it takes them so long to find their extra cash, they miss dinner entirely.

My eyes zoom to the very back, where Colin carries a tray, three tacos wobbling, his roommates trailing him. I expect him to plop down at the nearest empty table, but instead he circles around it until he reaches a table full of girls from the tour.

Cute girls, I might add.

I groan, and Lakshmi whips her head to me.

My fingers tighten on my tray. "Let's sit with Colton."

Lakshmi purses her lips. "Looks like he already found people to sit with. Besides, we need to save seats for Natalie and T."

"Okay, in that case, get us a table. I'll be right there." I march with a little too much gusto toward Colin, but no one notices my approach, because every girl at that damn table has goofy smiles on and lovesick heart eyes. There are no more seats, but that's no problem for Colin. He perches on the edge of the table, casually leaning toward the girls, his smile set to *stun*. His three roommates stand there awkwardly, glancing at one another, before shrugging and taking a nearby table without Colin.

". . . and then this one time . . ." Colin's voice booms above the cafeteria din as though he's trying to create his own version of a mic drop. "I put on black pants. White shirt. And lingered outside like the valet of a swanky restaurant."

My eyes widen, and alarm bells ring in my ears. Is he really telling them his valet-parker-con story? I ram my tray against his back, not in a subtle way at all, and six sets of eyes narrow in unison as Colin twists his attention to me.

"Oh. Hey, Fiona." He gives me a curt nod. "Have you met Sydney? She loves Hearts for Vandals as much as I do." He points to a girl with frizzy red hair and a millennial pink hoodie who chatted his ear off about the lead singer when we first got off the bus. She ducks her head and smiles, eyelashes batting. "And Cassidy." His finger shifts to a tiny girl with far too much blue eye shadow. "And Emi—"

"So nice to meet you all, but, uh, Colton needs to be going now." I shift my tray to one hand and tug on his shoulder with the other.

He doesn't take his eyes off Sydney, even though he addresses me. "Can we catch up later, Fiona? I'm kind of in the middle of something."

I turn to the girls. "Whatever he's about to tell you, it's a lie. He's really good at that. Lying. Oh, and breaking hearts." I tick off on my fingers. "Cheating, on girls and on tests, I'm sure."

He shakes his head but remains totally calm. "I've never once cheated on a test. A test I myself took, I mean."

I kick his shin. "Seriously. Come on." I lower my voice. "Before I start telling them that you still wet your bed at night."

He makes a grand show of rolling his eyes dramatically. "And here I thought I'd left my ball and chain at home with my dad," he says, and the girls giggle. "See you all later." He winks at each one in turn, then picks up his tray to follow me.

"For future reference," I snap. "Here are the rules. No talking about your past cons, no matter how much hyperbole you add."

He scoffs. "There's no hyper—"

"And no flirting."

A giant grin plays on his lips. "Does that include flirting with you? Because you seemed to enjoy it last night."

Now it's my turn to scoff. "I did not!" My voice rises an octave, so I clear my throat. "We need to lay low. Stay under the radar. Blend in."

"Flirting is *how* I blend in. It's how I infiltrated the school and became the most popular guy ever in, like, a week."

"Again with the hyperbole. This isn't school. It's a mission. And I'm in charge, so you have to play by *my* rules. Laying low means staying away from the rest of the campers. Got it?"

He sneers and says in a mock-childlike voice, "Yes, Mom."

Lakshmi's waving at us to sit at her table, and although I have no intention of actually doing that, when I glance around, I notice every damn table is occupied. I have no choice but to lead Colin toward her. "My roommate." I stab my finger toward her in a voice fit for a funeral. "My *fourth* roommate."

He flicks his eyes between Lakshmi and me. "Where are Natalie and Ti—"

"Teagan," I say fast as I sit down, "and Natalie are grabbing cash from the room."

Lakshmi glances at her watch. "They've been gone for a really long time. I should probably go check on them." Her chair scrapes as she stands up.

"No!" I grab her shoulder and push her back into her seat with a little too much force. "I just got a text!" I dangle my phone toward her, showcasing only a blank screen with no evidence of a text. "They're on their way here."

"Oh. Good." Lakshmi hesitantly takes a bite of food but continues glancing toward the door.

I bang out a hasty group text under the table while Lakshmi occupies herself with a bite of her pizza.

Fiona: This buzzkill over here was about to go check on you. Abort mission and come back.

Natalie writes back instantly.

Natalie: FFS. Tig needs time to do all the hacking prep work. Not to mention we still need to go over the plan details one more time.

There's a vibration on the table next to me. Colin snatches up his phone and reads the texts since he's also part of the group convo. The corners of his lips quirk upward slightly as he types back.

Colin: Yeah, and it would be good if you told me what the plan actually is. Before we have to do it.

I start to type a comeback, but only manage to bang out the letter *I* before stopping with my finger raised above the phone.

He arches his brow at me. Checkmate.

I told him I'd tell him info when he needed to know it, and I guess that time should be now.

Colin: How about this: the three of you meet me in the hot tub at 2:30am. We'll have several hours to get set up AND plan while your roomie sleeps.

I glance over at Lakshmi and catch her watching this entire exchange play out on our faces. She's practically biting her lip in excitement at whatever she thinks we're trying *not* to say aloud.

My fingers fumble under the table with a new text.

Fiona: But we need to sleep. Tomorrow's a big day.

Colin: Tomorrow won't even happen if we don't get organized today.

We make eye contact, holding each other's gaze for a brief moment, and Lakshmi lets out a little squeal. I sigh. He's thinking like a true criminal. A man after my own heart (except for everything else about him). We can still get a few hours of shut-eye before 2:30 a.m., and coffee will do the rest.

I bite my lip. This was supposed to be *my* mission. My heist. My crew. But my control keeps slipping through my fingers like sand, and we haven't even started yet.

As I lie in bed, listening to the grating sound of Lakshmi's CPAP machine next to me, it finally hits me with a gut punch so fierce, the wind flies from my lungs. I might never see my dad again.

I can't contact him. Not now. Not while running from the law. Maybe not ever again.

If I find my mom, I'm going with her, wherever she's been hiding, whatever she's been doing. Which means I'll be hiding, too.

A lump lodges in my throat, and hot tears press against my eyes. I hadn't meant to choose my mom over my dad when I started this mission, but that's exactly what I've done. I always intended to choose *both*. The grief at the thought of never hearing his voice again is too much to bear.

I let the tears slide out of my eyes and stain my white pillow and the awful bedspread I got stuck curling up in. I let my throat hitch and the panic rise until I'm gasping. I allow myself to plummet into this pit of despair because it's the only chance I have to let it all out, let it overtake me. In one hour, when the clock hits 2:30 a.m., I have to pull my biggest con yet.

I have to convince myself that I'm okay.

After a while the tears slow and then cease, leaving only the faint evidence of my weakness stained across my cheeks. A swipe of concealer instantly erases my vulnerability, and a shaky breath morphs into normal ones.

I grip the counter in the bathroom and stare at myself in the mirror. *You can do this,* I tell myself. *You have to.*

I lift my mom's necklace to my lips and kiss it. She's my future now.

With that thought echoing in my brain, I gently shake Natalie and Tig awake. The three of us slip out into the bright hallway. I squint against the fluorescent lights and readjust my pajamas over my string bikini (thanks, Natalie). We safely parade through the hallways, since Tig temporarily disabled the cameras before we snuck outside.

The scent of chlorine coats the air when we reach the indoor pool. A RESTRICTED AFTER 9 P.M. sign just begs me to thwart it. Dark windows surround the basin, reflecting back the eerie, turquoise water. In the circular hot tub, Colin outstretches his arms along the tiled edge as bubbles pop around his torso.

Heart pounding, I force myself to look away from his bare, tanned chest and focus on the piles of lounge chairs ringing the pool. The hot tub gurgles like frothy soup, steam billowing toward the high ceiling. Blue lights catch on the ripples.

Despite my request that everyone wear bathing suits, Tig defies me by keeping her black hoodie and fedora on. She immediately starts unzipping her roller suitcase and setting up various electronics on the nearby vinyl lounge chairs. She stretches a long extension cord into an outlet for some juice.

"Let me know if you need any help." Natalie offers Tig a comforting smile, and Tig glances at her just long enough for her shoulders to relax ever so slightly. I nod encouragement at Natalie for her ace flirtation attempt.

She carefully lifts her pajama T-shirt (conservative) over her frizzy wig. "Please, no splashing. I can't get this precious face masterpiece wet. Not the best disguise choice now that I have a civilian roommate to get ready in front of." She shrugs out of her shorts and gingerly steps into the water. Hopefully the steam doesn't make her nose fall off.

I groan and strip down to the sparkly gold bikini I'd rather burn than wear. At least my mom's necklace provides some semblance of class. I plop into the water and try not to make it seem like Colin has won this round by suggesting this ridiculous location.

His calf presses softly against mine under the water while the bubbles inflate his bathing suit like a balloon rising to the surface.

Thanks to our stage 5 clinger back in the room, I haven't gotten any updates yet from Natalie on what she and Tig accomplished while I was off turning my enemy into a cohort. (And an escaped convict.) So I start there. "What did you guys get done yesterday?"

It takes Natalie a little extra time to drag her gaze away from admiring Tig, who's fluttering around to the various electronics, plugging small devices into a variety of laptops, and typing away with the sophistication of a maestro leading an orchestra. "A little recon mostly. Here's my mark."

Natalie reaches behind her to grab a phone and holds up a photo of a pretty, young security officer with a similar bone structure and dark olive skin tone to Natalie's. "Amy Cleary. Twenty-five. Been working at the amusement park for two years. According to all the Facebook spamming she does, she's on tomorrow from two p.m. to closing. Oh, and it's her cat's birthday today. She made him a cake out of cat food." Natalie clicks to show another picture, this one of an elaborate cake that could pass for a chocolate wedding cake if it wasn't made of ground-up fish guts.

I give her a thumbs-up. "Good choice. How long will it take you to turn into her?"

"Twenty minutes maybe?" She taps on her lip. "I mean, after I take some time to shadow her and learn her mannerisms."

"Wait." Colin's head turns back and forth between the two of us. "If she's on the schedule tomorrow, how are you going to get rid of her?"

I grin at him. "We're not. *You* are."

He laughs to himself. "I should have guessed."

"You keep her distracted while I take over for her," Natalie clarifies.

Colin holds up his hands. "Whoa there. I don't even know what we're stealing. If I'm going to help, I need to know everything."

I shift. He's right. About this heist, anyway. "The most popular ride is a mild water coaster with a pirate-and-sea-chantey theme. Back when the park first opened, they tried to be real authentic with their decorations and used actual human skeletons for props."

His brow shoots upward. "Morbid."

"Yep. Eventually the amusement park wised up that immortalizing dead people for shits and giggles was . . . not the best tourist draw. And so they replaced them with plastic replicas. Though some people think one original skull remains. Sort of."

Colin snaps his fingers. "Wait, I know this one." He pauses for dramatic effect. "But not for long."

"Well, no, it's technically already a forgery. Whether the skull in question is supposed to be real or not is meaningless because my mom already stole it. And now we need to steal her version since it contains a clue to her whereabouts."

"Okay, switching out a skull from the most popular ride at the most popular amusement park in the world." He scratches his chin. "On second thought, maybe I was better off on house arrest."

I elbow him in the ribs under the bubbles. "Here's how it's going to work. This is a four-part heist. Part one: smuggle in the skull."

Natalie swirls her finger in the water. "You can't exactly waltz through the security line holding up a skull prop like it's Yorick in *Hamlet*."

"Points for the literary reference," Colin says. "But I need more here. How exactly are we doing that?"

I wave my hand dismissively. "That's the easy part."

"Let's just say I have more costume changes than a Hearts for Vandals concert," Natalie adds.

Across the way, Tig's electronics zing to life, and her eyes grow fierce, her fingers tapping rapidly.

I clear my throat and lower my voice. "Part two: identity theft."

Colin rolls his eyes. "I'm really liking your dramatic delivery. If your career as a criminal fails, you can always narrate audiobooks."

I stand up and cross my arms, water dripping down my bare stomach. "And that concludes all the info I'm willing to tell you."

He tugs on my elbow. "Hey, sorry. I was just kidding. Sit back down, okay?"

I sit down, but only because I'm standing right in front of him in nothing but a potentially see-through bikini. "Part two involves you and me stealing two other random IDs and finagling our way through an underground tunnel system." When I see his brows knit together, I clarify. "It's used by employees to get around the park without being seen."

"And transport garbage in a noninvasive way for guests. I've heard it has quite a fantastic odor," Natalie adds.

"The tunnels are also where they house all the costumes and uniforms for the employees. Away from the garbage, I promise."

"Costumes which I assume we'll be stealing?"

"Not stealing. We'll be scanning them out legitimately with the stolen IDs! We need a security officer uniform for Natalie and a maintenance worker uniform for me."

"Part three," Natalie says in a voice that seems filled with awe, "is all Tig's show. The last two days she's been planting viruses on various control room employees' computers."

Colin leans forward. "That doesn't sound easy."

Tig glares as though to say it was a piece of cake for her.

Natalie rushes in with details. "Well, my good friend Amy Cleary helped here. On her friend list, we found another park employee, Jamison Alameda. And on *his* friend list, Tig contacted a few folks via email until one of them took the bait and clicked."

"It's always easier to fool someone who isn't well versed in technology and security protocols than someone who is," I add.

"Right. So once his friend clicked on the email, it planted a virus on his computer that allowed Tig to gain control. She then sent an email to Jamison from the friend. Naturally, he clicked on it because it looked legit. I mean, it technically was. And voilà! Virus planted on his computer. From there, we sent out a few work emails to plant that same virus on the other employees' computers. Long story short, she basically has control of the entire control room all remotely from her own laptop."

Colin's jaw drops. "Yeah, like I said. That doesn't sound easy."

Tig dons her first proud grin at this and bows.

I just hope the script Tig wrote to gain access to the control room computers is as good as the one Johnny had written before he got hauled to jail.

"And right now she's simply setting up a coordinated attack on the computers that will go off at exactly four p.m. tomorrow. The ride will shut down. Everything will go black."

"And we go into action."

"Part four: action. Colin, you'll distract poor Amy from her security post. Disguised as a security guard, Natalie will usher the riders off the ride. And I'll step in disguised as a maintenance worker to assess the situation . . . By our estimation, I'll have only a few minutes to pry my mom's skull-prop forgery off the wall and replace it with mine."

Colin looks at each of us in turn. "Is now the time I say the obligatory line, 'What could go wrong?'"

I press my finger to his lips, and he clamps his mouth shut. "Shush, you. Nothing will go wrong. This is the plan my dad and I have been working on for months. It's foolproof."

Except for the fact that I had to cut out the getaway driver from the scenario. He was also supposed to be acting as a distraction by causing a commotion in another area of the park while Natalie occupied the real security guard. And my dad was supposed to play the charismatic fake security guard.

Our new version of the plan is better.

It has to be.

CHAPTER 14

I'm in a bad joke where someone asks me, "Fiona Spangler, you've just broken your former worst enemy out of house arrest. What are the two of you going to do next?" And I reply, "I'm going to (steal from) an amusement park!"

With a team of FBI experts on my tail, possibly. Or at least according to the police blotters Tig hacked into after Natalie batted her (false) eyelashes and begged. They've expanded their search to Southern Cali. Hence the horrible character-ear headband concealing my hair and the oversize sunglasses that cover my eyes and most of my cheeks. Every time someone swings their head in my direction, my blood turns to ice. Rule #10 of the con code: The best way to blend in is to dress like everyone else. But it takes a concerted effort not to dart my head squirrel fast after every step or speed up past the surveillance cams.

Because our hotel has shuttles every fifteen minutes to the park, the counselors gave us free rein today to come and go as we please, though Hot Dave is stationed at the hotel lobby to track us leaving, and Ugly Dave's waiting just inside the entrance to track us coming in. Thankfully, Lakshmi was too excited about all the funnel cakes and princesses to wait for our slow asses to get ready, so she took the first shuttle with Sydney and her friends, and we made plans (that I intend to break) to meet up later.

Before we reach the entrance, Tig veers off toward the bathrooms just outside the park. With a backpack full of laptops and other hacking devices, she can't actually enter. She just has to be *near* the park to latch on to the network, which means a fun-filled day holed up in a bathroom stall. The only place where there are no security cameras to capture her misdeeds. Colin thinks I'm super jealous. Rule #11: Criminal activities involve hiding out in a lot of gross bathrooms.

Natalie waddles toward the line, rubbing her swollen belly and bracing one hand on the small of her back as though she can't stand upright for too long. An auburn wig grazes her shoulders. Operation Sixteen and Pregnant is in full effect to smuggle a cloth-wrapped skull inside the park.

The good thing about going through security with no tools or weapons is that I have nothing to hide. I'm going to have to steal all my tools once inside the park. The guard scrutinizes my brick phone charger and the two sets of wireless earbuds. But in order to preserve battery life on the earbuds, we'll have to communicate the layman's way until it's go time: via text messages.

With a tug of my bag's zipper, the attendant waves me through the line, and tension eases from my shoulders. A tingle spreads through my stomach. The same feeling I always get before I pull a job. The hot sun beats down on me as I casually stop beside Colin to zip my bag.

I glance up to check on Natalie's progress through the gates when my eyes land on a guy standing alone by a cookie shop on the main path, checking his phone but lifting his eyes every few seconds. Twenty feet away, a woman sits on a bench with a paperback novel in front of her nose but not turning the pages. Farther down the street, the woman selling balloons keeps glancing around instead of trying to engage customers.

Panic climbs my spine, and I grab Colin's arm and squeeze. "Undercover agents are here, trying but failing to blend in."

Colin's expression fills with pure alarm, as if I just whipped out a hand grenade and tossed it directly into his mouth. "How do you know?"

Because my dad showed me how to spot them. "They generally stay in one location, try to appear busy, like they belong, but they're really keeping their eyes on their surroundings." And being a single adult at an amusement park without towing around a little kid would mean you're either on the sex offender registry or the FBI agent roster.

I cup my hand over his ear and whisper the locations of the three I spotted. His eyes flick to each one, his face growing paler.

A hand braces on my shoulder, and I jump, letting out a yelp that sends several heads swiveling in my direction. I spin around, heart thrashing, and amp my legs to run, but it's only Natalie, not an undercover cop.

Her mouth opens in a wide O, which must be a moan. I bite my lip. *Don't oversell it, Nat.* She braces her hand against me and starts panting. "I don't know how preggos do it. I've only been with child for twenty minutes, and I desperately want to vomit everything I ate."

Calm. Stay calm and act normal. My pulse keeps amping. Through gritted teeth I say, "Bathroom, now."

I hike my backpack higher on my shoulder; it contains all the supplies to transform her into someone else. Actually, a few someone elses. It requires concentration to place one foot in front of the other and walk like a normal person instead of someone fleeing to safety. Once inside, I shove the backpack at her and collapse against the door in the handicapped stall Natalie and I squeezed into. My eyes adjust to the dull khaki walls and floor that remind me far too much of prison uniforms.

"What's going on?" she asks.

I lift a finger to my lips, then get out a sheet of paper and scribble the evidence away from eavesdroppers in adjacent stalls.

"Shit." Natalie purses her lips at me, then reaches into the makeup container and grabs the putty. A dollop elongates my chin, and two more give me hooded eyes. She readjusts my character ears to cover more of my forehead. "There."

But it doesn't seem like enough.

For a moment, I worry the FBI agents will spot Colin instead. I tell myself I only care because we're in this together, whether we like it or not. I promised him a family, and I intend to keep that promise. But I've also gotten used to him being around . . . and working together so far hasn't been as bad as I thought it was going to be.

While Natalie transforms herself into the second of three different people today, this time reverting back to her Teen Tour disguise, I plop onto a chair right outside her stall door and try to calm myself down.

A few minutes later, Natalie hands me the backpack with the forged skull prop and frowns at me. "We're going to rock this. I promise. Don't look so worried."

"What if we fail, Nat?" My voice comes out soft. "Then I'll never find my mom and—"

"Have we ever failed before?" She sounds so confident, but I hate to remind her that we have. Only once.

Only when Colin beat me himself.

"Have a little faith. And—what's the phrase now? Don't stray from the plan."

Her words coax a small smile to my face.

"Speak to you at three thirty." She jets off to stalk Amy Cleary and memorize her mannerisms so she can take over her life for five or so minutes. I try not to choke on the lump blocking my airway as she struts away, her new butt jiggling.

I hope when I leave the restroom, I won't be exiting straight into an FBI ambush.

Swarms of people surround us, some tugging screaming children covered in character ears (probably a doomsday cult—that I've apparently joined). Balloons float in the air, pulled on strings that cover the sky (pollution). Characters weave in and out of groups of tourists, each with a friendly wave and a frozen fabric smile. A beautiful castle looms in the distance, and the scent of baked cookies drifts from the pathway, making my stomach gurgle.

We beeline straight for the pirate ride for a stroll down recon lane so when 4 p.m. rolls around, we'll be locked and loaded to pull off the switch in the dark without, well, a hitch.

"Ahhhh! Hey, guys!" There's a loud high-pitched voice oozing with excitement screaming behind me. "Fiona! Colton!"

We both freeze in place. There's a choice: run or hide. But I don't get a chance to make either, because Lakshmi reaches us, huffing and puffing. She bends over and braces her hands on her knees. "Yay! I can't believe I found you! And looks like I was just in time to join you on the pirate ride!"

I glower at her. Fan-freaking-tastic. "What happened to Sydney and the other girls?"

"They wanted to go on the free-fall-drop ride, and I'm such a wimp." She lets out a shaky laugh. "Besides, I want to hang out with you more!"

"The feeling's not mutual," I mutter before I can stop myself.

Colin clears his throat. "*Fiona . . .*"

When I catch Lakshmi's bottom lip quivering, my stomach sinks. One thing criminals should not have is a conscience, but mine loves to show up in spades at the very worst times. What I really need is for Lakshmi to go away so we can perform illegal activities in peace (ignoring the other people on this ride, of course), but she's like a punching bag: always coming back for more. Guilt seizes control of my mouth, and I try to save face. "If it makes you feel better, I don't want to hang out with *him*, either." I poke Colin hard in the chest in retaliation. He catches my finger and holds it for a moment before depositing my arm at my side.

A smile bursts onto Lakshmi's lips as if she just got an inside joke. She gives me a wink, and the joke's on me. She thinks my attempt to shake her was actually a way to covertly *flirt* with the guy she thinks I have a crush on. *Please,* if my covert game was that bad, I'd have been caught ages ago.

I can't exactly kick her to the curb now. So Lakshmi flanks me on one side while Colin pushes in on the other, my very own ménage à blah. We migrate like cattle in a maze of metal gates that herd the crowd into single-file lines. My smartwatch counts off the minutes. Each step I take in the dank dungeon of a queue is like an ice pick in my chest. The *tap tap* of Lakshmi's impatient foot echoes my thumping pulse. The blast of air-conditioning in the waiting area makes me shiver, and I long for the days when I pulled heists with people I trusted implicitly, whose flaws I knew how to use to our advantage.

I'm not even sure I trust myself after the way I faltered in the rain with Colin.

When we reach the front, plastic boat-shaped cars glide along the coaster track in the murky black water, rising up and down as the customers hop from the wooden plank into them. Drops of water streak the seats. Colin slides in first. My feet land with a hard thump, and I rest my butt on the plastic ledge. My skirt shifts, causing my bare thigh (thanks, Natalie) to press against the douchecanoe next to me. As the other douchecanoe slides in beside me, Colin nudges his thigh into mine for a brief second, a silent message I can't interpret. No wonder I can't decipher my mom's clues; I can't crack anything.

With a lurch the boat jerks into motion, crawling along the rickety tracks. I remove my sunglasses once we enter the tunnel and get ready to study as much as possible so I have it all memorized by the time the heist rolls around. The atoms in my veins dance at the prospect of a heist. A manufactured blast of sea salt hits my nose. Screams and shouts of glee mix with the turn of the gears and the cheesy music of fiddles and guitars. Colin wraps his long fingers around the plastic hull while Lakshmi's white knuckles shake. "I'm scared," she whispers.

The only reason I don't kill her right here is because murder would not help me stay incognito.

When Colin sits upright, I tilt his head to the side and cup my hand against his ear. "We need to ditch her. Immediately."

His cheek grazes against mine as he maneuvers to whisper in my ear. His warm breath sends goose bumps down my neck. "If we do it too early, it'll just make her desperate to find us again. We've got to make sure leaving us is *her* idea, not ours."

Damn it, that actually makes sense. I cross my arms and sink into the hard back of the seat while Lakshmi strings her arm through my elbow and screeches. The boat brings us into a dark cavern filled with posed skeletons that light up when we pass. Mist floats upward to surround our boat in a ghostly ambience. The scent of barbecue seasons the air while dancing skeletons encircle an illuminated fabric flame. The song blasting recounts tales of debauchery, rape, and murder, and other things that might lead to thousands of skulls. A real cheery number. Gonna have to put this on my next workout playlist.

"It's coming up," I tell Colin. Thanks to illicit YouTube videos and a variety of internet photos, I've done a lot of virtual recon over the last few months. But this is my first time seeing it in the flesh. Or, well, lack thereof.

"Oh my God!" Lakshmi grabs my arm and lets out a bloodcurdling shriek. Wilhelm scream, I've found your replacement. "The skulls look so real!" She forcibly pushes my head in the opposite direction of the skull forgery to ensure I don't miss seeing the scene of dueling skeletons fighting with bones on the other side of the river.

The dreary pirate song recants how killing and stealing is an excellent form of currency. Kind of like my life now (minus the killing). I spin to see the forged skull whipping by as the boat glides past it. Two crossbones meet below it. And a few feet away, right where the schematic maps Johnny managed to track down show it, is a doorway hidden behind two skeletons having a feast.

"Smile!"

We turn just in time for Lakshmi to snap a photo of the two of us looking horrified.

"Oooh!" she squeals. "It's super Instagram worthy!"

I widen my eyes at Colin. Posting on Instagram with a girl who will probably tag us with a million identifiers? #Coast2CoastConnect TeenTour #Fiona #Colton #PirateRide #NextStopGrandCanyon. She might as well send the image straight to the FBI.

Colin must be on the same page, because he asks, "Can I see it?" When she hands it to him, his thumb subtly swipes across the device to delete. "Oh crap. I think I deleted it by accident."

My shoulders relax.

"I'll just take another!"

I shake my head fast. "Not today. I'm, um, having a bad hair day."

Colin nods. "I can confirm she's having a terrible hair day. Seriously, one of the worst."

I elbow him hard, and he lets out an *oof*. The ramp rises up up up and then plunges down into a small pool of murky black water. My stomach doesn't even budge, but the drop forces a high-pitched scream from Lakshmi that makes my own blood curdle.

When the ride stops, I tug Lakshmi's arm and force her out of the seat. She wobbles on shaky legs like a newborn calf taking its first steps. "Ferris wheel next. I've planned it out, and if we hit that one in precisely ten minutes, there should be no line. From there we have to go to the racing cars and the jungle ride and—"

I stifle a groan. Of course, the one variable in a heist you can never plan for: well-intentioned leeches thwarting you unknowingly.

I lean close, whisper in her ear, and try not to cringe at what I have to say. "I really want some time alone with Colton." I blast Lakshmi with a glare that sends two messages at once: Leave us alone and *leave us alone,* the last version followed by a couple of implied eyebrow raises.

She lets out a sniffle and flicks her eyes between us as though she's mentally imagining us making out. "On second thought, I'm going to see if I can find Natalie and T for the Ferris wheel."

My stupid chest cinches tight at the sound of her defeated whine. It takes extra internal coaxing to force myself into motion instead of folding her into a hug. "Great," I say through clenched teeth. "See you later." I grab Colin's hand and tow him in the direction of the witch ride before I ruin everything by being nice. As soon as we round the corner, I relax. Alone, at last. I immediately curse myself; being alone with Colin should not be a relief.

Bright sunlight forces me to squint at the large crowds in line for the witch ride. Off to the side of the line, concealed by a blue door that appears to be part of the painted scenery, is a corridor that leads into the underground tunnel system. Entry requires an employee badge/key card and a lot of stealth. We only have one of those. Well, *I* only have one of those. Colin has a lot of bravado instead.

"Okay, there's the entrance. Do you see any marks?"

Colin struts toward one of the photographers. A pretty female photographer, of course, with great big blue eyes. Straight out of a cartoon. It's a wonder she doesn't have tiny birds perched on her arms, chirping. Her badge dangles from her belt.

I inch closer to eavesdrop, pretending to study my phone like any good undercover FBI agent might.

"Hey there." Colin leans against the white railing beside Miss Beauty Queen. The railing surrounds an array of gorgeous pink and purple peonies, the perfect photo backdrop.

She beams at him, pushing her dark hair out of her eyes as though to see him better. "Would you like a photo?"

"I sure would." He positions himself in front of the flowers, looking like a social media influencer modeling a product and living his best life. Hashtag YOLO. His grin is so infectious that several people pause to look at him. The photographer even pauses for a moment, clearly forgetting what she was supposed to do. I should remind her about that . . . and the fact that he's underage.

"Wait!" he gasps to himself. "Fiona! Get in!" He coaxes me over with a wave of his palm.

I widen my eyes at him when the smile on the photographer's face falters just a little at the sight of a girl joining him in the photo.

"Smile wide, okay?" He nudges me with his elbow. I have to resist the urge not to stomp on his foot.

I play along, though, smiling as best I can. Colin slides his arm around me, his warm palm skating down the bare skin. I shiver but remind myself it's only because there's a slight breeze . . . somewhere.

The photographer snaps the photo and then glances at the camera to check it. She gives him a grin, but hers is no match for his. "Great, let me scan your wristband, and the photo will appear in your account by the end of the—"

"Can I see it now?" He bites his lip and looks up at her beneath his lashes. "Please."

"I'm scheduled to upload these in—" She checks her watch. "Oh! Only ten minutes. It should be in your account in no time."

"Oh man. Ten minutes?" Colin's whole face deflates as though he's seriously dejected by this news. "Here's the thing. My sister's dying." He nods toward me, and my mouth drops open. I quickly correct myself and give him the requisite glare that all sibling rivals (and scorned rivals) must portray. "And this might be the last photo of her ever." He swallows hard, eyes welling up. "I need to make sure it's perfect. So I can remember her by it." His voice cracks on the last word.

The photographer twists to me with a horrified expression. Thankfully my sputtering cough at Colin's cover story sells the image of me dying. Probably of whooping cough. Disregard the fact that it's basically extinct these days.

"Please. This is her last trip. Tomorrow, she goes into hospice care." He sniffles and sounds so goddamn devastated, I have to resist the urge to check my pulse and make sure it's still ticking.

The photographer's hand flies to her mouth. "Of course. Of course. I'm so very sorry to hear this." She avoids my eyes, too afraid to look at the girl who might only have a few days left.

We crowd around her camera, the two of us leaning in to see the adorable photo. We honestly look so happy with the way his arm casually rests around me. Even my smile looks real, not something put on just for show. I definitely don't look like I'm about to keel over.

"Hmm, do you think the lighting is weird right here?" He points at the corner of the photo.

While she leans in to scrutinize the sun glare, my hand snakes out and yanks her key card from her belt.

As soon as we thank the photographer and walk away, I jab him in the ribs. "You just had to kill me, didn't you?"

He shrugs. "Girls love a sob story."

"But that one made us stand out. We need to blend in. Now she's going to remember us."

"You're paranoid. It'll be fine. Send the image to Tig."

I sigh and take a snapshot of both sides of the ID to send to my favorite microserf.

Tig texts back a thumbs-up emoji, and I kind of love that the girl stays silent even in the written word.

Tig will now hack into the park's system and update the records to replace Kate Sinclair's ID photo with mine.

And maybe this whole plan will succeed.

CHAPTER 15

After snagging another ID—without metaphorically murdering me this time—we sit on a hot bench a few feet away from the tunnel entrance door. The California sun reflects off the cobblestone walkway that's embedded with tiny particles of glass, making the ground sparkle like diamonds. A slight breeze carries the scent of roasted nuts from a concession stand, and people crisscross in front of us, each heading to a different ride, a constant stream of strangers trying to get out of each other's way. The sickly sweet music blasting from a nearby ride plays on a loop, and after only five minutes, I want to gouge my ears out. If the US Army ever runs out of torture devices to get enemies to blab, I'd recommend playing them a few bars of the magic-carpet ride theme song.

I glance at my phone and then the tunnel entrance. As soon as Tig gives us the signal that she's updated the IDs in the system to match our photos, we need to slip into the tunnels and grab two uniforms: a security guard uniform for Natalie and a maintenance worker uniform for me. From there, it's a matter of Colin distracting Amy while Natalie and I slip into our disguises and wait for Tig to cut the lights. Then we barge in through the maintenance door, and Natalie will keep everyone calm and distracted while I pretend to fix the lights issue while really switching out the skull under the cover of darkness.

The plan is all timed out, and we're using up almost all our contingency time. If even one step goes a minute too long, the whole thing might fall apart, since Tig's script to cut the lights is set to a timer that can't be adjusted.

I fiddle with my phone to distract myself. We have about forty-five minutes to get these uniforms and change into them. I bite my lip. "According to the schedule, Tig should have been done with the ID hacking fifteen minutes ago. Do you think she's having trouble? Is that why she's not responding?"

He shrugs. "Does she ever respond?"

"Good point." I sigh. "We can wait five more minutes, but that's it."

Rule #12: Heists involve spending a lot of awkward quality time with people you'd rather never see again.

"Maybe we should use this time wisely instead of sitting here." I turn to face him. "Here's your crash course in all things stealth," I say, and he rolls his eyes. "As soon as we go through those tunnel doors, act natural. No showing off. No making a scene. No smiling at cute girls."

He scoffs. "If I'm not smiling at a cute girl, then I'm not acting natural!"

I ignore this and the way my stomach squeezes at his mention of smiling at cute girls. "Just don't make eye contact with anyone except the clerk at the costume warehouse, okay?"

"Okay, but I'm counting you in that no-eye-contact bullshit. And I definitely won't smile at you, either."

My cheeks burst with redness, because did he just imply that I'm cute?

My phone vibrates with a text, and I nearly leap off the bench. But my face deflates when I see who it's from.

Lakshmi: Where are you guys? I miss you!
Let's meet at tilt-o-whirl in 5?

I groan, and Colin snickers over my shoulder. I shield my screen from him to type out a reply.

Fiona: Can't. Too busy making out with
Colton.

I squeeze my phone, a bitter flavor lingering in my mouth. The words look just as awful as they taste reading them back.

Colin snatches the phone right out of my hands, and his eyes widen. "Whoa. Usually if I'm involved in making out, I like to, you know, *be* involved."

My cheeks get hot, but I'm sure it's just from the temperature outside. "Calm down." I hope he doesn't notice how high-pitched my voice gets. "I had to tell her I liked you, because it was the only thing that would get her to back off for a while."

A wicked grin crosses his face. "Suuuuure." He drags out the word in a singsong way. He looks as though he's one step away from writing *Fiona loves Colin* all over his yearbook and then holding it up for the entire grade to see.

I shift uncomfortably on the sticky bench. "It's a ruse! I swear!" I hope I don't seem *too* defensive, but when he keeps looking at me with that little smirk of his, I open my mouth again, my words coming out in a rush. "Just like when you pushed my hair aside in the rain and—"

I clamp my mouth shut. Oh God, why did I say that? I bolt from the bench and start pacing in front of him. Anything to stop my heart from beating so fast.

He stays on the bench, watching me. *Studying* me. After a moment, he grabs my wrist and pulls me to a halt. "Okay, I—I get it. I . . ." He lets out a sigh and rakes his free hand over his shaved scalp. "I approve of the ruse, okay?" He bites his lip. "Will you please sit back down? You're making a scene."

I glance around and notice several people staring at us. I plop back down with a heaviness I hadn't meant to carry. "Let's take a cue from Tig and sit here in silence." I cross my arms for emphasis.

Thankfully, Tig texts a moment later. It's a single emoji of a woman shrugging with only one hand. "What the hell does that mean?"

Colin shrugs with one hand in response.

I text Tig: Does that mean we're good to go?

A minute passes, but there's no further response from Tig.

Tension coils in my shoulders. "What do we do?" I don't want to risk using the ID if Tig hasn't successfully accessed them on the backend to change out the photo and identifying information to match us instead of the people we stole these from.

Colin checks the time. Thirty minutes until he has to distract Amy and thirty-five minutes until it's showtime, folks.

Thirty-five minutes isn't a lot of time to slip inside the tunnel doors, find the wardrobe room, check out two uniforms, find Natalie, change, alter my appearance—ugh.

"I think we have to go for it," Colin says.

"But—"

"Either we risk it, or we risk not getting your mom's clue at all."

Blood whooshes in my ears. When I stand, I wobble on shaky legs. My hands are slicked with sweat, and there's even more pooled in the crooks of my elbows. It must be due to the heat. It can't be nerves. It can't.

We weave more aggressively through the crowds than we really should, considering we're trying to go unnoticed. I bump into one woman's shoulder, and she yells angrily for me to watch where I'm going. I slide off my character ears and reluctantly drop my sunglasses in my backpack.

At the tunnel door, I grip the ID in shaky fingers and hold it up to the sensor. The door beeps an angry red, and cold panic races up my spine. I wipe my palm on my shirt and try again, but the door blinks red a second time. "Why would it turn red?"

"Maybe Tig's still working on it so it's temporarily deactivated?" Colin knocks my arm aside and shoves his ID at the door. An eternity passes in the two seconds it takes for the sensor to turn green.

We let out twin breaths.

"Do you think a one-handed shrug meant that Tig could only access one ID instead of both?" I pull the door open.

He bites his lip. "Hope so."

Colin starts to race down the steps, but I clear my throat, and he slows his pace. A guy in a duck costume zooms past us, fixing his head on as he goes. The air gets steadily cooler the farther we descend inside, and I shiver when I was sweating like crazy only moments ago.

Our eyes adjust to the dull lighting and the gray drear that decorates the tunnels. It's a stark contrast to the bright and bubbly exterior, where every inch of the park has been carefully painted to look new and pristine. Here, long brown pipes line one entire side of the gray hallway, and the stench of garbage makes me gag.

There are unmarked doors along the corridor that each lead to a different ride. For emergency purposes only, of course. (Or for heists, depending on your perspective.)

I glance down at my phone, where there's an image of the tunnel schematics Tig found. I nudge Colin in the ribs when we pass the next unmarked door, a silent message for *That's the one that leads to my mother*. Or, more accurately, her forgery.

"Wait, is that it?" He says way too loudly, and I have to nudge him again as an employee with a clipboard walks by us and nods in greeting.

We pass by a cafeteria filled with gabbing employees and a studio for filming quick Instagram content. We make a pit stop at the maintenance closet to steal some supplies for later. Crowbars, a portable drill, a hammer, and flashlights land in my backpack.

We continue down the tunnel until we reach the wardrobe hall.

Every role and job here has a specific costume, from the characters down to the guy who slops mashed potatoes onto your plate at the diner. Employees pick up their costume each shift at the wardrobe center and return their soiled ones at the end of the day.

It works similar to a library, where employees come in, locate their costume, then scan the bar code at a checkout counter. Our plan was to check out the uniforms in a legit way by scanning our new IDs and then smiling when our photos pop up on-screen. But if my ID doesn't work, Colin can't check out two different uniforms. And since we're not sure what Tig's text means, it's probably too risky for him to check out even one.

So we have to steal these for real now.

I'm not sure why that idea scares me so much.

A woman sits behind the desk in the entrance of the wardrobe room, typing away on a computer, a fluorescent light above her head exposing all her freckles and flaws. A sign above her reads NO GUESTS, NO EXCEPTIONS. I keep my head down, shuffling past her as though I've done this a thousand times, but Colin chooses this moment to wink at her and shoot her his most magnanimous grin. As soon as we round a corner, I glare at him.

He turns up his palms. "What? You said I was allowed to smile at her!"

"I said nothing about winking," I deadpan.

The costumes are grouped by theme, so we skip the various princesses and witches and head straight to the adventure section. We pass by pirate costumes and jungle costumes, each one neatly hanging from rows of garments in a colorful array, until we find the ones in the back—the ones that aren't cool. A security guard with a little bit of jungle flare in the form of a palm-frond print on the trim and a safari-chic maintenance worker. Complete with a ridiculous safari hat.

I grab one of the maintenance worker outfits in my size and turn it over in my hands, brushing my fingers against the sturdy fabric. We have no real plan on how to smuggle these out of here illegally, so I scrutinize the fabric for any obvious traps. There's a bar code with a raised bump beneath it affixed to the tag of every single piece for the uniform. The safari-style maintenance worker uniform contains five pieces alone. If we walk out of here without scanning these, the alarm will surely blast.

I tug on one of the tags, but it doesn't budge, sewed on too tightly.

Before I can even try to rip it off, there's a high-pitched blip, like a police siren being turned on and then immediately off. Red lights blink from devices on the ceiling and douse the room in flashes of scarlet.

"Attention!" An announcement filters in through speakers. "This is a mandatory ID check. Please report to the front of the room for verification."

My skin turns to ice, and the uniform falls out of my hands.

Colin launches into action. "Quick, grab the uniforms and stuff them in the bag. We're going to have to make a run for it."

We hastily shove the uniforms into my backpack on top of the skull and all the tools. I zip up the bag and stand, heart beating.

People stream past us, walking casually toward the front. If we run, we won't be able to stop. We'll have to keep running until we flee the tunnels. We'll have to run until we outrun whoever might pursue us.

We have to run straight out of the park.

Colin's eyes widen at something behind me. "Security's coming."

We have just enough time to kick the backpack into the rack of clothes before a security guard looms over us, looking burlier than ever. My gaze shifts from the muscles bulging out of his shirt to the gun fastened to his belt. Gulp. I'd make two steps before he flattened me like a pancake. The queasy look on Colin's face indicates he's thinking the same thing.

"Up to the front." He juts his chin, and when I glance that way, the blood drains from my face. They're searching everyone's bags. "Get in line."

"Wh-what's going on?" I manage to stammer.

"Security breach. One of the employees reported a stolen ID. Need to check everyone as a safety precaution."

Oh shit. The photographer's ID. The fact that I'd tried it at the tunnel door must have alerted them to the possibility that the culprit might be in the tunnels somewhere. That must be why it was deactivated in the first place—it had already been reported stolen when Tig tried to hack it.

One-armed shrug. One ID activated.

"Okay, we'll head there in a sec." Colin gives him his signature smile.

"Now." The guard stares down at us with a menacing gaze.

My hands shake, itching to lift in surrender, but I force them to stay down. Colin and I march toward the front, the security guard's boots stomping behind us. With every click of my heel, my pulse ticks up.

We must have hit this place right before a shift change, because there's a long line of employees streaming from the front of the checkout counter all the way to the back wall, and we have no choice but to stand at the end of it. Roughly forty people in front of us, and the security guard, who keeps his eyes trained on us.

Everything's silent except for the blips and bleeps from successful ID checks and the groans issuing from the annoyed employees about to miss the start of their shifts.

I bang out a text to Tig: Pls get my ID working stat. They're checking everyone. T-minus ten minutes until we're united with handcuffs.

This time she responds instantly with a screenshot of her computer screen showing an *Access Denied* message.

A lump swells in my throat.

Fiona: Try harder!

Three more people check out. The line moves forward. The walls close in on me.

Fiona: Let me see what you're doing.

I call Tig via FaceTime. I keep the sound off because she wasn't going to say anything anyway, but she picks up and sets her phone beside her so I can follow along. Colin watches over my shoulder. Tig plugs various devices into her laptop, seemingly to run cracking software of some kind. Binary code flashes on her screen at light speed. But the error message pops up once again: *Access Denied.*

"Crap," I mutter, and the person in front of us swings around to squint. I lower my voice and lean even closer to Colin, so close that I can smell his coconut suntan lotion. "Can you talk us out of this?"

His face pales, and he shakes his head, a wounded expression twisting his brows together. The most confident guy I've ever met. The cocky guy that claimed he could weasel his way into anything. That same guy cannot assure me that he can keep us safe.

"Double crap."

A few more people pass through the security check. We move forward, about halfway to the front. I start to picture the cold slap of handcuffs. The experience of the elusive park jail, where they take truants and drunks. The face of Ian O'Keefe when he hauls his ass down here to swoop us back to San Fran.

The disappointment that I'll never find my mother again, and I won't be able to face my father.

"Please, Tig," I whisper into the phone.

On the screen, her fingers flex. She unplugs the devices she just plugged in and tries another combination. She pulls up several new scripts and executes one via the command line. The script runs much more slowly than the last. 1% complete. 3% complete.

Security validates two more people's IDs. My heart is in my throat.

7%. 12%.

I string the charm on my necklace back and forth on the chain, faster and faster to combat my nerves.

16%. 21%.

Eight people ahead of us. Panic climbs up my spine in full force.

27%. 35%.

Bleeps and blips pass the next person. My hands shake, rattling the phone. Colin grips his own phone with white fingers.

44%. 51%.

The girl in front of us clears her throat, and I nearly throw the phone into the air. I let out a little yelp, but so does Colin.

58%. 62%.

Two more people move forward.

73%. 76%.

The next person clears security in less than a second. Five people ahead of us.

81%. 85%.

Four people left. Oh God. I've maneuvered in and out of heavily secured museums with more stealth. And now a measly ID is going to be my downfall. And worse still, I'm going to get Colin caught, too, breaking my promise to protect him.

89%. 93%. 95%.

Three people pass. Only one person ahead of Colin.

99%.

The next person in line, a girl in her mid-twenties with her hair stuffed in a bald wig, laughs at something the security officer scanning her badge says.

99%.

Bald wig asks him about the weather.

99%.

"Be prepared to run. Or grovel," I whisper to Colin. We don't have the costumes, or the skull, but we have no other option except to try to escape.

99%.

There's a beep, and the guard's scanner turns green. Baldy waves goodbye and exits safely. Colin takes a hesitant step forward.

One. Two. Three. Six security guards surrounding us. Fifteen hundred pounds of muscle.

Gulp.

99%.

"ID?" the guard asks Colin.

"Oh, um." Colin fumbles for his wallet, and the guard sighs heavily.

"Please have your IDs out and ready to go." He's addressing Colin but looking at me.

I keep clutching the phone, making no move for the ID.

99%.

Colin continues to fumble for his ID, clearly dragging this out as long as humanly possible. My stomach twists with knots.

"Any day now." The guard blows out his bangs from his face in annoyance.

"Sorry about that." Colin extracts the ID from his wallet and slowly passes it over to the man.

99%.

Crap crap crap.

The man lifts the scanner just as the screen on Tig's computer changes to 100%.

The light on the scanner turns green, and I wipe sweat from my brow that Colin passed this test. But then I glance at Tig's screen, and my stomach drops to the floor. Her screen shows a side-by-side view of my ID and Colin's. Colin's ID contains his photo, while mine contains a giant red X over it and the word *Deactivated.*

"Miss, please step forward and hand me your ID."

There's nothing to save me from this. My ID won't turn green no matter how slow I go. "I, um . . ." I swallow hard. "I don't have one."

Colin lifts his head, shoulders straightening. "Oh, yeah. Sorry about that." The nerves he had moments ago dissipate, and that cool, confident manner of his takes over. He laces his fingers through mine and pulls me toward him. His warm palm offers my sweaty one a little bit of comfort. "She doesn't work here—she's my girlfriend." He says it with absolutely no hesitation, like this is something he's said a million times. "I was just showing her around." He turns to me and gives me the most lovesick grin I've ever seen. For a moment I lean toward him, falling right under his spell like I did outside school in the rain.

The guard's eyes narrow. "Excuse me, but we have a breach in security and you neglected to mention that you brought an intruder in here?"

Colin shrugs. "It's my first day. I didn't realize—"

"You watched a training video. You signed a document acknowledging—"

Colin rubs the back of his neck. "Guess I should have paid more attention to that video, huh?"

"Sir, I'm afraid I'm going to have to report this incident to HR."

Colin swallows hard but nods before ducking his head.

"Miss, come with me. You need to leave these tunnels immediately."

Colin squeezes my hand. "I'll see you later, okay?"

"Backpack," I whisper through gritted teeth.

I follow the guard straight out of the wardrobe room and through the hallways, where we pass by room after room undergoing the same security review to find the culprit that they're unknowingly about to escort out. Once the guard punts me all the way into the bright sunlight, I lean against the side of the building, tension still wound in my shoulders as I wait for Colin to return. He's still going to have to get those costumes out unscathed somehow. He can only scan one.

Ten minutes later, he still hasn't returned, and my texts have gone unanswered. Maybe Tig's rubbing off on him. We only have five minutes to meet Natalie and start distracting Amy.

Someone taps me on the shoulder, and I nearly yelp. When I spin around, there's a giant pig character waving at me.

I shake my head. "Not interested. Go find a child or something."

The pig lowers his head and pretends to cry into his white gloves. I roll my eyes.

"Calm down. It's me."

I squint harder and then burst out laughing. "Colin?"

"It was the only way I could smuggle the backpack out of there. Inside this giant pig head. Literally crushing my own head right now."

"Oh my God. I need to capture this forever for future blackmail purposes." I fumble for my phone.

"Yeah, yeah. I got the other uniforms by the way. Had to rip off all the security tags, but they're here. Also crushing my skull. Now help me ditch this costume."

I lift my brow. "Is this the part where you strip?"

"If your fantasies are to watch me slowly yet seductively remove a pig tail from my torso, then yes." He pauses, then tilts his head to study me out of giant fabric eyes. "Are you okay? I was worried you got caught."

My heart amps faster. "You were worried about me?"

He rubs the back of his fabric-covered neck with white gloves. "I mean—yeah. Of course. You're vital to this operation."

Something in my chest cracks. It's the same thing I said to him after the truck escape, but now I can feel the sting. "Right."

"So, what do you say? Let's ditch a pig and then steal ourselves a skull."

He knows just the way to a girl's heart.

CHAPTER 16

With the stolen uniforms in my bag and less than ten minutes until Tig cuts the power, we weave through a crowd stopped to watch a parade of singing men dressed in animal costumes and head toward Amy Cleary and her soon-to-be replacement. On the way, we place our earbuds in our ears and connect on a four-way call. Well, it's technically four-way even though the fourth person only breathes heavily in response. I thought cracking my mom's clues was hard, but deciphering what Tig means when she sends a haircut emoji followed by a number nine proves to be impossible.

"You want nine haircuts?" I guess, and Tig clucks her tongue.

Colin rolls his eyes, nearly crashing into a mother pushing three screaming kiddies in a stroller as wide as a tractor and seemingly as heavy. "She probably means your hair looks stupid. Nine times stupid."

Another tongue cluck.

Natalie lets out an exasperated sigh. "The power gets cut in nine minutes."

Tig confirms that Natalie's correct with silence rather than an emphatic yes.

For every group text that Tig sends, I receive a private text from Natalie full of heart-eyes emojis. List of things that turn Natalie on: fedoras and ineffective communication.

I pick up my pace. "Natalie, we're roughly ten seconds away from—Oh, I see you."

Natalie sits on a bench across the way, a thick paperback book cracked in front of her face. I wouldn't have recognized her if she hadn't already texted a photo of her new-and-improved appearance. She's already done half the battle of transforming herself into Amy Cleary: freckles dotting her nose, hemp-colored hair knotted into a tight bun at the nape of her neck, prosthetics giving her a dimple in her chin and hooded eyes. The only thing missing is the security guard uniform, which jostles in my bag. Sunglasses and a baseball cap conceal her from the real Amy Cleary, who stands a few feet away at a security kiosk, helping point a family of four in the right direction.

"Okay, Colin." I pat him on the shoulder. "It's all you now. Talk Amy's ear off and keep her distracted for the next fifteen minutes or so."

"Remember," Natalie adds, "she likes tabby cats, all the shows on the CW network, and to rant about feminism all over social media."

His face goes pale. "Great, all things I know zero about."

Still, he looks casual as he approaches Amy, hands slung in his pockets, hips angled as if he doesn't have a care in the world. My stupid heart does a flip-flop, which is weird, because I've never been nervous for a heist. Not once.

I straighten my shoulders, feeling a little more confident after the uniform fiasco. The hard part is over. Colin can charm this girl in his sleep. I can slip in anywhere unnoticed. We've got the rest of this heist down pat.

"Oh my God!" A girl runs toward me with the speed of a linebacker, tackle-hugging me like I'm the long-lost sister she hasn't seen in ten years. Lakshmi's intense embrace forces me to stumble backward and crash into Colin, who in turn crashes into Amy's podium. "I totally didn't think I'd see you again today! Yay!"

She lets go of me and wraps Colin in a similar bear hug, tugging him away from Amy.

"I missed you guys so much! I couldn't find Natalie or T. Or Sydney and her friends. I've been wandering around all alone and now . . . !" Lakshmi wipes sweat from her brow to indicate the hardships she's endured the last few hours, so empty and abandoned.

Amy shuffles away from the podium, robbing us of the opportunity to distract her. No no no. We can't let her out of our sight.

"Guess what!" Lakshmi's fingers fly fast on her phone. After a moment, she hops up and down, her braids flopping. "I just got us line skip passes for the pirate ride. I want to go on it again!"

A text vibrates, and Colin and I glance down at our phones.

Tig: 7 minutes

Colin sets his greatest weapon on Lakshmi. "We're in the middle of something here, though, so if you can just give us a few minutes, we'll meet up with you on a different ride. Promise, okay?"

Lakshmi dismissively waves her hand and laughs. "You guys have done enough sucking face for today. Take a five-minute break and ride with me." She lowers her voice to sound authoritative. "I'm not taking no for an answer here."

"Six minutes thirty seconds, guys," Natalie mumbles in my ear.

Shit. Shit. Shit. Colin has to distract Amy before she walks too far way. Natalie and I have to change into uniforms. And we can't do any of that with Lakshmi blabbering. What would my dad do?

He'd find a way to ditch Lakshmi without giving her any reason to follow.

I dredge up the memory of the guard shoving my dad into the back of a prison van and whisking him away from me. Hot rage boils through my body and makes me straighten like an arrow. Out of the blue, I slap Colin across the cheek with an open palm. "You cheating bastard!" I cry in my best impression of a shunned girlfriend, imagining how Jessica Sanchez feels now. "You kissed another girl!"

Lakshmi gasps and backs away a step. Colin's eyes widen, and he rubs his jaw. Natalie giggles in my ear.

"Um, yeah." Colin rubs the back of his neck, looking sheepish. "When I said we were in the middle of something, I meant an argument. Not, you know, making out."

"Because he was making out with someone else! I just need to be alone!" I channel every teenage girl in every cliché movie and force my voice to hitch. Too bad I don't have a bedroom door right now, because the moment definitely calls for a hard slam. Instead, I turn on my heels and run, my hands still curled into fists.

"Excellent improvising and subterfuge. A little overdramatic on the acting, though." Natalie shoots me a thumbs-up from her bench, and my stomach squeezes again. Because I'm not actually sure I was acting there.

We run into the restroom to change.

Thanks to Colin's earbuds, I can hear Lakshmi launch into him. "Why would you kiss another girl after you just made out with her? That's incredibly smarmy."

Colin's answer comes a second later. "I'm a jerk, I guess."

"Ditch her," I coax him via the earbud as Natalie and I squeeze ourselves into the handicapped stall. "You need to be distracting Amy right now."

"Trying," he whispers back, then says louder to Lakshmi. "I need to find that other girl. We'll do the ride later, though, okay?"

Natalie and I scramble out of our clothing as my eyes adjust to the dim restroom lighting.

"No way," Lakshmi says. "I'm not letting you be a jerk again. Fiona *likes* you. A lot!"

I freeze while zipping up the ugly tan maintenance worker jumpsuit. "I don't. At all."

Natalie purses her lips and squints at me. Tig also sucks in a sharp breath, her version of a condescending laugh.

Lakshmi continues to prattle on. "You need a grand gesture or something to win her back. Like in the movies!"

"Not interested in getting her back. I just really, uh, want to find that other girl." For a guy that normally waltzes through life dripping with confidence, Colin sure sounds flustered.

"And I want to make friends, but somehow that seems impossible." Lakshmi sounds so dejected, and I worry she's on the verge of tears.

"Oh no. Please don't cry. Let's just—"

A wail rings out. "Is something wrong with me? Why doesn't anyone want to hang out with me today?"

I help Natalie button her security uniform and glance at my phone in the process. My pulse spikes. Four minutes.

"Of course we want to hang out with you, it's just that we all have our own things going on and—"

"Then let me be part of it. Let me in. I could have comforted Fiona. I could help *you*. Please."

"I know, but—"

Lakshmi's sobs grow louder. Remind me to slip her some Midol later.

"Calm down. We'll hang out with you later. We'll—oh shit. One second," Colin says to Lakshmi. A moment later, a text pops up.

Colin: Amy's heading toward the pirate ride!
I'm too far away to stop her.

I let out a growl of frustration and type a response. Tig, any chance you can whip something up, another distraction this area?

Three little typing bubbles appear, and I pray it's Tig, but then I glance over and see Natalie fiercely typing on her phone. Explosion on another ride. Malfunction maybe. Anything but a blackout.

Tig texts back a smiley-face-wearing-sunglasses emoji. I press my lips together.

The lights in the bathroom flicker off, the whirr from the air-conditioning ceases, and a few people shriek.

"Oh my God," Lakshmi says through Colin's earpiece. "Look! All those rides just stopped! I think the power went out."

I let out an aggregated scream that just mixes with the commotion in the now pitch-black bathroom. My phone provides a faint glow as I type. She said NO blackouts.

Natalie shoves our old clothes into the bottom of the backpack. "She probably wasn't equipped to do anything else on such short notice."

Colin sends a text. It worked. Amy ran in the other direction, but I lost her in the chaos.

Natalie tugs on my arm. "Maybe this is even better. She'll be totally distracted now. Let's get out of here."

My chest trills, my muscles jittery. I run through the plan in my mind, but already I'm crossing out too much, skipping over steps, leaving huge gaps in the setup. We're not ready. Not yet. We need to adjust the plan and—

Natalie tugs me toward the tunnel entrance. My stomach swirls faster than the fastest roller coaster.

"Look, Colton!" Lakshmi shouts. "The pirate ride looks like it's still working. Let's use the fast passes before it fills up."

"Ugh." I groan. "You have to go with her. You have to make sure she doesn't see what's about to happen. Block her view."

This is bad. If Lakshmi sees anything at all, I have no doubt she'll blabber about it to the entire camp. And all of Twitter.

"Okay, fine. Let's go," he tells Lakshmi.

I try not to focus on the way my stomach churns as Natalie and I barrel through the crowds and descend through the tunnel door beside the witch ride, using Colin's stolen ID. Although Natalie looks like Amy, we didn't have time to alter my face like we'd planned. Another mistake.

Three minutes left.

The usual adrenaline that rushes through my veins before a heist doesn't appear, too weighed down by the bog of fear and uncertainty. It's supposed to be thrilling to do something really wrong and get away with it. But I can't shake all that's riding on this. Not just finding my mother, but the desperate need to prove to myself I'm not a total screwup. I can still carry out a mission successfully even though my last attempt resulted in me getting stranded in the rain empty-handed and empty-hearted.

I need to make sure I'm still worthy of making my parents proud.

"Wow, those fast passes really work! Got on the ride in less than ten seconds," Colin says, clearly for our benefit. The sea chantey plays faintly through my earpiece.

Natalie and I head toward the hallway that leads to the emergency exit for the pirate ride. My timer ticks down, and my pulse ticks up.

Three.

Two.

One.

Oh God. No turning back now.

I brace myself for the quick snuff of the lights blinking out. The inevitable collective shriek from the crowd. The glide to a stop and confusion that will rise into panic.

It all hits at once, sharp and loud.

". . . going on?"

"Is this normal?"

". . . broken . . ."

Then panic. Shrieks emanate from Colin's headset, Lakshmi's the loudest. "Oh my God! Oh my God! We're going to die!"

The panic's like a disease: contagious. In seconds it seeps into my bloodstream, rings in my ears, makes my steady legs wobble like Jell-O. Natalie bursts through the doors, and I have to coax my feet into action. Our pupils widen to adjust to the stark blackness, a sharp contrast from the saturated hallway. Tiny glows of light dance in the distance like a rock concert where everyone's holding up their flashlight app during a slow ballad. Although this time the music consists of a cappella screams and hushed panic. Without the A/C blasting, a rush of sweltering heat stifles us.

"Everyone calm down!" Natalie moves into action and shines her flashlight toward the stopped guests. "We're going to fix this and have you out of here in a jiffy."

"What's going on?" someone yells.

"Electronic malfunction. I'm going to evacuate you in an orderly fashion."

You can't fail. I point my flashlight at my feet. *You have to switch the skull prop.* I place one foot in front of the other and traverse a rocky terrain of, well, rocks made out of wood and foam. *You can't get caught.* A small hill causes the landscape to wobble under my feet, or maybe that's just my vision going unsteady. To my right, skeletons encircle a table and pound glasses filled with shiny amber beer (lushes). And just beyond that, the skull in question hangs at the far end of the scene, above the display of a sleeping skeleton in a lavish bed, looking darker and drearier and decidedly deader than any of the other skeletons in here. It rests on a shield of crimson, as if it's still bleeding its secrets after all these years. Two crisscrossed bones mark an X on the spot like buried treasure.

Natalie marches toward the nearest boat. "All right, everyone! Please step carefully onto the side where I'm standing." She starts with the only boat that's connected to the land. All the other boats have a much wider berth of water on either side of them. She'll march everyone through the maintenance door in groups. Once we're done with the switcheroo, we'll rip off our uniforms in the darkness and mingle with the evacuees as part of our exit strategy.

"Guys . . ." Colin's voice is a whisper, barely audible in my earpiece. "I'm right in front of the skull."

I freeze mid-step behind the bar. This is no *bueno*.

"Who are you talking to?" Lakshmi asks Colin.

"No one. Hey, stop, don't touch my headphones."

"Keep her distracted," I hiss. "Don't let her see anything!"

The crowd keeps causing a commotion, and Natalie continues guiding the first boat's passengers to safety on dry land, the boat rocking as the stopped guests demand to be let out faster, some crying claustrophobia. But this is all good. It helps cover the metallic sound of the crowbar scraping against the back of the skull as I wedge it behind with sweaty fingers.

Touching it sends a rush of nostalgia through me. Mom bracing her hands against mine, moving my thumbs to show me how to properly mold the clay. Helping me twist the clay in my palms until it warms and I can knead it like dough into any shape. Dipping my fingers into a cup of water to keep the clay moist until I'm ready for it to air harden into the consistency of bone. "The trick to getting the perfect shape is to pay attention to the details," she said.

The eye socket dips a millimeter on the left eye, probably from some dingbat poorly handling the skull while nailing it to the wall. My mom managed to re-create even the mistakes, not just the perfections.

Determination floods my veins. Squaring my shoulders, I pull back on the crowbar with all my strength, grunting in response. The skull loosens, and one of the four nails goes flying.

"All right, first boat group! Please head on through that doorway and turn left. Follow the stairs up to ground level."

I pop another nail loose. Two down, two to go.

My elbows shake from exertion, but I keep going. Tig's blackout won't hold much longer. Another nail comes free.

Before any of Natalie's first group of evacuees can flee, the emergency door swings open again, and another flashlight beam joins the fray.

"Everyone, please calm down. We've got the situation under control." A woman's voice. She shines the light toward her face, and I catch a brief glimpse of her features. Amy.

The real Amy.

My stomach clamps up.

The real Amy's flashlight sweeps across the scene and lands on Natalie.

"Excuse me!" Amy marches toward her, and her hand goes to her waist. "Who are you? I need to see your security credentials!"

"What do I do?" Natalie whispers.

There's only one thing she can do. "Run."

"No, wait! I have a better idea!" Colin's voice is sharp and clear.

And then a second later, I see a shadowy figure rise in the boat and leap into the murky water. The splash is so loud that everyone freezes for a second. Until Colin's splashing starts.

"Help!" He flails his arms frantically, slapping them against the water. "Help! I can't swim!"

Chaos ensues. Lakshmi's piercing scream rips into the air. Someone else dives into the water to help Colin, but he's flailing too much to be rescued easily.

I war between sagging in relief at his clever distraction and groaning that he managed to be clever.

Amy has a choice. Continue toward Natalie to catch her or help the direr situation of a potential drowning. With a sigh, she shouts, "I'll get a life ring!" She runs back toward the emergency exit, cutting off the fleeing group again. Slim chance that when she returns, she returns alone.

Natalie rushes toward me, and together we pry the last nail off the wall while Colin covers our sound with his frantic splashing. His distraction won't last long.

"Nat, start stripping back into your regular clothes."

"But—"

"Our exit strategy is compromised. Amy saw you. We need a different way out."

"And that way is?"

I bite my lip. "No idea. I just know we can't look like this."

As I affix the replica skull I made onto the wall using just one nail instead of the four I'd planned, Natalie shrugs out of the uniform and rips the prosthetics off her face. She shimmies into her new clothes and then takes the skull from me to place everything into the backpack, uniforms and all, while I change out of the maintenance jumpsuit. Natalie settles her giant wig of massive hair back on her head.

She blinks at me. "Now what?"

What, indeed. My shoulders tense, worry seeping into every crevice in my body. We can't go out through the maintenance door. And we can't stay here. The only way out is . . . on the ride itself.

My fingers settle into the scratchy fabric of the backpack, and I lock my elbows as I hoist it. "Follow my lead."

She switches on her flashlight, but I yank it out of her hands and shove it down on the floor. Darkness leaches my vision like inkblots.

I trace my hands on the dusty bones of the skeletons to help guide me toward the far edge of the island. Most of the boats are kept a good six feet away from the scenery, but the boat closest to the land is now free of people thanks to Nat's evacuations. We climb into it, boat wobbling, my knees scraping over cold plastic that resembles wood.

Colin's flailing continues. A few more people jump into the water to try to help. We could do that, sure, but I worry they'll take everyone in the water for questioning or maybe to an infirmary. We can't risk that.

Natalie and I maneuver over the seats in the empty boat and then climb into the next one, landing directly beside two people. They scoot over and look at me like I'm crazy. "Hey! What are you doing?"

"Sorry!" I make my voice sound desperate. "My friend fell in the water!"

They immediately scoot over to let us pass. The people in the row ahead of us do the same and even offer their hands to help us climb over the divider into their seat. We scale the next two rows, and when we reach the back, we jump over a foot of water to reach the next boat. The boat Colin jumped from.

The boat Lakshmi's in.

I fall into her row, sinking onto the hard seat and crossing my arms over my chest while the backpack wobbles on my knees.

Lakshmi screams in horror at the sight of us. "Where—where did you come from?"

"We were a few rows in front!" I jut my thumb behind me and try to sound panicked. "I heard Colton's screams. Is he okay?"

"But—" Lakshmi opens her mouth and then snaps it shut, her brow furrowing in utter confusion. Then she shakes it off and tackle-hugs me. "I'm so scared for him!" Tears leak from her cheeks onto my lap.

"Me too." I allow myself to settle into her embrace, relaxing for the first time in hours. "Me too," I whisper again, only this time I hadn't meant to say it out loud.

I place my hand over my mouth and let out a sob just as the emergency door swings open and Amy shuffles through with an army of crew members. They manage to lift Colin out of the water and bring him to shore. He sprawls out on the rocky terrain, arms spread wide, chest pumping raggedly in a grand show of weakness.

The lights switch on, harsh and bright, but the ride stays stopped. My eyes widen at Natalie.

"Your nose," I whisper in haste.

She covers her nose with her hand as she digs into the bag to find the prosthetic. A pretend sneeze provides the cover she needs to fix it back on.

The medical crew lead Colin out the emergency exit along with the rest of the people who jumped in the water.

Amy stands at the edge of the scenery, her eyes sweeping over everyone. "Did anyone see where the security officer went?"

"You're the security officer!" someone shouts. Amy studies everyone, scrutinizing every face. Natalie and I paste on our best innocent, confused expressions.

"Damn it," Amy mumbles to another security officer. "She must have exited through one of the other doors. If she went all the way down to ten, she could have gotten out by the carpets."

"I'll send a crew to look there," he says, and Amy nods.

"Folks, we'll be starting up the ride in a second to get you all out of here. Sorry about the disturbance, but we'll be handing out some free food vouchers as you exit, to make up for the mishap."

The security crew leaves. The lights dim. And somehow we've managed to make it out of here with the skull in hand *and* some free dinner.

CHAPTER 17

Natalie opens the bathroom door to shocked silence. Her fake dark curls drip small puddles of water onto the taupe carpet, and a white towel hides the curves she usually conceals with disguises. "No word yet?"

Tig's fingers fly fast across the keyboard, hacking into whatever systems she can to try to find any info about what happened to Colin. But the concerned look on her face and the way her tongue lolls out of her mouth in concentration provides all the updates she has: a big wad of nothing. His burner phone went kaput once it sank to the bottom of a six-foot-deep water ride. A pit of worry swims deep in my gut. What if they run his fingerprints and connect him to his past?

I pace the hotel room, creating tread marks on the carpet with my heavy footfalls. When I convinced Colin to uproot his life and help me, I promised him the one thing I thought I could truly offer: protection. If he joined my crew, he'd become my family. I'd have his back, always. And yet I failed. I got him caught.

Lakshmi reaches toward me but then snaps her hand back on second thought. She bites her lip and wrings her hands. After a moment, she holds her phone out to me. "Did you see this?"

Technical malfunction shutters popular ride for hours.

The article's posted on a national media site. Embarrassment creeps into my veins. Oh God, if it's posted here, anyone might see it. My *dad* might see it. If he knew how royally we screwed up that heist, he'd be so disappointed in me. Ugh.

There's a sharp knock on the door, and I jump in surprise, almost dropping Lakshmi's phone. I shove it into her hands and race toward the door while everyone else springs to their feet.

When I twist the knob, the smirk on Colin's face offers me the first sense of relief I've felt in days. "Miss me?"

We circle around him, but before he even has a chance to speak, Lakshmi's cell phone buzzes. She frowns at the screen. "It's my grandma. I have to take this. Don't tell us anything until I get back. I want to hear it all!" She heads into the hallway to take the call. Clearly she doesn't trust me not to eavesdrop. (Smart girl.)

I dead-bolt the door against Lakshmi's inevitable return and wheel on Colin. "What happened?"

He shrugs. "Mandatory medical exam mostly. And then a shit ton of paperwork. And then Abby had to fill out a shit ton of paperwork. And then she spent hours trying to get in touch with my parents, but couldn't, because Adam and Marsha Buttz technically don't exist in real life. Though Marsha does have a lovely voice mail message."

Natalie clears her throat. "I'll call Abby later and pretend to be Marsha." She pats him on the shoulder. "Glad to hear my son's okay."

"Wait," I say. "Security didn't suspect you at all?"

He shakes his head. "Honestly, they were more worried about me suing them than anything else."

I squeeze my eyes shut as tension drains from my shoulders. He's safe. We're all safe.

"So, what does the clue say?" He looks to each of us.

"We haven't even had a chance to look yet thanks to Clingy McGee." I lift the skull from the backpack with greedy fingers and hold it high in the air as if I'm reenacting the opening scene of *The Lion King*. The rest of them huddle around the skull like it's a holy grail about to grant us eternal life. The hazy light filtering in through the curtains blurs the surface of the skull. I flip on the nearest lamp and blink against the sharp pop of light exposing all the cracks in the clay . . . and all its secrets.

You were my first and my last and my past. A melody and a felony and a tragedy in propensity. The second chance future is hidden within.

I scan the carving again for any spark of familiarity, but it reads like all the other nonsense my mom spewed instead of relaying sage parental advice. My first instinct is to immediately pick up my phone and call Dad to tell him what I've found. So we can try to decipher it together. But the anvil in my gut drops to the floor at the realization that I can't rely on him anymore. I shove the skull at Tig. Natalie leans in, too. For a brief moment, Natalie's finger entwines with Tig's before they both jerk away.

A calming hand lands on my shoulder, and when I spin around, Colin's staring at me with an intensity that makes me shiver. "You okay?"

"Yeah, I—" I swallow past my dry throat. "I need time to make sense of it."

He gives me a small, crooked smile. "Well, how much time do we have before the next heist?"

This, I can focus on. “Eight days, and zero of that week includes alone time to crack the clue without the harshmellow crowding on me.”

“We’ll find time.” Colin bites his lip. “But I think what’s more important right now is having the proper time to plan the next heist. So it, you know, goes halfway decently.” He glances up at me from beneath his eyelashes. “Which means telling me what the next heist is.”

I nod. He’s right. “That guitar I’ve been carrying around? It’s a replica of the one Eric Clapton gave to George Harrison who used it to write ‘While My Guitar Gently Weeps.’ It’s currently on special display at the Gibson Guitar Factory.”

He snorts. “So the most famous guitar in the world?”

My mom used to tell me tall tales about how the guitar—nicknamed Lucy—was stolen in the seventies and Harrison went to great lengths to retrieve it. He refused to put it on display or part with it until his death in 2001 when his estate inherited it. *Or so they think*, my mom used to say with a weird glint in her eye.

“We’re going to get them to take the guitar off the wall and hand it to us.” I pull back to give him my widest grin.

He sputters. “And how—”

“By tricking them into thinking they were supposed to ship the guitar to another location. There’s a Gibson Brands showroom in LA. When the Nashville office discovers they messed up and LA needs Lucy that night thanks to backdated emails Tig’s already planting”—we glance at Tig, and she gives us a thumbs-up—“they won’t be able to take the usual precautions. They’ll have to put someone on a plane and hand deliver it. Then we distract that person outside long enough to switch the guitars.”

Colin purses his lips. “But what if they call the LA office?”

“We’re going to pretend to be the LA office and call *them*.”

"Tig's going to mask my number." Natalie holds up her phone in demonstration. "When I dial the Nashville office, it'll look like it's coming from LA. I'll impersonate the CEO and ream them out for not sending the guitar. I'll insist one of the interns hand deliver it." She lifts her nose in the air, affecting an air of snootiness.

Colin nods. "I like it. And let me guess, I'm the one acting as the employee who will be hand delivering it?"

I laugh. "It's a small office. We'd never be able to convince them of that." I pat his hand. "Once the intern exits the building, you just have to distract him or her long enough for me to perform a little switcheroo while the intern's back is turned."

Sinking onto the bed, Colin taps his finger against his lip. "The plan's okay except for all the holes and assumptions."

I splay a hand against my heart. "I think that's the highest compliment you've ever given me." I purse my lips. "But we need to be perfect this time. We were sloppy with the skull and barely got out of there without getting caught."

There's a twist to the doorknob and then a sharp knock.

"The Barnacle has returned." I groan and shove the skull into my suitcase. Natalie sidles closer to Tig on the bed and leans in to whisper something. Tig digs her laptop from her bag, settling it on both their legs, their thighs pressed together.

Colin glances at them for a beat too long. "I should go. My roommates probably think I died in a six-foot moat." He heads toward the door, and I sink onto the desk chair.

One step closer, but still so very far away.

The next morning, Natalie, Barnacle, Tig, and I are getting ready for breakfast when Natalie gasps so loudly while scrolling through her phone that Lakshmi drops her curling iron.

We all look at her expectantly, and she widens her eyes at us while hiding her phone behind her back.

My pulse spikes at whatever she must have seen on her screen.

Lakshmi laughs and lunges for Natalie. "Let me see! Let me see it!"

Natalie scrambles to her feet to back away, but all that does is give Lakshmi the opportunity to reach behind her and swipe the phone away. Her eyes widen when she glances at the screen, then back at me, then at the screen again. "Oh my God. That looks just like you and Colton!"

She hits a few buttons, and the volume blasts on a video clip.

I march over, trying not to let it show how much my hands are shaking, and snatch the phone from her. She's already rewound the video to the beginning and leans over my shoulder to watch with me despite my protests.

Colin's mug shot graces the news segment. The photo shrinks to one side of the screen, and a new photo emerges, my high school yearbook photo, where I look entirely too much like a goody-goody in my pristine uniform, nude lips, and cheery smile. Remind me never to let Natalie give me a makeover when it might be immortalized in print.

I freeze, panic climbing my spine. Until now, my story had only hit the police blotters and local San Fran and Reno news. The scroll on the bottom of the video flashes the words *Be on the lookout: Colin O'Keefe and Fiona Spangler* and also our heights and weights. Which they *so* got wrong. Both cameras and the FBI add ten pounds.

Lakshmi increases the volume on the phone even more to drown out the laughter coming through the wall from the campers in the next room.

". . . escaped from house arrest . . . ," the news reporter says. A new image pops on the screen, this one of the empty box of black hair dye from the lost backpack. The yearbook photo reappears, now photoshopped to give me long black hair as the reporter explains my possible change in appearance. Colin's hair has been darkened as well, even though it was dark to begin with. "Eyewitnesses believe the two may be traveling together in Southern California . . ." A new photo fills the screen, this one taken from the side, of a girl with long black hair standing in the shadows near the pirate ride. Right location, wrong person.

Blood whooshes in my ears, and my fingers twist my necklace. I can still see the roller coasters from my hotel window.

The FBI knows where we are . . . but maybe this means Dad does, too. Glass half-full and all that. I can't get a message to him myself, but at least now he'll realize I'm finishing the mission we both started.

Lakshmi gasps at the screen. "That's so weird how much those people look like you guys!"

"Yeah, that's why I gasped initially! Those criminals *do* look just like you." Natalie lets out a hearty laugh, as if she finds this coincidence hilarious. "But clearly one has a different first name, and your last names are way different, too," she points out, so Lakshmi won't miss it.

"Crazy!" I flop onto the bed as if I don't have a care in the world, even though my heart is thumping faster than most marathon runners'. "But at least neither of us have a permanent record," I joke. "Yet." I punch the wall behind me. "These loud-ass girls in the next room might convince me to murder someone."

Lakshmi steals one last glance at the phone before letting out a laugh of her own and passing it back to Natalie. She buys it. For now.

But the video is already going viral within my small circle of (mis)trust. A peek at my Facebook page shows all the concerned and worried messages from the people who never cared about me in high school until I may have run away with the guy everyone couldn't wait for to return.

Vance Whitford: Damn you two. I hope you're not eating double doubles without me. Also, I'm assuming this means we have a clean slate and I don't owe you any more favors?

Olivia Rossdale: OMG. I hope you guys are okay. I'm not sure how I'll get through school without you next year!

Jessica Sanchez: You bitch! I trusted you! You ran away with MY boyfriend! He was going to come back to ME in the fall!

Amelia Thomas: Jessica, you weren't actually dating him so . . . might want to edit that comment there. Fiona, if you're reading this, I'm very impressed. And a little concerned! Hope you're YOLOing it up and all that.

I snicker. Of course Vance only cares about the favors and the burgers, and Olivia's freaking out about how she's going to have to attend every single class next year like a model student and not a truant one. And Jessica appears to still be brainwashed by Colin's magnanimous smile. At least Amelia is taking her role of president right and setting everyone straight.

While Lakshmi heads down to breakfast early to talk Abby's ear off about her thoughts on the tour so far, I alter my face with Natalie's help: nose a little longer than usual, cheekbones shifted higher, severe winged eyeliner and excessive contouring. The changes shouldn't be too jarring in person, but when you compare photos of the new me and the old me, there will be clear differences. She helps Colin, too, rushing to his room to give him a more prominent chin.

By the time breakfast begins, Tig has erected a fake Facebook page for incognito me with photoshopped pics dated to place me at a scene far away from my past crimes. All Google searches for our fake names, Fiona Queen and Colton Buttz, lead to the curated sites she populates with random info: backdated newspaper articles about me winning school art awards, my grades accidentally leaked and better than I could ever achieve, an ex-girlfriend still hung up on Colton according to her fake Snapchat account, a blog Colton maintained to chronicle his Hearts for Vandals obsession.

Natalie trails her finger down Tig's arm in thanks, and Tig's cheeks combust in a blush.

Word of mouth fills in the rest as Natalie deflates any rumors of us looking like Colin and the other Fiona by regaling the rest of the campers with stories about fake me as if she's drafting an entire novel of fan fiction starring her best friend. "This one time," she tells James Kennedy while chewing a bite of maple French toast, "Colton broke his leg on a class trip to a horse stable. And he wasn't even riding!"

Colin turns bright red. "It was muddy. I slipped."

Natalie slaps her hand down on the table. "And oh my God. Remember the time that Fiona and her ex Travis rocked the homecoming dance by performing this amazing choreographed routine that involved crazy flips." Natalie leans back, shaking her head fondly at the nonexistent memory. "Oh man, people are still talking about that."

"Oh yeah?" James raises a bushy eyebrow. "Let's see."

I stow away my glare at Natalie and push my chair out from the table. In the thin aisle between the buffet stations and our long table, I stand up. The campers scoot their chairs in, each head turning to watch me expectantly. Colin wears an amused expression while Lakshmi claps in anticipation. Dancing is not one of my many talents, but the flips I can handle.

I raise my arms in the air, point my toe, and perform an adequate back walkover back handspring step out. After I stand, I throw in a little shimmy and a twirl, which I hope satisfies the dancing part of Natalie's requirement. Then I blow on my fingertips as if I'm cooling off a smoking gun.

Lakshmi claps louder and squeals. Colin rolls his eyes and shakes his head at me.

When I slide back into my seat next to Lakshmi, I say loudly, "Now let's see if that other Fiona can do that."

The other campers laugh, and the scandal instantly shifts into a crazy coincidence of an inside joke. Still, with our faces plastered on the news and on social media, I worry we won't be able to keep up this ruse for long.

CHAPTER 18

Over the next week, we perfect the roles of model campers to prevent anyone from getting suspicious, arriving five minutes early for each counselor check-in, staying snuggled in our beds when the Daves conduct room checks, acting as photographers for all the perky photos the other kids take at scenic overlooks by the Grand Canyon, where the most scenic things Natalie looks at are Tig's eyes (sans glare). The two have been sitting together on the bus, trading giggles, while I play along with Lakshmi, squealing at all the camper gossip she tells me, like how Lexi and Anderson may or may not be hooking up in the back of the bus (spoiler alert: they definitely are). Lakshmi's good side, here I come! The teen tour provides the best disguise of all as it glides right through the FBI checkpoints, and the agents only give a cursory glance at the camper roster.

I haven't been able to crack the skull clue, but only because I haven't had a moment alone. I've tried to turn it over in my mind while lying in bed, but it's too difficult to decipher a complicated clue without using a pen and paper to make cross outs and notes. I also haven't had a moment to even start on the forgery of the ancient book after the one I spent weeks on was confiscated by the FBI. I can't risk working on either on the bus, in the hotel room, or anywhere anyone could walk by and see. And by anyone, I mean Lakshmi.

So I lay low.

And wait.

But all that does is give me ample time on the long drives to dwell on my dad, stuck in a jail cell, no way out. And my mom, waiting at the end of the rainbow, hoping one day I might find her.

I rattle a heavy breath, and Colin glances over at me from the next seat. Bronze light from the caramel-colored sky filters in through the window and makes him look like he's gilded in copper. Without a word, he plucks one of the earbuds from his ear and passes it to me over the walkway like an olive branch. When I take it, our fingers brush, and he wraps his around my hand for the briefest moment, squeezing tight, before pulling away.

The small act of compassion almost breaks me completely.

I settle his earbud into my ear and lean close to him, our heads nearly connecting across the aisle. I let the soft melody of the rock ballad lull me, eyes closing, breath evening out. But I can't concentrate on the lyrics because I'm reciting my own mantra. *I'm going to find my mom. And maybe, together, we can rescue my dad. Somehow.*

I'm still playing the Model Camper role when we stop for the night at some campground in the backwoods of Oklahoma the next day. I grit my teeth against all the complaints that lodge in my throat—*What? No bathrooms?*—and lug one of the C2C-issued tents to a spot at the edge of the clearing. The tall trees that circle the campsite and cast my spot in shadow provide the protection to stay hidden. The wind rustles my hair, carrying the scent of pine, woods, and barbecue from a nearby campsite.

I spread my arms out to the side and twirl in the open air. No security cameras that could identify me in an instant. No elaborate plans to deal with right now. No undercover FBI agents combing the woods. No internet service. It's the first time in a long time I've actually felt free.

Or at least like we might not get caught.

It reminds me of the last trip I ever took with my mom, right before she disappeared, when the three of us pitched a tent near a lake in Washington State and I thought nothing would ever be better than that.

I wish I hadn't been correct.

The counselors pass out plates of lukewarm pizza into our waiting palms, since the hot-dog delivery never showed. My stomach lurches at the sight, a reminder of the school election and the rivalry that used to exist between Colin and me.

The weird part is I can't pinpoint which day it stopped.

"Sleep with me!" Lakshmi hops in front of my Bear Attraction Lodge—blocking my optimal exit. All at once the feeling of being trapped returns, crushing my lungs, and I hug my arms to my chest like a shield.

From the red bandanna draped over her boxer braids and the hiking boots that cover her feet, it seems she takes camping as seriously as she takes every other excursion we've been on. Around us, campers work in tandem, sliding metal poles through the slits in the dirt-streaked tarps. A few of the girls shriek as their structures collapse on top of them. Within seconds, Colin's tent stands proud and unwavering, and even a little cocky. He parades around the duos, dispensing advice as if he not only has to be the best at everything, he has to let everyone know it.

Thankfully boys are on the other side of the campfire. Sometimes playing by the rules has its perks. It can repel mortal enemies.

I skid my new sneakers along the ground (forever defying Natalie's dress code of wedges and short skirts), sending up a cloud of dirt over my bare ankles. "I promised Natalie . . ."

"I think she plans to sleep with someone else. Figuratively and literally." Lakshmi giggles and jerks her arm to where Natalie aligns solar panels in a patch of sunlight to charge Tig's electrical equipment. Once set up, Tig places her oversize headphones over Natalie's ears and then presses her cheek against Nat's to listen as well.

They're working on both of the next heists simultaneously. Although perhaps the "work" part is optional for Natalie. For the Gibson Guitar Factory heist, Tig has been hacking into their system and planting backdated emails between the LA office and the Nashville office, marking them as read so they go unnoticed.

For now, anyway.

For the Hesburgh Library heist in Notre Dame, Natalie's been doing remote recon with the help of Tig hacking into security feeds. She won't have time—or the opportunity in such a low-traffic place—to tail her mark and mimic her mannerisms on the day of, so she needs to do it in advance.

"Oh my gosh! I just had the best idea," Lakshmi exclaims. "You should get your guitar from the bus and serenade us all tonight! Your hand seems way better now!"

I freeze. I can tell you exactly where the famous Lucy guitar got a slight dent in the back—from Eric Clapton—but I cannot for the life of me tell you what a G chord sounds like. "Um, it's electric. And there's no electricity out here . . ."

"Tig has solar charging panels, though! Look!" She points right in Tig's direction.

"But they don't work on . . ." My eyes shift at movement in my peripheral vision. Natalie's waving me over excitedly, and I welcome the excuse. "Hold that thought," I tell Lakshmi, and drop the tent just in time for my knight in shining handcuffs to swoop in and help her. I stomp toward the (soon-to-be) lovebirds' setup. The two perch on a fallen log, Natalie bopping her head to Tig's tunes and Tig engrossed in a textbook filled with complicated math equations and grids that form swooping parabolas.

Natalie beams a smile at me and points at Tig.

I groan. "Oh no, did she convince you to forgo speech, too?"

Natalie pulls the headphones around her neck and nudges Tig with her hip. "Show her."

Tig tilts her textbook toward me and wiggles her hand over it.

I squint at her. "You're showing me that . . . you really like studying?"

She traces over two letters she's written on the open page. *Ag.* Then she leans back, crosses her arms, and delivers me the most obnoxious eyebrow raise I've ever seen.

"Ag? As in, *Ag! I have cramps*?" It shames me that I have to use so many words to communicate with her, while she gets to trump me with a single gesture.

She sighs, blowing her bangs out of her face, and shoves the heavy book at me.

"Flip to the back," Natalie tells me as she stares so lovingly at Tig. I feel like I'm invading a private moment.

Markings and crossed-out words fill the white paper on the inside cover. *You were my first and my last and my past. A melody and a felony and a tragedy in propensity. The second chance future is hidden within.* Taking guidance from the line about first and last, Tig circled the first and last letter of each word longer than two letters to get *yuweftadltadptmyadfyadtypytesdcefehnwn.* From there, she tried a few ciphers each with the key *FIONA* like I did with the last clue, but she crossed out all those attempts. Then she tried the word *past* as the key, because the first sentence indicates first, last, and past are all important and connected. The Bifid cipher and the *PAST* key decrypted the code to a few letter sets: *YWCAHA PMAGAB BAADDL YUERDR DTYDRD RTQISQ PC.*

The line *the second chance future is hidden within* led her to the *second* set of decrypted letters, thanks to the blatant use of the word *second*. The rest of the phrase—*is hidden within*—made her locate the letters hidden within the second set. There are only two letters in the center. So *PMAGAB* reduced down to only *AG*.

I straighten, a mix of excitement and disappointment warring in my body. Disappointment because I wasn't the one to decipher this, that Tig found a way to be stealthier than me. And excitement because *AG* is the answer and because maybe I'm not alone without my dad to help me. Maybe I *can* do this without him. *We* can.

Even if the very idea sends little volcanoes erupting through my body.

Even if I can't ever tell him what I found.

AG . . . Ag . . . I rack my brain for what *AG* might refer to but come up blank.

I drop the book at Tig's feet, but she doesn't even notice. She's too busy finding excuses to touch Natalie: helping her readjust the headphones, pushing her hair out of her eyes, holding her hand. I whip my head to look away, heart thumping.

Scrambling back to my tent, I stop short at the sight of it already set up. With someone inside. And Lakshmi's across the way, helping Ugly Dave unpack marshmallows. At least I kept my promise to Colin about the s'mores.

My heart beats faster.

I kick the lump and earn a low-pitched groan. When I crawl inside, a musty scent attacks my nose. Colin rests on my inflatable pillow, hands clasped behind his head, legs outstretched. He waggles his finger toward his chest, coaxing me to lie down next to him.

"Don't tell me you want to sleep with me, too? Because Lakshmi has dibs."

"Been there, done that. I'm mostly in your tent now to piss you off."

"Mission accomplished!" I flop next to him, curling close, then stroke my fingers along his forearm to accomplish the same. Instead he stills at my touch. I snap my hand back, and he inches away from me.

Awkwardness creeps into the space between our bodies like a wedge.

I clear my throat. "Tig deciphered the second clue. A. G."

His head perks up, minty shampoo drowning out the scent of pine. "Any idea what it means?"

I bite my lip. "An address, maybe?" But none of my previous addresses match. "A location we once hit?" I don't say the worst guess of all: Combining *AG* with the rest of the clues might just equal nonsense. Like all my mother's musings.

"Hopefully, it will make sense once we find the next two clues," he says.

Hopefully.

"Speaking of which . . . you still haven't told me what the last heist is. I know the guitar's in two days, but then what?"

A few days ago, I hesitated when he asked for more info about the guitar, but this time I tell him without missing a beat. "It's a book Christopher Columbus once owned. A book bound in human skin." I purse my lips. "Or, well, a replica of a book bound in human skin. So not *as creepy*."

Colin leans in, and a shadow from the sun hitting the tent casts him in the perfect ratio of chiaroscuro. "First a skull, then a book bound in human skin. Are we sure this is a heist and not some sort of weird form of ancient human trafficking?" He laughs to himself. "Just to be clear. We're not peeling any humans and turning their skin into leather to replicate the book, right? Though I do seem to have a good candidate sitting right next to me." He pats my shoulder.

"Hey, don't look at me." I shrug. "My mom chose these items. Besides, there's a guitar! That's not morbid."

My mind flashes on Mom's weird collection of oddities. A pickled finger. A petrified rat king. My umbilical cord blood, stolen from the lab she'd paid to store it.

He tilts his head. "You two are a lot alike, you know."

His words tear through my chest. They're words I always wanted to hear, but they're also words that scare the shit out of me. "H-how?"

"You don't do what anyone expects you to do."

My hand flies up to grip my necklace, clutching it tightly. His words swim through me, buoying me upward.

"What about you?" My voice is quiet, barely a whisper. "And your mom?"

He absentmindedly lifts the photo of her from his back pocket and studies it for a second. "I wish I knew." He swallows hard. "I wish I got to know her."

We lock eyes for a long moment, the spell only broken when he rakes a hand over his shaved head.

I clear my throat and fumble for something, anything, to cut the silence. "But here's the thing about the third heist." My words come out in a rush. "I'm not even sure there's going to be one." I bite my lip. "The FBI confiscated the forgery of the book I made. I need to re-create it, but I've had zero opportunity with Lakshmi wanting to braid my hair and make friendship bracelets every two seconds."

He taps his lips with his finger, and I try not to look at how plump they are. "Can you create it in one night?"

"The previous one took me weeks . . ." I sigh. "But I guess I'll take whatever I can get."

Rule #13: Always create forgeries that can't be traced back to you. Hence the stolen pages. But I will smash rule #13 in the proverbial kisser. It's more important to get the clue, get out of there, and find my mother before the FBI does. If that means I can't use a stolen sheet of paper from the 1400s to create a better forgery, then I'll just have to use artistic tricks to fool the library until we safely vacate the premises.

"Tomorrow night, I'll find a way to keep Lakshmi out of your hair."

My first instinct is to snark, and a million comebacks fight for proximity to my lips. But instead I let my voice go soft. "Thanks." I meet his eyes. "I appreciate it."

Outside the tent, I hear shrieks as two of the girls claim they just spotted a bear when it was only a tree, based on a third girl's claim.

"Um, guys?" Natalie pokes her head in the tent, looking grave. She thrusts her phone at me, an article already loaded onto the screen despite her phone showing only one bar of cell service. Colin leans over my shoulder, placing his thumb over mine to shift the screen between our pressed-together faces. We read the headline in silence, save for the racing of our pulses.

Search Expanded into East for Escaped Fugitives

Authorities now suspect escaped convict Colin O'Keefe and his accomplice Fiona Spangler were spotted at an amusement park in Southern California following an incident that occurred at a popular ride. A warrant is now out for their arrest in connection with vandalism and trespassing. Authorities believe the two might be in Oklahoma but heading toward Tennessee. The search for the fugitives has been expanded.

The hair on the back of my neck prickles. Tomorrow, the bus heads from Oklahoma to Tennessee, with the FBI hot on our tail.

CHAPTER 19

After a night of mosquito bites and a day of nature-trail hiking/tripping over fallen sticks, all I want to do is crawl into a real bed in our new hotel and curl up in fluffy blankets (sans bedspread this time). But Colin promised me the time I need to re-create the book forgery, and this might be the only time I get, so when there's a pounding knock against my hotel door, I leap to my feet. Darkness filters in through the gauzy curtains, casting the entire room in shadow.

Lakshmi rushes out of the bathroom. "It's probably Abby. It's almost lights-out."

Natalie places her palms on Lakshmi's shoulders and pushes her down onto the bed. "Listen. We need you to act cool."

Lakshmi's head darts around squirrel fast, from me hovering between the beds to Tig on the chair, innocently surfing the web . . . or so it seems. She's currently hacking into the hotel system and remotely unlocking one of the rooms.

"What? Why?"

"Fiona has somewhere to be tonight, and we're going to cover for her." Natalie grins.

I grab my backpack from the floor. It's loaded with all my art supplies plus a few Diet Cokes to help me battle the night.

"Fiona? Ready?" Colin's voice calls from outside.

Lakshmi's eyes widen. "But I thought he cheated—"

I look away, my cheeks heating. I hate having to play the role of woman scorned but dumb enough to go back to the douchebag who scorned her.

"He wants to make it up to her." Natalie tacks on a little swoony sigh. "They just need some time alone to work it out."

Lakshmi leaps off the bed and starts pacing. "Oh God. This is completely against the rules. If you guys get caught, we're *all* getting in trouble."

My confidence level for her being capable of staying silent hovers around 0 percent.

"By the time Abby checks on us, Fiona will be snuggled in bed fast asleep." Natalie shoves a bunch of towels beneath the covers and tucks a black wig inside so a few strands peek out.

"Please," I beg without intending to. It's the first genuine thing that's come out of my mouth since I met her.

Lakshmi studies my face for a few seconds before letting out a big sigh. "Fine, but you owe me. And if you do get caught, I'm claiming I had no knowledge of this."

I give her a strained smile. "Wouldn't expect anything else from you."

I turn to the door. My bag of supplies weighs heavy on my shoulder, my necklace an anchor grounding me. The itch of creation tingles all through my body. Something inside my stomach starts to churn. But it can't be nerves. This whole ruse isn't even real. Colin's just my excuse to get out of this room, but he won't actually be escorting me on this all-night adventure in forgery.

Colin's wearing a white T-shirt that hangs just an inch too short above his plaid pajama bottoms, revealing a sliver of the skin below his belly button. I hope this was Natalie's doing, too. Revenge by way of packing clothes a size too small. I stare for a beat too long before forcing myself to look away.

Dark hair swinging, Abby rounds the corner and stops short at the sight of us. "Lights-out in fifteen minutes. I'll be doing room checks."

"Just had to chat with Colton for a sec. See? We're standing in the hallway since he's not allowed to be in my room."

Her mouth stays in a straight line. "See you at the room check, then."

I swallow hard. She's definitely going to be checking for me, specifically.

Abby disappears into one of the rooms a full minute before the text from Tig appears. Room 640.

"Thanks for the alibi. See you tomorrow?" I veer toward the elevators to get to room 640, but Colin stays in step with me. I groan. "Your room is back that way."

"My roommates snore." The steel elevator door distorts his good looks like a fun-house mirror, which suits him.

"So do you." My insides are a swirl of nerves, and I shift the backpack from shoulder to shoulder.

The blinking lights above the buttons illuminate numbers in a sequence: *7, 6, 5* . . . a countdown to my next prison sentence. Trapped in a room I can't leave with a boy I don't want. When the elevator arrives, we step inside. "I need to concentrate. Which means I need to be alone."

Colin rakes a hand over his buzzed scalp. "Oh come on," he says. "I thought you'd want some company. Trust me, it's lonely as hell to be stuck in a place by yourself with no one to talk to."

The way he says it, I wonder if *he's* the one that doesn't want to be alone.

Sure enough, room 640 opens with a simple twist of the knob, showcasing a beautifully made double room, a cookie-cutter replica of the rooms in the hotels we've stayed in so far, all the same dumb chain. Color me impressed at Tig's hacking skills. A thin beam of moonlight traces Colin's outline like a graphite-pencil drawing, but then he switches on the lamp, and I blink against the flood of yellow light.

I spread a towel over the closest bed and dump my bag of supplies onto it. The pitter-patter of paintbrushes and packets of boneware moist clay is like a symphony to my ears. "What about Abby?"

"Taken care of. Recorded audio of me that my roommates can play for her to verify I'm in the bathroom."

"Smart." Then a thought hits me. "Ugh, everyone's going to think we're doing something in here that I've never even done in real life." My cheeks combust. I probably shouldn't have said that. Out loud. To a guy who might use that ammo against me one day.

"Don't worry, I'll tell everyone the truth: that I wouldn't touch you with a ten-foot pole." His eyes flash with amusement.

The tension drains from my shoulders. "Please also tell them that I'd rather be eaten alive by rabid alligators than touch you."

"Only rabid alligators?" He raises a brow. "Regular ones wouldn't suffice?"

"As a last resort, maybe," I say, and he laughs.

Somehow I'm smiling now, too.

But on second thought, maybe letting everyone think something's going on between us isn't the worst idea. After all, we've already planted the seeds with Lakshmi by letting her think I have a crush on him and we're using tonight to potentially get back together. "Actually." I bite my lip and avoid his eyes. "Maybe we should let people make their own assumptions about . . ." I wave my finger back and forth between our chests to indicate *us*. "Even if that's what they assume."

He meets my eyes. "Are you sure?"

"Yeah, it's the easiest alibi." I still can't look at him.

"Works for me, then."

"I should . . ." I gesture at my backpack, and he waves his hand as though to say *proceed*. The snap of blue rubber gloves is like a second skin, transporting me back to the first time my mother taught me to create a perfect replica of a masterpiece. I had rushed home from school and flown down to our studio basement, which was somehow always flooded with light despite the lack of windows.

"It's not about showcasing *your* skills." She squinted one eye as she filled in a canvas with a burst of color that replicated the brushstroke of the original Caravaggio next to her. "It's about showing off *theirs*." She stepped back and studied her work, then jabbed a sharp finger right above the brushstrokes. "There. Tell me what I did wrong."

My heart skipped with the chance to impress her. I turn my head from the Caravaggio to my mom's version. Each one had a zigzag brushstroke done at an angle with a tilted brush. The color matched exactly. As I studied them, my chest constricted. "I don't know."

Mom plucked a fine hair from her paintbrush and, with tweezers, applied it to the wet paint. She pulled it off again. When I glanced between the two paintings, I gasped, finally seeing it. In the original, there was what looked like a scratch but was really a paintbrush hair that had gotten stuck and then been removed.

To create a precise forgery, you couldn't just look at what was in front of you. You had to look at what was once there, too.

Now, I lay out the photos of the Christopher Columbus book,

rendered on four-by-six glossy paper from a portable printer Nat brought. A 180-degree view of the book animates as I sweep my eyes from left to right over the photos. Colin's staring at his own phone when he glances up at me with a devious smile. "Have you researched this book at all?"

"Only about a million times." Our target—or should I say *mark*, considering the book was once human?—is believed to be bound in the skin of a Moorish chieftain.

Colin clears his throat and starts speaking with the voice of a narrator. "'The practice of binding books in human skin peaked in the nineteenth century as a way to identify medical books.'" He shakes his head to himself. "Because nothing says, 'This book contains diagrams of human anatomy!' more than binding it with human anatomy."

I shrug. "People were so damn literal back then."

Colin continues paraphrasing. "The (un)lucky skin donor was usually a medical cadaver who probably thought donating his body to science would result in medical breakthroughs, not readers judging him for all eternity don't-judge-a-book-by-its-cover style."

I raise a brow in challenge. "Well, guess what they bound books about law out of?"

His eyes widen. "Don't tell me . . ."

I look him straight in the eye. "Criminals!"

Thank God I only have jail to look forward to if I get caught.

"Oh God." Colin's face turns gray. "Another popular pastime was to write an autobiography and then insist that your manuscripts be bound in your remains when you die."

"Imagine the options," I say. "Casket. Cremation. Or bookbinding. What'll it be? Remember, fiction lives forever!"

While I don't have any human skin to work with, I do have a brand-new hardcover journal Natalie bought. The pages inside were blank, but under the guise that I've been writing in my nightly journal before bed, I've been painstakingly hand printing every letter and symbol on the pages splayed open at the Hesburgh Library. It was the only thing I could do in Lakshmi's presence without raising her suspicions. I only have a few pages of lettering left to complete, so I tackle those first. Colin watches the steady progress of my swooping typography that ranges in size as it cascades down the page.

Once the lettering dries, I dip my fingers into a cup of water to keep the clay moist as I press it onto the journal cover. Clay gives me the second best medium to create the look and texture of leather made from human skin. The first best medium of course would be cow's leather, but Natalie couldn't find one the exact shape on such short notice, and vegan leather is too difficult to play with.

As my mother taught me, the trick to getting the perfect mold is to pay attention to the details, the way the texture has little bumps like chicken skin but long scratches toward the edge, probably due to age. I need to re-create this book in all four dimensions: appearance, texture, size, and the last dimension—history.

I'm concentrating so deeply, I don't even notice the shadow darkening the glass-covered desk until Colin's sharp breath whirrs in my ear.

My hand slips, creating a large divot. I curse. I'll have to patch it, which is always a risk. Anytime you add something to the surface, the seams might show through. "What are you doing?"

"I wanted to see how you worked."

"You're blocking my light!" I say, and he backs up a few feet so I can focus.

But for some reason, the only thing I can focus on is the question I just asked him. *What are you doing?* Not now, in this moment.

But how'd he even get here? "Hey," I say. "Can I ask you something I've been wondering for a while?"

He nods.

"Why'd you start doing cons in the first place?"

He lifts one of my steel tools off the desk—the ones that look more fit to be on a dentist's table than an art room—and holds the wire loop sgraffito up to the light, silver metal glinting. "Teenage rebellion?"

I roll my eyes. "Teenage rebellion is cigarettes and breaking curfew. Not evading the FBI on your many crime sprees."

Colin stays silent for several seconds, his chest puffing in and out. "My mom died when I was three. Now that I've outgrown my nanny, it's just me and my dad, but he's never around. He's always at the office or chasing a lead." His shoulders shake. "At first I thought maybe the cons would get his attention, make him remember I exist."

"But they don't," I guess.

With a sigh, he scoots the reclining chair over and lounges next to me, feet kicked up onto the desk right next to my wrist. The once-purple bruise on his ankle has faded to yellow green. "All it got me was an empty house. You know, when I was first arrested . . ." He swallows hard. "I thought . . . maybe. *Maybe* now he'll spend more time here. Maybe now he'll realize that what I really need is a good role model or something." He shakes his head. "I'm such an idiot."

I reach for him, cupping his hand with my clay-covered palm. "You're not an idiot. You're one of the smartest people I know."

"I'm not so sure about that." He gives me a lopsided grin. "After all, I agreed to go on a crazy mission to help someone who refuses to even call me a friend, even though getting caught would mean trading in the big, lonely house for a tiny, lonely jail cell."

I squeeze his hand, after realizing I'm still holding it. I know I should tell him what he wants to hear, what I want to say: that he *is* a friend. That, somehow, he's become one of the only people I trust. But I find myself deflecting. Wimping out. I can steal expensive paintings with enough bravado that no one would ever suspect me, but I can't tell a guy how I'm feeling. "Why'd you agree to help me?" I ask instead.

He pulls his hand away and picks at the clay on his skin. "Because it's not about getting caught anymore. It's about continually proving to myself that I don't need him. That I'm better than him. Better off *without* him."

There's an electric pulse in the air, something that's making us look at each other with a new intensity. I ruin it with a joke. "But you can't even gloat. And you *love* to gloat."

He laughs. "That is true."

"Hey," I say, my voice going softer. Now that we're talking about some things we've never said before, I risk asking another question that's been bothering me for months. "Whose fake IDs were you transporting? That day I got you arrested?" Was this all a lie, and he really did start a fake ID scheme, or is there someone he valued more than himself when he protected that person at the expense of his own freedom?

He flinches at the reminder of how I got him arrested. "I'm not sure I should say."

"You have a lot of stuff hanging over my head. I'll keep your secret."

He bows his head and takes a deep breath. "Tig."

I startle. She hadn't mentioned any of this, but of course that would have required her to talk. "I don't get it. Why would she need fake IDs?"

Unless . . . she didn't. Natalie had bragged about our plan to her in an attempt to impress her. And maybe Tig found a way to impress Natalie right back by using the opportunity to take Colin out for the count.

He shrugs. "No idea, but she didn't mean harm by it." His eyes meet mine. "Only you did."

I bite my lip. "That's not—"

"There's something else I haven't told you." Suddenly his face takes on a new intensity, and my stomach winds up in response. He breathes in sharply, like he's about to say something huge and needs a swift boost of courage, but nothing comes out of his mouth. He clutches his phone so hard, I think he might snap it in two. Pain crosses his face, his brows knitting, and for a moment it seems like he's fighting an internal battle I can't see.

"What?" I prompt.

"It's—" The tension knotting his face suddenly deflates, and he sighs, a heavy sound, like he's disappointed in himself. "Something I read in my dad's files once. Something about your mom."

His words puncture the air and drive straight into my gut like arrows. My hands shake, and I put down my tools, waiting for the bad news that will match his grave face.

"Right after my dad busted your dad, he brought home a ton of old case files to sift through. I'm talking piles. When he took a phone call in the other room, I took the opportunity to snoop a bit."

I'm on edge, my body still, not even breathing.

"There was one case file from the nineties. Back when your mom was a teenager."

I lean closer, strung like a marionette on his every word. My mom had me when she was twenty-three. She'd met my dad when she was twenty-one. She had a whole other life before us but rarely talked about it. I always assumed her life didn't truly begin until she met Dad, but the grave tone of Colin's voice makes me think that maybe this wasn't a beginning but an ending of sorts.

"She ran with a different crew then. A guy and two other girls. Jeremy. Nikki. Amanda. Has she told you about them?"

I shake my head, my whole body coiled tight.

He lets out a sigh, as though he was afraid of that. "They did a lot of big heists—art museums, banks, you name it. Plus whatever my dad's files don't know about. They were pretty slick . . . until your mom messed up and got caught."

A small shudder ricochets through me. *She got caught?* My head twists, back and forth—*no no no*. "But—"

"She struck a deal." He meets my eyes. "Immunity for her crimes in exchange for ratting out her crew. She sold out her friends to save herself."

"No." I leap to my feet, the taste of dust like a desert in my mouth. "No way. She'd never sell out anyone."

"Never, ever turn your back on your crew." Mom pressed her hands on my seven-year-old shoulders and forced me to look at her. "They're your family. Stronger than blood."

"If I hadn't said anything, then I would have been expelled, and I didn't do it!" I tried to shrug out of her grasp, but she held on tight. A little too tight. She didn't say a word, just studied me with such intense concentration that it forced me to look away.

Stacie Holmes, my best friend at the time, had snuck back into the classroom during recess while I stood watch at the door. It was school-book-fair day, and she dug through each kid's backpack until she found the money their parents had sent. It was a huge jackpot: $120 total in profit, all fanned between her pink, sparkly nails.

It didn't take long for the students to notice the missing cash and the teacher to question each student individually. Some kids had spotted me heading back inside during recess because I hadn't yet perfected my stealth, and the teacher told me, point-blank, that if no one came forward, then she would have no choice but to report me. Expel me. I'd be a second-grade dropout.

I squirmed in my seat, thinking only of my parents. If I got caught, it might shine a beacon on their illicit activities. We were flying under the radar, but as soon as I got in trouble for stealing, the seal would be broken, and we'd forever seem like criminals in the community's eyes.

So I did what I had to do to protect the people I loved. I sold out Stacie to save my parents. I thought I was doing the right thing, but the look in my mother's eyes made me flinch.

"But you helped. You're as much a part of it as she is."

She wasn't mad that I stole something. Of course not. She was only mad that I'd betrayed my crew. It's the only code of con we truly abide by.

"No," I say again, my voice louder this time. "There's no way she turned in her team. It's just not possible."

I stab my metal tool back into the book and avoid looking at Colin.

"They each got twenty years for their crimes. Well, not Amanda. She got forty, thanks to her escape attempt."

My mom never uttered a word about her former crew or the way she threw them under the bus so easily. When she scolded me for doing the same when I was seven, was it out of guilt over what she had once done . . . or fear? Fear that one day, I'd rat her out, too?

My throat hitches, and that small escape of breath may be the most incriminating evidence of all.

It reveals he got to me.

CHAPTER 20

A loud phone ringing blasts me out of a deep sleep. My eyes fly open, stinging and burning. Hazy light splashes in from the bone-colored sheer drapery while mumbled words echo from somewhere in the room. My head throbs as if I pressed my ear against a speaker at a rock concert. The slam of plastic hitting plastic makes my teeth snap. A phone hanging up?

I pull the covers over my head and sink deeper into my feathery pillow.

Hands rip the covers away and shake my shoulders. Colin stands over me, purple crescent moons hanging under his eyes. A mountain of crinkled blankets rises to a peak from his bed. "We have to leave. They've started wake-ups."

Wake-ups mean head counts. Shit, if they catch us out of our rooms, we'll be kicked off the tour. And then it's bye-bye, alibi. Rubbing my wrist over my sweaty brow, I swing my legs over the edge using muscle memory. My head pounds steel-drum hard.

Colin sweeps his arm over the desk and swipes all my art supplies into my bag. Open paint tubes descend, clacking against one another and likely creating an abstract installation piece no one will ever see inside the bag. A wet squish makes my heart squeeze.

He reaches for the imitation book.

"Wait!" My voice comes out all scratchy. "It's not dry yet. I only finished the cover"—my eyes fly to the clock—"one hour and forty-two minutes ago." Acrylic paints in burnt umber and sepia blend over the clay surface to give the faux book the perfect look of rot and decay. The dappled texture will give me nightmares for weeks.

I slide the cardboard that the book sits on toward me gently, dipping my thumbs into paint splatters. The book wobbles, and I grit my teeth, my shaky, sleep-deprived hands threatening to ruin the whole heist.

"Now's your chance to really use your stealth-mode skills," Colin says.

"And yours." I raise a brow. "Still waiting to see them in action."

"Who needs stealth when you've got charm and persuasion?"

I roll my eyes. "Yes, your cockiness is utterly irresistible to girls with no taste."

He plugs a set of earbuds into my phone and pushes each one into my ears. A pair of blue earbuds stream from his own ears. He presses a few buttons on his phone, accepts the call on mine, and in a flash we're on a three-way conference with silence, or rather, Tig. "We need you to hack the security cams and guide us through the halls." Colin's voice echoes a moment later through my receiver.

No response. I give Colin the side-eye. He's suggesting the girl who seems to have taken a vow of silence be our GPS announcer? "Because this went so well at the amusement park."

"Please?" Colin begs Tig, and I cringe inwardly for him.

"These must be your excellent persuasion skills in action."

He ignores me. "What if next time, I get Fiona *and* Lakshmi out of your room for the night?"

The clack of a keyboard echoes through the phone. Deal accepted. A little part of me squeals inside, because what this really means is that Tig wants to be alone with Natalie. Despite sharing a tent while camping, nothing happened between them except a lot of *z*'s (Tig) and a lot of angst (Nat).

After two minutes, Tig finally stops typing. I wait for the quiet whisper of the word *clear*, but instead a text pops up showing a screenshot of our empty hallway. Great, we're doing the charades equivalent of a daring escape. Colin twists the metal doorknob and pokes his head out, looking left and right.

Tig clucks her tongue as if to say, *You don't believe me?*

I place one foot in front of the other like I'm walking the balance beam and scoot sideways out the door, sliding my butt against Colin's crotch because it's the only way to fit myself and the cardboard through the cramped space. His strong hands brace against my hips to steady me.

"Which way?" I ask on the off chance she'll actually answer. There's a staircase three doors away, another at the far end of the hall, and an elevator directly in between both.

She makes an *uh-uh* sound with her throat.

"*None?*" The tempo of my pulse increases. All routes must be compromised. "I thought you said it was clear." My eyes fly to the door behind us, now locked. We can't stay here, either; we're sitting ducks. The walls close in on us from all angles, but my criminal mind calculates an exit plan *despite* feeling like I'm halfway dead. Adrenaline takes over, and I steel myself for the escape. Elevator's too slow and with too many variables: civilians who may step on and have eyes that can witness things. "Far staircase," I say.

Colin tugs on the cardboard. "This one's closer."

"All the camper rooms on my original floor are on this side of the hallway. If we emerge from the closer stairwell, we could be walking right into a trap."

As if to confirm, Tig sends a screenshot of Abby pushing open the door to the closer stairway on my original floor, which means she's on her way up to this one since there are a few camper rooms here.

I beam a triumphant smile at Colin that earns a laugh from Tig. We march with calculated steps to the far staircase. The book wobbles precariously, and I shift the cardboard to keep it steady, like balancing a marble on a tilting surface. All we need is a trio of lasers sweeping through the hallway to add just a little more danger.

We reach the end of the hallway just as another door at the opposite end opens. I catch a brief glimpse of Hot Dave's dark hair and long legs stepping out of the room across from our stolen one as I slip inside the stairwell and seal us in. "That was close."

I pause to readjust the book when Tig gasps and slams her hand hard on something, as though to spur us faster like a horse jockey. My legs kick into motion, each step threatening to ruin the whole operation. Colin bypasses his own floor to help me to mine. Sweat glistens on the back of my neck.

"Is the coast clear on this floor?" I snap.

The line goes dead.

I call back, but it just rings and rings. She must have run out of prepaid minutes on her burner. We yank out our earbuds, and Colin cracks his neck side to side before wrenching open the door to my floor. He cringes as he pokes his head out, then relaxes a fraction. "Clear. Thank God."

The last few feet to my room feel as dangerous as traversing a minefield. One door opening and this whole operation will explode. I count down like a rocket about to take off. Four steps. Three steps. Two . . .

Colin pounds on our door with a fist. I rock in place, keeping a firm grip on the book. When Natalie swings the door open, the relief that seeps from my shoulders is enough to make me keel over. I didn't get caught, by Abby or the FBI.

"Aww, how sweet. You escorted her back on her walk of shame." Natalie winks.

"Oh thank God." Lakshmi stands there, wrapped in a towel, black hair dripping. Tig bites her lip and holds up her dead phone, then chucks it into the metal garbage can.

A door down the hallway flies open. The stairwell. Shit. I bump past Colin, poking him in the ribs with the cardboard, and flee into the safety of the room. Colin squeezes inside after me. A yelp forces me to spin around in my own room.

Lakshmi tugs her towel tighter around her chest. "There's a boy in our room!" Her eyes land on my masterpiece. "And a weird-looking book?"

I clutch my stiff, trembling fingers harder onto the cardboard.

"Art project," Colin says fast. "She's trying to get into a prestigious program for fall."

"Yeah, I, uh, need to submit my portfolio by, um, next week." Oh God. She can't possibly buy this.

But then Colin sells it the only way he can. With charm and gusto. "She's so goddamn talented. I love watching her work." He glances at me with a look of pure awe that makes my cheeks heat.

I slide the book beneath the bed in futile desperation that Lakshmi subscribes to the theory of out of sight, out of mind.

A wrinkle creases her forehead as she glances between Colin and me. "Wait. I thought you two were, like, doing something *other* than art projects all night." A blush spreads on her cheeks—and mine. And Colin's.

"We, um, we . . ." I have to force myself not to say *um* again. "We weren't doing art projects *all* night." I also have to force myself not to cringe at my horrible delivery. I pat his shoulder in what's supposed to be a romantic gesture but sends the message of *not even buddies* instead.

Lakshmi's head rotates from him to me with a look that could be the poster child for *skepticism*.

"Hey, it's okay." Colin turns to me and looks deep into my eyes as he tilts my chin up with the tip of his index finger. "You don't have to be embarrassed. This is my walk of shame, too."

His arms wrap around my waist, and he pulls me closer, so close his breath sends my hair dancing. The flashback of us almost kissing in the rain a couple of months ago comes back in full force, robbing me of air. It was the one time I got played. This time, we're both complicit. He leans down, and I rise on my toes. This is a con, I tell myself. A quick peck, that's all. Just enough to sell this.

But right as our lips meet, there's a loud knock on the door.

We scramble out of the embrace, my heart pounding loud in my ears. Colin rakes his hand over his buzzed hair.

"And now I must hide." He runs past Lakshmi into the bathroom.

Lakshmi keeps looking from me to the door with her big brown eyes as if she can't make sense of what just happened.

The door bangs, louder this time. "Ladies, it's Dave!"

This could just be a routine wake-up call, but if the counselors reached Colin's room first, they'd be searching for him. Possibly in girls' rooms . . . and the most obvious place to hide a stray boy is in the bathroom. Wobbling on shaky legs, I twist the bathroom doorknob and slip inside the steamy room. Colin stands in the center, raising a brow. "Came to finish what we just tried to start?"

"You know how I feel about bathrooms." I start the shower. "You may be good at advanced planning, but you need to work on your impromptu skills."

Outside, the door swings open. "We're all here. See?" Lakshmi's voice shakes like she's announcing to the entire room she contracted Ebola overnight.

"I'm in the shower!" I shout. Right in Colin's ear.

Silence for a few seconds. Colin and I both stare at the door, our chests stilled. There's a whole room of space, but somehow we're standing right next to each other.

"He's not in the main room or balcony!" Hot Dave yells, likely to another counselor in the hallway.

Sweat gathers in the bend of my elbows. Colin's shoulders tense.

"Oh, hi, Abby!" Natalie calls way too loud, clearly for my benefit.

"He could be in the bathroom with her," Abby says, her accent growing thicker with the volume of her voice. Angry bangs ricochet off the bathroom door. "Fiona, I need to check in there!"

"One sec!" I shout. "I'm not decent!"

"Damn straight," Colin mumbles.

We both beeline for the shower. Hot water scalds my skin. I cringe and bite my lip as I douse my hair under the boiling stream. He frantically twists the knobs until the water cools. My clothes cling to me, showing off every curve. Little droplets stick to Colin's eyelashes while his abs poke out of his now-translucent white shirt. Just like that day in the rain.

He must be thinking the same thing, because of the way he avoids my eyes.

"Shampoo," I whisper. He uncaps the travel-size bottle and dumps half the contents over my head. I lather for a few seconds until I get it nice and soapy and alibi-proof.

"In case you forgot, people don't wear shirts in the shower..." The smirk playing on his lips would be the perfect target in a shooting range. "Or pants."

"Feel free to take yours off." Instead I stick my head out of the curtain and drape the front over my neck to conceal my tank top. I nudge my spaghetti strap down my shoulder so it appears bare. "Get down so your silhouette doesn't show through."

He lies down on the bottom of the white porcelain basin and covers his eyes against the pounding water.

Another knock. "Fiona! Now!"

"Tell her I'm in the gym," Colin whispers.

My hand threatens to slide off the knob, but I reach out of the shower and twist it anyway, offering Abby a grand view of my soapy head and nothing else. "Sorry, I was trying to finish."

Abby's eyes narrow as she takes in the scene. Me, in the shower, seemingly alone.

And a concealed guy, unknowingly sending goose bumps up my legs as his wrist accidentally grazes my ankle.

"If I ask you to open up, I need you to open up. We can't find Colton. You wouldn't happen to know where he is, would you?" The way she says it indicates she's pretty sure I know *exactly* where he is.

I furrow my brow. "Have you checked the gym? He told me last night he was going to work out this morning."

"He needs to clear that by me." She slams the door shut.

I lean my head against the cold tiles and string my silver charm back and forth on my necklace chain. I might be home free, but Colin still has to get back to his room—post workout, of course.

He stands up, forcing me to brush my chest against his so I can fit under the showerhead to wash out the shampoo.

"Look at us"—his eyes trace the length of my body, drinking in all my curves the water has so graciously revealed—"sleeping together, showering together . . ."

"Don't you dare say *getting* together." I switch the water to ice cold and step out of the shower as he yelps.

In order to help Colin get back to his room safely, Natalie quickly disguises him in a long brown wig and the maid's uniform we used in the Hotel Galvez heist since we're staying at the same hotel chain. Hopefully his roommates will think the way he escaped Abby's wrath after our "sleepover" is epic and not . . . suspicious. When he leaves, I shut the bathroom door behind me and lean against it, heart thrashing, thinking thoughts I should not be thinking. All the feelings I've been keeping buried beneath the surface rise, memories of all the glances I've stolen in his direction or the smiles that pop onto my lips, unannounced, when I talk to him. After a proper shower, I push my dripping hair out of my face and reapply my thick black eyeliner—my go-to disguise these days. But the problem is I still recognize myself in the mirror.

CHAPTER 21

"I'm going to do it. I'm going to kiss her." Natalie squares her shoulders, balls her hands into fists, and juts her hips out with a runway strut as we walk to the bus two days later. Gray clouds scuttle in the sky like fluffy dust bunnies.

I blink at her, partly surprised she's worrying about this and not everything that's about to go down in less than an hour at a certain guitar center, but Natalie has always been one to prepare for a heist by clearing her mind and focusing on something else. Or, in this case, some*one* else.

"You should go for it. She's definitely into you." I've already told her about Tig's desire to spend a night without me and Lakshmi.

She puffs out her chest, the cool breeze sending her long, frizzy (fake) hair flying in all directions. "I'm not going to chicken out this time. I'm not."

"I have a lot of rules when it comes to cons, but the most important one is: The only thing you're going to regret is not trying."

She marches onto the bus with a new determination, and I follow after, my steps a little heavier, but I'm not sure why.

I plop beside Colin, and he gives me a head nod before glancing out the window and watching as downtown Nashville sweeps by outside the bus windows, fog descending over the boxy office buildings. We arrived at a hotel just outside the city late last night, and this is our first chance to see the beautiful city in daylight. Across the aisle, Natalie drops a quick kiss on the tip of Tig's nose. Wow, I guess when she said she was going to kiss her, she meant *right now*. Tig captures Nat's face in her palms, and the kiss turns real. A pang of jealousy threads through me, and I find myself inching a little closer to Colin. But I quickly snap back to a normal distance, bending over to dig into my purse to cover.

As the bus idles at a stoplight a little bit later, Natalie stands up and hovers over us. "Come on, switch with me," she says to Colin. "I need some girl time."

I raise a brow. "Didn't you just have that?"

She rolls her eyes. "Of the platonic variety."

When Colin stands up and vacates the seat, I feel a twinge in my chest. His cologne still lingers like an afterthought even as Natalie slides into the seat he vacated. "You look like you had a fun bus ride," I say.

As the bus resumes motion, she leans into the backrest and sighs. "The kiss was *amazing*! Butterflies and fireworks and fairy dust and every other magical cliché."

"I'm really happy for you." My voice cracks on the last word.

Natalie leans back against the velvet seat and swoons a bit. "I feel like myself when I'm around her. She's bringing it out of me. I've never felt more connected to the person I was trying to hide."

"Wait. She actually talks to you? Not just glares?"

"She's just a very private person, but when she trusts you, she lets you in. She stays quiet to help stay forgettable, and it's a hard habit to break. But last night, we whispered for hours. She really opened up to me. And so . . ." Her teeth snag on her lower lip as she fights back a smile. "I want to show her my real face. Not quite yet. But before we find your mom, I think."

No wonder the two hit it off: Natalie hides behind her disguises, Tig behind her silence. Yet together, they can be themselves. I nibble on my inner cheek. "Wow." I swallow hard. For three years she's been my best friend, my partner in crime, and my wingman. And she's never once shown me what she looks like without a disguise. Sure, there were pictures of her from *before* hanging proudly in her living room and showcasing her eighth-grade scowl in all its non-glory. But even at school, she'd always at least conceal her hair. As a fellow con artist, I respected her desire to keep her identity a secret, but I always thought I'd be the first to see.

"Maybe I'll even show you, too," she says with a grin, and I hate the way my shoulders relax.

The bus slows to a stop behind a long line of cars. Traffic stops for minutes at a time and the campers start to groan at the lengthy delay. It's only when we reach the front of the traffic queue that I see them. The black cars. The shiny badges. The jackets that say *FBI* in big white letters on the back.

An FBI checkpoint.

My pulse slams into my neck. Colin yanks me out of my seat and tugs me through the aisle, despite Abby's warnings to sit down.

"She's going to throw up!" he announces and pulls my hair out of my face in preparation.

I cover my mouth with my hand and try not to look any campers in the eye as we beeline for the tiny bathroom at the back of the bus.

Just as the bus door swings open to let on an agent, Colin and I launch ourselves inside the bathroom.

Inside, my shoulder juts into Colin's chest, both of us maneuvering to press our ears against the door. Outside the bathroom, Abby warns everyone to stay in their seats. A stomp ricochets through the floor and indicates expensive men's shoes have entered the bus. A hushed exchange follows.

Abby's shrill voice penetrates the thick plastic separating us from jail. "I assure you, this is a teen tour. We're not harboring any criminals."

". . . take a look around . . ." The agent's voice floats through the door. His footsteps grow louder.

Colin's hand finds mine and squeezes. Our fingers lace together as if we're both trying to hold on to freedom. I clamp my mouth shut, afraid even a tiny whisper will give me away. I don't even make a joke about our love for restrooms.

Everything stays silent except for the *thump thump thump* of men's dress heels making their way to the back. My skin prickles with goose bumps.

The footsteps stop. There's the unmistakable static of a walkie-talkie coming to life, sounding loud enough as though it's right outside the bathroom door. "Agent Olsen. You're needed back at base immediately."

Once the agent exits, the bus moves past the FBI cordon, and the commotion starts back up. I fall out of the bathroom and sink into the three-seater. A sensation of vertigo makes my head spin. When Colin scoots next to me, his eyes zone out, and his face is blank except for the tightness winding at the corners of his lips.

"Was that for us?" I ask.

He bites his lip. "I doubt it. Otherwise they wouldn't have left without checking everywhere."

I swallow hard and nod. He's right. The FBI aren't stupid. If they were looking for us, they would have been more diligent about searching, asking questions, catching us.

The two of us stare forward, and I try not to freak out in the ten additional minutes it takes to reach the guitar center. The FBI weren't here for us. But the guitar is.

"Ready to make history?" Colin asks in a cheery tone, clearly trying to lighten the mood.

I suck in a deep, encouraging breath. No time for nerves. I need to go all in now. "Personal history, yes. But not anything that will go down in the books."

Tig's electronics are all charged, organized, and tucked into her backpack so she can slip out to the restroom and be ready to intercept calls within minutes. Thankfully, the famous Lucy guitar is on display on the last part of the three-hour tour, so we've got a lot of time to pull this off, and we're way more prepared than for the amusement park heist.

We've got this.

I grab the guitar, which I brought with me under the ruse that I want to get it tuned. Totally reasonable, I'm sure. But right after we step off the bus, I pretend to tie my shoe. While everyone's back is turned, I shove the guitar behind a decorative bush off to the side of the entrance.

"Wait, where's your guitar?" Lakshmi asks as we head into the foyer, squinting at me.

I groan. "Abby made me keep it on the bus."

"Oh man. That sucks."

She studies me for a beat, but the line moves forward and I clear my throat. She spins around and starts following them without another word.

Inside, high ceilings and slick white walls surround us. A glossy wood floor leads toward a large open space filled with guitars and blowups of famous rock records. Gray metal beams ring the ceiling and shoot in columns at intervals to give the entire place an industrial vibe.

But my eyes fly right to the two police officers standing guard just beyond the ticket booth. The steady *tick tick tick* of my pulse increases in tempo.

I ditch Lakshmi and sidle up to Colin again. "They have to be here for us. Police right after an FBI check seems too coincidental," I whisper into his ear as we wait in line for wristbands.

He stares forward as though he's seen a ghost. "I stand by what I said on the bus. If they're here for us, wouldn't they stop us? Especially by now?"

I try to still my shaking hands. He's right. He has to be right. They're probably just here for standard security. I'm being paranoid.

I can barely concentrate as our pretty, young tour guide introduces herself as Kaylee, an intern here at Gibson and full-time music student over at Vanderbilt University. She tacks on a giggle and way too much pep that grates on my fraying nerves. Her blond hair cascades down her shoulders in curly ringlets.

Kaylee leads us to the first factory stop to show us how the guitar bodies are cut from blocks of wood. I spot four more police officers—each keeping watch in a corner of the room. Watching only our tour group.

Apprehension knots in the base of my throat, and the words *Abort! Abort!* echo in my mind like a gong.

"This is weird, right?" I say over the squeal of the wood saw into Natalie's ear.

She scratches her jaw with her thumb and forefinger. "I'm not sure why they'd need four different officers to keep watch over a teen tour . . ."

Tig suddenly shoves her phone under our noses. She's managed to hack into the security feed, and it shows a view of the employee parking lot, where fifteen police cars are lined up.

My mouth goes dry as dirt. The three of us exchange glances.

"All right, my friends," Kaylee says, and I almost gag. "If you look to my right . . ." She flourishes her dainty hand toward the guy sitting at the wood saw, gold bracelets sliding down her forearm. "My pal Jimmy over here is going to show you how we cut the neck." She goes so far as to draw her finger across her neck and make a screeching sound.

"Not that kind of neck cutting," Jimmy says, and they both guffaw. Jimmy takes over by describing the process, and I hustle over to Colin. "Sweet-talk that girl and try to get info out of her."

"Okay." He pulls himself together and struts in that confident way of his around the group and heads over to Kaylee. I stay at a distance, slinking into the shadows to prove there's nothing going on between Colin and me if her romantic-competition radar is set to *threat* levels. It takes a concerted effort not to turn my head between him and the police officers who stand as stoic as royal guards. Colin says something to Kaylee, and her head instantly falls back in laughter, coral lips stretching wide.

He's smiling, too, all eyes on her, and something turns in my stomach that wasn't there before.

Lakshmi steps beside me. "Wait, I thought you two got back together. Why is he flirting with that chick?"

"He's not flirting," I say defensively, even though he totally is. He has to. "He had a gazillion questions about the guitars and couldn't wait until the rest of the tour to ask."

Her brows knit. "He doesn't play, though."

I shrug. "No time like the present to start."

They talk. And flirt. And talk. And flirt.

An eternity passes before he comes to stand beside me again. He gives me a slight shake of his head, the universal sign for *not here*.

It's not until the tour group starts to move toward the next room, where we can see at least two more police officers through the open door, that he motions for me to hang back in the empty hallway. Thankfully, no officers stand watch here, but probably because there's nothing to steal except the door handle to the bathroom.

Colin's voice is a whisper, so low I have to lean close to him. "There's been a tip-off. They know someone is planning to steal the guitar, so they've taken precautions."

The news hits me like a gut punch. "But—how?" I cover my mouth with my hand. "Oh my God. Do you think the FBI knows as well? Is that why they had a checkpoint ten minutes away?"

A muscle in Colin's jaw tightens. "I have no idea. But I have to assume so."

"Shit." I start pacing back and forth in front of him. "Did they know it would be *today*? Or do they just know it'll happen here eventually?"

"I asked Kaylee that. She said officers were here the last few days, too. So I think they know it's coming, just not exactly when."

My shoulders relax a little. That means they don't know it's *us*. And maybe the FBI checkpoint is just a coincidence. The latest blotter did say the search was expanding into Tennessee.

He rakes his hand over his shorn scalp. "We have to abandon the plan. We can't go through with it if—"

I stop him short. "No." I press my lips together to keep the tsunami swirling in my chest at bay. "This is our only chance! If we don't get this clue, I'll never find my mother."

He shakes his head. "We'll find another way. It's too dangerous."

"I need to make sure I have every advantage here." An idea rockets through my mind, and I squeeze his wrist in excitement. "And we *have* the advantage here. They think someone's going to steal it from the inside, but we're going to do it outside. We've already planted all the seeds in email." I start pacing again, the idea fully solidifying in my mind. "We can do this, Colin. We're good enough to make the switch without getting caught."

He sputters a cough. "Were you not at the pirate ride heist? That was a disaster."

"Because we weren't fully prepared. We were in scramble mode for that one. But this one? We've had time to properly lay it all out. We've talked over every detail." My words grow more confident with every syllable. "And I've done heists that are almost as difficult and never got caught. The only reason *you* got caught at school is because I meddled."

His face looks strained as he considers. He buries his head in his hands, his shoulders shuddering. "It's not that I don't think we can do this. I know that under the right circumstances, we could pull this off. But—"

"I can't let my mom down," I snap, my voice growing harsher. "I can't let my dad down, either, for that matter. Giving up on this clue will be doing exactly that."

Colin's body tenses, and he makes a muffled noise that sounds downright frightened. "But, Fiona, you don't understand—"

The faint squeak of sneakers makes me pull my head up as a shadow elongates.

"Shh," I hiss, but Colin must think I'm trying to shush him as part of the argument, because he keeps going.

"Doing this heist today would mean almost certainly getting caught." His voice rises in volume, pure terror evident in his words.

I grit my teeth. "Hey, stop."

He shakes his head, ignoring my pleas, his face growing intense. "No matter how stealthy we are. This whole place is under hyper-scrutiny, but especially the guitar."

Lakshmi rounds the corner.

"If we steal this—"

I don't think. I just shove him to the wall and press my mouth against his in order to shut him up.

He hesitates for a second before his mouth starts to move against mine, gentle at first, but then faster, more insistent. The kiss grows deeper. The flavor of cinnamon travels into my mouth, and I curse him for tasting this good without it being premeditated.

Tingles gather along my skin as he trails his fingertips around my ear, skates along the edge of my jaw, and traces the delicate curve between my neck and shoulder. I shiver as his touch grazes all the way down my arm, leaving goose bumps in his wake. In the distance, I hear the sound of retreating footsteps.

An alert lights up in the back of my mind, big neon letters flashing *Stop! The ruse is over!* Instead, my own greedy fingers scramble for the bottom of his shirt and slide under to reach the bare skin of his lower back. My palms brush the knobby bones of his spine, and I smile into the pause he takes to release a tiny, shuddering breath. Our mouths reconnect, the kisses growing fiercer. Heat sweeps across my chest, radiating outward.

His teeth gently nip my lower lip, sending a wave of tingles throughout my body. Damn, he's a good kisser.

My knees buckle when his lips abandon my mouth and drop tiny kisses along my jaw. "Hey," he whispers when he reaches my ear, his voice velvet and soft. "If this was your attempt to disorient me so I go with your plan, it's kind of working."

"We'll go with that excuse, then," I whisper back as his fingers knot into the hair at the back of my neck. "Rather than the fact that I needed you to stop talking before Lakshmi overheard."

He nibbles at my earlobe. "If that's what you need to tell yourself."

His lips find mine again, and this time we kiss without excuses, just the two of us finally making up for all the time we'd been conning ourselves out of what we really wanted. The kisses are slow this time. He plants gentle pecks before he pulls back to look deep into my eyes. "Do you trust me?"

There was a time when this question would have elicited a laugh. And another time when I would have hesitated, my stomach churning as I debated the answer. But now I don't even need to think. "Yes."

"I don't think we need this clue. If we find the last one, maybe it'll all be enough to figure out the entire puzzle. Tig was able to decipher the previous clue. Between the four of us, we can find your mom."

I suck in a big gulp of air. A tear flees down my cheek, but Colin wipes it away with a sweep of his thumb. He pins me with a gaze so intense, my guard shatters to pieces, crackling onto the floor like ice shards melting. Maybe he's right. It's not giving up; it's getting out of here unscathed. It's ensuring I'm still free to find my mother and not caged behind steel bars like my dad.

"Okay." The word scrapes across my gravel tongue. "Let me text Nat and Tig and tell them to stand down."

He slides his hand into mine, our fingers interlocking, and tugs me back down the hallway. He doesn't let go for the rest of the tour.

CHAPTER 22

We file onto the bus to head back to our hotel just as rain starts to splatter against the windows, a steady pitter-patter echoing in my skull. The fake guitar hangs on the back of my shoulder, useless now. I start to slide into the seat beside Colin, but Natalie plucks the back of my shirt and pulls me across the aisle from him. Tig shuffles beside Colin and plugs in her earphones.

"Details." Natalie wags her hand toward her chest. "I needs them."

I affect a snooty accent, lifting my nose in the air. "Whatever are you talking about."

"Something tells me the hand-holding PDA going on wasn't part of your ongoing ruse for Lakshmi's benefit." Natalie taps her lip. "Oh, I know—it's the look on both your faces!"

"Shhh!" My eyes widen. "What look?" A bolt of lightning slashes across the sky as though to provide emphasis to my ominous question.

Natalie flicks her eyes toward Colin across the way. "*That* look."

Colin's got a goofy smile, biting his lip as he scrolls through his phone. Just the sight of him sends my stomach swirling with nerves.

"And this one." She taps my nose.

The bus starts moving, the heavy growl of the engine roaring beneath my thighs. "I kissed him. And I want to do it again."

Natalie clucks her tongue. "Damn it! I thought you'd hold out until next week." She reaches into her purse, takes out a fifty-dollar bill, and throws it across the aisle toward Tig. "You won."

I gasp. "You bet on me? And you *lost*?"

She shrugs as thunder booms in the distance. "I guess Tig knows you better than I do. It must be all that observation she does." Her voice gets stronger. "So, I'm guessing it was a good kiss?"

"The best one I've had, and I'm not just saying that because the only other kiss I had was with a random dude that slobbered all over my chin at a party."

"Ah, this is so exciting," Nat says in a dreamy way. "Me and Tig. You and Colin."

The bus pulls into the hotel parking lot just as the rain dies down to a few drops that splash into puddles on the pavement. All of a sudden, Colin leaps over Tig and jabs a finger at the window beside Natalie. "Look. Outside," he says through gritted teeth.

"Let me guess. It's rain . . ." My voice trails off. Several black town cars are parked in the parking lot, inconspicuous, unless you've spent your life hiding from unmarked FBI cars. Cold panic races up my spine. I failed Criminal 101: Check your surroundings.

A man in a sharp black suit gets out of a car and stalks toward the lobby, ducking his head against the drizzling rain. Dark floppy hair and chiseled movie star face. The same face that greeted me in the middle of the night when my dad was arrested.

Colin's dad, Ian O'Keefe.

FBI checkpoint. Heightened security at the guitar center. And now his dad, in the flesh. This isn't a coincidence; this is an ambush.

I'm sure there are a gazillion more agents keeping watch around the perimeter. I press my palms to my temples, trying to dull the pounding there. The instant we step off the bus, we'll be recognized.

But the fact that they didn't arrest us on the bus or at the guitar center leads me to believe they still don't know where we are, just that we're nearby. They're probably just checking every hotel in the area.

We might still have a chance to make it past them unscathed.

A whistle at the front of the bus draws our attention toward Abby. She waits until everyone quiets down. "You have two hours to relax before the special surprise tonight."

"I hope it's not a room full of FBI agents," I mutter, my voice strained. Anything to cut the tension and elicit a spark on Colin's face again. But his face is ghostly white.

Abby pauses for dramatic suspense. "A poolside luau party!"

She waits for the applause, but we all just blink at her.

"I need two volunteers to help me set up." She cranes her neck for all the hands I'm sure she's expecting will rise, but no one makes the effort. She purses her lips. "Please, guys. This will be fun."

Still no one responds. *Don't pick me. Don't pick me.*

She sighs. "Lakshmi? You did such a great job helping at the cookout that it would be fantastic if you could help again."

Lakshmi looks around the bus, her face falling, before her goody-two-shoes nature gets the best of her and she nods. Abby picks one of Colin's roomies to help as well, and everyone stands up, gathering their belongings.

Colin turns to me, his eyes wild and scared. "How are we going to get past my dad and his team?"

"The same way we get through every other con. Stealth and disguises." Stealth and disguises, a con artist's two best friends. "Walk in with your head down, no eye contact. You're just a kid on a teen tour. That's all."

Since we checked in last night, our suitcases are already in the hotel, along with Natalie's arsenal of disguises, which means we can only work with what we've got on the bus.

There's a girl in a pink hoodie, Tig's fedora, a guy in a baseball cap so dirty I suspect he sleeps with it on, and a bus full of sunglasses, including the pairs we're already wearing.

"You take Tig's fedora," I say, and he starts texting her. "I'm going for Sydney's hoodie."

As the front of the bus starts to disembark, I reach over and tap Sydney on the shoulder. "Hey, I'm freezing. Any chance I can borrow your hoodie?"

She looks at me like I'm crazy. "Don't you have one in your room?"

"I can't wait that long. I'm literally going to freeze to death right now." My teeth clatter together for dramatic effect. "Plus, I don't want to get wet."

Sydney rolls her eyes. "It's barely raining. I think you'll survive."

"Hey." Colin places his hand on her shoulder and shoots her his most adorable smile. Damn, he's so sexy when he does that. "That's super sweet of you to offer her your hoodie." He does a little swoony sigh and, ugh, I also do a swoony sigh. "That's my fave trait in a girl: generosity."

Sydney dissolves into a series of giggles and pushes her frizzy red hair behind her ear. "Really?"

"Yeah." His voice is laced with diamonds, and he holds her gaze like she's the only thing in the world. "I'm realizing now we haven't had much time to chat. Maybe we can connect at the luau later? We still haven't talked about our fave Hearts for Vandals songs."

He sounds so hopeful. So in love.

I want to punch her.

And maybe tell Colin not to flirt in front of me again, even if he *is* doing it to help me escape the FBI.

"Oh wow." She nods way too vigorously. "That would be amazing."

Sydney pulls the hoodie over her head and tosses it to me without looking back. I throw it on, getting a whiff of rose-scented perfume, and tuck my hair inside the pink jacket, letting the hood itself cover my head. Any other color hoodie and this would look suspicious, but thankfully hot pink helps sell the image of teen girl and not wanted criminal.

Colin picks up the fedora from Tig's empty seat and tosses it onto his head with a suave little flip.

My feet splash in puddles, sending water spraying up around my ankles. My pulse beats in my ear like a drum at a heavy metal concert. But I make it a point to look down and do what I would normally do if I was walking into a hotel and no one was here to arrest me.

Each step takes years. The ornate hotel lobby in shades of beige and gold stretches for miles rather than feet. It feels like the gazes of every damn person in this place weigh heavy on my back. I spy Lakshmi standing with Abby by the front desk and breathe a sigh of relief that she's not already in the room. We need to talk about this where she won't eavesdrop. We reach the elevators, and I jam my finger on the button again and again as the other campers groan at my impatience. Each elevator seems to mock me with their perch on a high floor.

Sydney's busy gabbing at Colin, trying to get his attention, but he's staring at the way the numbers on top of the elevator descend from ten.

When the elevator doors slide open, I launch myself inside, nudging other campers out of the way in order to slink toward the back. I don't dare breathe as the rectangular box propels us upward.

At my room, I wrench open the door and pull Colin inside. Natalie and Tig are already pacing inside. I nearly collapse onto the bed. "Shit, guys."

"It can't be a coincidence." Natalie twists her hands in her lap, her voice grave. "The FBI must know we're here."

"And that we were going to grab the guitar. But that was the one piece of evidence they hadn't confiscated from my house!"

Colin bites his lip, sets down Tig's fedora, and sinks onto the bed with such heaviness, the mattress caves. "This is really bad."

"How could they have found out?" Natalie drags her fingers over her face. "We've been so careful to cover our tracks for the rest."

We made all purchases using prepaid credit cards and burner phones. We did all the planning in Nat's backyard only hours before the tour. There was no way it could be traced back to us, not that soon anyway.

Tig crosses the room to where Lakshmi's suitcase is perched on the little luggage rack. She unzips the main compartment and starts rooting around in the clothes.

"Tig, what are you doing?" Natalie sidles up to her. "We need to figure out our game plan here, not search for outfits to borrow."

Tig rummages in the side compartments, pulling out random toiletries in superorganized bags, but doesn't seem to find what she's looking for.

I try to tamp down the panic by sucking in a hard breath through my nose. "We need to leave this tour. Immediately."

Colin nods. "But how? They're everywhere."

Tig starts digging her nails along the inner rim of Lakshmi's suitcase, and after a moment, there's a little snap. A hidden compartment opens, and Tig gasps. She pulls out two items: a notebook that looks like it's been well loved and a black wallet case. She flips open the wallet to reveal a shiny gold badge.

Lakshmi's not a camper; she's an FBI agent.

The news hits me like an atom bomb, a bolt of tension that sparks through my body and sets my skin ablaze.

Tig flashes an ID that indicates Lakshmi's really twenty-three years old. She juts her hand on her hip as though to say *I told you so*. She sets both on the table and then backs away from them, a disgusted look on her face.

"Wait." Natalie slaps her hand down on the desk, the sound so loud my teeth clatter together. "Is this room bugged?"

We all clamp our mouths shut. Tig gets out her laptop and bangs the keys with furious strokes. She plugs in various devices that blink red red red. After a few minutes, she shakes her head, and the horrible weight in my stomach shifts slightly.

I grab the notebook and start flipping through it. Lakshmi's neat, girly handwriting chronicles every decision we've made, every piece of evidence she's found. Our mannerisms. Our likelihood to flee the tour at each of the stops. The entire amusement park heist, boiled down into detailed bullet points with time stamps that don't miss a single step.

Recommendation for Guitar: FBI checkpoint right before reaching Gibson and heightened security at the factory. Light a fire under them so Fiona thinks she has *to steal the guitar then and there, or else we'll get to it first. Suggest the police officers keep an overbearing watch in the first few rooms, but as she makes her move, we'll call in an emergency elsewhere that will force the police to vacate. This will allow her to make the switch without any fear of getting caught.*

Holy shit. They never got a chance to call in an emergency because I never made my move.

I keep reading and then grow queasy when she guesses our plan for the book heist.

With a glass room, alarmed glass cases, and the tour in a confined space, they can't attempt to swipe the book in a stealthy way. They'll have to cause chaos. Perhaps set off the alarm electronically so that everyone has to flee. They'll use that as their distraction for Fiona to make the switch.

My fingers go numb. That's our exact plan.

Recommendation: No FBI presence. Fiona needs to believe she's solving the clue on her own since she's the only one who will know where the clues lead once deciphered. We need her to act as bait and lure her mother out of hiding.

I set the book on the nightstand, and Colin picks it up to peruse.

I start pacing. I consider myself the queen of stealth, yet somehow Lakshmi managed to be stealthier than I am. She found time to write detailed notes without ever exposing said notebook to her three roommates. Maybe she hid it in a towel on the way to the bathroom and wrote furiously while the shower fogged up the mirror with steam. Or maybe she just wrote it during all those times I tried to avoid her, giving her ample time to chronicle everything she's learned about me.

And even at the amusement park, when I thought I'd gotten rid of her, she probably worked with her team of undercover agents to follow my every move. I'm sure she also snooped through our luggage the same way we just searched hers and filled in the rest of the details that way.

No wonder the FBI didn't catch us at the amusement park or at the checkpoint today. They didn't *want* to catch us. They just wanted us to think they were getting close. Or maybe to smoke my mother out of hiding with strategically timed news articles indicating I'm making my way through her clues. That must be why they released the BOLO alerts but with the wrong photo of me.

The world tilts, knocking reality askew and sending all my control cascading off the side of the planet. A blast of hot and cold alternates across my skin, feeling like sweltering icicles burning frostbitten fingers. "But . . . how'd she even know about the tour?

We booked it only two days in advance, and only broke Colin out of house arrest twelve hours before."

Colin lets out a heavy, shuddering sigh and sets down the book. "I know how."

I whip my head to him, raising my brows. Tig stops zipping up Lakshmi's suitcase.

He bows his head, avoiding my eyes. "I struck an immunity deal and tipped off my dad about this whole plan the day you cut my anklet."

CHAPTER 23

Colin's confession about tipping off the FBI is a punch to my stomach, leaving me gasping. "*What?* Y-you sold us out?" My voice breaks. This can't be right. I must have misheard. I *must* have.

Tig shoots Colin both middle fingers, and Natalie backs away from him, shaking her head in denial, frizzy hair rattling.

"You got me arrested! I was pissed!" Colin buries his fists against his sides, as though he's preparing for a cage match.

My knees get wobbly. A headache brews behind my eyes and blots out all thought. He's staring at me, eyes big and wide, and waiting for me to say something. The way he ducks his chin like he's taking cover indicates he expects me to explode. My fingers curl, itching to slap him across the cheek once again, this time with the kind of force behind my punch that would send him flying. Knock some sense into him. Push these horrible words back into his mouth and rewrite history so I never heard his betrayal.

My jaw clenches. "I told you guys it was a bad idea to invite him into our crew." My words are laced with a venom so poisonous, Colin slinks back.

I violated the real number one rule of being a criminal, above anything else: Never let yourself be betrayed. And he got me twice! God, if my dad were here right now, he'd be angrier at *me* than at Colin. Well, okay, he'd be pretty angry at Colin. I started to trust him. I kissed him! And ugh, I liked it!

Natalie marches to the window, yanks it open, and storms out into the fresh air on the balcony. She slams it shut again. Tig dons a look so fierce and jabs her fingers against her laptop with the hard strokes of a piano player. A moment later Colin's phone lights up with gibberish before turning to black and letting off a faint sizzle sound.

"I deserved that," he says with a little laugh that sets my skin on edge.

"When?" I grit my teeth, rage boiling deep in my gut. "When did you betray me?"

He squeezes his eyes shut, and his shoulders give off a tiny shake. "When I went upstairs to get that picture of my mom. All it took was two quick texts to my dad, the first to ask for immunity in exchange for being a mole and the second, after he accepted, to give him the name of the tour."

I spit hot air through my teeth. "God, I'm such an idiot."

"But I swear." He holds out his palms as though he's showing us all his cards. "I had no idea an undercover agent was on this trip. Honestly, I thought *I* was the only mole, but clearly my dad didn't trust me enough, so he hired a babysitter." His voice breaks on the last part, and he has to clear his throat to regain his composure. "Perhaps for good reason, because after a few days, I stopped giving him information. I guess he knows me well after all."

It feels like the room is caving in on me. "Yeah right. I'm not falling for your lies again."

"No, I swear."

I roll my eyes. "When? Right now, I assume?"

"Right around the time I stopped hating you." He moves into my line of vision, forcing me to look at him. "And started liking you instead."

The silence lingers for a moment, tension all around. Even Natalie steps back into the room and stews with us. These were words I craved once; even minutes ago that sentence would have triggered a smile so wide on my face it would have taken days to rub off. But now his words sound empty, just another attempt at charming someone he's already fooled too many times.

"Well, that's not entirely true, either." He swallows hard. "I've always liked you. From the first rumor I heard about you before I even started school. And then, once I met you, I liked that you challenged me. Kept me on my toes. *Understood* me in a way no one else did." His shoulders go slack like all the tension he's been carrying around has fled. "I got sidetracked for a bit when I was pissed at you and stewing alone for a month, but I quickly realized I was *never* on my dad's side. I've always been on yours."

He looks at me with a heartbreakingly wounded expression on his face, and I flinch. Everything coming out of his mouth sounds genuine, but so did all the other lies he fed me. When he reaches for my arm, I stumble back, still reeling from the metaphorical knife plunged into my gut. "Why should I believe you?"

"Because I think that's why the FBI showed up today despite what Lakshmi wrote in the notebook. As a warning to *me* to start giving them info again, or else they'd take away my immunity deal. But I don't care about that anymore. I only care about you. I want to help you find your mom."

"All we have is your word, and your word means shit," Natalie says.

"Okay. Well . . ." Colin rakes his hand over his scalp. "I'll call my dad and try to extend my immunity deal to the rest of you?"

I snort. "They'd never go for it. Why would they?" I pause. "Besides, they'd never extend it to my mom as well, and I can't sell her out like that."

"Then I'll tell you everything I know!" Colin says in a rush. He sucks down a big gulp of breath as though he's about to give a big, important speech. "The FBI already looked at the human-skin book but couldn't find a clue in it at all. They think there must be something in the existing text that only you'll be able to find. Something your mom told you once or alluded to. They've essentially hit a dead end until you find it and decipher it."

The air whooshes from my lungs. "What about the clue from the guitar? Do they know that one?"

He swallows again. "I'm guessing they do, but they haven't told me it."

Natalie crosses her arms. "Wait, how do you know this? When did you even talk to the FBI?"

"At every hotel there was a burner phone waiting for me at the front desk. I would sneak down and get it while everyone was getting ready for dinner each night. But shortly after the skull heist, I stopped picking up the burner or calling them. " He pleads with his eyes, his voice sincere. "I tried to tell you. That night with the book forgery? But I—" All the fight leaves his voice, like a balloon losing air. "I chickened out."

The walls curl in on me, cleaving me in two equal halves. One part of me laps up his words, soaks them in, replays the kiss between us and the way his hands gripped me so firmly, like he couldn't let go, and believes the look on his face proves everything that happened between us was real. That the electric feeling zipping in my veins when I'm around him pumps through his body, too. But the other part of me retreats as reality shatters. The memory of the kiss gives way to his conniving smirk and all the traps he set that I fell right into.

It's a choice. Continue to be mad at Colin and assume he's lying, that this whole charade is another con he's pulling on us with his charm as the ultimate weapon. Or listen to the part of me . . . which might be my gut or might just be my dumb hormones . . . that believes he's changed and will truly help me find my mom.

But maybe that's our advantage.

I bolt upright as the idea zooms through me, skin tingling. But this idea requires a leap of faith. I have to choose him the same way he claims he chose me. "Girl huddle. Quickly. I have an idea."

Natalie races over to me, but Tig takes her time crossing the room, using the opportunity to glare at Colin menacingly. He backs up to give us space, shoving his hands in his pockets.

"Do you guys trust me?" I whisper.

Natalie purses her lips. "Usually."

"I think I know how to use this to our advantage. But we have to be all in. Colin included."

Natalie's eyes widen. "You believe him?"

I meet her gaze. "I believe we should give him a chance to prove himself."

She nods, slowly at first, before becoming more aggressive. "Okay. I'm in."

Tig's glare morphs back into a normal expression, which I take as confirmation.

I spin to face Colin and raise my voice. "Okay, if you are truly on our side now, then you need to prove it."

Colin perks up. "I'll do anything."

"Lakshmi doesn't know we've discovered her true identity." I start pacing the room as the plan solidifies. "If we can start to feed her wrong information, then we can outsmart the FBI and send them down the wrong path to lead them *away* from my mother."

We have to con the very people trying to catch us for pulling cons.

"A heist within a heist." My words grow more confident. "Once we get the book, we pretend to decipher it within earshot of Lakshmi. Have the entire message lead somewhere far away from the ancient book in Notre Dame. Seattle or something. Whatever the farthest continental US city is."

Everyone nods along.

I turn to Colin. "You have to talk to the FBI. Make them think their ploy today scared you and you're back on their side. Give them wrong specifics about the escape plan."

"That's not enough, though. You need to play Lakshmi if this is going to work." Natalie points at me. "She's been clinging to you; you have to be the one to feed *her* wrong info. Maybe give her a sob story about your mother and a fond memory you have of the two of you in Seattle to plant that seed in her mind. That your mom might be hiding *there*."

I clench my teeth. "I'm probably not the best person for that. It has to be—"

"You," Colin says. "You're the only one that can feed her false info about your mom. I'll help you charm her. Coach you through it via an earpiece."

I don't look at him when I say, "Fine."

Natalie paces the room. "And we need an exit strategy. South Bend will be swarming with FBI agents. We need a way to get out of that city without being detected, because as soon as we fake decipher that clue, they're going for us. Even if we manage to evade them, they're going to be stopping cars, buses, trains."

Tig taps her phone as though to suggest she'll research the best way out of there.

Natalie bites her lip. "And new disguises. We can't use any of the wigs or supplies in my luggage in case Lakshmi snooped." She starts rummaging through her suitcase, probably to catalog what she already has so she knows what not to buy.

I unzip Lakshmi's suitcase to shove the notebook back in.

Colin crouches in front of me. "Hey."

I ignore him, my fingers tightening around the notebook.

"Does this mean you believe me? That you forgive me?" He looks so damn hopeful.

"I don't think I'll ever forgive you." There's a sudden stabbing in my chest. "And I don't fully believe you. Not when you're so damn good at lying."

He nods, swallowing hard.

"So this only means that I'm giving you a chance to do the impossible: Convince me."

We all huddle around Colin's cell phone in the hotel room and listen in while he makes the call. It rings several times before his dad picks up. "I see you got my message."

I can hear the croak in Colin's throat. "You probably didn't need quite the theatrics of fifteen police cars. One or two would have sufficed."

His dad responds with a snort. "I wouldn't call it a message so much as a warning." In the background on his line, there's a lot of shuffling and side conversations, and I assume others are in the room as well. "Care to explain why you've neglected to send any reports for twelve days?"

Natalie and I exchange glances, and then when I glance at Colin, he's staring at me.

The tightness in my chest loosens. He was telling the truth about this, at least. I do the math. He said he stopped contacting the FBI right around the time he stopped hating me . . . Twelve days puts us . . . the day of the bus ride where we leaned close and listened to the same music from the same pair of earbuds. Nothing special.

Except to him.

"I got paranoid," he says, his voice a little dejected, his eyes pinned on mine. "I was worried she was onto me. She wouldn't tell me anything about the next heists. And then I saw her talking to the front desk once, and I started freaking out that she knew about the phones you were leaving me. I figured it was best to lay low for a few days until she started to trust me again."

Ian O'Keefe clucks his tongue. "If you thought she was suspicious, that's exactly the type of thing you need to tell us about, not try to handle it yourself. Understand?"

"Yes, sir," he says, and looks away from me. So formal. So different from the kind of father-daughter relationship I have. *Had.* My throat gets tight.

"We'll give you a second chance." I notice his dad says *we,* as though it's the FBI's idea and not necessarily one he endorses or came up with himself. "But you need to cooperate from now on."

"Yes, sir." There's a slight pause before Colin speaks again. "But how did you know about the guitar factory? *I* didn't even know until the day of."

I recognize what this is. It's him saving face. He couldn't have told them this info if he didn't know it himself. It's smart, and his delivery of complete disbelief sells it. It's also a ploy to get his dad to admit he planted Lakshmi.

"I'm good at what I do, Colin."

I cringe for him. Because his dad's words imply that Colin is not good at the role he's been given. Ian won't offer any more details, and of course he won't tell Colin about Lakshmi. He doesn't trust him enough.

"Do you know the clue? If you tell me, I can—"

"No way." Ian's voice is sharp and hard. "If she even suspects you know the clue, this whole plan falls apart. And if she can't decipher the message without that clue, well, she'll have to come to us."

"But—"

"Now get off the phone and come to room 343. I need you to tell me everything that happened in the last twelve days."

"Yes, sir." He hangs up and bites his lip before leaving the room . . . and taking with him our chance to eavesdrop on what he tells them.

CHAPTER 24

"Over here." Colin juts his chin toward a deserted patch of grass hidden between two elm trees. I hesitate for a moment before following him. We're at Old Hickory Lake, just outside Nashville, on this idyllic day when none of us should have a care in the world except the warm air on our skin and the soft lap of the waves.

It's been three days since Colin confessed and then retreated back into the FBI's good graces with a lot of groveling and a few apologies. Within an hour of Colin knocking on his dad's door like the prodigal son returned and reinforcing his commitment to the squad, the black cars disappeared, and so did the agents in question. I just hope the trap he set with his pledge of loyalty was for them, not for us.

We've been laying low, walking the line between trying to show we were spooked by the FBI's antics and moving forward with our plans for the book heist.

All our plans. Including the part where we need to hoodwink the FBI themselves.

In order to do that properly, we need to plant the seeds.

"Number one thing to do when charming someone—" Colin

plugs an earbud into my ear and tucks my hair over it, fingers sliding gently over my ear. The shady elm tree sprinkles diamond-shaped shadows on his shorts and tee. "Make them think *they're* your entire world. They're interested in themselves, not you. So take an interest in them."

"Easier said than done." I wrinkle my nose against the peaty scent of algae. "Unless you're you, of course. Or my dad." My voice cracks. "I don't have the requisite winning smile."

"You do to me. The smile, I mean." Sunlight drops glistening spotlights on both the ripples in the lake and the dimples indenting Colin's cheeks.

I look down at my feet and kick a pebble toward the lake edge, swallowing hard. A few days ago, that compliment would have made my skin warm, but now the feeling wars with the cool sensation of lingering betrayal. "Actually, on second thought, it's probably better if you give me this advice from a distance. So we can check if the earbuds are working."

He squints at me. "They're Beats by Dre. Of course they're working."

Still, I tap my ear and use the excuse to walk away, concentrating on putting one foot in front of the other and not the bevy of tears swarming to my eyes.

The grass tickles my ankles, and the warm summer breeze blows my short hair around my face. I don't dare look back at the boy I left behind as I circle around the lounge chairs facing the glittering lake. Laughter, the vibrating motor of a speedboat, and the tinny sounds of Sydney's portable speaker blasting the latest Hearts for Vandals song fade away the farther from the lake I flee.

I lean against the bark of a large oak tree, its thick leaves shading me from the hot sun. A quick look around confirms no other campers are within earshot, most too busy taking kayaks and paddleboats and trying to get their crushes to notice them. A few girls lie on towels, tanning by the dock, and some of the boys engage in a fierce game of volleyball down by the shore. Lakshmi casts a fishing line into the lake.

"Okay," I say. "Can you hear me?"

The faint hint of the Hearts for Vandals song carries through before Colin's voice drifts into my ear. "Yep, like I said . . ."

No one trusts me to be able to talk Lakshmi into believing our misdirections without Colin coaching me through it, Cyrano de Bergerac–style. But the problem is I flinch every time I hear his voice.

"Let's talk body language. You've got to smile. A smile is infectious. Contagious. If you're smiling, then your mark will feel a little bit happier, too."

"I'm well aware of your smile and how you use it as a weapon," I snap. Trees rustle as a gust of wind powers through. "Tell me something new."

"No crossing your arms. Relax your legs. Don't fidget. Lean toward her. If you seem confident in your own skin, she'll be drawn to you."

I drop my hands to my sides from where they were crossed at my chest.

"Use a soothing tone of voice," he says in his ridiculously velvet tone. "Make her feel calm in your presence." His voice is a lullaby, soothing all the anger boiling in my veins.

"So no swearing at her. Got it."

"And don't forget eye contact. Look at her as though she's the only person in the world. Hell, pretend she's famous. If you ran into your fave celebrity, how would you act? You'd be excited to see her; you'd hang on her every word; you'd want to watch her every move."

The hair on the back of my neck starts to lift. Every conversation, every interaction we've ever had floods into my mind. His siren-song smile. His eyes locked on mine, smoldering. Listening to me. Knowing me sometimes better than I know myself. The way he made me feel like I was the only person in the room that mattered.

He claims there was a turning point for him. That his feelings grew, and he could no longer squash them down. But he was still using these charm tactics right up until he confessed. He'd been using them in the hallway seconds before I kissed him.

How can I trust that any of what happened between us was real?

"Compliment her," he continues. "Acknowledge her accomplishments. Latch on to her interests and—"

I purse my lips. "I have no idea what her interests are."

"Exactly. You haven't been paying enough attention to her. Start by picking out a positive observation about her and pointing it out. Tell her you love her shoes and ask where she got them or something."

A light breeze snatches my hair and blows it across my eyes in a wild tangle. "Okay. That sounds somewhat reasonable."

"Repeat it all back to me."

"Um." I push the hair out of my eyes and kick a clod of dirt with my shoe. "I love your shoes."

He chuckles. "No, the advice. Not the compliment, though it did make me feel good about the sneakers decorated with an ugly checkered pattern Natalie bought for me. Even if they are pink-and-purple checkers."

"They're statement sneakers." I bite my lip. "But to answer your question: Be nice. Compliment her. Ask her questions."

"Avoid showing any sort of weakness or vulnerability," he adds.

I let out a sharp laugh. My weakness and vulnerability have

been written all over my face ever since he shoved an ice pick into my chest. I can't listen to him say any of this anymore. "I'm ready."

"But—"

"I'm ready," I say through gritted teeth, and roll my neck. I solidify that thought by texting the group the signal for Natalie to alert Lakshmi that she can't find me. In this case, the signal is a merman emoji.

"Okay then," he says after reading the text. Dejection laces his voice.

I slide against the tree to wait to be found in a ridiculous game of hide-and-seek. Tapping my finger against my thigh, I repeat his words of wisdom in my mind. *Smile. It's about her, not you. Don't show weakness or vulnerability.*

But how do I slip in the fake info about my mom if this is about befriending Lakshmi? I can't be like, *Hey, girl, what's your fave hobby?* And she goes, *Horseback riding!* or something. And then I reply, *That's so interesting. By the way, I think my mom's hiding near a tiny creek in Hoodsport, Washington, a tiny fishing village about two hours west of Seattle. Spoiler alert, I'll soon be handing you the GPS coordinates on a silver platter.*

We chose Hoodsport not simply because it's on the outskirts of the farthest major city from Notre Dame but also because the story I'm going to tell her is real. It's a gamble for sure. My mom could very well actually be hiding exactly there.

Thick trees sway in the distance, leaves jangling in a metallic shake. Puffy white clouds lurk across the sky, looking almost like snowcapped mountains rising above the trees. The image is overlaid by one of another lake. Another place. Another time.

Back when I still had a family I could talk to. When their laughter was something I took for granted. When their love for each other and for me permeated the air and buoyed me upward. I close my eyes, and I'm back there at beautiful Finch Creek, steep mountains rising in my panoramic view.

Large evergreen trees cast dark shadows on the muddy grass. I was nine years old, on the verge of ten and ruling the world, or so it felt.

"Fiona, hon." My mom slid beside me on a large, gray rock, pulling her thin legs up to her knees and following my gaze out to where the sunset lit the water on fire. Dad was busy setting up the tents a few feet away, grunting against the hard strike of a hammer. Mom stared at me with those piercing eyes of hers, the ones that always seemed to be trying to x-ray me to uncover my secrets or to send me a telepathic message I couldn't quite decipher.

I shifted under the weight of her uncomfortable stare. "It's so beautiful, isn't it?"

She placed her palm on my shoulder, just a simple touch. "We'll have to enjoy the calm while it lasts."

I nodded, closing my eyes. The crisp air iced my lungs and sent shivers through me.

Her voice dropped, and she spoke in a hurried tone. "We should do something to remember us by."

I laughed. "You mean remember this *by."*

She looked confused for a second but nodded. "Yes, this. This moment. The three of us together. No one after us. What's ahead of us still a bit uncertain."

"Okay. I'm in. What should we do?"

She tapped her fingers on her knees, which were slick and glossy with bug spray. "A carving? In a tree, maybe?" She fumbled in the box of supplies beside her and pulled out a hunting knife, small and sharp. Deadly. "You want to do the honors?"

I took the knife in shaky fingers and held it gingerly between my thumb and forefinger like a person might hold a rotten apple. But Mom cleared her throat, and my fingers slipped to the hilt, gripping tightly. I checked back to confirm, and when she nodded, the nerves dissipated. I braced one hand against the scratchy bark, and with my other, I carved the only thing that made sense at the time. Six letters. Our initials. Forever branding this place as ours.

She pursed her lips at my carving and snorted once. My heart beat faster. Did that mean she didn't like it?

She held out her palm for the knife, and when she took hold of it, the way she gripped the hilt with white knuckles made it seem as though she was clutching the most powerful weapon in the universe. She studied the tree for several long beats, like she was Michelangelo and could liberate the image hiding within by carving.

And then she set the knife against the other side of the bark.

When she painted, she lost herself. She wouldn't sleep, eat, sometimes barely even breathe until she got the image down on the canvas, whether it was one from her mind or a copy of someone else's mastery. And when she carved that tree, the same fevered frenzy took over her. Glazed eyes. Triceps bulging. Sweat beading down her back.

My mouth parted, my eyes glued to her every move. It was like a dance, the most mesmerizing performance I'd ever witnessed.

When she finished, she stood back and nodded to herself. I gasped at the beauty.

Two long lines converged up the length of the tree to a vanishing point to create what looked like a road in the distance of the image. Four separate lines fanned out, two on either side of the original two, creating what looked like walls. The walls had a pattern of horizontal rectangles cascading across their surface. At intervals, long poles rose vertically and interrupted the whole image.

"What is it?"

"Nothing. Or maybe everything," she said.

I never found out what the image meant. If it was a real place, another one of her twisted clues, or just a figment of imagination she had to free from her mind. But that trip was the last one my family took together. It was the last one where my mom acted like a mother and not a person on the verge of fleeing. It was the only time my life felt somewhat . . . normal.

The sting in my throat starts slowly but swells faster than I can stop it. I suck down desperate gulps of air to try to quell the tsunami about to explode. But it's too late, and I'm too helpless. Big fat tears rush out of my eyes. My gulps turn into sobs, and suddenly I can't catch my breath.

"Fiona?" Colin whispers in my ear. "You okay?"

I can't speak. All I can do is succumb to the racking sobs.

"I specifically said *not* to cry," Colin says in a tone of jest, and even that doesn't break the tension.

"Oh my God, Fiona!" A new voice precedes the rush of footsteps and the arms that engulf me in a hug. "What happened?" Lakshmi shrieks. "Are you okay?"

I nod through escaping wails. Then shake my head.

"Oh, it's okay. I'm here for you. Cry it out." She pulls my head against her shoulder and lets me release all the emotion I've been holding back.

Because my mom's gone, and it's looking less and less likely that I'll find her. Not without trading the FBI my secrets for the guitar clue. And my dad's gone, trapped behind steel bars, probably for the next ten years. I have no idea what comes next for me if I can't succeed in this mission. And the one guy I trusted had been working against me.

I let it all out. Directly on Lakshmi's beautiful silk shirt (funded by the FBI). I don't stop until my throat's raw. My eyes burn. And I'm more vulnerable than I've ever been in my life, with the guy who broke me, listening, and the girl who's only here to catch me, comforting me.

"What's wrong?" She traces her palm over my hair, smoothing it down.

"My mom," I say, my voice cracking on the word and a new rush of tears sliding out of my eyes. It goes against everything Colin just tried to teach me, but if I don't salvage this situation, if I don't succeed in conning Lakshmi, then I'm at even more of a loss than before.

"Fiona, stop," Colin coaches. "You can't just launch into it. You have to ease—"

I ignore him. "This lake reminds me of the last time we were together. As a family, I mean. One of the most magical days of my life."

"Quick," Colin says in my ear. "Pretend you don't want to talk about it. It'll only make her more interested."

"It's silly." I frantically wipe away my tears, listening to him for once. "It's just a lake. It's not the same."

"Now ask her about something else. Anything," he coaxes.

"Did you catch any fish?" My voice is still incredibly shaky.

Lakshmi studies me with a look of utter concern, her lips pursing. "Fiona, if you're this upset about something, we should talk about it. Where was the other lake, exactly?"

"Near Seattle. Well, more like two hours away, but still." We agreed not to give her too many details on location quite yet. Just enough to get her mind churning, but not enough to send out a search party.

"Reminisce about how beautiful it was, make her truly interested in it, but keep it generic," Colin suggests.

"God, it was so beautiful. Mountains in the background. Clouds in the sky. Crystal-blue water and perfect weather." Can't get more generic than that.

"Sounds amazing," Lakshmi agrees, her eyes lit with a glint of interest. "What was so special about that day?"

Now I take his advice without being prompted, almost involuntarily. A small smile pops onto my lips. "My mom and I—we decided that it was the most perfect place to escape." I let that word linger in the air for just a beat as the lump in my throat shrinks. "There was just a peace to it. And a simplicity. A fishing rod. A tent. A knife, and you'd be set."

Her brows shoot way up, but then she corrects herself, and her face morphs back to one of concern. "You mentioned this was the last time you were all together. How old were you?"

"Nine? Ten, maybe? It was right before my mom left." I make sure not to say she disappeared. I'm just a girl that was abandoned by her mother, not a girl whose mother went on the lam.

Lakshmi strokes her chin, taking this in. I can see the wheels turning in her mind.

"Quick, thank her! Make it seem like you really needed this chat, but now it's over." Colin's voice in my ear prompts me to throw my arms around her. "Thank you. I never feel like I can talk about this stuff to Nat. She's got a normal family life. Two parents. Annoying siblings. The whole shebang. She doesn't get it."

"And T's not exactly the best person to talk to, either," she jokes, and we both laugh. "Seriously, you can come talk to me anytime. I'm here for you."

I smile through gritted teeth, hoping it looks genuine . . . and not like I know the only thing she's here for is to use whatever I say against me.

When I return to my friends . . . and Colin . . . my eyes sting, and there's still a hitch in my throat.

Colin stands in a copse of trees with his hands shoved in his pockets, looking completely out of place and unsure he still belongs in this convo. In this group. With me.

"Good job." He places a palm on my forearm, and I reflexively shrug out of his touch, stepping backward. He snaps his hand back and shoves it into his pocket, studying his feet.

"We still need an exit strategy," I blurt in an attempt to distract myself. It's probably the wrong time to discuss this, but the rest of the campers are still laughing on the lake, not skulking through the woods like us. "As soon as we pretend to decipher the clues, we have to flee. And they'll be vigilant to find us."

Tig digs out her phone, scrolls through some saved links, and then shoves it at Natalie. Natalie squeals and wraps her arms around Tig. "Wait. When did you find this?"

Tig whispers something in her ear, and Natalie scoffs. "And you didn't bring this up until now?!"

Colin rolls his eyes and snatches the phone out of Natalie's hands. He purses his lips. "Okay, not a bad idea. But how do we even know what planes will be there that day?"

He shows the phone to me. North Liberty Aviation in South Bend, Indiana. A small airport for private planes. No major security team and there might not even be TSA agents, though Tig will create some fabulous fake IDs just in case. If we can get our new identities on the roster of a private plane, we'll be golden.

Tig waggles her fingers for the phone and types in a few more things. She tilts the phone screen toward us, showing us a hacked-in screen with all the flights scheduled to take off that day. She points to one particular section on the screen.

Hearts for Vandals Private Tour Jet. 11:49 p.m.
Destination: Teterboro, NJ. Gate 1.

Private Owner. 11:55 p.m. Destination: Bahamas.
Gate 2.

Tradewinds Charter Company. 12:30 a.m.
Destination: Jacksonville, FL. Gate 1.

Private Owner. 12:21 a.m. Destination: Roswell, NM. Gate 2.

Jetstream Charter. 12:57 a.m. Destination: Bellingham, WA. Gate 1.

Natalie plunks her finger on the screen. "I vote Bahamas."

"We're going to have to decide that night. Whichever flight gets us closest to wherever my mom's really hiding." I turn to Colin. "You'll have to convince the private owners or the charter folks to let us on somehow."

"I can probably do that." He scratches his chin. "But we should back it up somehow and get ourselves on an official roster so we have tickets in case we're wrong about private airports not having proper security."

Natalie gasps. "Wait! Hearts for Vandals is playing at Notre Dame that night! If we can convince them that we're contest winners for their flight or something, we'll be able to get past TSA. And from there we can decide if we ditch them for another flight or stick with the boy band." She turns to me. "Can you create fake VIP passes to get us into the concert?"

I shrug. "If you can keep Lakshmi away from me for a few hours, then yes. I've got all the supplies here already."

Colin drops his head into his hands. "I can't believe our best option for escape is convincing the most famous band in the world to let us ride on their private jet."

I pat him on the shoulder. "Hey, at the very least, this holds up with your alibi of being obsessed with them."

We spend the next two days preparing as much as possible. I seize every spare minute that Natalie manages to distract Lakshmi to work on fake IDs. Tig uses her hacking skills to dig up information about the private jet owners—one a billionaire in town for business and another a frat boy who just turned twenty-one and finally received access to his trust fund. The latter will be far easier to convince than the former, but Colin plans to kill me all over again with another sob story about how I'm dying and need an urgent flight out for a heart transplant to hopefully convince the billionaire. The charter companies are both running tours, mostly targeted at the elderly, but there's no specific age limit. A few backdated emails "proving" we've paid for the tours in question should do nicely here.

I have no idea which flight we'll end up with, and that scares me. It means I don't know my mother well enough to even guess.

But despite all the scurrying and planning we're doing behind Lakshmi's back, with only two days to go before the library heist, we still need to keep up the ruse of good little campers. So on a tour of Graceland, I try my best to pay attention. As our guide blabbers on, Colin slips a slim black device into my palm. A string of headphones wraps around it. Rule #14: When attempting subterfuge, don't look immediately. Wait until you're away from Lakshmi or whatever other FBI agents they've planted here.

"What's this?" I whisper.

He tilts my head to the side and his warm breath coats my ear. I try not to shiver. Or cringe. "My way of showing you I'm trustworthy. You once checked if I was wearing a wire. This time I actually did."

I squint at him, trying to make sense of what he's saying.

"It's my conversation with the FBI last night when I was giving them my report. So you know exactly what I told them. And because I got you a bit of info in exchange as well."

I want to rush through the ornate entryway right then and listen, but I force myself to be patient. Not be suspicious. I wait a whole thirty minutes before I excuse myself to the restroom. I settle into a stall and stick the buds in my ear, closing my eyes against the bright fluorescent lights. I have to grip my necklace for comfort as I press play.

There's static and some rustling for a few seconds before a dial tone comes on. The sound of it startles me so much that I let out a small gasp, and the woman in the stall next to me asks if I'm okay.

The phone rings four times before a man says, "Hello?"

I can hear the croak in Colin's throat. "Hi, Dad. Checking in for my nightly report."

His dad responds with a snort. "Wow, five days in a row now. I'd say I'm impressed . . . if this wasn't the exact deal you agreed to."

Colin sucks in a shaky breath.

"Did you learn anything today? Anything at all?"

Colin sighs. "Nothing. Not one thing." His voice rises in frustration at the end of the word. "She refuses to tell me anything, no matter how close I get."

"Then get closer. Do what you're good at. Smile. Make her feel—"

"I've been doing that. It's not working."

I pause the recording here, my heart pumping painfully. Water splashes in the sink as the woman who was next to me washes her hands, and I let the sound drown out my thoughts. It takes a moment of courage before I hit play again.

"I need something else. Something that would really make her think I've got her back. Something she wants."

"Like what?"

Colin's voice changes to one of confidence now that he has his dad's attention. "Info about her father, maybe. She's worried about him and misses him so—"

Ian laughs. "How are you going to get that info, if not by talking to me? If you tell her that, you're exposing our deal."

"I thought about that. But I can tell her I called the correctional facility. Posed as you or something to get him on the phone. I think if I'm able to tell her a small tidbit, even if it's just that he's okay, she'd start to trust me again."

Ian considers this for several excruciating seconds. I lean forward on the toilet seat, chest trilling.

"Are you sure you can sell that?"

Colin's voice is shaky at the doubt in his father's voice. "I have to."

"Okay, in that case, I do have a message from her father that I've been keeping in my back pocket."

"A real message?" I can hear the excitement in Colin's voice.

"Yes, I visited him last week and explained that I wanted to get a message to her under the ruse that I wanted to get her to stop. He said to tell her, and I quote, 'What happened to our talk about hotel rooms and boyfriends?'"

Colin and his dad part ways under the agreement that he'll continue to give reports every night.

Two emotions fight a war on my face: the smile that emerges at my dad's inside joke and the tear that slips out of my eye because I miss him something fierce.

I clutch the recording to my chest, savoring this small piece of my dad. How he knows me way too well and how, given the opportunity to tell me anything in the world, he went with something that would make me feel loved rather than spur me onward. Though I guess making me feel like he has my back does exactly that.

But there's something even more important in this message from my dad.

It proves Colin really is on our side. I can truly trust him.

CHAPTER 25

Despite Colin earning back my trust and my quick, muttered *thank-you* when I handed back the recording device, I've still felt a little weird around him. He keeps glancing at me expectantly, and I keep avoiding his eyes. Because the thing is, earning trust back and earning his way back into my heart are two separate things. And he's only managed one so far.

The problem is I'm not sure what it will take to earn the other.

But I don't have much time to dwell because the day after Graceland is the last heist, and I need to throw all my energy into that. While Lakshmi showers, we pack our "go" bag and make sure she has no opportunity to snoop inside it before we leave the hotel room. Colin slips me a handwritten note at breakfast, and I make an excuse to go to the bathroom before I read it in a stall.

Told my dad the message from your dad worked and you confided the escape plan to me.

The "escape" plan we fed to the FBI was that we'll lay low until 3 a.m. and then flee by train to Chicago, figure out our next move from there. We also had Colin plant the idea that my mom might not emerge from hiding unless she knows I'm the one finding her. Translation: Keep the FBI far far away.

> *He agreed to not send any agents tonight. He's going to let me keep up this ruse and accompany you to her location until she comes out of hiding. I promised to check in every hour once we escape.*

I flush the note down the toilet. Hopefully, this means the FBI will let us walk out of here at 3 a.m. without any issue. From there it's just a matter of *not* going to the train station, as we led them to believe. We figured the safest way to leave was if the FBI knew about it and let us.

On the way to the bus, we exchange glances, and this time I don't look away as quickly as I have been. Lakshmi clears her throat, and we stumble onto the bus and try not to make anything obvious during the fifteen-minute ride to the Hesburgh Library at Notre Dame.

Our voices carry across the quiet atmosphere of the library. The wooden chairs surrounding the study carrels are probably older than the now-defunct card catalogs. Light gray walls and a geometric carpet draw my eye to the black shelves packed with books that are stacked like dominos in a row.

"Follow me to the rare books collection," our librarian tour guide says, pressing a wrinkled finger to her equally wrinkled face. A cloud of white hair circles her head like a halo. She ushers a few of us into an elevator. "We pride ourselves on housing the rarest collection of books, from medieval manuscripts—"

"Bound in actual medievals," I whisper, the sound of the hydraulics covering my words.

Colin keeps close, his body curving toward me, and mine replies with the same answer for a second before I take a step away.

"—and even an entire collection on sports research," the guide continues.

"Are we going to see the book bound in human skin?" Lakshmi fans herself with a brochure, and her fishtail braid flops on her shoulders as she bounces on her toes.

Shut. Up. Lakshmi. I grit my teeth together. This must be a game to her. Make it harder for me to steal the very thing she needs me to steal.

"We'll get to that in a minute, dear," the tour guide says. The elevator door opens, and we all wait outside a room enclosed in glass while the tour guide descends back down to escort the next group of campers. Rectangular glass display tables secure the rare books. My eyes immediately settle on the little green blinking lights at the very bottom of each case. A sign above the door reads RARE BOOKS, SPECIAL COLLECTIONS, SPORTS RESEARCH.

"I'm going to find a bathroom." Natalie pivots on her heels and beelines down the hall, despite the fact that there are two bathrooms flanking the elevators. Her backpack drags, heavy with tools. I lift my eyes to the security camera and give it a wink. Tig rigged them by looping yesterday's footage back through the feed. Doesn't matter, though. The FBI needs us to succeed in this heist and won't be stopping us. Cutting the feed is all for show.

"Now, children," the tour guide says once everyone has reached the second floor. A few groan at her use of the word *children.* "The books I'm about to show you are very delicate indeed. You may look, but please do not touch. Fingerprints on the glass cases will disrupt the experiences of the next tour group."

Colin stands so close, and I catch a whiff of the spicy cologne he picked up at a rest stop in Louisville. The group files into the rectangular room where rows of display cases sit on thrones of steel legs. Books rest splayed open in each one. Overhead lights drop spotlights onto the tomes. The students start to spread out, but the tour guide waves everyone toward the first display. The human book.

"As your camp mate already pointed out"—she lifts her chin toward Lakshmi—"we sent this book to a medical examiner in New York City to determine if the binding comes from traditional sheep leather or from the human skin. Since the test requires examination of DNA and touching the surface could contaminate it, examiners removed a small sliver from the inner flap that had been covered by a glued-down page."

"Spoiler alert," one of the campers shouts. "It's human."

Several students, including Lakshmi, lean in, oohing and aahing at the seemingly morbid artifact. Except, of course, the version on display here is another one of my mom's excellent forgery achievements.

Across the way, Colin lifts a phone to his ear. "Hello?" The cue: Natalie calling him to signal she's ready to be someone else. But also to give him an opportunity to act out his role.

The tour guide stops talking and glares at him. Her finger lifts to her mouth: *Shhh*. Abby crosses her arms and stomps toward Colin.

He slaps at the air, waving her away. "Is she okay?" His face falls.

Abby stops in her tracks, hovering in front of him. Every head swivels in his direction, including the tour guide's. Everyone's except Lakshmi's. She only has eyes for me.

"Dad, hold on a sec." He cups his hand against the phone and peers up at Abby, his face grave. "My—my grandma's in the hospital." He lets out a strangled wail. "I need to . . ." He doesn't finish, just heads toward the doorway. Abby doesn't stop him.

Colin hustles beyond the glass, pressing the phone against his ear and whispering something nobody will ever hear because there's no one on the other end. He disappears around the corner.

While everyone's preoccupied with Colin's ruse, Tig starts tapping away on her phone. She's already done the hard work of hacking into the security systems and planting scripts that will instantly cause every alarm in the building to go off. Once she remotely accesses her laptop, it'll take a quick second or two to execute the scripts.

Ugly Dave cranes his neck at the group. "Where's Natalie?"

Tig clutches her bladder and points toward the entrance.

Abby checks her watch. "Still? I'm going to check on her." She snaps her fingers at both Daves. They perk up to handle the group while she stalks away toward the bathroom, dark hair swinging.

Shit. And I mean that literally. Time to enact contingency-plan A. I leave my perfect spot in the middle of the group and weave through the other campers, muttering, "Excuse me," in a rush to cut Abby off at the door. "Abby, wait!"

Abby stops and spins around, one foot outside the door. She's still wearing her resting-bitch face, otherwise known as *I see right through your bullshit.*

"You should know . . ." I look around, then lean in conspiratorially toward Abby, making her duck closer to me with a waggle of my fingers. "I think she caught the stomach bug I had the other day. It was pretty awful. She might be in there for a while."

Abby's face pales, but she nods. She slips out of the heavy doors and pulls them shut behind her.

Rule #15: There are boring parts to being a criminal. Sure, we swoop in and grab expensive jewels right out from under your nose, but in order to do that, we have to plan for everything. Which means risk management: identifying anything that could go wrong and coming up with a plan to mitigate potential dangers. Not exactly glamorous but still necessary. My dad even made me audit a college-level risk management course as part of my criminal training.

Thankfully, we already accounted for Abby being a nosy beyotch. I picture the scenario unfolding exactly as planned: When Abby enters the restroom, her steps will trigger an iPod rigged to play an audio clip of Natalie saying, "Fiona? Is that you? Can you tell Abby I'm not feeling—" The track then dissolves into heavy moans and the sound of liquid splashing into a toilet basin. Once the door shuts, the trigger resets for the next person to hear just in case someone entered the bathroom before Abby.

If that doesn't fool Abby, she'll duck her head under the locked stall to find scarecrow legs stuffed with doll cotton, wearing the exact same pants and cowboy boots Natalie wore today. Any follow-up questions Abby asks to nonexistent Natalie will be answered in a loop of moans.

A few seconds after both Colin and Abby leave the room, an announcement comes on the PA system. "Estelle LaMar, please come to the front desk. You have an emergency phone call."

The tour guide's face drops. My stomach squeezes. I force myself to look away, studying the square plaster ceiling tiles above us. This is the worst part of any con. The people who get hurt in the process. Even if it's just emotionally. Even if it's just temporary.

"Dears, please stay put for one minute. I'll be back in a jiff. Have a look around," she says, because after all, why wouldn't she? Everything in this room is under an alarmed glass case. She shuffles out of the room, running as fast as her old hip can take her. Good thing Notre Dame is out of session for the summer, and the library is short staffed.

When she reaches the front desk, she'll pick up the phone, and a boy disguising his voice as a man's will keep her talking as long as possible. Colin will use the info we extracted about her from across the web, mostly in press releases from the library illustrating all the Good Samaritan work she does. He'll claim he's calling from her credit card company because there's been suspicious activity on her account. He'll list a few of the legit purchases Tig sussed out and then buffer it with outlandish ones. He'll drag out the process to "close" her account as long as possible. If that starts to fail, as a last resort, he'll suggest she cancel all her other credit cards right then.

The heavy doors open a minute later, and "Estelle" comes back, but with some slight adjustments to her appearance. This cosplay version is hunched over more to account for Natalie's extra inches of height. Her shoes are now trendy Toms instead of the sensible flats she wore two minutes ago. For days Natalie and Tig have been monitoring the employees here by hacking into the security cams to case the place and do recon from afar. And this morning, Tig's quick hack of the surveillance footage showed us Estelle's outfit. We cobbled together a replica as best we could in under an hour. The black cardigan we "borrowed" from Lakshmi while she was in the shower fits Natalie a little too tight in the boob area, stretching across her chest instead of being baggy. Natalie-as-Estelle clears her throat. "Sorry about that," she says in her best impression of an old lady, which sounds too much like Natalie to my own ears, like a concert pianist that skips an entire bar of music but keeps on playing, and only his teacher notices.

"Is everything okay?" Lakshmi sidles back up to Natalie in disguise.

My pulse thumps.

"It's fine, dearie," Natalie says. "Just the credit card company." She straightens and swings her arm too fast, too agile, in the direction of the opposite side of the room. "Now, if everyone will follow me, let's take a look at this book from the sixteenth century." She gestures toward the display case at the far end of the room that houses a book about witchcraft, probably written by people who thought there were actual witches back in the day.

Tig stabs at her phone.

Instantly, every alarm in the building switches on. A loud wail screeches, and everyone's hands rise up to cover their ears. A little lightbulb affixed to each alarmed glass case blinks an aggressive red color, and short little whoops ring out, adding to the symphony of sound. The lights in the room switch off, and floodlights spring to life instead, each one blinking.

"Everyone, please evacuate immediately," an announcement blares. "This is an emergency."

Although I can't see him, Colin and Estelle have most likely hung up—her to evacuate, him to intercept the call from the alarm company, which Tig has routed to his phone instead of the main desk.

"Everyone!" Natalie shouts. "Please follow me in an orderly fashion."

Tig runs out of the room, nearly knocking Natalie aside as she does so, and soon the thunder of student footsteps follow as panic ensues. Sydney screams louder than the alarm and grabs James's hand with white knuckles. He doesn't look like he minds. The Daves try their best to calm everyone down but ultimately give up and join the fray of fleeing guests. Only Lakshmi and I remain calm, but Natalie moves over to her.

"Do you smell smoke? We have to go!" She grabs Lakshmi's hand, tugging her out of the room so fast that Lakshmi trips and rolls her ankle in the process. Natalie needs to jet out of here as fast as possible in case Estelle decides to come back and check for stragglers rather than evacuating.

"Ouch! Hold on!" Lakshmi stops in the hallway, rubbing her ankle, but as she bends down, her eyes land on me.

I pretend not to notice.

I quickly pull my trusty lock-picking tools from my back

pocket. I resist the urge to sigh with nostalgia at all the good times we've all had together and make quick work of unlocking the case with a few twists of my tension wrench and Bogota rake. I can't hear the beautiful little *click* in all this noise, but the tools slide into place. A little tug and twist and the case pops open.

In any other circumstance, I'd make sure to be stealthy. I'd be quick as a fox as I lifted the book from beneath my waistband and switched it out with the one under the display. But there's no point in being stealthy when the FBI knows I'm doing this. I switch the book on display and the replica with a sleight of hand and a lot of prayers.

CHAPTER 26

The four of us squeeze into the three-seater at the back of the bus. Lakshmi plops into the row right in front of us and closes her eyes in a ruse that she's sleeping.

My head's still swirling, my muscles locked and on edge, but I force myself to power through the script we wrote and practiced while Lakshmi helped Abby set up for the picnic lunch at the lake.

I make a grand show of flipping through Mom's forgery and letting my breathing increase. I desperately want to take my time, scrutinize every page, but I need to concentrate first and foremost on this ruse for Lakshmi. If we succeed in fooling her, there will be plenty of time later to comb over every inch of this thing.

To play up the ruse, my tongue clucks, and I grow more and more dejected as my eyes blur over everything my mom painstakingly copied.

"Anything?" Colin prompts.

I lower my voice to a whisper . . . but not low enough that Lakshmi won't be able to hear us. "This one's not like the others. There's no clue obviously written in it."

"Maybe there's something already in the text. Something that your mother would know you would recognize," he suggests, basically saying what the FBI thinks verbatim.

I make a big, dramatic sigh. "Okay, let me read more closely."

Tig silently sets the timer. Twelve minutes twenty-eight seconds. That's the amount of time we deemed appropriate for me to read closely and find the "clue" hidden beneath the front cover.

Everything goes excruciatingly slow as the clock ticks down and I keep turning pages for no real reason. I'm too nervous to truly concentrate on finding the real clue. My pulse amps in the process. I've always been crap at convincing anyone about anything, and now our entire plan relies on my delivery for the next few minutes.

Three.

Two.

Tig stops the timer before it reads *one*, and I let out a gasp. "Oh my God!" I say a little too loudly. A few girls two rows ahead spin around, so I deliberately lower my voice. "Tig, can I borrow your lighter?"

"We can't use a lighter on the bus." Natalie chastises me but obviously doesn't follow through with her concern.

Tig unearths a lighter from her pocket and hands it over. She doesn't smoke, of course, but procured said lighter yesterday. She even made a point of flicking it on and off in the hotel room until Lakshmi yelled at her to put it away and Natalie grumbled that pyromania is not a great hobby to adopt.

I drag my nail across the pages to make a scraping sound. Colin clucks his tongue. "What are you doing? You can't pull up the lining. That might ruin it!"

We scripted this out, each of us grabbing lines in order to convey all the exposition so Lakshmi could follow along as much as possible. No doubt the FBI tested the pages, looking for hidden messages, which is why we have to pretend the hidden message is in a place they couldn't have checked without damaging the book and making me suspect it was tampered with.

"Trust me. My mom and I used to pass messages to each other this way." (Not true.) "I thought it was just a fun game at the time, but now I realize . . ." I pause and swallow hard, just like we practiced. Just like Colin coached me. "She was training me."

I lift up the page with as much noise as possible and then hold it to the lighter.

To make invisible ink, mix a little bit of lemon juice with water and then heat the paper a little to show what was written. I hold a random piece of paper to the flame to give off the right odor.

"Look! That's the clue!" I say, staring at nothing but a slight burn mark. While I rustle through the book again to make noise, Colin grabs the burned paper from me and quietly folds it into a neat square, then slides it into his pocket.

"Okay, so what does that give us?" Colin says. He's playing the role of recap right now. "We have a few numbers: Forty-seven. One twenty-three. Eleven." Hopefully, Lakshmi realizes that 123 is the new clue we just found.

"And then a bunch of words or random combos," Natalie adds.

"And a missing one," I point out. I wait a beat before clucking my tongue. "Maybe the numbers all go together? An address? A date?"

"Coordinates," Colin suggests.

"Okay, hold that thought for a second. Let me try to run the ones that aren't plain numbers through a decryption tool and see what I get."

"Good idea." Natalie slaps her hand on the book. "Put them in the order that your mom hit up those places. Which was first? Hesiod?"

"Yep." I could reveal the order to Lakshmi, but I can't hand her *all* the pieces on a silver platter. She needs just enough to figure out the rest herself.

I normally like to decipher these by hand, using the exact methods my mother taught me. But for now, I type *hesiodagd52nd* into a few wrong online ciphers—Nihilist, Gray, Beaufort, Autoclave, etc.—so it's not too obvious I know which is the correct one in case the FBI manages to search through Colin's phone's history somehow. I force a huge sigh out to show I'm not getting anywhere.

"Keep trying," Natalie coaxes in a warm voice.

I type again and wait for the results, then sit up a little straighter. "Hold on, I may have something with this cipher."

Colin laughs. "L-E-Z-E-X-H-A-N-Z-W-H doesn't sound like something." But it should be enough for Lakshmi to figure out we used a Vigenère cipher.

"I need to run it through a common dictionary attack. One sec." I copy the new mix of letters into a common dictionary attack cipher and gasp. "Oh my God."

Natalie's eyes widen. "Water? That's the answer? But it's so vague . . ."

"It's not. It's my mom's way of telling me how to work with the remaining numbers. Forty-seven. One twenty-three. Eleven. And whatever we're missing." I turn to Colin. "Maybe these *are* coordinates for a place near water? Quick, what's the longitude and latitude of a place near Finch Creek in Washington State?" I rattle off the address from memory.

Tig pulls up the answer faster than any of us. Her screen shows the coordinates of 47.3400934°N, 123.1176541°W.

"That's it!" We picked this because the coordinates contain two numbers already: eleven and forty-seven. We decided the missing clue from the guitar factory could point to thirty-four somehow, and that leaves the one we just made up: 123.

We took a risk with this, making up a legit answer even though we have no idea what the real answer might actually be. It's quite possible the FBI already deciphered it and got something else.

"Finch Creek?" Natalie clucks her tongue. "How'd you know that?"

"Because it was the last place my family ever went on vacation. I doubt she's hiding there, in the woods, but I bet she left me a clue as to how to find her at our old campsite. We marked a tree with our initials and this cool carving she did—if I can find that tree, I can find her."

Good luck, FBI. There's got to be millions of trees surrounding Finch Creek.

I notice the unmarked black car the instant we pull into the hotel lot. There's another toward the back.

A guy in plain clothes—jeans and a T-shirt—chats on his cell phone on a bench outside the lobby, and though he's wearing mirrored sunglasses, his eyes are on us.

And he's most likely not alone.

I nudge Colin in the ribs, and his head swivels so he can look at what I see. His face pales.

"I thought he promised to keep the agents away?" I whisper.

He swallows hard. "He did."

Shit.

My pulse beats loud in my ears. Of course they're not going to let us just walk out of here at 3 a.m. Now that we deciphered the clue, they don't need us anymore. Even as bait to lure my mom out of hiding. Their guns can do that just fine.

Which means we can't wait until 3 a.m. or even another hour. We have to escape right now.

The sense of urgency running through my veins pulls me to my feet. On wobbly legs, I push my sweaty hair out of my face as I get off the bus and enter the hotel. I wait for the elevator with the throng of campers, the weight of my necklace grounding me like a hot dish of comfort food. When the doors open, I squeeze inside, making sure to twist just right to avoid staring directly at Lakshmi, who stands in the lobby plucking various brochures for places she's never going to visit. Her fellow agents likely encircle her the moment we're out of sight. They'll probably march right up to our room after she debriefs.

The plain white key card digs into one palm while my other flies to the necklace bouncing against my clavicle. Inside my room, I grip Colin's shoulders. "We have to get out of here. Now."

"Had the same thought," Natalie says, tapping her phone. "Tig's hacking into security now."

Our backpacks are already stuffed with new disguises and not much else. We still have no idea where my mom's clues lead. They could very well lead right to the very place I just sent the FBI.

Tig's mouth flops open. She holds up her phone, and our faces pale.

The agents are everywhere.

Stationed at the bar. Reading a newspaper in the lobby. There's even one huddled in the parking garage.

"How the hell are we going to sneak by them?" Colin rakes a hand over his head. "Escaping a hotel can't be easy."

Natalie and I exchange glances, and the twin smirks that pop onto our lips tell me we both had the same idea. We escaped a hotel once. We can do it again the same way.

"We hide in a cleaning cart, and Natalie dresses as a maid to wheel us out of here."

Colin blinks at me. "I see many holes in this plan. Like the fact that we don't have a maid's cart." He ticks off on his fingers. "Or a maid's uniform."

"Yes we do!" Natalie rummages through her luggage. "I used it on another heist, and we decided to pack it just in case it came in handy. And look at that! It did." Natalie starts pulling her shirt over her head and replacing it with the uniform top.

Colin looks away and crosses his arms. "Okay, but I stand by point number one. No maid's cart."

"Well, not yet. Not until you sweet-talk a maid when she's inside a room and we push the cart away. Then all you need to do is swipe her access card and join us inside the cart."

He purses his lips. "This plan keeps getting worse."

Natalie heads into the bathroom, and when she emerges a minute later, the pants are on, and her frizzy wig is gone, replaced by a dark wig with a bun at the nape of her neck. "Okay, I'm ready. Let's do this before Lakshmi gets here."

She starts to head toward the door, but not before smashing her phone. We follow suit, stomping the life out of those devices with the stilettos Natalie packed for me.

Tig and I shrug our backpacks on and carry Colin's and Natalie's for them. I drop the broken cell phones beneath the silver cover on a discarded room service tray someone left outside their room. A cleaning cart idles a few rooms down. Colin cracks his neck side to side and heads over to it. The three of us hang back, waiting. Listening.

He steps into the room being cleaned. "Excuse me, miss?"

"Sir, you can't be in here."

"Won't touch anything. Promise. I just—this is going to sound so weird." He rattles out a shaky breath. "But I think we might be related?"

Thank God we're a few feet away so she can't hear the giggles that erupt from me and Natalie. That's what he chose as a distraction?

I wave Natalie and Tig forward, and the three of us tiptoe past the room. A quick glance reveals that the maid's an older woman, possibly in her sixties, and her furrowed expression indicates she's incredibly confused.

"Excuse me?"

"Did you have a son?" he guesses, and I hope like hell he guessed right.

Natalie braces her hands on the handles of the cart and pushes it a few feet away. I cringe at the squeaking wheels.

"Yes," the woman answers skeptically.

"He's my father. I know, I know—it's crazy. I only just found out yesterday, and I had to come and meet my—" There's emotion in his voice. "Grandma."

"I don't—No. Not possible." She speaks with a thick accent.

"It is. I just found out. *He* just found out."

"Are you telling me my son cheated on his wife? She's infertile."

"Shit, guys," I whisper. "Better pick up the pace."

Natalie pushes faster, and I start grabbing towels from inside the cart. I toss them in the corner of the soda machine area and say a small apology to the laundry staff that will have to wash those again. As we wait for the elevator, Tig and I squeeze into the cart, knees bent at odd angles, while Natalie hides the backpacks on top under a few more towels.

It was cramped when I rode in the cart alone, but this is like claustrophobia on steroids. My elbow jabs Tig's ribs. Her knee whacks my nose. And Colin's not even here yet.

He rushes toward us just as the elevator doors open. We all squeeze inside the elevator. "Well, I may have just broken up a happy marriage." He eyes the cart skeptically. "How the hell am I supposed to fit in there?"

"Uncomfortably," I mutter.

He hands Nat the key card and then folds his body beside mine, pulling his knees up to his chest. Our limbs are all entangled, and Colin manages to take up more space than the two of us combined. There are body parts I can't even identify jabbing my back.

Every bump of the cart makes me knock into both of them. My body aches from contorting at such odd angles.

"Freedom in one, two, three."

There's a beep as Natalie swipes the key card at what is likely a restricted area that leads to the back entrance, just like last time. She wrenches open the door.

"Excuse me, miss?"

The cart jerks to a stop. We all freeze, my pulse amping.

"Where are you taking that cart?"

A second passes. And then another. I wince on behalf of Natalie. A moment later, she finally responds. "I wasn't taking it anywhere. I just needed to step outside for some fresh air." She sputters a cough. "My asthma's acting up."

The man who stopped her doesn't say anything for a full minute, probably studying her intently, and my heart is in my throat. Inside the cart, Colin grabs my hand and squeezes. I do the same for Tig.

"Okay, only a minute, though. We're fully booked tonight, and I need all rooms ready in time for check-in."

"Understood," she says.

"Actually, I'll join you," the manager says, and it takes all my effort not to suck in an obvious breath.

There's a beep when she swipes again. The door opens. They both step outside.

And we're abandoned.

We can't move. We can't leave. But we're sitting ducks here.

I count to sixty seconds in my head, but there's no sign of the door opening again, Natalie, or even the manager. I count another sixty. Then a third.

After a fourth minute, the door pops open again, and Natalie pulls the curtain on the cart. "Quick, come on. In the middle of that manager guy chastising me for slacking on the job, he noticed someone milling about in the restricted area. An FBI agent stationed here, I'm guessing. He's escorting the guy back to the lobby, but I'm sure it's only a matter of minutes before the FBI find a way to replace him."

I take a deep breath. And make my second daring escape from the FBI in only a few weeks.

CHAPTER 27

The thing no one tells you about running from the law is that it involves very little running. Actual running would just draw attention to us. So we walk casually until we flag down a taxi a few blocks away. A nervous flutter warms my belly and bubbles over into a laugh. We did it. We actually evaded the feds.

Natalie, Tig, and I squeeze into the back seat while Colin takes the front. The first cab drops us off clear across town, and we immediately flag another cab a block away to take us halfway back to where we started. We switch cabs three more times until we finally near the venue for tonight's Hearts for Vandals performance.

Taking a cue from our last escape, we hole up in a gas station bathroom with four hours to go until the concert begins. Natalie doles out our party favors.

A chic sandy-colored wig with cascading waves straight off a runway for me. A sophisticated side part of light brown hair for Colin to give him an older, douchier appearance. A fishtail braid in cobalt blue for Tig. And Natalie—

"This is what I look like. For real."

I gasp. Instead of a heavy wig of curls, a short bleach-blond pixie cut jars me, snipped short to make wig application easier. A tiny yet perky nose commands attention at the center of her face, one she can easily build up into other shapes. Crystal-blue eyes peer out from deep-set sockets, rounded out by a heart-shaped face. Her thin lips look so bare without their usual plump. This is my favorite version of her yet. Natural.

"Does it look bad? Should I put on a wig?" She runs a hand over her hair that's only a few millimeters longer than Colin's buzz cut. "I just figured no one would ever recognize me like this."

Tig's fuchsia lips stretch into a smile. "You look perfect." They're the first words I've ever actually heard come out of her mouth. And they're the best words she could have said.

Natalie beams, and her shoulders relax. She strips off her maid uniform without a care and changes into shorts and a Hearts for Vandals tee. Something completely inconspicuous. Tig and I replace our shirts with Hearts for Vandals tees as well, and Colin slides on a gray blazer and designer jeans. He has the decency to completely turn around this time.

Once we're all in new disguises, we stand in the middle of the bathroom and glance at one another expectantly. Their eyes flick toward my backpack, which contains the book.

They're right. Now that we're finally in a safe place, I should try to find my mom's last clue . . . but there's something I need to do first. Before I comb through this book. Before I find my mother. I need to let Colin know that I'm on his side, too.

I take slow, methodical steps across the small bathroom space. We do love our bathroom rendezvous after all. Four gray walls surround us, and two onlookers watch my every move. The scents emitting from the toilet provide the exact opposite of ambience, but somehow this is the perfect place for me to stand on tiptoes and press my lips against his. For real this time, not because of some ruse.

We've been in sync for weeks, even before he admitted what he'd done, and we're in sync now as our lips part in unison. His hands hesitate for a moment before encircling my waist. I lean into him and let myself finally give in to everything I've been feeling for weeks and everything I tried to forget in the last few days. He tastes like mint gum and possibilities I never thought could be mine. His teeth capture my lower lip and bite gently before he plants drops of butterfly kisses along my chin and up my jawline. His warm breath lands against my ear and sends goose bumps down my arms. When he speaks, his voice is a whisper. "Does this mean you forgive me?"

"Yes." I pull his lips back to mine.

We kiss for another minute or two, each one growing more intense than the last, until Natalie clears her throat with a loud *ahem*.

When we pull away, we're both wearing sheepish grins. I notice Tig and Natalie are holding hands, too.

With Colin at my side, I start to thumb through the book more carefully and methodically than I did on the bus earlier. The FBI's right. There's no obvious clue in this one like the others. It's not written in English but instead Latin calligraphy. I'd painstakingly copied every letter based on images uploaded to the internet multiple times, first for practice, and then finally to re-create both versions of the book I made. I've memorized every curve that belongs on those pages.

And every curve that doesn't.

It's subtle at first. Difficult to see if you don't know to look for it. An extra dip on one letter. A minuscule rise on another.

"Quick, I need paper."

Tig quickly unearths a notebook from her bag and rips out a sheet. I set it on top of the page and copy all the various extra curves and swirls from each individual letter.

When I pull back and squint to eliminate the spaces between the marks, the entire message becomes clear.

Vertical dashes on the left side make a straight line. In the center, the various curves create the illusion of an oval. And on the right, a horizontal line of dashes on top meets with vertical dashes up the side.

It's a number: 107.

"One oh seven!" I say out loud. "That's the last clue." I sag in relief. I figured it out! My dad would be so proud of me. Hopefully my mom will be, too.

Wow, we weren't too far off with our fake-out of 123.

Natalie bites her lip. "Guessing it's like the others and has no connection to anything else?"

At first glance, it all appears to be completely unrelated. *107. Hesiod. 2nd. Ag. 47. 11. D5. 92.5.* Plus whatever we're missing.

I press a palm to my forehead, trying to dull the pounding in my temples. A heavy fog settles over my brain. "I have no idea."

Tig opens her laptop to show a million ciphers she's run on the existing clues. She adds 107 to the mix but comes up with nothing.

Colin squints at her work. "Wait, Natalie, repeat what you just said."

"Um." She taps her lip. "I asked if the clue has any connection to the others?"

Colin snaps his fingers. "Maybe that's it! The key to this. There *isn't* a connection to the others. We have to solve each one individually."

"But I don't know what any of them mean. It's all just . . ." My voice trails off. My mother wouldn't have been able to ensure we'd find *every* clue she left. So maybe she made sure each one had enough information to find her. I get out my new burner phone I packed in my bag and pick a clue at random. I type in *what does Ag mean?*

Google tells me it's short for the word *agriculture,* which isn't any help. But Google also supplies other frequent searches people have done.

What does Ag mean in text?

What does Ag mean in slang?

What does Ag mean in chemistry?

It's the last one that ignites a bulb in my brain. All those chemistry postcards my mother used to send me pop into my mind, each one depicting a drawing of the periodic table and nothing else. I thought it was just her trying to make up for missing my education. Or maybe a new art style of hers, Art Nouveau Chem or some other name she might give it. But maybe it was more than that. It was her preparing me for this moment.

When I click on the search term, I discover that Ag is the chemical compound for silver. And the number 47 rests in the corner of its periodic-table box. Two of the clues, right there.

"Silver!" I jab my finger at the screen. "It's silver! Check the other clues."

It all works out.

107 = Atomic weight for silver.

11 = Group 11 for silver: otherwise referring to a group of elements based on modern numbering known as "coinage metals" due to their usages in currency.

D5 = Period 5 and d-block: There are seven periods in chemistry, and silver belongs in the fifth. And the d-block is on the middle of the periodic table, encompassing elements in columns 3 through 12.

92.5 = The weight to classify silver as "sterling."

Hesiod = Author and creator of the Silver Age of man.

2nd = The Silver Age is the second of five ages according to Hesiod.

"But what does *silver* mean?" Colin reads over my shoulder.

I purse my lips. "I haven't gotten that far."

Tig wraps her fingers around the charm on my silver necklace and taps once.

Blood pounds in my ears. Of course. *Silver.* My necklace.

My heart fills. A few weeks ago, I was worried I wouldn't be able to solve this without my dad's help, but I have a crew here. I know all too well that your crew is stronger than blood.

I scrub vigorously at the metal with my shirt and twist the flame-shaped jewelry in my palms. Everything looks the same as always. No hidden clues that could unlock my entire world. But of course, there wouldn't be anything visible on the outside. It would be hidden, just like the treasure.

"I think there's a clue inside."

Colin and I both reach for the door to the Jewelry Center at the same time, and he snaps his hand back. It only took a quick Google search to locate one a few blocks away. Tig and Natalie hung back at the bathroom so as not to have four fugitives out on the street at once. We still have over three hours before the concert starts.

"Sorry, you go," he says. I start to pull the door open when he reaches out again and stops me. "No, wait. Let me get it for you." He bounces on his toes, head darting, eyes sweeping to mine and then hastily away.

Eek. He's nervous after our kiss earlier. And nerves are the one thing that could kill a con artist on contact.

Glass counters form a maze throughout the store, colorful gems sparkling beneath spotlights. An overexcited woman tries on engagement rings next to a guy who looks like he might pass out. Several clerks eye us suspiciously as we pass. Colin juts his chin toward the back, and I follow his gaze to a counter that sits in front of several gritty drill machines.

When I spin and lift my hair to allow Colin to remove the necklace from my neck, his fingers graze my skin, sending electric bolts of tingles down my back.

An old man comes out of a back room, pushing the loupe onto his forehead to look like he has a third eye. He shuffles over, taking his sweet time. "How can I help you?"

"We need you to melt this." Colin lifts my necklace into his palm, standing so close his warm breath sends the hair on the back of my neck flying.

"I think there's a message inside," I add.

The man holds the necklace up to the light, squinting at it through his lens. "My, it's exquisite. If I melt it, it'll be ruined."

"That's fine," Colin says fast, and then tilts his head to me. "Is it?"

My chest cinches tight. This necklace is my last link to my mother. Removing it permanently feels like removing an arm. I suck back my strangled cry and nod.

The man takes the necklace into the back, where the sound of a machine grinds. Every molecule that connects my body feels coiled tight like a spring, ready to explode. Colin leans against the counter next to me, arm brushing mine.

A few minutes later, the clerk returns and sets down my silver chain. It coils on top of the glass. "You were right." Wrinkles shift on his face to make room for a smile. "This was inside." Next to the chain, he places a small glass vial, the kind amusement parks fill with grains of engraved rice. A miniature roll of paper curls inside the glass.

Both of us reach for it at once. Colin pulls his hand away to give me access. I squeeze the tiny glass.

The clerk clears his throat. "Do you want the melted-down silver? It needs to cool, but—"

Colin looks at me. My mother's charm, my prized possession, is now just a puddle of liquid chemicals. Even the sentimental value is gone. When I find her, I'll create new sentimental memories. "No."

Even though the melted silver is worth something, Colin slides a hundred-dollar bill toward the clerk.

"Hold on, I'll get you change," he says.

But we flee before he even finishes his sentence. Around the back, we huddle in the shadow of a building. With shaky hands, I unscrew the tiny black cap that seals the vial and shake the glass until the paper slips out onto my palm. Black text in size three-point font covers the front.

South Fourth Street Station. G subway line. Williamsburg, Brooklyn.

Tension drains from my shoulders. Not Seattle. Not Finch Creek. I swallow hard. Not anything I knew her well enough to guess.

"A subway station?" My mind spins through the recesses of my memories, searching for a spark of recognition. All I come away with is a furrowed brow.

Colin's already tapping away on his phone. "Weird, there is no South Fourth Street Station on the G line. Or in Williamsburg. There's a Broadway station, though."

I snort. "Then that isn't weird at all. It's another clue."

"Wait, no, I don't think it is." Colin's fingers hastily scroll through an article. "Check this out." He clears his throat. "'Rumors of an underground museum in an abandoned subway station . . . a gallery of sorts that displays illegal art installed on the walls. No one knows for sure if it's true, where it's located, who started it, or how the artists are invited.'"

My body thrums. "I think we know who can answer all of those questions: my mom."

"Guess that's our answer, then. Hearts for Vandals tour jet, here we come." It's heading to Teterboro airport in New Jersey, which is the closest destination to Williamsburg of all the flights.

"Oh crap." Colin purses his lips. "Rumor has it police have put some security systems in place in an attempt to catch the people trying to sneak into the abandoned station, whether to view the art or leave behind more."

I wave my hand dismissively. "Good thing we have tons of experience evading the police."

Four identical VIP passes dangle from our necks as we walk up to the Hearts for Vandals concert. I constructed each during several too-long shower sessions where I spent more time painstakingly cutting out images with an X-Acto knife and hand lettering with ink than conditioning my hair. Frizziness was just a sacrifice I had to make. To further ensure our ruse goes off without a hitch, we purchased four legit concert tix via a ticket-selling app and an untraceable disposable prepaid Visa card.

Once we're past security, Colin leads the charge, waving us through the crowd as though he has the entire arena layout memorized. Which of course he does.

I have to admit he looks amazing in the gray-blazer-and-designer-jeans combo. It takes all my effort not to stop him in the crowded hallway and press him against the wall to do all the naughty things running through my mind. But although we've been pretending he's my boyfriend through this entire trip, now that he may actually be, we have to pretend we're not together. After all, a smarmy radio station representative can't be dating a screaming seventeen-year-old superfan.

We reach the VIP area, and the bouncer takes one look at our passes and nods, and I lift my chin in victory. That's the problem with being a forgery artist. You rarely get to take credit for your excellent work.

Colin continues strutting through the hallway until we reach the greenroom. He doesn't even hesitate before he pushes the door open and does a complicated handshake with the guy in the doorway as though they've known each other for years instead of ten seconds.

The four heartthrobs of Hearts for Vandals lounge on plush leather couches, each with varying degrees of long, floppy hair. Jackson's the main cutie, but the other guys have swarms of nervous teenage girls vying for their attention, filling this room up with more hormones than ninth-grade sex-ed class. A long refreshment table stretches against a back wall, filled with bowls of food sorted by color: green M&Ms, red Skittles, and what appear to be potato chips made from purple potatoes. Guys in suits and blazers mill about on the outskirts, each with a phone or walkie-talkie pressed to their ear.

Tig lets out a cough, and Colin follows her line of sight toward a guy with slicked-back hair and a glitzy silver blazer talking to a woman with a clipboard. Walt Windsor, manager extraordinaire for Hearts for Vandals. According to an article in *Rolling Stone* six months ago, he's super into astrology, exists on a diet of legumes and wheatgrass, and will only sleep on 100 percent silk sheets. Not the most helpful bit of info, but we'll use what we can. Natalie affixed Colin's ear with a clip-on earring in the astrological sign for Aries.

Colin beelines right toward him, motioning for us to follow.

I smooth down my skirt and turn to Natalie, trying to give her my best *oh my God I can't believe I'm here* face. She fans her hand in front of her mouth in equal excitement. It's still weird to see her real appearance. Tig doesn't change her normal stone-faced expression at all.

Colin leads with his hand stretched out. "Hey, mate," he says in an epic fake British accent. I withhold my urge to side-eye him, but he insisted the accent would help sell this. And because he can't do anything without being awesome at it, he mastered the dialect with only a few hours of practice. "Nigel Smythe here. From WRQA 106.3."

Walt studies him up and down suspiciously before he lands on the Aries earring, and his eyes sparkle. He reaches out and shakes Colin's hand somewhat tentatively.

"Wanted to introduce you to the contest winners and confirm everything's good to go for the jet tonight?" Colin hits him with his gorgeous smile, and I notice that the face of the girl with the clipboard lights up at the sight of it. Stay away, lady.

"I'm sorry, but what contest?" Walt eyes him up and down one more time. "And how old are you?"

Colin laughs as though he's heard that one a million times. "Thanks, mate. Best compliment I've heard all night." He pats him on the shoulder like they're now old pals. "Didn't you get my email the other day? Or the one from Tommy last week explaining the whole shebang?"

Both backdated emails have already been planted into Walt's account, of course. Tommy's the account manager at the record label, the one person Walt might actually trust.

Walt squints at Colin before pulling out his phone and scrolling through. His brows shoot up when he undoubtedly finds the email from "Nigel" from two days ago, introducing himself and explaining that he'll be accompanying the contest winners to the show tonight as well as on the plane ride from South Bend to Teterboro, plus tomorrow's show in New York City. Walt lets out a little squeak as he goes farther down and finds the email from Tommy, which explains that the record label hooked up with the radio station to put on the contest, and though it's short notice, he expects Walt to work out all the details.

Walt rakes a hand through his hair, and his shoulders tense. "Sorry, yes, yes." He loosens his collar. "Had a momentary lapse there, but of course everything's all set for the flight tonight. Remind me again the winners' names?"

Colin rattles off our new fake names that match the new fake IDs.

"Fantastic," Walt says. "If you'll just excuse me for a second, I have some business to take care of. Please enjoy the refreshments until the show starts." He motions his hand at the table of food and then runs to an office to scramble.

And just like that we've got a foolproof exit strategy and back-stage seats for Colin's "favorite" band.

CHAPTER 28

After spending an unbearable two hours screaming my head off as Hearts for Vandals shimmied onstage, and then another hour or so backstage elbowing the other giddy teens for prime real estate in Jackson's breathing space, I deserve the peace and quiet of the plane. I make an excuse about being tired, and Jackson doesn't even blink as he turns his attention to the rest of his fan base joining us for this three-hour flight.

The requisite news articles of our disappearance and APBs hit the web as I settle into my seat. This time all four of our pictures appear, and I have to laugh at the class photo they used of Natalie in her pink wig and fluorescent-yellow contact lenses.

Authorities are seeking information on Fiona Spangler and Colin O'Keefe, who are believed to be traveling with Natalie Babineaux and Tig Ramirez, last seen in South Bend, Indiana, on the Coast-to-Coast Connect Teen Tour using fake identities.

"I'm so worried about them!" Abby Ito, head counselor on the tour, said when questioned. "They went straight up to the room, but no one ever saw them again! We can't seem to get ahold of their parents, either."

Video surveillance footage captured the four escaping out a back door in a laundry cart.

The group is suspected of stealing prized artifacts from several locations, including the Hesburgh Library. Authorities believe they are heading to the greater Seattle area via train and may try to hitch a ride out of Chicago.

"Well, bright side, they bought our ruse?"

Colin bites his lip. "Now we just have to hope they don't find that tree at Finch Creek before we find the subway station."

I flick my chin over to where Jackson lounges on a plush leather chair, tilts his head back, and snags a grape in his teeth while no less than six giggling girls dangle branches over his face like he's a Greek god. Really glad my excuse about being tired got me out of that one. "I'm surprised you're not going gaga over Jackson like all the other groupies on this flight," I joke to Colin.

"My fandom may have once been super strong, but there's something else I'm much more into these days." He squeezes my hand, and for a moment, I can relax.

I tilt my head against the window, watching stars sparkle in the night sky. A whole world out there I've never explored, and yet the plane flies on, keeping me prisoner. The stale air reaches out like claws around my neck, choking me with claustrophobia. But the real problem isn't the feeling of being trapped. It's that the tour's already over. The heists are done. But I can't ever go home.

Whether I find my mother or not, this is my new forever. I won't ever hear Dad's voice again or rule the roost back at Amberley Academy. I can't let my hair grow long or go back to blond. Once we evade the FBI, I'll always be on the run.

I'll be just like my mother.

As soon as the flight lands, we part ways with the band under the ruse that "Nigel" will be escorting us to our swanky hotel for tonight. I'm forced to let out a few requisite squeals as I tell Jackson I can't wait to see him again tomorrow for the next concert.

My shoulders tense as I weave my way through the airport, keeping my head down, making sure not to look at any of the security cameras around until we launch ourselves into a waiting taxi. Our cab cruises through the deserted streets of New Jersey, empty at 5 a.m. We change cabs a few more times, first stopping at an Amazon locker in Hackensack to pick up a bunch of supplies we overnighted that we knew we couldn't risk bringing through airport security. Finally, the last cab glides toward Williamsburg.

We file out and open our identical bubble umbrellas. The clear plastic distorts our features enough to fool any security cams. Town houses in various shades of brick line the deserted street, dark except for a few scattered lit windows. Rain drums at a slant against the buildings and sneaks beneath our umbrellas, the sound pinging off the metal garbage can a few feet away.

For the next few blocks, our marching feet slosh in puddles. According to research we found on the internet, all the pedestrian entrances to the old, abandoned G station in Williamsburg are boarded up, long rendered invalid. The simplest way to get to the abandoned station is to slip into the dark tunnel that stems from an active station and combat mold and rats until we reach the old station's entrance. But Big Brother is watching the entrance, so we need to find another way into the tunnel.

Like a service entrance that Tig found on a schematic map.

Tig stops short in front of a boarded-up recessed doorway. She checks her phone, then the door, then pats the pristine wood with her palm. The surrounding wooden planks boast years of grime, weathering, and faded graffiti, but a few planks look brand-new.

"This is it?" I ask, and Tig nods. "But . . . it's boarded up? You said this was an active service entrance."

Tig glares at the wooden boards as if they personally offended her and holds up her phone. A screenshot of a surveillance image dated yesterday shows the same doorway, only without the new-looking boards.

"So these weren't here yesterday?" Panic races up my spine. "That's coincidental . . . and suspicious."

We shut our umbrellas and crowd into the tight alcove, cramped shoulder to shoulder. I place several flashlights in a row at the bottom, shooting enough light upward for us to see.

Colin pries out each shiny nail that secures the wooden board to the entrance. A rusty door with a simple lock chain hides behind the unwelcome wooden plank. I step forward to inspect the lock, pursing my lips at the simplicity of it. I fit one of my glinting silver tools and twist. The lock opens easily. Too easy.

I push the door open. Inside, red laser beams crisscross from wall to wall in a dark corridor, each one a moving trip wire. They're the kind of maze only an Olympic gymnast could conquer with ease. One wrong step, and we won't even have enough time to cover our ears from the alarm before police swoop in and haul us away for life.

"This wasn't mentioned in any of the research we did on the plane," Natalie whispers.

"Oh, good." My eyes lock on a sweeping red beam that probes the dank entryway. "So that trigger alarm right in front of our faces is just our collective fantasy?"

I bite back a growl and turn to Tig. "Can you cut the power?"

In the glow of the flashlight, she looks scary-story-ghost pale. She shrugs and starts changing settings on her laptop. After a moment, her eyes widen, and my stomach coils with dread.

Tig shoves her laptop into Natalie's arms and beams a circle of light on the point where the first laser starts. She waves it around as if to say, *Look, you see that?*

I cross my arms with impatience. "Yep, it's a laser maze all right."

Natalie squints. "The glistening stuff around the projector box?" she guesses. "It looks . . . glued on."

Tig shoots her a finger gun. *Bingo.*

"Which means you can't hack it to cut the power, because it's not part of the real security system?" I guess. All of us turn our heads to the sweeping beams. One of us has to get across and shut off the projector box.

Blood drains from my face. Colin can't charm his way through this one. Tig's stealthy with machines, not real life. Natalie's a master of disguise, but not a master of anything else.

I swallow. "I've actually conquered one of these before."

What I don't mention is that my mom installed it in the house for practice when I was nine. And out of the thousand times I practiced, I only ever beat it . . . once.

The others step back, clearly resigned to hand me the reins of this police trap.

You can do this, I coax myself.

I crack my neck from side to side, and then jump up and down in place. My nerves congregate in my cells, vibrating at high frequency.

It takes me a good seven minutes to recognize the sequence of sweeping probes—it's the same pattern I practiced with as a child. It's not twenty beams each moving randomly. It's three beams with alternating patterns.

Banishing my nervousness, I enter a zen zone. Eyes zoomed. Sounds ignored. Mind focused. I square my shoulders before lifting my leg over the first sweeping laser.

It's like a dance. My mind calculates each twirl several moves ahead while my feet follow along to the count of eight. I contort my body into a back handspring as a red beam passes mere centimeters from my nose. No time to catch my breath, instead I flip over, ducking underneath another beam, then dropping to the floor for a millisecond, army crawling while a glowing red line chases me. Before it catches me, I hop to my feet and sweep my torso forward like a head-swinging dance move in a music video.

One beam glides upward, so I duck down. The next zooms across, and I fit my body into the tight triangle of space. Then I sink low until I only have two more beams left. I've got this.

When I reach the end, I stand on tiptoes and scrutinize the box creating the lasers. It *is* glued on. That fact, combined with the recognizable pattern, gives me confidence that this box wasn't planted here by police trying to keep people out . . . but rather by my mother, making sure the right person got in.

With a flip of a switch on the side of the box, I deactivate the lasers and let out a breath when the glittering red lines disappear.

I wave my friends forward.

"How did you—?" Natalie squints at the box.

"I think my mom planted it," I say, and they all nod. "I hope so, anyway."

We yank open the service entrance, and together we descend the rickety steps that take us lower and lower into the dank subway tunnels. The squeak of rats and water sloshing through pipes cover the sound of my raging pulse. It smells worse than the garbage tunnels at the amusement park.

We reach the dark depths of the abandoned part of the subway station. I expect brown sludge to hang from the arched ceiling like stalactites and years of piled-up trash to conceal the subway tracks, but the place looks pristine. The glistening tiled floor smells

Pine-Sol fresh. A shiny wood stain coats the benches propped in the center, each looking newly sanded and refurbished. And the walls. Oh God. The walls. Glorious paintings cover the subway tiles. Cartoon pigs squealing. A photorealistic mural of the city at night that gives me the best view I've seen so far on this trip. An intricate sketch of two rats crawling on top of each other.

I spin around, my mouth open in awe of all this gorgeous artwork, on display but hidden from spectators. No one can view it or experience it, defeating the entire purpose of a gallery. I feel a strange sort of camaraderie for an artist who can never take credit for what she's created, just as my own forgeries hang in galleries, attributed to someone else. The articles indicated that a variety of artists must have found their way down here to leave their mark based on the various art techniques used, but as I scrutinize each mural, I know they're all my mom's. She can adjust her technique to mirror anyone's, and that's exactly what she's done to conceal her involvement down here.

My fingers itch at my sides, gripping the tube of my flashlight tighter. I imagine trading the light for the thin reed of a paintbrush, squeezing my mark into the space between the murals.

"What are we searching for exactly?" Natalie shifts from foot to foot, craning her neck at all the art.

When I stand at the far end of the platform, facing straight ahead, I see it.

Two long lines converging to a vanishing point to create what looks like a road in the distance of the image. Four separate lines fanning out, two on either side of the original two, creating the walls. A pattern of horizontal rectangles cascading across their surfaces. At intervals, long poles rise vertically and interrupt the whole image.

The carving my mother did into the tree at Finch Creek. It was this subway station.

She knew, even then, that she was leaving. And worse still, she knew exactly where she was headed.

I stop short, my flashlight pointed at the wall. Before me stands a painting of a young girl with mischievous eyes and colors that shouldn't exist in nature, yet the painting insists they belong. Phthalo blue and manganese purple highlight the cheekbones. Alizarin crimson plumps the lips with a hint of vermillion. Cadmium yellow and Hooker's green comprise the unexpected flesh. Despite the intense use of color, the hues in this painting are faded, dustier than all the rest.

"Holy shit," Colin says, pointing his flashlight at the same painting as mine. "That's you."

My heart thumps in my chest. The girl in the painting looks like she's about to roll her eyes and make a snarky comment. Because I was. My mom snapped this exact pose of me only minutes before she fled my life forever. For a moment, I'm sidelined by both her cruelty and her brilliance. She hid everything in plain sight and armed me with all the information to find her.

Your age when I left, now with the standard term. Paint an inch thick, bugs instead of eyes. You belong on the surface. Or so it seems. It all makes sense, the photo of me the day she left, painted an inch thick on subway tiles where bugs might crawl over my eyes. I'm on the surface—the wall—but only in appearances. Beneath the tiles, there's more.

"This is it," I say, my voice echoing off the high ceiling. "If there really is a stash of all the art she stole, it will be here."

We descend onto the tracks to get closer to the walls, each of us jumping off the platform like no one in their right mind would do in a working subway station.

I wield a crowbar. "Stand back, guys."

They point their flashlights at the wall. A battle cry rips from my throat as I raise the crowbar and thrash it into the tile like a golf swing. The painting's eye—*my* eye—cracks in two. Shards drop onto the floor and mix with the years of decay. I allow myself one moment to mourn, throat constricting, before my weapon smashes into the painting's mouth.

All the pent-up anger about my mom surges out of my veins and into my swing. My crowbar punctures the tiles again and again, splinters of ceramic flying like confetti. Dust rains down on us. When a gap widens in the wall, I toss down my crowbar and wipe sweat from my brow.

"That was hot," Colin says.

I stick my hand inside the hole and graze something smooth and long. When I try to lift it, my arms give out. "A little help?"

Colin nudges me aside. A large canvas covered in plastic wrap crinkles as he heaves it out of the hole and rests it on the subway floor. I gasp at the gorgeous Renaissance painting, preserved in perfect condition inside the wrapping. *The Concert* by Johannes Vermeer.

Colin and I lug another plastic-wrapped painting out of the hole in the wall. *Christ in the Storm on the Sea of Galilee* by Rembrandt van Rijn.

Natalie bends down to inspect them. "Wait, are these . . . ?"

"The Isabella Stewart Gardner heist." Tingles dance along my skin. In 1990, thieves liberated thirteen paintings from the museum in Boston worth a total of three hundred million dollars. No, not *thieves*. I clamp a hand over my mouth. *My mother*. And her crew: Jeremy, Nikki, Amanda. She was just a teenager then.

The other eleven paintings still at large from the Gardner heist join the first two on the platform.

The real human-skin book, guitar, and skull prop follow.

"Sweet." Colin lifts a violin over his head, which must be the rare 1727 Stradivarius that was stolen from a renowned violinist's apartment in New York City back in 1995. Another notch on my mother's criminal timeline. "You learn guitar, I'll learn this, and together we'll create the greatest band that ever played on stolen instruments."

I snatch the violin case from his hands and peel off the plastic wrap. "Don't break anything. I don't know what my mom's intentions are for these things."

He squeezes my hand, and the two of us share a smile at all we've accomplished together.

"Incoming!" Natalie balances a box of six wobbling Imperial Fabergé eggs. Exquisite jewels and precious metals surround each of the ovals, all neatly preserved in Mom's careful wrapping.

My heart pounds. In 1918 thieves pillaged the czar's palace in St. Petersburg and stole fifty-two of the eggs. Most have been recovered, but eight remain at large, believed to have been sold to private investors, and then stolen several times.

We don't just have a fortune on our hands. We have the most wanted pieces of missing art in history. Selling these would make us the richest people in the world. Why would my mother go to extreme lengths to steal these precious items only to bury them in a wall for years? It makes no sense, not when she could have fenced the art and set up a trust fund legally, if that was her intention.

"Wait." Natalie bolts upright. "Do you guys hear that?"

We freeze. My heart pounds, but I hear the sound of footsteps growing louder and louder.

"Someone's coming!" Natalie whisper-shouts. "We have to hide!"

My pulse revs. I scramble after my friends into the hole in the wall, and we cling to one another in the dark space.

"No need to hide," says a female voice. "I see you got my messages, Fiona."

I'd recognize that voice anywhere.

My mother.

CHAPTER 29

My mom. In the flesh. Standing in the same room as me. The stolen art around me becomes worthless compared to the sentimental value of getting my mother back. "Mom?" I ask, voice quivering. I have to make sure I'm not hallucinating. That I haven't been dreaming this up for so long that my subconscious decided to give in to the fantasy. That she's really here and won't ever leave me again.

She pushes her stringy, washed-out-blond hair behind her ears, revealing the hard lines etched around her mouth like an artist's pencil marks. When she hunches forward defensively, bones protrude from her shoulders at sharp points. Her smile shines like a beacon in my memories, but now her thin lips barely fit on her gaunt face. Time was the cruelest thief of all. If this were an art critique, I'd have to describe her the only way that makes sense: cadaverous. She looks one step above a corpse, like she gave all her life and energy into the forgeries and left nothing else for herself.

Mom's bony wrist points a scrawny finger at me, and little pieces inside my chest meld together, like I'm whole again. I crawl out of the hole and climb onto the platform, my steps echoing like bombs. The features on my face wobble as all the emotions I've held back for years break free. A tear cascades down my cheek, but I don't bother to hide it.

I fold my arms around my mother's skinny frame and squeeze. The scent of lavender and something else, maybe tequila, engulfs me. My throat gets tight. My mom. My role model. But her body retreats from mine in incremental centimeters. A shiver runs down my spine. This is a one-way hug, me wrapped around her, her arms hanging limply at her sides.

I step out of the hug. Mom stands stiff as a stranger, her eyes narrowed over my shoulder. At Tig. At Natalie. At Colin.

A fierce need to protect my friends overwhelms me. Mom's wild eyes flick to me, still stuck in the angry squint, and she leans in close to my hair. "We need to take what we can and run."

So many questions pound against my forehead, but, my voice cracking, I ask the most pressing of all. "Why? Why did you do all this?"

"Because they were about to catch me." Her eyes dart around the room, squirrel fast, as though she expects FBI agents to spring out of the walls. "I had to go. Before that happened. Before they took me away from you."

"But—" I suck in a deep breath. "You took yourself away from me."

Her hands suddenly reach out and grip my shoulders in tight claws. "Don't you see? I had to. It was the only way for us all to stay safe."

These are the words I've been longing to hear. They should make sense. Finally connect like all the clues she left me.

But the problem is I can't decipher this new piece of information. Dad and I were safe this whole time. The only reason we got caught is because we were following *her* trail.

I pry her hands from my shoulders. "Where were you this whole time?"

"Here." She practically spits the word, as though it should be obvious. "Fake name. Fake identity. Basement apartment. Waiting for you." Her tongue pushes out one side of her cheek and a wave of utter nostalgia hits me so intense, I nearly collapse right there. This was the face she used to make when she was angry. "I was going to send you the first clue on your eighteenth birthday." She barks a harsh laugh, the first spark of life I've seen in her. For a moment, her eyes light up with an electric blue that sends a wave of longing rocketing through me before her face descends into the chiaroscuro of shadow. "But it seems you beat me to the punch."

The child long dormant in me fights back tears. I finally have my mom back, and she's practically spitting her disappointment at me. She's even mad I one-upped her. My heart cracks into two clean pieces. I followed her clues. I did what she wanted. And I still didn't make her proud.

Hands land on each of my shoulders. Colin and Natalie. My allies. The ones who had my back this whole time, even with Colin's betrayal. Tig hangs back, but she's there for me, too, in her own way.

The straight line of Mom's lips evolves into a grimace directed at my friends (my allies).

I angrily wipe a hot tear from my cheek. "But why didn't you take Dad and me with you?"

Mom crosses her arms in a protective stance, as effective as a bulletproof vest. "You would have been a burden. I couldn't bring you here until the trail ran dry."

Her words puncture my heart like she stabbed a knife straight into my gut. Me. *I* would have been a burden, not Dad.

"But I waited for you in order to claim this legacy, didn't I? I didn't have to do that." She blinks at me as if expecting something.

A thank-you, maybe. Or for me to get my butt in gear and haul her "legacy" of million-dollar paintings out of here. Will I still be a burden to her once we flee? Will she find a way to ditch me again if she deems the situation too dangerous? She's resorted to great lengths in order to stay away from me in this warped sense of protection.

There's still so much I don't understand.

Suddenly her hand encircles my wrist, as tight as handcuffs. "We can't stay here. We have to run. Not them." Her words turn cold. "Me and you. Only us."

I tug my arm free. "Mom, wait—"

Mom doesn't blink at my words. "Did you learn nothing from what I taught you? If they're after you, you run. That means away from people like them." She glares at my friends. "You can only trust blood."

But that's the thing. My dad and I had been after *blood* for years, and she kept running from us. Yet this whole summer, the other three people in this tunnel had my back. They gave up their *lives* for me with no promise that we'd make it out of this unscathed. Hell, they didn't even care about getting a cut if we retrieved the stolen goods. All they cared about was helping me reunite with my mother. And okay, sure, maybe Natalie and Tig were in it for each other as well.

And Colin—although he may have had an ulterior motive initially—he relinquished that immunity offer. He chose me over his own freedom.

I don't want to be the kind of person who abandons the people she loves in favor of a life in hiding. Or the kind of person who rats out her friends in order to save herself. I'd rather go down with this ship than take a lifeboat and watch it all sink without me.

This whole time I've been chasing a memory of my mother that didn't exist, a treasure I tried to claim as mine.

But it wasn't. It was stolen.

My mother abandoned me years ago. Now it's my turn to do the same. The only way to save my friends *and* myself is to let my mother go for good.

The tears I've been holding back stream down my face. Now I have to do the hardest thing I've ever had to do in my life—I have to look my mother in the eye as I turn my back on her plan. "Mom, this is my boyfriend," I say, seemingly out of nowhere. But she needs to know who he is to fully understand everything I'm about to say. I point to Colin, and he straightens. But my mom only spares him a cursory glance before her eyes start to roam along the art again. It confirms everything I suspected. She doesn't really care about me. In fact, I'm not a real person to her, just an imperfect copy.

"His dad is the head of the Northern California branch of the FBI's white-collar-crime division."

She freezes.

"I'm giving you a one-hour head start to get out of the city before I call his dad and give him your location."

Her eyes widen, scared and rabid. She doesn't hesitate, she grabs the nearest treasures—a Fabergé egg, a Rembrandt, and several more paintings—whatever she can fit inside her scrawny arms. She runs out of the tunnel with her arms stuffed, without so much as a goodbye.

I collapse onto my knees on the grimy subway floor and three sets of arms engulf me, rubbing my back, running fingers through my hair, and whispering that it will be okay. It has to be. Because they are my family now.

When the hour is up, I clear my throat, desperate to disguise all the emotion swirling behind my lips. "Colin, call your dad."

He blinks at me. "Wait. You were serious? I thought that was just a threat before."

I hold his gaze. "I want to strike a deal. We turn in this stolen art and tell him everything we know about my mother. Remind him the only things we stole were replicas, and we'll turn those in, too." I swallow hard. "And in exchange, I want immunity for the five of us. My dad included."

Turns out this entire time I was on a mission to rescue the wrong parent. But I can fix that now. I can fix everything.

Colin gets out his phone and makes the call.

EPILOGUE

"You got this, kiddo."

Dad's voice buzzes in the earpiece. Some dads indulge in their kid's pastimes by cheering from the sidelines at games, but my dad is by my side once again and helping me with another con.

I take a deep breath as I round the corner onto Sixteenth Avenue and come face-to-face with an amazing hidden wonder nestled between apartment buildings. Two brick structures conceal an elaborate staircase hidden between them: 163 steps covered in mosaic tiles, each one hand glued by local artists and neighborhood residents to create a swirling ocean that rises through a garden until it reaches the sun at the very top. It takes my breath away.

"Remember. Just act like you belong. As long as you don't look suspicious, no one's gonna—"

"Dad!" I whisper-shout as my feet slap the first step. "I think by now I'm the crowning expert in heists *and* scavenger hunts. You just enjoy the fresh air and the lack of handcuffs and let me do the hard part."

There's a groan in my ear. "You do realize we got fresh air in prison, right? Only an hour of it a day, but still!" In my earpiece,

I hear him take a deep breath. "This is lovely, though. Have I said thanks yet?"

"Only enough times that I've already considered it your new catchphrase." I smile, savoring his voice in my ear and sucking a big gulp of fresh air myself. After all, neither of us would be tasting this kind of freedom if it wasn't for me . . .

And Colin.

Thinking of him sends a new resolve coursing through me. I pull my shoulders back and climb the beautiful secret staircase hidden in this residential neighborhood. A unique but rarely visited tourist attraction in San Francisco, and the perfect place to hide the first clue.

Now that our journey is done, another one begins. Find the sound of the ocean; thankfully, you don't have to break in.

Sure, I could have created a clue that required a complicated cipher in order to solve it, but I don't want Colin to have to work *too* hard to find the treasure at the end of this scavenger hunt. After traveling the country together to steal concealed clues left behind by my mom, it seemed like a creative scavenger hunt was the very best way to get my message across to him. Three clues. Three locations. Three chances. Just like our summer heist-fest. And my dad was happy to help me plant the clues, even if he doesn't quite approve of the reason for said clues. After all, no dad is ready for their seventeen-year-old to have a steady boyfriend.

I race back down the stairs and hightail it to the waiting getaway car idling a few blocks away, mostly because we couldn't find a parking spot on this street and we've had enough run-ins with the law lately without adding a parking ticket to the mix.

I slide into the passenger seat. "Step on it!"

Dad rolls his eyes at me. "If by 'step on it' you mean slowly merge into traffic and then drive the speed limit, you got it."

"You'd make a terrible getaway driver. I hope this doesn't mean we're aligning with the right side of the law now."

He scoffs. "For traffic, yes. For everything else?" He winks.

I relax into the seat, glad my world's back to normal. Somewhat. I get out my cell phone to bang out a text but see I have a few missed ones already.

Colin: Hey, what's the big surprise? Where are we meeting? I thought you said to be ready by three?

I roll my eyes. It's 3:02. Crimes can't always be punctual. I scroll to the next text.

Natalie: Tig asked me to be her girlfriend! She actually asked! With words!

I'm not sure which to reply to first, but I always have Natalie's back, so I send a gazillion confetti and heart emojis to her and then some to Tig, plus a requisite warning that if she hurts my gal, she answers to me. On second thought, I send the same thing to Natalie. To Colin, I reply with:

Fiona: Hidden out in the open you'll find your first clue, a beautiful art installation the community grew. Reach the top and you will see, the next step to reaching me.

As Dad swerves through traffic to the next destination, three little dots appear and then disappear. Finally, Colin's response comes:

Colin: Nothing is ever easy with you, is it?

He tacks on a smiley emoji and then adds:

That's what I like best about you.

Dad weaves the car along the coastline, the breeze flowing through the open windows and sending my dark locks flying around my face. I could let it go back to my natural blond color now, but I've gotten used to the choppy black bob Colin fashioned for me out of necessity rather than skill. Maybe I'll go back to blond when school starts up again for the two of us in a few weeks. Or maybe I'll embrace the new me now.

As Dad drives, I try to savor the things I thought I'd lost. The two of us, together. The scent of salt wafting from the ocean. Our three-story Victorian house, forever in need of upkeep.

We pull up along a jetty located on San Francisco Bay, and Dad manages to steer the car into a space.

"Good. I could use a little help on this one." I unbuckle.

Dad scoffs. "And here I thought you only wanted me to be your chauffeur."

I wave my hand dismissively. "And moral support. You can never have too much of that."

Dad gets out of the car and stretches his legs. A ginormous structure greets us, constructed out of carved granite and marble from a demolished cemetery. The Wave Organ's exactly the type of morbid curiosity my mom would have loved. The sculpture creates a semicircle facing the ocean, complete with a terrace and benches.

Concrete pipes as well as PVC pipes jut out into the water at various elevations. When the waves crash against the pipes, they create gurgling musical notes that harmonize with a sound similar to putting a conch shell against your ear.

It's a magical place, created by both nature and man. It's the perfect setting for this clue.

"Where should I put it?" I ask Dad as I step over the cobblestones.

He purses his lips. "How about nowhere? As a dad, I have to say that, right?"

"As a dad, you have to support my dreams, and this is one of them. Making a boy I like go through extreme and unnecessary lengths just to hang out with me."

"Over there, then." He points to the longest pipe, the one that stretches over the makeshift benches and appears to dangle precariously over the ocean.

I affix this clue plus a five-dollar bill to the underside of the pipe, right above the seating, so if Colin sits down to glance at the ocean and looks up, he'll find it. The money is because I'm a twenty-first-century kind of girl, and I'm not going to let a guy pay for himself on a date.

Now it's time to get cheesy on you, one last task before we rendezvous. Find the treasure at the edge of a maze and a mirror, you have to look closely and it'll all become clearer. The treasure's not an object but the person writing this note. Yes, I called myself a treasure, but I'm your treasure—so feel free to gloat.

Dad shakes his head at me as we stride to the car. "Not the romantic words I would have chosen."

"Would you have preferred something hidden within a book bound in human skin?"

I expect him to laugh at the ridiculousness of Mom's clues, but instead a sad expression washes over his face.

"Hey, I'm sorry for mentioning her." I grab his hand, squeezing tight for a second before letting go. The love of his life chose a life on the run rather than one with him. That's not something you can easily get over. Or legally separate yourself from, if you choose to do that one day. Even if you *are* a rock-star lawyer as your side hustle from your *real* job of running cons.

Dad sucks in a shaky breath. "It's okay. I need to . . ." He swallows hard. "I need to move on. I know that."

But it sounds like he's having a difficult time convincing himself of this.

The lump that lodges in my throat and makes it hard to breathe indicates I am, too. There's still one mystery she left behind.

Where is she now?

She evaded the FBI again, on the run once more, and a little part of me feels relieved that my grab at freedom and safety for my loved ones didn't result in iron bars and an unflattering beige jumpsuit for her. True, if she was behind bars, I could visit her one day and maybe finally say all the words I couldn't bring myself to utter in the subway tunnel. But with her on the lam, I have to let her go for good.

We get in the car and stay silent for most of the way to the final location. When Dad pulls up in front of Pier 39, I place my palm on his shoulder. "Are you going to be okay?"

He squeezes his eyes shut for a moment but nods. "I've been trying to find the right time . . ." He rakes his hand through his dark hair. "But nothing seems right. Or perfect. Or—" He stretches over me to unlatch the glove compartment and then pulls out a tiny, velvet box. His hands shake when he presents it to me.

I squint at the box and then at him. For some reason, I hold my breath when I open it.

Nestled inside, resting on delicate white silk, is a beautiful silver chain with four flat circle charms dangling from the center.

"To replace the one you lost and represent the people you gained."

Tears press against my eyes, and I hug it to my chest. I never thought I'd be able to replicate the sentimental value of the necklace my mom gave me, but as I string this one around my neck, it already feels like it belongs with me more than that one ever did. I wrap my arms around Dad. "Thank you."

"You're welcome, hon."

I raise my brow and tap one of the charms. "Any clues hidden in here?"

He laughs. "Wouldn't the FBI like to know . . ."

I laugh, too, then gesture toward the pier up ahead. "I should . . ."

Suddenly Dad's face gets serious. "If he tries anything—anything at all—I'll kill him!" He presses his lips together. "Well, actually, I don't condone violence, so maybe I'll just ban him from coming over on a school night. And I'm banning both of you from hotel rooms!"

I roll my eyes. "Dad, you can trust him now." I don't even hesitate when I say the next part. "After all, I do."

Dad smiles. "Have fun, hon. But not *too* much fun. And remember your curfew! I'll be waiting up!"

"Of course I have the one father in the world that doesn't care at all if I stay out late on an illegal crime spree, but a date? Gotta be home by ten."

"Nine thirty!" He gives me a devious smile. "And remember, don't stray from the plan."

"I won't." I get out of the car and give Dad a tiny wave. A burglar usually wears all black for a con, and I've donned a little black dress in compliance. I guess Natalie's sense of style rubbed off on me—after all, she helped me pick out this ensemble.

I waltz down Pier 39, passing by young children licking ice cream cones and families looking out at the water. I stop in front of a nondescript building and pay my five-dollar admission fee. Inside, a psychedelic array of flashing neon lights sparkles between columns of mirrors. The entire place is lit with black light that turns everything inside the colors of an Andy Warhol painting. Rave music pulses in my ears and in my veins, creating a trippy experience that's as much enchanting as it is disorienting.

I weave my way through the maze, bumping into tall columns and shrieking once when I accidentally knock into another person that I thought was just a reflection. I find a spot to wait toward the end, surrounded by mirrors that produce an infinite number of Fionas across my vision.

After twenty minutes I check my phone, but there aren't any texts. Does that mean Colin's doing well? Or doing so badly he doesn't want to admit it?

Or maybe he's decided this whole thing isn't worth it, and he's backed out completely . . .

But a few minutes later, he comes huffing through the maze, out of breath, and at first tries to tackle my reflection before finally wrapping his arms around me and pulling me into a hug.

I laugh. "Did you run here from the Wave Organ?"

He rakes his hand through his hair, growing back a little by now. I still can't decide if he looks better with hair or without. "Practically. I didn't want to wait any longer to see you."

"You saw me yesterday."

"For a second! And our dads were there! And it was at the FBI office signing papers!"

I wave my hand dismissively. "Still counts. Even if it's no gas station bathroom."

As does the fact that Colin's dad took a week off work to spend time with him the way he's been craving. I did manage to pry Colin away for a few hours tonight. Until nine thirty, apparently.

Colin spins around, taking in the crazy scenery. "So what is this place?"

"The site of my next con," I say matter-of-factly.

He raises a brow. "What are we stealing?"

I have to smile at this, that he's already game for more despite all we've been through. "Something of yours."

He pushes me against a mirror, every part of his body settling into mine in a delightful tease. "I hope you're not about to say something cheesy, like you're going to steal my heart."

I wrap my arms around his back, resting my palms between the ridges of his shoulder blades. "Already have that."

He grins. "My soul, then?"

"I may be bad news sometimes, but I'm not actually the devil." I blow a warm breath into his ear, the kind of torture a devil might actually deliver.

His lips trace along my jaw, and heat trails in his wake. "My dignity? Pride?" He quirks an eyebrow. "Wallet?"

I sink my mouth into his, softly at first, then fierce enough to make up for the last few days without his lips against mine. "A kiss."

ACKNOWLEDGMENTS

Like Fiona relies on her con crew, this book wouldn't be what it is today without my crew.

To Holly West, thank you for seeing the potential in this story and guiding me to the right way to tell it. All your editorial suggestions took this book to a new level and I'm so grateful to be working with you. Neal Caffrey would tip his fedora at the result!

To Brent Taylor, thank you for championing this book and being a rock star agent. Your enthusiasm is always a welcome dose of encouragement. Thanks as well to the rest of the Triada US literary team for all your efforts.

To Jean Feiwel, Lauren Scobell, and everyone else at Swoon Reads, thank you for supporting me and my books. Liz Dresner and Lesley Worrell, thank you for the fantastic cover art and interior design. Lindsay Wagner, thank you for shepherding my book through the publishing process. Brian Luster, thank you for your keen eye and exceptional copy edits. Kim Waymer, thank you for overseeing the printing process. Kelsey Marrujo and Madison Furr, thank you for all your publicity efforts. And a big thank-you to everyone else at Macmillan who helped along the way.

To Chandler Baker, Diana Urban, and Lauren Spieller, thank you for being fantastic critique partners and for all our brainstorming sessions, writing sprints, and gchats. Thanks also to my other early readers, Jen Hayley, Naticia Hutchins, T.A. Maclagan, and Jim McCarthy: Your feedback was invaluable.

To the Swoon Squad, thank you for your fabulous wisdom, solidarity, and reassurance. Special thanks to Shani Petroff, Samantha Hastings, and S.M. Koz for your feedback on the first one hundred pages. Thanks also to Novel Nineteens and the 2020 MG/YA Graduates group.

To Meredith Moran, Kathryn Pearson, Erika Shenker, Crista Finocchio, Chelsey Wolf, Amanda Simon, Melanie Doyle, Denise Jaden, my Pokémon Go friends, and my Covet Fashion house—thank you for friendship, support, and distraction. And to Jeremy Samon, Nikki Facchine, Stacie Ehrenfeld, and Amanda Goodman, thanks for letting me borrow your names and for being part of my real-life travel camp adventures at Ivy League Day Camp that served as inspiration for the setting of this story.

To my family: Becca Levine, Eric Levine, Casey Levine, Eliza Levine, Rowan Levine, Daniel Preiser, Marta Pagan-Ortiz, JoAnne Preiser, Richard Preiser, and my parents Nina and Steve Silberberg: Thank you for all your love, encouragement, and for putting up with my terrible jokes. I hope you all skipped over the kissing scenes.

To my favorite husband, Josh, and my favorite daughter, Quinn, thank you for being my favorite people in the entire world. (That line was suggested by Quinn.) I love you both!